A VERY NORTHERN KILLING

VERY NORTHERN TALES BOOK ONE

J. C. O'NEILL

JCONEILLAUTHOR

“This is Nox Section. They’ll show us no mercy. So we’ll give them none.” — Sinclair

ABOUT THE AUTHOR

During Covid lockdown, J. C. O'Neill's wonderful sister-in-law was diagnosed with breast cancer. J. C. started to write a preposterous story to keep her amused. The story became a novel, which then grew into a trilogy. A Very Northern Killing is the first book in the series.

J C O'Neill lives and works and writes in Sheffield, South Yorkshire. She was born in Cumbria, so is a true Northerner. She has three kids, a dog, a Mr O'Neill and a fondness for McVities chocolate digestive biscuits. She is not to be confused with the evil Sheffield author, C. J. O'Neill....

Also By J. C. O'Neill

A Very Northern Death

To Be Published Tuesday July 25th 2023

A Very Northern Heart

To Be Published Tuesday October 31st 2023

www.jconeillauthor.com

First Published in the U. K. By jconeillauthor

First Edition First Printing

Book Cover and Illustrations by Cathy Stanford

CIP Catalogue record for this title is available from the British Library

Trade Paperback ISBN 978-1-7392579-0-3
eBook ISBN 978-1-7392579-1-0
Hardback ISBN 978-1-7392579-2-7

Created with Vellum

This book is dedicated to my beautiful, brave sister-in-law, Andrea.

I know a place that's blessed by beauty
High from the moor to the rolling sea
Long is the sky and deep the waters
I live in God's own country

Excerpt of Song to the North by J. C. O'Neill

PROLOGUE

Thunder crashed overhead and rain, like heavy tears, fell from the dolorous sky. A woman staggered over the cobbled alley, her hand plunged and groping in her sopping pocket. Her fingers closed on the heavy iron object, the elusive key. She paused, studying the door with intense concentration.

"Keep still, damn you," she muttered. After the fourth attempt, she managed to unlock it. She fell inside and lay, quiet, on the stone flags for an entire minute before dragging herself to her feet. She stumbled heavily against the oak door, and it slammed shut. "Shhh," she whispered, putting her finger to her lips. "Shhh. Don't want to wake...." She looked over her shoulder. Her eyes became wary, melancholy. "Wake the dead..." she whispered. She was standing in a dark corridor in a run-down church in a dilapidated area of a Northern city. Something shifted and sighed in the shadows. A murmur of dust rose from the floor as if long skirts had drifted by. The woman clenched her eyes tight shut and crept, blinded, up the grubby passageway, feeling along the walls. She located a doorway and edged into the room, closing the door as quietly as she could. "Don't wake the dead, Jess," she muttered, her head against the warped boards. "Don't wake the dead."

Jess opened her eyes and flipped the light switch. She looked around her small, bare room. It contained an unmade bed and an empty wardrobe. A pint glass, half filled with water, stood alongside a cheap plastic lamp on a lopsided bedside table. She stood, swaying slightly, looking at the glass of water.

"So," she said. "Do I sober up? Or do I actually sleep? Decisions, decisions."

"Good evening, Sister," said a cool voice behind her. Jess leapt in fright and spun to face the speaker. Another woman sat on a low chair in the darkest corner of the room.

"Holy Mother, you gave me a fright!" exclaimed Jess. She peered into the gloom at the newcomer. "Miss Whelan?" The woman frowned.

She was of middle age. She wore a neat tweed suit with a matching blouse in a neutral colour. Her hair was clean and medium brown. It was of medium length. Her shoes were sensible, tasteful, but not ostentatious. Everything about her was admirable. But nothing about her was desirable. And certainly not memorable.

"Or shall we say good morning?" said Miss Whelan. She looked pointedly at her modest watch. "It is, after all, almost three o'clock."

"What do you want?" demanded Jess. "I am very, very busy!" The woman in tweed looked her up and down with a slow and appraising gaze.

"Busy destroying your liver," she observed calmly. Jess

shoved her hands into her damp trouser pockets with an air of defiance.

"I am doing everything that The Order demands," she replied loftily. "I care for the destitute, the poor, the lowly. I do the best that I can, in my particular circumstances...." Miss Whelan folded her hands over her sensible, brown leather handbag.

"I'm happy to leave the affairs of this part of Manchester in your hands, Sister," she said.

"Then, again, what do you want?" asked Jess.

There was a long silence. Miss Whelan looked very uncomfortable.

"There has been a development," Miss Whelan began. "With the Belle Witch." Jess's eyes grew round.

"She's come into her powers? She's begun to bleed?" Miss Whelan gave the most subtle of squirms.

"The girl has begun to bleed... but...." She paused, agonised.

"What?" demanded Jess. "What?"

"Nothing," said Miss Whelan. She looked at Jess. "Absolutely nothing. That's the problem. She's not the Belle Witch." Jess's mouth fell open.

"So, the Order's been fussing over this girl for eleven years, and she's the wrong girl? She's not the Queen of Witches?" Jess couldn't resist a smirk. "Bit of a faux pas?" Miss Whelan looked very disgruntled.

"It's give or take a hundred years, for goodness' sake," she said. Anyone can make a mistake when there's one hundred years leeway." Jess continued to grin.

Miss Whelan stood and approached Jess.

"I need to talk to your Great Grandma," she said briskly. Jess's face fell. She backed away.

"No. I'm not letting that old bag into my head. No!"

"You have to obey The Order," said Miss Whelan sharply. "You made a vow."

"I was sixteen!" exclaimed Jess.

"Old enough to make a promise. Old enough to make a deal. And a deal is a deal!" snapped Miss Whelan. Jess continued to shake her head. Miss Whelan tutted in frustration. "You have no choice, Jess," she said. Miss Whelan made an impatient gesture. Jess's world went dark.

WHEN JESS AWOKE, her head was throbbing as if it would burst. She groaned. Her right hand was clenched. This was a familiar part of the experience. Jess didn't open her hand but kept it tightly shut. She didn't want to look at it. She sat up slowly from where she lay on her narrow bed. Miss Whelan was back in her chair, watching Jess. She did not look pleased.

"Well?" said Jess. "What did the old bat have to say?"

"You shouldn't speak so disrespectfully of the dead," said Miss Whelan irritably. "Especially not someone of your Great-Grandmother's reputation."

"You haven't just been booted out of your own brain," replied Jess sourly. She reached inside her shabby black jacket and retrieved a damp packet of cigarettes. She shook one out onto the bed and put it in her mouth.

"Don't you dare, Jessica Pendle-Howard!" cried Miss Whelan. Jess looked at her as she pulled out a black zippo lighter and lit the cigarette.

"I'm not at school anymore, Miss Whelan," she said, inhaling deeply. "And I am just clinging on to sanity by my fingertips." Jess held up the cigarette. "As I say to my flock; whatever gets you through the day.'"

Jess regarded Miss Whelan sharply through the smoke. "What did my Great Grandma say?" she repeated, all levity gone. Miss Whelan looked back at Jess. She seemed scared.

"The Belle Witch is here. But not on this side of the Pennines."

"She's in the East?" said Jess. "Oh, dear. Are you going to go and find her?" she asked. Miss Whelan shook her head firmly.

"You know very well that we have no dealings with the Pagans," she declared. "So, there's a storm coming. A great storm." She regarded Jess.

"What?" said Jess. "There's more?" Miss Whelan hesitated.

"She doesn't know. Whoever is the Belle Witch, the Queen of Witches. She doesn't know she's the Belle Witch. There is a darkness that clouds everything. We can't see who she is; we can't see where she is, how old... Your Great Grandmother could see nothing. Except...."

"Except what?" said Jess slowly.

"The Beautiful Wolf. He has not done his Penance," said Miss Whelan. Now it was Jess's turn to look frustrated.

"This Penance thing again? It's nothing to do with me!" she cried. "Their Penance is not my problem."

"But your blood runs in their veins, Jess. So that does make them your problem, as far as The Order is concerned," insisted Miss Whelan. Her face hardened. "That family has still made no atonement." Jess shook her head.

"For goodness' sake! No one knows what the nature of the atonement is. Or what they are to atone for," she replied, frustrated.

Jess's shoulders slumped, and she rubbed her left hand through her short, black hair. "Bit of a problem, this whole ancient curse thing," she said. She looked up. "So, Great Grandma has no big plan? We just have to wait for the storm to come?" Miss Whelan nodded, her lips pursed.

"We cannot go into the Pagan East," she said firmly. "We cannot cross the Pennine mountains. That was the agreement."

"Oh, come on. Everyone knows rules are for breaking," said Jess, a wicked smile breaking out over her tired face. Miss Whelan drew herself up, and Jess cursed quietly as she remembered Miss Whelan's history.

"That's what my sister thought," said Miss Whelan bleakly. "Twenty-six years ago. She thought she could unite the West and the East, by blindly wandering over the Pennines." For a moment, Miss Whelan's face lost its calm control, and grief blossomed over her features. "Oh, Brigid," she said quietly, her face turned towards the shadow.

Miss Whelan quickly recovered and glared at Jess. "The Order may turn a blind eye to your antics, Jess," she said sternly. "But you will have the Church of England inspecting you if you're not careful." Jess looked around the room.

"I think the Church of England has forgotten me and Gramps exist," she said sadly. "Us and this dirty little church. In this dirty little piece of the North." She looked at Miss Whelan. "So, bring on the storm, I say. Let the rains come down. It might wipe some of us clean."

After Miss Whelan had gone, Jess looked down at her clenched right hand. She shouldn't look at it. She should just wash it. Who cared what a dead old witch thought of her?

Jess slowly opened her hand and looked down at it. She began to smile. A tear ran down her face, a face that looked so much older than it should. A red letter X lay over her palm. It was drawn in bright scarlet lipstick, and the edges of the letter curled with a confident flourish.

"Love you too, Nana," whispered Jess. She wiped her tear away. "I miss you. And I love you too."

CHAPTER ONE

The old woman was dying. Even Mac could see that, gazing, transfixed, through a gap in the disposable hospital curtains. She'd been wheeled in by an indifferent porter and a stressed-looking Accident and Emergency Department nurse. A short, blonde hospital doctor in scrubs that looked two sizes too large for her had taken the brief and damning bedside handover. Neighbours had called Police as they hadn't seen the woman for a few days. Door broken down, found moribund on the floor, barely breathing. Chest X-ray showed huge, metastatic tumour with effusion. Dying. Wouldn't survive even insertion of a chest drain. Quick shipping off to the Clinical Decisions Unit; to die there and not make A and E figures worse. The doctor sighed and took the notes.

"Well, there's hardly any staff on this morning. I'll see what I can do..."

"You should have gone home at midnight last night, Charlie. It's almost nine in the morning, and you're still here," snapped the A and E nurse.

"The Registrar called in sick at the last moment. Eddie asked me to do a couple of extra admissions."

"Well, Eddie Lam left over an hour ago, and he was meant to be working nights. Unlike you. Go home, Charlie." The staff nurse walked away, shaking his head.

"Hang on..." called Charlie after him. "Matt! She's got no end-of-life drugs on this chart! Nothing!" The staff nurse turned round briefly.

"Sorry, Charlie, but what the Hell do you expect after last night's fun and games? Not my fault. Go home!"

There was a loud crash and a scream from further down the ward. There seemed to be a few problematic patients keeping the scanty nursing staff on their toes. Through the gap in the curtain, Mac watched as the doctor's face slowly crumpled and tears started to flow. Deep, dark patches under her eyes smudged her face, pale with fatigue. She grabbed the drug chart and wrote angrily and rapidly. She then carefully read what she had written, once, twice. She seemed aware in her exhaustion how easy it was to make a mistake. The doctor turned to the old woman who lay in the bed like a panting, fragile bird. Her eyes were wide with distress beneath her hissing oxygen mask.

"Lily, my name's Dr Charlie Hart," she said gently. "I'm going to get you medicine to help with your breathing. Is there anyone I can call to come and be with you, Lily?" The old woman shook her head, unable to spare air for any answer.

Dr Hart walked to the entrance of the small four-bedded bay and looked, hopelessly, for a staff nurse. A red-haired, short, barrel-shaped staff nurse barged into view. "Lianne, thank goodness," said Charlie. "Can you check me some morphine, please? The lady in 4 b's dying. It's to ease her breathing."

"Well, if she's dying, she doesn't need it!" barked Lianne, brow furrowing, barely stopping in her angry progress past the room.

"No! We're stopping her from feeling like she's drowning."

"I'm too busy. Find someone else."

"There is no one else! Just check it for me, and I'll give it then. Please, Lianne..." Lianne rolled her eyes dramatically and drew a set of keys from her pocket.

Without another word, she marched into the clinical room. Mac could see into the room as they unlocked the controlled-drug cupboard. With Lianne's maximal annoyance, they counted glass vials and drew up the morphine dose so carefully prescribed by the crumbling Dr Hart. Mac again watched as Charlie and Lianne checked the old woman's identity. Lianne twisted the woman's arm to look at her identification bracelet, causing the dying woman to wince. Mac grimaced at this tiny, miserly cruelty. He glanced across at the woman lying in the bed at which he sat. He was surprised to see that her eyes were open. Sally had finally awoken. She, too, was staring through the gap at the curtains. She took in the terrible rapidity of the woman's breathing, which spoke of the inevitability of death. Sally, however, seemed detached rather than distressed.

Dr Hart administered the morphine and then sat slumped at the bedside. Mac and Sally listened as the woman's breathing eased slightly, saw her relax as the morphine took its effect. But her eyes were still terrified, full of emotional pain, still full of the fear of death. Mac frowned as he saw the doctor look around her as if she was about to do something illicit or forbidden. But all she then did was take the old woman's hand. The doctor took a slow, deep breath, and then her brow furrowed as if she herself was in pain. She then breathed out slowly. The old woman's eyes cleared and closed as if falling into a gentle, trouble-free slumber.

"It's OK, Lily. I'm here," whispered the doctor. "You're not alone. It's a lovely morning. Spring's here; I can see the sparrows in the trees outside. The rain's cleared, and I think we'll have sun later." She gently stroked the nicotine-stained hair and fingers as Lily's breathing carried on. It strained less now against the fluid that pressed on her lungs. Mac turned to Sally, but she held her finger to her lips, indicating that they shouldn't talk yet.

Through the curtains, Mac saw that the old woman had now slumped into an uncomfortable position. The small doctor pressed the call button, and the alarm flashed and beeped. No one came. The doctor sighed and tried to move the woman, to ease her breathing, but struggled. The bed was an ancient model that had somehow found its way back onto the ward. The bed head needed adjusting manually, and the doctor couldn't keep the old woman upright and adjust the bed at the same time. Still, no one came, and the woman slid further down the bed, her breathing coming in laboured gasps.

Mac stood and pushed the curtain open. The doctor looked up, her face distressed. Without a word, Mac grasped the mechanism that raised the head of the bed and pulled it into place. They quickly manoeuvred the woman up the bed between the two of them. She laid her head back in clear relief. Mac nodded once and turned to go. The doctor then reached out and put her right hand on his forearm. Mac felt a jolt pass through him as if she had administered a small electric shock. He looked down in surprise at the small hand. It was just a hand. Trained to observe, he saw dry, chapped skin, bare ring finger, unpainted nails that were bitten down to the quick, even bleeding in places. The doctor saw him looking and pulled her hand away. In a curiously childlike gesture, she put her hand behind her back, embarrassed.

"I just wanted to say thank you," she said quietly. Still silent, Mac nodded again and returned to his place at Sally's side. The doctor pulled the curtains shut.

Half an hour passed, and the woman's breathing slowed and eventually stopped. Charlie stepped out and talked with the nurse in charge before returning to confirm death and document in the notes. By now, Mac could see that she was struggling with profound exhaustion. She staggered slightly on her slow progress down the corridor and out of Mac's view.

He turned again to Sally, who was now looking at him, her face sallow and drawn against the white pillow.

"What happened, Mac?" she said.

"You were right," said Mac. "Maya was taking something. She was taking Code Blue."

CHARLIE HART SLIPPED into the packed resuscitation bay of the Accident and Emergency department of the Northern General Hospital. The entire staff of the department had been summoned to an emergency meeting. Doctors and nurses stood, talking quietly. Charlie went to stand next to the male staff nurse, Matt. He stared down at her grumpily but then smiled and tousled her hair. He then poked the nurse standing in front of them.

"Oi, Carmella, give Charlie a chocolate. I know you've got one." Carmella looked down her nose at the two of them.

"I don't know what you're talking about, Matt."

"Come on, Melli," Matt said. "Charlie's been here all night. She looks like one of your patients after they've spent a whole shift with you." The nurse sniffed in disgust but slipped her hand into her pocket and handed Charlie a soft toffee, which Charlie took gratefully.

"Thanks, Melli," she whispered, and Melli flashed her a warm smile.

A tall, dark-haired doctor looked up from his notes and surveyed the room with a haughty stare. The gathered staff became quiet.

"Thank you for coming. For those of you who don't know me, I'm Dr Fergus Eaton, lead consultant of the Emergency Department," he said. "The morning team will have had a handover from the night staff, so you may have some idea of what's going on. It seems we have a Public Health emergency on our hands. Detective Inspector Decker of the South Yorkshire Police will address us shortly." He indicated a man with dark, greying hair standing next to him. Intelligent brown eyes glittered in a friendly but creased and worn face. The officer nodded to the gathered crowd.

"Y'alright?" he said in a quiet, measured voice.

Dr Eaton continued. "As you know, in the last few months, we've been aware of a new street drug. It's known by many names, but most commonly as 'Code Blue.' This is due to the blue tinge in the eyes of those under the influence of the drug. It apparently gives a prolonged high, with an intense feeling of transcendence and well-being. It's not physically addictive and has no hangover effect.

"What's the problem, then?" quipped Matt, provoking a murmur of laughter.

"The problem, nurse Marston," said the unsmiling Dr Eaton, "is that it's now been taken for long enough to get more data on it. It appears that, for most people, it is initially safe. However, one in ten thousand doses will produce severe side effects. The more you take, the higher the risks. Malignant hypertension, cerebral bleeds, complete psychotic breakdown. Last night, a mother and father were murdered by their teenage son, who had taken Code Blue. A woman was brutally assaulted, also by a man who had taken Code Blue." Dr Eaton paused and looked down. "She may need an operation," he said, unable to look at his colleagues while he said this.

Despite all his years in the Emergency Department, Fergus Eaton had not been prepared for what he'd seen during the night shift from Hell. He breathed in sharply and looked up again. "And a woman was attacked and seriously injured by her former partner. Again, Code Blue seems to have been taken." He paused. "I know it was chaos here, but I assume someone stitched up the wounds on that woman's head and arm?" he asked.

IN THE CLINICAL DECISIONS UNIT, Sally sat up. "I need to get out of here," she said firmly. She threw back the covers of the bed.

"You're bleeding," said Mac, knowing better than to touch Sally. The dressing that covered the wound on her right upper arm was soaked in blood. Her sudden movement had dislodged the fragile clot over the deep wound. It had not been stitched. Sally looked at him.

"I need to get out of here," she repeated. She opened the door of her bedside cupboard and dragged out her clothes. She started pulling on her trousers, and the movement caused more blood to flow down her arm, between her fingers and onto the lino floor. Shaking his head, Mac walked onto the ward corridor and then into the clinical room, the door of which had been left ajar. He grabbed some tape and gauze dressing packs and returned to Sally. Mac knew that nothing he could say would stop her from going. Ripping open the packs, he made a thick wad and moved towards Sally, who flinched away.

"Don't touch me," she said in a monotone.

Mac stood very still. After nearly four years, he'd become used to this. "I need to place the gauze pads on your wound to apply pressure and stop the bleeding," he said in a calm and reasonable tone. "If I don't do this, you will continue to lose blood. You, therefore, may become weak and not function efficiently." Sally looked at him, then nodded.

"Do it," she said, holding out her right arm and looking straight ahead. Mac tore strips of tape and hung them from the nearby cupboard. He pressed the fresh gauze over the existing soaked pad and efficiently wrapped long pieces of tape around Sally's arm to pull the dressing down and stop the bleeding.

"Press here," he ordered. Sally held her left hand over the wound dressing and looked at Mac.

"You did this in the army," she stated. "Stopped bleeding." Mac nodded tersely.

"It needs stitches," he said. Sally turned away.

"I need to get out of here," she repeated, heading for the curtain.

"Let's not discuss your head injury either, shall we?" muttered Mac as he followed Sally.

BACK IN THE A and E department, Dr Fergus Eaton turned to the Policeman standing next to him.

"Inspector Decker?" Decker stepped forward.

"First, can I say how grateful we are for your professionalism and care," he said in a deep, slow Yorkshire accent. "It sounds like you had a terrible time last night. We'll do anything we can to support and protect our medical colleagues." There were a few smiles and nods from the gathered staff. "I can't say much, but it looks like this is a Sheffield-based gang manufacturing this stuff. It hasn't turned up in Leeds or Manchester; however, the word's out, and people are now coming in, hoping to buy it. It seems they release 10,000 doses at a time, only on a Friday night. And each week, the price goes up. It started at five pounds a tab. It's presently at eighty quid a pop." There was a muttering of surprise.

"I thought it wasn't addictive," called out Matt. "Why are they paying eighty quid when it's not addictive?"

"It's not physically addictive," said Decker. "But the high you get is insanely addictive, psychologically. No one will talk to us. And that's a big, big problem. We hear that the man running the game is a tough guy. Ruthless. No one who works for him will breathe a word. And the people who've taken it? Take it once, and it's all you crave from then on. No one will talk in case it turns off their supply." He shook his head. "The people brought in here, you've seen them; raving about angels."

"Screaming like demons, more like," piped up Matt. "Before their heads go pop."

Dr Fergus Eaton closed his eyes and rubbed a hand over his exhausted face. He couldn't get the images from last night out of his mind. A young man had been howling in one of the bays, blood trickling from his eyes and nose as his deadly blood pressure refused to come down. It had taken three police officers and a staff nurse to hold him down. An ashen-faced registrar had been sitting on a stool between the open legs of an unconscious woman, desperately trying to stop the flow of blood that poured from her.

"She needs to go to the Jessop Hospital, to Obs and Gynae!" the Registrar had shouted.

And then there had been Her. The skeletal woman who had been brought in minutes after her former partner, whom she had savagely assaulted. She, too, had required four people to restrain her. The skeletal woman had looked at Eaton, her blue tinged eyes glowing, and had started laughing.

"You killed him!" she said gleefully. "You gave him Tazocin when he told you, again and again, that he had a penicillin allergy." Eaton had frozen in horror. How did she know that? That had happened over twenty years ago, right at the start of his career. He looked wildly around him to see if she was speaking to someone else, but her wide, glistening gaze was fixed on him. "Tazocin!" she had shouted. "Piperacillin! I can see him! He's standing right next to you! Blew up like a balloon, airway tight shut. 'Can't breathe, can't breathe!'" She mimed gasping for air and grinned again wildly. "Little Mikey Sharrow." Dr Eaton's mouth had hung open. That had, indeed, been the man's name. "You dropped the glass Tazocin bottle in the sharps bin. You hid it, you coward!" yelled the woman, her mouth pulled into a rictus of a smile.

"Sedate this woman!" Eaton had shouted, pointing with a trembling finger at the writhing, heaving figure.

"What the hell do you think we've been doing?" exclaimed the sweating staff nurse. "She's got enough benzos on board to take out a rhino!"

Eaton's mouth had twisted down. "Rapid sequence induction," he'd announced. "Anaesthetise her. Now! She's a danger to everyone."

"You can't do that!" objected the staff nurse. "The psychiatric team are on their way." But Eaton had marched to the resuscitation trolley and was tugging at the drugs box. *Propofol*, he'd thought, *propofol will shut her up*.

"Hold her still!" he'd snarled to the policemen. He'd slipped a green cannula into the taut, bulging vein on her emaciated right forearm. She had glared at him.

"Brown hair, gold earring, name of his kid tattooed on his arm!" she had hissed. "He's standing behind you!" Eaton had let out an inarticulate cry as he slammed a large bolus dose of anaesthetic into her vein. Her eyes had closed, and her body had abruptly dropped, flaccid, onto the trolley surface.

That shut her up!

CHAPTER TWO

"Are you alright, Dr Eaton?" came a voice from nearby.

"What?" Eaton shook his head and took his hand from over his eyes. Decker was looking at him, friendly concern in his eyes.

"I said, are you alright? I think you've had a long night," said Decker gently. Eaton looked around. His colleagues were staring at him, waiting for someone to continue. For once, he was lost for words.

"I'll leave you... in... in... the capable hands of Inspector Decker," he mumbled and lurched towards the door of the bay. Once he was in the corridor, he sucked in a deep breath. It was not like him to lose control. He saw a small, blonde figure slip out of the resuscitation room. Sudden, irrational anger bloomed inside him. What was Charlie Hart doing, still being here? “Charlie!" he shouted. The woman started and turned towards him. He angrily gestured for her to join him in a curtained trolley cubicle. She reluctantly trailed towards him, her head down. "What the Hell are you doing? You should have gone home at midnight. If you work over your allowed hours, it's me, your consultant, who gets into trouble. Well?" he demanded. She looked up at him.

"There was a woman, dying..." she began.

"There's always a woman dying around here," Eaton ground out. "In case you hadn't noticed, it's an accident and emergency department." Charlie's eyes started to fill with tears. Instead of making him back down, Fergus Eaton found himself becoming more furious. He could have stopped himself, but he made the decision to let her have it, all his anger and frustration and fear.

"This is what's wrong with the Medical Profession these days," he said, his voice tremulous with anger. "Full of do-good females. All of you trying to make it all better. Terrified of making a mistake. Incapable of making a bloody decision! Grow up, Charlie! Do you think if you hand over part of yourself to everyone you meet, you can make it all better and take the pain away? Well, you can't. You'll end up flat-out and burned-out, and then you'll be dead. You'll end up killing yourself, just like your sister." Charlie said nothing, just looked at him in dumb, shocked surprise. This infuriated him further. "Or perhaps you think Charlie Hart is the only one who can take the pain away?" he snarled. "Well, believe me, you're not. There will always be some poor little sap ready to step up and take your place." He marched out of the cubicle and grabbed a leaflet from a nearby display. He flung it at Charlie. It glanced off her right shoulder as she cringed away, and it fell to the floor. "Workplace Well-being," Eaton continued, unable to stop his uncorked rage. "Call them! It's part of your duty as a doctor to take care of yourself–"

"Dr Eaton!" exclaimed a voice. They looked up to see Inspector Decker standing close by, his hands on his hips. There was an uncomfortable pause. "I think the young lass has had enough, don't you?" said Decker in a more reasonable tone. Eaton stood, breathing heavily. He took one last look at Charlie and then stalked off. Decker approached the pale and lost-looking Charlie. He picked up the leaflet and handed it to her. "I'm sure he means well," he said gently. Decker paused, looking at her. "However, speaking as a policeman, maybe he's got a point, Dr Hart? Maybe there's more to life than giving every piece of yourself away?" Charlie nodded and tried to smile. Decker patted her on the shoulder and then headed back to the resuscitation bay.

Mac and Sally left the Clinical Decision Unit without being challenged and followed the sign that said Exit. They made their way back through the eerily quiet A and E department. There seemed to be a meeting going on in the large room to their right. Sally pointed to the automatic exit doors at the end of the corridor that were activated by a green push button. She set off towards them. Mac hesitated. Sitting on the floor of a nearby cubicle to their left was the small blonde doctor they had seen earlier. Her back was against the wall, and her knees were pulled up to her chest. A shabby rucksack was flopped over at her feet. Her right hand clutched a leaflet, and her left hand shaded her eyes. She seemed to be crying. Mac stood still. The now familiar panic pushed gently inside his chest. He shook his head and walked over to the doctor.

"Excuse me," he said. "But are you alright?" The doctor looked up at him and tried to smile. She nodded her head.

"I'm fine, all fine," she said. She wiped her nose with the back of her hand. "Thank you," she said brightly. Mac nodded tersely and set off down the corridor.

Mac stopped. Ahead of him, Sally confidently slapped the green button to open the door. It remained shut. She hit it again. The door remained stubbornly closed. What was going on? Sally peered through the glass, looking for an approaching ambulance crew who might open the door for her. Mac slowly turned around and walked back to the cubicle and the young doctor.

"You seem distressed. May I accompany you to your car?" he asked formally. The doctor looked up, her eyes slightly glassy. She stood up abruptly.

"I'm fine, look," she announced. She then swayed, and what little colour she had drained from her face. Mac put out his arm, and she clutched at it. They stood for a few moments as the doctor drew in some deep breaths. Mac could feel her hand trembling as it rested on his skin. Her touch no longer had the quality of an electric shock, but seemed to hum against his flesh like a half-heard musical note. She appeared to feel it too, for she looked up, eyes widening, as if truly seeing him for the first time.

Through her fatigue and distress, Charlie saw a tall, strikingly handsome Black man. His generous mouth was straight and unsmiling, his tightly curling hair cut very short, emphasizing the sharp planes of his face. His large, intelligent eyes were deep brown and widely spaced, but a slight, furrowed frown seemed permanently etched on his forehead. *He looks like he's going to deliver a eulogy*, she thought. She looked down to where her hand rested on his muscular forearm, vibrating gently against the rich darkness of his skin. She shook her head and slowly lifted her hand away. She gave him another hesitant smile. "I really am fine," she said. "I just need to...."

She moved off, wearily and unsteadily, towards the Exit,

the crumpled leaflet still clutched in her small hand. The door finally opened as she approached. Outside, it had started to rain heavily. As she disappeared from view, they saw her light blue scrubs quickly darken in the deluge. *She doesn't have a coat,* thought Mac. He glanced down and saw the doctor's shabby rucksack. He picked it up and moved towards Sally, who was staring at him.

"I need to go home," Sally repeated. Mac nodded, distracted. They walked out into the rain.

CHARLIE STOOD by her old silver VW Polo, shivering and cold. She patted vaguely at her pocket and then groaned as she realised she'd left her bag in the department. She was so tired; the short walk back seemed like miles, and what if Fergus Eaton saw her again? She put her hands onto the top of the car and then placed her forehead on her hands. She was frozen and exhausted, and drained. Charlie felt tears welling up again. All she wanted to do was to sleep, to forget. A small sob escaped her. She jumped when a voice spoke close by.

"Excuse me." Charlie looked up. It was the man again. The one who had helped her with Lily and again in the A and E department. He was holding her bag out to her. "Are you sure you're safe to drive?" he said, his face still stern and unsmiling. He pointed towards a large Range Rover parked up on the kerb nearby, windscreen wipers waving lazily in the ongoing storm. "I can give you a lift," he said. Charlie regarded him. They were now both soaked.

"You're getting wet," she said vaguely. The man said nothing. He just carried on watching her, water streaming down his face. Charlie realised she probably wouldn't make it home safely. She nodded slowly. "Can you get me to Crookes?" she said. "It's not far."

Charlie slipped into the leather backseat of the Range Rover and shivered. The car pulled away, and Charlie was startled to feel the seat beneath her warming up. The woman sitting in the passenger seat didn't turn around or acknowledge her presence. Charlie could barely see her behind the high leather headrest. Charlie felt her eyes grow heavy in the thick, luxurious warmth of the car. She would close her eyes. Just for a minute....

MAC PULLED onto Mulehouse Road in the little Sheffield suburb of Crookes. He looked into the back seat and saw the doctor was fast asleep. Her head was slumped onto her shoulder, and her breathing was deep and heavy. He reached into the back and shook her leg, gently at first and then more firmly. She didn't stir. Sally looked at Mac.

"You said you'd get me home," she said insistently. "I need to go home." Mac nodded.

"I'll get you home, and then I'll try and wake the doctor again," he said. "Don't worry, I'll deal with it." Sally nodded and looked out through the windscreen at the heavy rain.

"You always do," she said.

"Pardon?" said Mac, distracted by the extra passenger.

"You always deal with it," repeated Sally. She looked at Mac again. "Thank you."

THEY DROVE in silence down the Manchester Road that led out of the West side of Sheffield towards the notoriously dangerous Snake Pass. The road narrowed and became more twisting. Mac eventually took a sharp right onto a rough track lined with birch and rowan trees. *Rowans Holt. Home,* Sally thought and started to relax. The car slowed and crawled over a tall, arching stone bridge, where a busy river flowed noisily below. The vehicle eventually emerged from the trees into a clearing. Mac glanced over at Sally and was surprised, as he always was, by the sudden softening of Sally's features into something like love. A large, imposing, yellowed sandstone manor-house stood close to a cliff edge. The house was very old, Elizabethan in origin, with square, mullioned windows and tall, twisting red chimneys. There would normally be a breath-taking view of the moors and distant edges spread beneath them; however, it was now hidden by curtains of grey rain.

Sally's face fell. In front of the house, a car had been parked. It was an old, battered Volvo estate. A man emerged from the vehicle. He was tall and broad-shouldered, with long hair that curled around the upturned collar of his shabby Barbour jacket. He stood, watching the car's approach, hunched against the rain. Mac cursed softly. He'd completely forgotten about the visitor, having made the arrangements a few days ago.

"Sally, I forgot to tell you. I found someone who can look at the damaged woodwork in the library," he said. Sally regarded him silently. Mac couldn't tell what she was thinking. He rarely could.

"Can he mend my house?" she asked.

"He can try," replied Mac. I haven't seen him for years, but we... we were in the army together. He was a carpenter before he joined up and went back to it once he left." Mac looked at the tall figure who stood watching the car. "He's a good man," he said quietly. Sally nodded.

"I trust you," she replied and opened the car door.

They ran through the rain to the large gothic wooden door in the side of the house. Mac gestured to the newcomer to join them. Sally unlocked the door, and they hurried into the hallway. The man's eyes widened as he looked around him. Mac smiled slightly as he remembered the first time he'd entered Rowans Holt. Polished, honey-coloured oak was everywhere: the floor, the doors, and the intricate panelling covering the bottom half of the large hallway's walls. A stunning, oak Elizabethan staircase twisted upwards to the left. Light suffused everything. As they stepped from the hallway, the man saw why. To their left was an enormous open-plan kitchen with a red-tiled floor and a wide wooden oak island. Hand-carved units surrounded a large range cooker which squatted in the cavernous, brick fireplace. Straight ahead was a vast living space with sheepskin and what looked like Persian rugs scattered over the polished wooden floor. Cashmere blankets in shades of soft grey and delicate pink lay over huge leather sofas and chairs. Pieces of sculpture and art were subtly lit and displayed to maximise the impact of their beauty. The main wall to their left, facing the distant peaks, was formed of an enormous, floor-to-ceiling, trifold glass window which showed the shifting shades of the wide, weeping sky.

Mac clapped the shoulder of the man and grinned. Sally hadn't seen this expression on Mac's face before.

"Nice to see you, Yorkie," he said. A slow, lopsided grin spread over the newcomer's face. He was in his late twenties. His deep-auburn hair was long and shaggy, hanging round his face and brushing over his collar. His clear skin had a Celtic translucency that went with the dark russet colour. His chin was square and firm and covered with at least two days of stubble, but it was softened by his wide, full mouth that seemed eager to pull into a gentle smile. His sleepy blue eyes sparkled gently with good humour.

"Good to see you too, Sir," he replied, in a broad Sheffield accent, shaking Mac's hand firmly. Mac shook his head.

"Those days are gone, Yorkie. It's just Mac now." His smile fell. "I'm sorry about your brother," said Mac. The newcomer frowned, his sunny expression turning bleak.

"No, you're not," he said, his voice suddenly becoming clipped. "And neither am I. I'm glad he's dead. In fact, it's a good thing we both had watertight alibis." After a pause, Mac nodded slowly. Being at his own court-martial had been a good alibi.

Mac turned to Sally. "Sally, may I introduce Ben, Ben Morton." The man held out his hand to Sally, who ignored it.

"Mac says you're a carpenter. Is that true?" she asked. Ben nodded, lowering his hand.

"Aye," he said.

"He says you're a good man. Is that true?" continued Sally. Ben cast a surprised glance at Mac before looking back at Sally.

"It's a constant battle. But I try," he said quietly.

Sally abruptly turned and made her way through the living space. Ben's sharp eyes took in the blood soaking the thick, cream silk of her right upper sleeve. Mac indicated they should follow, and Ben walked after Sally. He saw the back of her head and frowned again when he saw her hair was matted with blood. He looked at Mac, his eyebrows raised, and gestured towards the wounds. Mac merely shook his head firmly.

There was a corridor leading away from the lounge. They walked down the dark space towards an open doorway, then entered an old and (to Ben's eyes) beautiful library. Tall bookshelves lined three walls; behind the door and the walls left and right as you looked in. A long, brick-lined fireplace lay ahead, with soot-smoked walls and seasoned applewood logs piled snugly on the left. Two large, dark-green leather upright chairs stood, facing each other, in front of the open fire. Grey light smudged through the tall casement windows and over the heavy desk that stood in front of them. The quiet room smelled of old parchment and sweet, spiced apple smoke.

The wall surrounding the fireplace was also lined in panelling, but this was extensively scarred and torn. There was also damage, at hip height, to all the antique woodwork that lined the walls between the tall bookshelves. The desk drawers had been forced open brutally and lay splintered and ragged. It looked as if someone had taken a spike of some sort to the defenceless wood. Ben stood and turned slowly, taking in the damage, looking genuinely distressed.

"That's just a crime," he muttered. "To attack a work of art, a piece of history, like this...." He stopped, lost for words. Sally nodded at him, her eyes widening as she looked at his expression. For the first time, she seemed genuinely animated.

"You're right!" she said. "But I couldn't stop it from happening." Sally walked to one of the damaged walls and stroked it almost tenderly. Her brow furrowed. "Do you think... could you?" She paused and looked at Ben.

"Could I what?" asked Ben. "Recommend someone?" He breathed out heavily. "I don't know, it's specialist work...." Ben glanced around him. "It'll take hundreds of hours if you want it restored rather than replaced.... You could try Pete Morgan and his crew. But last I heard, they had a gig at a stately home near here. So, you could be waiting months, years even...."

"No," interrupted Sally. She glanced at Mac, then back to Ben. "I mean you. Someone Mac trusts, a good man. I don't want a pack of people in my home. Can you do it?" Ben stared at Sally. He didn't reply but went and knelt by one of the more seriously damaged panels. The image of a path wound through an intricate carving of woodland animals. A small rabbit had been torn, savagely, down its middle. Ben traced his rough fingers across the little animal and turned to Sally, his face burning with a mixture of fear and hope.

"I could do it," he said. Sally looked at him.

"This place is mine," she said with slight fierceness. "It's dear to me." She walked to the pile of dried applewood logs and selected one. She turned and abruptly threw it towards Ben. Without breaking gaze with Sally, Ben's left hand flashed out and caught the wood. They looked at each other.

"You're left-handed," Sally stated.

"So are you," Ben replied, holding her gaze. There was a pause. Sally frowned.

"Blood," she said. Ben looked down at his left hand. Bright scarlet oozed in a thin line around the hunk of wood. He'd damaged his hand as he'd caught it.

"It's nothing, don't worry. Just a scratch," he said.

A few drops of Ben's blood fell to the softly gleaming floorboards. Ben bent to wipe them away but paused, frowning. He could see no trace. The blood had disappeared. *It must have fallen between the boards*, he thought, even though he could see the planks were beautifully fitted and tightly sealed. The odd sensation flashed across his mind that the house had absorbed it. He shook his head. He was more tired than he thought.

"Show me what you can do," continued Sally, indicating the random chunk of wood that Ben now held. "You're a craftsman. You bring your tools with you," she stated. "You carry what is precious to you. In the car." Mac shifted suddenly. Sally looked at him. Mac looked uncomfortable.

"We left the doctor. Asleep, in the car," he said. Sally nodded.

"And you will deal with it," she replied with an air of certainty.

CHAPTER THREE

Mac carried the sleeping Dr Charlie Hart into the house. He held her close to avoid the rain, but cold drops still fell onto her pale, drawn face. She didn't wake or even stir. Mac laid her gently onto one of the large leather sofas. She looked tiny in her rumpled, outsized scrubs. Sally walked over to join Mac, and they both looked down at her. Mac pulled a blanket from the back of the sofa and covered her. He remembered her gentle care of the dying woman and wondered if that had been the cause of her tears. His mouth pulled into a straight line as he pushed away the feeling of sympathy that crept into him. Feelings only led to weakness, he reminded himself. Mac looked at Sally.

"As soon as she wakes, she'll tell us where she lives, and I'll take her home," he assured his employer. Sally continued to look down at Charlie, remembering what she'd seen at the hospital.

"She's a good woman. I think." Sally said quietly.

There was a buzz from a laptop that lay on a desk filled

with computer screens. Sally started and walked swiftly towards it. An icon was flashing on the laptop screen. An avatar appeared, and a low voice with a Scottish accent spoke.

"Miss Marshall, is Mac with you? I need to speak with him. Urgently."

"He's right here," said Sally, stepping aside. Mac leaned over the desk.

"What's the problem, Sinclair?" he said. There was a brief pause, and then Sinclair replied.

"I've got some news. You need to come back to base. Now." Mac glanced up at Sally and Ben, who looked on impassively, his arms folded.

"Can you give me any details?" he said, his brow furrowed. "I can talk."

"I need you back at base. Sir," was all Sinclair replied. A dark weight turned in Mac's stomach. There were very few explanations for Sinclair's closed manner. And none of them were good. Mac nodded and stood straight. He moved swiftly towards the front door.

"But you can't go!" exclaimed Sally. "Not after last night. And you need to sort out the woman!" She pointed to the sleeping Dr Hart.

"I'm sorry, Sally. I have to go," said Mac over his shoulder as he stepped into the hallway. “Morton can take the doctor home.” Sally and Ben heard the front door close firmly. They heard the car start and reverse, wheels spinning on the soaked gravel.

There was silence. Sally and Ben regarded each other. The rain stopped, and they both turned their heads towards the glass wall. Ben's heavy heart hummed with the almost-forgotten whisper of joy at what he saw: a glittering triple rainbow arching over the edge of the storm as it swept away towards the distant peaks. Shafts of warming sun studded the green and purple valley below them and meandered over the pool-pitted flagstones of the courtyard outside.

"Beautiful," he murmured. "Just beautiful." He pulled his gaze away from the shimmering scene. "I'll get my things," he said, giving Sally a half-smile. "The things that are precious to me." Sally nodded stiffly. She turned away from him and sat at the desk, pulling her laptop towards her.

A few minutes later, Sally looked up to see that Ben had walked around the house and was standing, looking at the view of the valley below. A gentle breeze caught at his long hair, and it circled around his head like a fading halo. Sally shifted in her chair as a memory pulled at her. Where had she seen him before? He was carrying the applewood log and a heavy wooden toolbox. He hefted them onto the long, low stone wall that separated the courtyard from the steep cliff. He opened the box and selected some tools before placing the heavy box on the ground as a low seat, sitting down, and starting to work. Now and then, he would glance up to take in the view, but his hands never paused. He looked content.

Sally was used to being alone. She mostly dealt with things, including Mac, remotely. She looked at the sleeping Charlie. All was quiet, but no longer empty. She was not sure how she felt about that. She returned to her work and was soon immersed. A few hours later, a hand placed a steaming cup of tea and a coaster on the desk beside her. She looked up to see Ben walking away towards the hallway. No one had made her a cup of tea since she could remember. Sally looked at the cup, then out at the courtyard where Ben had re-emerged, his own cup in hand, to continue working. She was not sure how she felt about this.

• • •

CHARLIE SLOWLY CAME AWAKE. She was absolutely starving. She also needed to use the bathroom. She hoped there was some cheese in the fridge.... But then Charlie remembered Eaton's angry face; flecks of spittle emerging from his tight and bitter mouth.

"Your sister is dead, Charlie!" Emily was dead. And Lily, poor Lily.... Charlie opened her eyes and sat up. Her head span in disorientation. Where was she? A blanket in shell-pink of unbelievable softness caught at her rough fingertips. Golden light drenched everything around her and a beautiful, heavy, expensive scent hung in the air.

"Where am I?" she said, out loud this time.

"Rowans Holt," a voice replied. Charlie turned her head in the direction of the voice. A tall woman was sitting at a desk of glass and silver that overlooked a vast window. She was in her late twenties and painfully thin. She was of mixed European and what seemed to be Chinese heritage. Her skin was the colour of imperial topaz, with a smattering of medium dark freckles over her nose and cheeks. Her straight hair was cut in a very expensive but severe style. It was shiny and coloured deepest brown, with the occasional flash of gold. Her large hazel eyes were slightly too far apart. Her top lip was thin, but her bottom lip was full.

"How did I get here?" asked Charlie slowly.

"In a Range Rover," replied the woman, not smiling, seeming to think the logical answer was what Charlie wanted.

"No," said Charlie. "I mean. How did I get here?" The woman's brow furrowed.

"Is your actual question: 'What are the circumstances

that have led to me being in your residence?'" the woman asked.

"Yes," said Charlie, slightly intimidated.

"You were sitting on the floor of A and E, crying. You were tired because Eddie Lam had asked you to stay on and work. My Security Advisor found your bag and then offered you a lift. But you fell asleep."

"Ah," said Charlie, memories echoing faintly of a handsome but unsmiling face and the faint smell of lemon cologne. Her right hand tingled faintly. "Then what happened?"

"Mac couldn't wake you. I needed to get home. So, we brought you here."

"This is your home? And who are you?" asked Charlie.

"I was the Concussion in bed 4a. Next to Lily."

"Oh," said Charlie, embarrassed. "I'm sorry you had to hear that."

"I saw it too," the woman replied crisply. "Your curtains are sub-standard." There was an awkward pause.

"May I use your bathroom?" asked Charlie. Sally stood up gracefully and led Charlie past the kitchen into the hallway. She indicated a door and silently returned to her front room.

Charlie opened the door, and her eyes widened. The bathroom was a modern take on an Elizabethan palace. The tiles had a Tudor knot and rose pattern, reflecting the rich carvings on the half-panelled walls. A white-oak sideboard held a large, grey marble bowl beneath an elegantly arched brass tap. The most enormous bath she had ever seen sat under a large, mullioned window, panes of pastel glass separated by fine flutes of stonework. Everything exuded luxury. The white towels were thick and soft, and the hand soap radiated the same heavy fragrance as permeated the ground floor. Her stomach rumbled loudly.

She returned to what she now thought of as 'The Palace' drawing room. The woman had returned to her work.

"I'd like to say thank you, but I don't know your name," said Charlie hesitantly. She felt unaccustomedly shy, a new sensation for someone who made a living by communicating with people in difficult circumstances.

"My name is Sally, Sally Marshall," replied the woman, turning again from her computer. "Now you're awake, Ben can give you a lift to wherever you need to go."

"Ben?" asked Charlie.

Ben entered the room from the courtyard at this point and looked at Charlie.

"You're awake!" he exclaimed, smiling. Charlie smiled back hesitantly.

"Hello?" she said, uncertain. Ben's smile widened.

"Sorry, I've been peeking in every now and again. You've been sleeping like a baby for the last five hours." He held out his hand. "Morton, Ben Morton. I'm a joiner and carpenter. I'm going to take you home." Charlie's eyes were caught up in the view from the window, and she gasped. "Beautiful, isn't she?" said Ben quietly. He looked, not just at the view but at the house around him.

Ben's face then fell. "God, you're pale! When did you last eat?" He looked over at Sally. "Have you not got a scrap for the lass, Sal?" Sally's face twitched.

"Sal?" she stated coldly.

"That's your name, isn't it?" said Ben.

"My name is Sally," came the reply.

"Aye, that's what I said." Charlie could see that Ben was

gently teasing Sally, who clearly was not used to being teased.

"If you do have something to eat, I'd be very grateful," said Charlie. "It's probably a day since I ate properly." Sally looked uneasy.

"You can look in the fridge if you like," she said slowly.

Ben and Charlie moved towards the kitchen. Charlie reached out and ran her fingers over the hand-carved surfaces and looked up to see Ben doing the same.

"Have you ever seen anything like this house?" she whispered excitedly. He flashed a broad smile back at her and shook his head.

"It's a fine house you have, Sal!" He called out. Sally just looked up at them briefly, then returned to her work.

Charlie figured out which of the cabinets held the fridge and opened it. She almost cried out in horror. A tub of unspeakable, and certainly inedible, low-fat spread sat forlornly next to a bag of rotted salad leaves. A plastic-clad pint of skimmed milk lounged, lonely in the door. And that was it. Charlie's stomach, having become excited by the prospect of food, complained loudly, and Charlie thought she might faint. Ben had grabbed the milk to make tea earlier but hadn't looked into the rest of the fridge.

"Oh Sal, have you nowt in?" Ben called, peering over Charlie's shoulder. Sally stood and came to join them.

"An emergency chocolate bar?" asked Charlie, confident that somewhere in the house was a forbidden, but craved, supply of carbohydrates..

"We'd best make a move then, pick up something on the way," said Ben.

Sally's face unexpectedly fell at these words. She

suddenly didn't want the silence to return quite yet. She wanted them to stay just a little longer.

"There's the freezer..." she suggested. "Maya...my ex." Sally had to take a deep breath before she could carry on. "She insisted it be filled up to the standard of a country house. She employed someone to do it. I haven't looked inside, but there might be something you can eat in there." Sally felt a bit overwhelmed. She didn't know what had come over her. She never disclosed information that she didn't need to. Knowledge and personal information were like currency, like gold, and she was a natural miser of this wealth.

Feeling shaken and unaccustomedly vulnerable, Sally led them into a stone-flagged larder that held an enormous chest freezer. She indicated that Charlie open it.

"There's also a store cupboard, just there." Sally waved with her long, slim hand. "Again, I've never looked in it." Charlie hesitated. She suddenly felt as if she was intruding into this odd, lonely woman's intimate life, looking before she did at the contents of her own house. Her hand hesitated on the freezer lock, and the thought *what if it's Maya in the freezer*? crossed her mind. She glanced up at Ben. She was sure the same thing had occurred to him by the look on his face. Gathering her courage, she flung open the freezer lid.

"Oh. My. God." Charlie breathed. The freezer was like a chef's paradise; baskets and neatly arranged boxes filled every inch of space. There was steak, chicken, lobster, sauces, pies, and frozen fruits. Charlie caressed the items, pulling them out and laying them carefully on a nearby table as she delved, like an excited pirate discovering a treasure chest. Charlie loved food. Loved thinking about it, planning it, shopping for it, cooking it and eating it. Especially when shared with other people. And wine. Lots of wine. "She's put stock in here!" exclaimed Charlie. "Real stock! All flavours. Oh my God, do you know what I can do with this? I can... hang on... if this is what the freezer looks like...." Charlie flung herself at the tall, wooden store-cupboard doors and wrenched them open. Her hunch was correct; the store cupboards over-flowed with all the things needed for a Cordon bleu chef's most outrageous of dreams. Ten types of rice, cans of oysters, every dried herb, vegetable, crustacean and spice imaginable stood to neat attention. Charlie felt on the edge of a small, but delicious, nervous breakdown. She opened a glass jar and helped herself to a handful of raisins. "Peaches in brandy. Who actually buys peaches in brandy?" she almost sobbed.

Sally realised that her mouth was hanging slightly open. She closed it and looked at Ben. He was watching Charlie with a big grin, obviously highly amused by her enthusiasm. His face was clear and open. There was no planning, no calculation, no defensiveness or lust; just pure enjoyment in someone else's happiness. She hadn't known that look on someone's face since.... Sally suddenly realised who Ben reminded her of and was almost undone. She felt her heart wrench itself into a new and nearly forgotten shape.

"Will you cook something for us, then?" Sally found herself saying. "Would that make you happy?"

"Very happy. And full," grinned Charlie, but then she hesitated. "Are you sure? You seem like a very... private person. I don't want to make you uncomfortable."

"You won't. This food deserves to be eaten," said Sally. "It was Maya who was the truly private person. And she's gone now." Sally felt a wave of anxiety sweep over her. She forced her voice to remain calm. "She's gone now," Sally repeated firmly. "It's about time I had some company." She wondered how much of a lie all of this was and found she couldn't tell.

"Butter! Oh my God, she's even put tins of butter in here!" yelled Charlie, as if she had just found gold. "You know what this means?" She looked at them triumphantly. "You're going to get my special risotto!" And she beamed as if she was gifting them the week's winning lottery ticket. Ben started to laugh, and even Sally found her face rounded in a deeply unaccustomed smile.

CHAPTER
FOUR

Two hours later, Charlie Hart found herself to be truly happy. Sally had led them to a wine cellar that would have graced a top London hotel and had, perhaps foolishly, told Charlie to help herself to anything. Charlie had avoided the more dusty and expensive-looking items but had chosen a few bottles of white wine that were proving to be very special indeed. It was only Saturday afternoon, and she wasn't working until Wednesday, so she could relax. She was sure she could persuade someone to put her up for a few nights. She couldn't face returning to her house. To the cellar. To the image of Emily.... Charlie shook her head as if she could dislodge the memories.

"Butter, garlic, mushrooms, rice," she muttered. A mantra of the moment to help her forget. "Butter, garlic, mushrooms, rice...." And it worked. She stirred the rice and added another ladle of fragrant chicken stock. She hugged herself mentally.

Charlie was cooking with the real-copper pan she had

reverently lifted from amongst all the other high-range copper pans in the pristine cupboards. Most of them had never been touched. *Why buy a ridiculously expensive kitchen if you don't eat?* She briefly thought. She already knew the answer. It wasn't a matter of food; it was a matter of control. Charlie eyed the defrosting ciabatta. *You know what would make this perfect?* She thought. *A bay leaf or two. If this is a cook's kitchen, I'm sure to find one close by.* No sooner had she thought this than there was a slow creak. A wooden door she'd barely noticed at the edge of the enormous window slowly opened. Checking the heat was set on low, Charlie walked to the door and gently opened it. She looked out onto an ancient, flagged stone courtyard and, sure enough, a small, dark bay tree crouched just outside. A low wall surrounded the yard. Straight ahead, a few meters beyond the wall, the ground fell away into a steep cliff. A path led away to the left, tracing round the house. Charlie walked down it, curious to see if the garden matched the grandeur of the building. The path led down some steep steps. She saw a crumbling red brick wall which, from where she stood, seemed to enclose an ancient garden.

"A kitchen garden?" she breathed. This house was like a fairy tale.

Charlie approached the wall and pushed against the wooden door that sat in it. It swung reluctantly open, and she stepped through into a massed tangle of weeds and overgrowth. At one time, the garden had been laid out with low stone walls into beds in rectangular patterns. A raised area sat in the middle of the ancient beds. *A well, at the very centre*, she thought. "You poor, lonely garden," Charlie muttered. "No one to love you." Charlie traced her hand over the stones. *I'll bet someone grew herbs just here*, she thought.

She breathed in the scents of rosemary and lavender. She felt her body relax for the first time that she could remember. She felt safe for the first time that she could remember. A tiny butterfly with wings of pale pink flew into view and fluttered around her head. She smiled, her face lighting up with quiet joy, but then her face fell. It was very early in the year for a butterfly. The little thing would probably not survive the cold night.

Charlie looked down and saw that her hands had been busy, without her knowing it. She'd cleared a space in one of the beds and revealed a small clump of primroses. She must have caught the index finger of her left hand on a hidden thorn, for a large drop of blood hung fat and heavy on the tip. As Charlie watched, the warm scarlet scrap fell to the earth of the beds and disappeared, eagerly consumed by the rich soil.

AT HER DESK, Sally looked up. "Hello?" she said. She thought she'd heard a sound, like a low, triumphant cry or a muffled bell. Sally looked around the room. All was quiet. She noticed that the kitchen door was open. Charlie must have wandered out to see the garden. Good thing she'd turned her risotto off before she left.

OUTSIDE, in the walled garden, Charlie shivered. It was only March, and the air was chilly despite the sun. From the front of the house, she heard a bang, as if something had slammed shut. She'd best get back. The risotto!

. . .

Sally glanced up again as a figure appeared in the corner of her vision. But it was neither Charlie nor Ben. It was Maya. She stood in the kitchen, staring at Sally. Sally felt her chest tighten until she could no longer pull air into it. The memories of last night's events pounded through Sally's head. Maya, Sally's estranged lover, had called Sally to her city centre apartment, saying it was life or death. Sally had gone to the apartment and had been shocked by Maya's appearance. She had not thought it possible for Maya to become any thinner, but in the months since their breakup, she had become even more cadaverous. Her hair had fallen in dark rat tails around her pallid face. Despite the dim candlelight of the unkempt apartment, she had been wearing dark glasses. Maya had demanded, once again, that Sally choose her or Rowans Holt. When Sally had tried to leave, Maya attacked her. Sally had knocked the dark glasses aside in the struggle and revealed the blue tinge to Maya's eyes. Maya had been unaware that Sally had asked Mac to accompany her. He had been waiting outside the flat, and only Mac's intervention had saved Sally. She had been assured at the hospital that Maya had been securely detained. But now, here she was.

Sally leapt up, and her chair crashed to the floor behind her. She struggled to catch her next breath. Sally was suddenly aware of the wounds to her arm and head. She felt a deep stab of fear, this blow falling directly through her heart.

"I've come home, Baby," said Maya timidly. "Are you pleased to see me?" Sally took a pace back, and, as if drawn by an invisible thread strung between them, Maya took a pace forward. "Don't worry. I'm not going to burn you," said Maya. Sally shook her head.

"I wasn't thinking that you would, Maya," she said in a small voice. Both women turned their heads as Charlie crashed through the kitchen door, smiling and clutching some dark, waxy bay leaves.

There was silence. Charlie looked between them and then slowly moved towards Sally. Unaware that she was doing it, Charlie took a stand between the two women. Her hand reached out towards Sally as if to shield her. Maya spoke, her voice now slow and dangerous.

"I thought you would be alone. You are always alone. Ugly and alone." Maya looked at Charlie with contempt, then back at Sally. "You bitch!" she spat. "I'm gone for a few days, and you already moved a new model in? A fat heifer! And you turned off the cooker to save her fat meal? You always let mine burn... always turned the cooker up higher!"

Sally's face was a frozen picture of horror. "Maya," she whispered. "But you've been sectioned. How did you escape? How did you get here?" Sally reached up and touched her right arm protectively. Maya's face twisted, but then she forced it into a smile.

"I've decided to forgive you," Maya said. "Let bygones be bygones. We can be together. Forever." Sally slowly shook her head, clearly terrified.

"We were over months ago, Maya," she said. "You need to go. Please leave my home."

"This is not a home! This is a cage!" screamed Maya. Ben appeared at the kitchen door.

"What's going on?" he said. He saw Sally's expression and stepped towards her; his face creased with concern. "Are you alright, Sal?"

"A man? You let a filthy man in? You are meant to be alone!" Maya's voice rose even higher. She strode towards the knife block and withdrew a large, Japanese-steel chopping knife, which spoke with a whisper of threatened violence. She swung her arm between Charlie and Ben as if deliberating which one to deal with first. Ben held his arms out from his body as if trying to soothe a scared animal. He, too, had unconsciously moved his body between Sally and Maya.

"Calm down now, Duck," he said in a slow, deep voice. "Calm down. Let's talk about this... just put the knife down."

Maya let out a screech and ran towards Charlie, the knife waving dangerously. Charlie leapt to the central island and used it as a barrier between them. Sally shouted out;

"Maya, stop! I'll talk, I'll talk!"

"It's too late for talking now, Sally!" exulted the incandescent Maya. "I'm going to kill the fat heifer. Blood is what you want, and that's what you'll get!"

"You are bonkers!" Charlie exclaimed. The ridiculous thought that this was not a medical term and not a very professional thing to say to someone clearly mentally unwell crossed her mind. Would Maya report her to the General Medical Council? Despite her terror, she giggled slightly. Maya's eyes widened.

"You think I'm funny?" she howled. Like a scuttling spider, Maya changed direction and ran at Sally. Ben ran after her. She flailed with the knife. Ben slapped her left shoulder, and her blow missed. She changed direction again and, this time, ran towards the cooker, reaching for the copper pan that held Charlie's risotto.

"Oi! Not my dinner!" raged Charlie. She picked up one of the copper saucepans and hurled it toward Maya's back with all her strength. It hit her, hard between the shoulder blades, and she dropped to the floor, squealing with pain. The knife scuttered across the floor, and Ben rapidly scooped it up. He slammed it onto the wooden surface and then grabbed Maya roughly. He was amazed by how light she was, how fragile her bones seemed beneath his grasp. Up close, he saw a fine down of hair covering her face and body.

Maya suddenly went limp. A look of cunning flitted across her face. She looked more closely at Ben and then at Charlie.

"Do you really think a Half Man and a Parasite will make you feel better, Sally?" she demanded. Maya's thin body twisted in Ben's hold, and she slid away unexpectedly. She flung herself at the knife on the sideboard and grabbed it with dogged determination. Maya hurled herself towards Sally with an inarticulate cry of fury.

CHAPTER FIVE

There was a loud crash at the front door. "Police!" came a cry, and the room seemed suddenly full of swiftly moving figures. There was a flash and a buzz, and a tazer deployed against Maya's contorting body. She collapsed and was swiftly cuffed. Charlie recognised Detective Inspector Decker, who stood, breathing heavily, in the doorway. He approached them slowly, hands raised.

"Ms Marshall. Sally Marshall? Are you alright? Do you need to go back to the hospital?" Sally looked at him.

"How did she escape?" she demanded. Decker looked apologetic.

"I'm sorry, Ms Marshall. She's proved to be a tricky customer." He turned to his officers, who were bundling a writhing Maya out of the room.

"You kicked his head!" Maya was screaming. "Then said he fell. And you! You! does your husband know about all the others...?" Her voice faded as she was dragged unceremoniously from the house.

"How do you know my name?" asked Sally to Decker, who smiled wearily.

"The inventor of the BanKin app?" he asked. "We know who you are." He looked around the room. "Don't worry; she won't escape the secure unit again. I'll make sure of it," he said confidently. "How long was she here before we caught up?"

"Minutes," said Sally. "But this is unacceptable. I will be considering legal action." Decker nodded slowly, and his shoulders slumped.

"You'd be within your rights, Miss Marshall. If no one complains, we, the Police, never learn." Sally glared at Decker.

"You can go," she said abruptly, her voice harsh and tight with fear. He looked at her for a moment, his face unreadable, and then he nodded. He handed over a card.

"You still need to make a statement about last night, Ms Marshall. I understand you don't want to press charges, but a criminal act still took place. My number, Ms Marshall," he said. "For when you feel up to an interview." He nodded once more, then turned and left the house.

There was silence. Charlie heard a soft drip. Looking down, she saw blood pooling on the floor below Sally's right arm. Sally swayed, and her eyes glazed over. Ben caught her as she began to fall. He lowered her to the floor. Within moments, Charlie was on her knees next to Sally.

"Get me some scissors, Ben," she said in a calm and professional voice that neither Ben nor Sally recognised. Ben pulled open drawers until he found a large pair of Sheffield steel shears. While he was doing this, Charlie located her work bag that Mac had brought in when he had carried her from the car. She opened it, slipped on a pair of disposable gloves, and threw a pair to Ben. Charlie cut up Sally's blood-soaked right sleeve and found the saturated dressing. She looked up and saw that Ben had lifted Sally's silk blouse and was running his hand over Sally's abdomen. "What are you doing?" she exclaimed. Ben looked back at her.

"I was an Army Medic," he replied. "Secondary survey. You know how easy it is to miss a stab wound." Charlie nodded, surprised.

"Don't worry, I'll manage," she said. "Close your eyes, Ben," Charlie ordered. She unbuttoned Sally's shirt and carefully checked Sally's chest and ribs for damage and any sign of puncture wounds.

"Don't touch me," muttered Sally.

"I'm not going to let you bleed to death in front of me. So, sorry, Sally, no," said Charlie, kindly but briskly.

Sally heard a great rushing in her ears and knew she was close to passing out.

"I'm going to be sick," she whispered. Charlie grabbed the pan that she'd thrown at Maya.

"Help me get her on her left side, Ben," Charlie ordered. "Now, hold her while I check her back." Sally's stomach heaved, but there was nothing to bring up. She retched, and, as she did, she felt Charlie's hands on her back this time, professionally checking for signs of a puncture wound. Too many people didn't realise they'd been stabbed if the blade was sharp and fast enough. A tiny-looking wound could hide a torrential internal bleed.

Charlie started to examine Sally's head, tutting at the deep scalp laceration. Charlie rapidly but carefully palpated, exposed, and examined down the rest of Sally's body and limbs. She pulled up the blood-soaked dressing again and frowned at the deep, seeping arm wound. She gently stroked Sally's hair.

"You've had a massive shock," Charlie said soothingly. "I assume these wounds are from last night. It's all going to be fine. We'll get you to A and E for stitches, and you'll be right as rain."

"Stitches?" gasped Sally. "No! I'm not going back there. Never again!"

"But your wounds are really deep," said Charlie, calmly but insistently. "You'll have nasty scars, and they may not heal properly. Wounds like these can't just be steri-stripped."

"I'm not going!" announced Sally. Charlie looked at the stubborn line between Sally's eyebrows and realised there was no persuading her.

"Is there nothing you can do?" said Sally, looking up at Charlie. Charlie sighed.

"I'm half cut, Sal. The GMC really would have something to say."

"Well, I'm good at keeping secrets," replied Sally. "And I can guarantee I won't sue." Charlie shrugged.

"Ok," she sighed. "You have been warned.... Ben, keep the pressure on her arm. I'll see what I can find in my bag."

Charlie emptied the contents of her work bag onto the kitchen island. She was shocked by the number of empty crisp and Twix packets she'd accumulated. However, she also had a fair bit of medical equipment, stuff you found at the end of a shift, deep in your scrub pockets. She generally threw them into a plastic bag and mentally promised to return them at the next opportunity. Which never seemed to come.

"So, we're in luck!" declared Charlie delightedly. "As well

as two green cannulas, a fifty ml syringe, a three-way tap, and this thing that I'm not sure what it does!" she waved a piece of plastic-enclosed equipment. "We have syringe, needles, local anaesthetic in a plastic vial (only just out of date) and, best of all, sutures!" Charlie swayed slightly, a mixture of fatigue and alcohol, but recovered. Ben gave her a measured look and then leaned over to look at the scattered items. He picked up a suture packet.

"Three-oh silk. That'll do for scalp. Shall I do that if you do the arm?" Charlie looked at him. Ben gazed back. "I've probably done more scalp wounds than you," he said softly. "We served the locals too, in Afghanistan. I've seen far more than my fair share of deep and dirty wounds." He looked at Charlie's uncertain expression. A smile tugged at the corner of his mouth. "You can watch me put the first one in if you like," he said. Charlie shrugged.

"It's not up to me," she replied.

Ben and Charlie looked at Sally. She sat on the floor, looking closed and vulnerable. They instinctively stepped away, giving her space. Sally stood and looked between them. She turned to Ben.

"Put me on the island," she ordered. "The light's better there." Ben put his hands around her waist and lifted Sally. She was light, but her bones contained a firm strength that Maya had lacked. He stepped away again, waiting. Sally sat with her head down. "I know that I need to be mended. So to speak," said Sally. "But I'm scared. Of needles. Of anything medical. Since..." She pulled in a deep, shuddering breath. She would not talk about the bad thing now. "Maya always says that I have no feelings." Sally continued, her head still down, her voice hesitant. The room was silent. "But, I have feelings. I have so, so, many feelings. I just don't know what to do with them." Ben and Charlie said nothing, just listened. After a while, Sally continued. "These emotions rise up. And I feel as if I'm going to die. So, I just... close down." A small tear made its way down Sally's face and hung on her top lip. She wiped it away impatiently. Charlie approached her.

"We'll be gentle," she said. "If you feel overwhelmed, that's OK. That's normal. You don't have to say anything. Just raise your left hand." Charlie demonstrated. "Like this." Sally nodded, tears now streaming down her face. The adrenaline-inducing events of the last day had left her feeling drained and uncharacteristically exposed.

Charlie couldn't help herself. She took a deep breath, gently took hold of Sally's hand and held it. Sally looked at her, surprised. Sally then gave a low gasp as she felt the sharp pain of her distress ease and fade. There was a long pause.

"How do you do that?" whispered Sally. "You did it to Lily, too. I saw you." Ben looked quizzically between the two women.

"Am I missing something here?" he asked. Charlie shook her head.

"I'm not doing anything, Sal. You're doing it all yourself. You're braver than you know." There was another long pause. Sally then nodded again. She held out her right arm.

"You can start now."

"Ok,' announced Charlie, trying to diffuse the tension in the room. "Let's get these wounds thoroughly cleaned, and then let's do this! Now, can you confirm your name and date of birth? Do you have any allergies, are you taking any medications, and do you have any blood-borne viruses, as far as you know? And Hell, while we're at it, what's your darn blood group?"

Charlie started injecting local anaesthetic into Sally's arm wound, being as gentle as possible.

"What's this BanKin app?" she asked, trying to distract Sally. Sally's breathing was fast, and her eyes were staring at the opposite wall.

"It's an app that can enable all your banking accounts to talk to each other. Across a secure individual network. Artificial Intelligence. A.I.," said Sally tersely. Charlie grimaced.

"That sounds complex. And very clever. I only have one bank account, and I avoid looking at it at all costs. Ben? do you know about BanKin?" Ben slowly shook his head, all his attention on the anaesthetic he was injecting and the difficult suturing job he was planning on Sally's thickly-haired scalp.

"I don't even have a smartphone," he said vaguely.

"Does it take up a lot of your time, running the app?" asked Charlie, gently placing the first interrupted suture through Sally's gaping arm wound. Sally shook her head.

"I sold it. To The Company," she said through gritted teeth.

"The Company? Or a company?" asked Charlie.

"The Company. I work for a company that calls itself 'The Company,'" replied Sally, her eyes still wide. "American. My boss thinks he's very amusing."

"What did you get for it?" asked Ben quietly. "If you don't mind me asking?" Sally didn't reply. Her mouth melted into a small, triumphant smile, despite her distress. She moved her gaze around the room, drinking in the beauty of her home.

"You got Rowans Holt? And all this land?" said Charlie.

"Smashing. Clever lass," muttered Ben approvingly. He bent again to his delicate task. "Now all you have to do is make another App, and you can buy half of Sheffield," he joked gently.

"I'm working on something, actually," said Sally quietly. "Something special." But she said no more.

Charlie continued placing seven interrupted sutures in Sally's arm. She glanced now and again at Ben. His worn but handsome face frowned in concentration at the work at hand. His hands were nimble and efficient as they worked with sure skill. Sally, in turn, observed Charlie as she worked. She was around five foot five, much shorter than Sally. Her clear-skinned face was soft and round and pretty, with a gentle mouth that was mobile and expressive. She had long, honey-blonde hair, haphazardly tied back with a cheap, black elastic band. Her hair had clearly not been cut for many months. Sally noted that her large-eyed gaze was direct and friendly, but she had a habit of pulling her chin in as if scared someone was going to aim a blow at it. Sally was not used to being touched, but she felt that Charlie's small, rough hands were warm and kind. She realised she felt safe, cared for. She didn't want the feeling to end.

Sally's small, tightly controlled world suddenly felt upended and unreal.

"What you did to me? To Lily. Is it magic?" asked Sally, suddenly. She felt stupid as soon as the words were out of her mouth. Charlie just smiled softly, not looking up from Sally's arm.

"There's no such thing as magic, Sally. And if there were,

it would all come at far too high a cost. All we can hope for is a little life. And the tiny pleasures we find there." Charlie finally tore her gaze away and looked up at Sally with a big, beaming smile. "Like doing seven, perfect interrupted stitches." Sally, however, squirmed.

"Seven?" said Sally.

"What's wrong?" asked Charlie, looking alarmed.

"It's the thought of an uneven number of stitches in my arm. It makes me feel really uncomfortable," said Sally miserably. Charlie smiled again.

"I'll put them a bit closer together, and then you can have eight."

"Evenly spaced?" Sally couldn't help herself saying. Charlie nodded patiently.

"Evenly spaced," she agreed. Sally then twisted her body.

"I'm already planning on doing six, an even number," said Ben reassuringly. There was a pregnant pause.

"Could you make it eight?" burst out Sally, closing her eyes and hating herself.

"Eight perfectly spaced stitches coming up," said Ben, his eyes dancing with amusement.

"How long were you and Maya together?" Charlie asked quietly as another stitch went in.

"A while," replied Sally, her face still drawn. "I'm not sure. It's. It's a blur."

"Is she the type you normally go for?" said Charlie, her brow furrowed as she concentrated on her delicate task. "If you don't mind me asking...."

"I don't have a type," Sally lied. "She's the only person I've ever... been with."

"Was it always like tonight?" Charlie asked gently.

"No. No," replied Sally mournfully. "Sometimes, it was

violent and unhappy." Charlie paused in disbelief and stared at Sally, who calmly returned the stare and slowly raised her left eyebrow. Charlie threw back her head in laughter, carefully holding the curved needle away from both her and Sally.

"You had me for a moment there!" Charlie announced, thrilled. "And I thought you didn't have a sense of humour…." Despite herself, Sally smiled.

LATER, they sat around the cleaned island and ate risotto. It was slightly stodgy, but nothing white wine and butter couldn't sort out. In fact, Charlie insisted, there was nothing in life that couldn't be sorted out with butter and an excess of white wine. Sally noticed that Charlie only gave her a tiny portion of food. She watched in amazement as Charlie wolfed her food down with such evident pleasure that it was infectious. Sally asked for more, much to her own surprise. She was even more surprised that she actually enjoyed the sensation of food in her mouth and belly for the first time in years. When Charlie again spooned a modest amount onto her plate, she asked.

"Are you worried about re-feeding syndrome? Do I look that bad?"

Charlie looked at her with raised eyebrows as if shocked that she'd read her mind.

"What? What's the matter?" asked Ben, unsure what the exchange meant.

"Charlie's scared I'll get sick if I eat too much. She thinks I've been starving myself for too long," replied Sally.

"Well, I have seen more fat on a chip, lass," said Ben

frankly but with a warm smile. He waved his fork. "Don't be stingy, Charlie; feed her up!"

"Traitor..." said Charlie, but she smiled too as she added another modest spoonful of risotto and a slice of buttered ciabatta to Sally's plate.

As they pushed away from the island, full and satisfied, Charlie finally asked Sally the question she'd longed to know the answer to.

"So, where is it?" Charlie asked intently. "The chocolate? I know she had some." Sally felt a thrill of anxiety. Was this a betrayal if she told? It was Maya's secret. Her shame. Should she tell this sunny, smiling woman? Woman of appetites. This woman who held the dying, kissed the newly dead and gently closed their fixed, half-mast eyes? Sally slowly raised her arm and pointed to the topmost cupboard in the kitchen. "I knew it!" exulted Charlie. "I didn't get a distinction in Psychiatry for nothing!"

In the end, she bullied and cajoled poor Ben into getting it for her; the large box of very expensive chocolates in a genuine silk-velvet, heart-shaped box. Complete with red satin ribbon. "Only six months out of date!" Charlie sighed, perusing the treasures spread out before her. She selected a caramel and a Turkish delight and relaxed back in her tall chair. She slapped the island top enthusiastically. "My God, everything tastes so much better on a few hours' sleep and a bottle of wine!" Sally grinned and felt another tiny wall crumble in her heart.

CHAPTER
SIX

Sally looked at Ben. "And what have you been doing all this time?" she said, suddenly relaxed. Ben walked into the hallway and retrieved the applewood. He held it out to Sally, who took it and looked at it, perplexed. A woman's face had been carved into the wood, seeming to grow from within. Her eyes were large, intelligent, and beautiful. Her mouth was caught, forever, in a half smile. She looked as if she was about to speak. Sally frowned, overwhelmed by the skill displayed. Her fingers ran over the golden wood, caressing smooth lips and high cheekbones.

"It's excellent," she murmured. "Perfect. Who is she?" Ben looked taken aback.

"It's you!" he said. Charlie came over and peered at the carving.

"That's amazing," she exclaimed. "Sal, it looks just like you!" Sally shook her head.

"I don't look like this," she objected. "This woman is beautiful." *And I'm just ugly*, Sally thought. She heard Maya's voice whisper inside her head. *You are ugly, inside and out,*

Sally Marshall. No one will ever love you. Except for me. Ben shook his head.

"I just carved what I can see," he said simply.

Sally felt self-conscious and overwhelmed. She turned the wood over in her perfectionist's hands and spotted a slight discrepancy on the reverse of the object.

"There's something here..." she said, frowning. She was eager to distract them from her raw pain. "What have you done? I don't really want your signature...It's a small rabbit?" Ben's face fell.

"Oh, it's all right, lass," he said quietly, not looking at either of the women. "I put the bunny on everything."

"Well, I don't particularly want Benjamin Bunny on everything you do in my home, Benjamin," said Sally archly.

"I'm not Benjamin," muttered Ben.

"What?" said Sally.

"I'm not Benjamin," repeated Ben. There was a pause. "I'm Benedict. It's my son. It was my son. My son was Benjamin." *Oh God*, Sally thought. *His son...was...Don't tell me. Please don't tell me.* "He's dead," said Ben, his head twisting softly away towards the shadowed side of the room. "Benjamin's dead." *Please don't...*"One year, two months, eight days, six hours, twenty-four minutes and..." Ben glanced up at the second hand of the kitchen clock. "Thirty-two seconds ago." Silence fell over the table. Sally felt her mouth dry up, as if filled with dust.

"Well, let's drink to Ben!" announced Charlie after a slight pause. "Do you have a picture? Come on! Let's have a look at him. Was he as handsome as his dad? Did he like football? Was he an Owls man or a Blades chap?"

Ben paused, taken aback. His announcement was usually a conversation-killer. He was not used to a follow-up, to actual interest in his child. He looked at Charlie. This was a woman who dealt with the dead. He could trust her with Little Ben. He reached clumsily for his old phone.

"Well..." Ben said, sniffing slightly. "Some of the photos, at the end, don't capture him. But, he has this smile...." And, before he knew it, he was swept up in Charlie's admiration and questions about the dead, but ever-present, Benjamin Morton. Charlie Hart accepted his hair loss. She laughed at the number of nurses he had persuaded to sit on his bed one slow Saturday afternoon. She excused his Mum's deadly stare at the camera. She appreciated Benjamin. Cheeky, naughty, lovely... perfect Benjamin.

Ben was vaguely aware of Charlie's gentle hand on his shoulder. And as he talked and cried and laughed, Ben felt a tight knot of ice in the centre of his chest start to melt. He felt the terrible pain ease. Ben hadn't spoken about his son to anyone since the dark night of his son's death. He felt a surge of gratitude towards the two women and the beautiful house which had enabled this to happen.

Sally sat and watched the interchange, feeling adrift and uncertain. She was unfamiliar with the emotional ebb and flow. But she could see Charlie's small hand on Ben's shoulder; she could see his pain visibly ease. Eventually, they stopped talking and looked at her. Something was about to happen.

"Well, we probably need to go," said Charlie. "It's been lovely to meet you." Ben looked uneasy.

"She's had a serious head injury, Charlie," he muttered.

"You'll need to call a taxi," said Sally, knowing they could not. There was little phone signal, and her Next Generation computer network firewall meant there was practically no accessible Wi-Fi in her home. "You've both had too much to drink to drive the Volvo."

"So we have!" announced Charlie. By her glazed expression, she was approaching the state that Sally had seen her in this morning at A and E. Ben, likewise, looked a bit dazed. He reached reluctantly for his phone.

"Hmmm, no signal..."

"Oh dear," said Sally, not feeling sorry at all. "Why don't you stay?" she asked as if this was a normal thing for her to do.

Ben thought about Sally's head injury. She shouldn't be left alone tonight. He also thought about his cold, dark flat, filled with the half-carved projects that he listlessly started and never had the heart to finish. The empty beer bottles, the unmade bed. His marriage had not survived the death of his son. Should he stay here for one night, or return to where he would sit, drinking, until he fell into a fitful, nightmared sleep?

Charlie thought of Sally's head injury. That she shouldn't be left alone overnight. Charlie also thought of her empty little house in Crookes, Sheffield. A house, not a home. A non-home. Filled with the memories of the daily struggle that had been her existence, living with Emily. The secrets and the longings crowding each corner of every shabby room. Should she stay here for one night, or return home? Back to the lock on her bedroom door. Back to the pile of cheap paperbacks she escaped into each night, forgetting the day just gone, not imagining tomorrow.

There was a long pause. "I do think I need to go to bed," Charlie nodded, fatigue and wine warring in her tired mind. "Can I use the master bathroom?" She waved her hand in the direction of the downstairs bathroom.

"Oh, Sweet Pea," she heard Sally softly declare. "That's not the master bathroom. That's not even the mistress bathroom...."

In her dreams, Charlie would remember walking upstairs and being led to an en-suite bathroom that felt bigger than her entire house. She would vaguely recall Sally opening a wardrobe filled with cashmere and silk socks, pants and guest pyjamas. They whispered against Charlie's skin like sweet relief to her troubled bones. Safe and warm, Charlie slept better than she had done in years.

Sally showed Ben to his room. A four-poster bed stood at the centre, with a richly carved headboard that was hundreds of years old.

"Because of your head injury, I'll be checking on you in the night. If that's alright?" said Ben, suddenly awkward without Charlie's sunny presence. Sally just looked at him, then nodded once before turning and disappearing down the long corridor.

Ben, however, didn't sleep or prepare for bed. He sat, looking out of the dark window. He sensed a vague malevolence deep in the distant city and was unsure where it was or what it meant. He felt he was waiting for something. He then heard a faint cry. Ben quietly opened the bedroom door and peered into the dim corridor. He was reminded of when his son had called out in the night, afraid of the dark. It came again, an urgent cry of distress. He hesitantly padded over the floorboards and then down a small staircase. He stood, uncertain, outside Sally's room. The door was ajar. Again, she cried out in the dark, clearly struggling with a nightmare but unable to awake. He felt so sorry for her, all alone in this place. Her warm flesh torn apart by someone whom she had once trusted.

So, he went to her. And the woman who was falling landed in the wide arms of the man who had nothing. Within moments, she was quiet. And he was asleep. And that's how Charlie would find them the following day. Ben, fully dressed, one booted foot hanging out of the bed. One hand gently placed on Sally's sleeping head.

CHAPTER
SEVEN

It was Friday night. They came in the dark, hushed and excited; some on foot, some slow in crawling cars, lights off, engines idling. They fumbled their way to the disused steel works. They all knew not to bring mobile phones. The word was very clear on that. Anyone found with a phone would be branded and banished. No one could bear that. Not once you had transformed.

The girl clung to the hand of the young man who pulled ahead, eager and alive. He looked back at her and said,

"Spud says it's like nothing else. You see angels, actual bloody angels!" She smiled, finally feeling excited rather than scared. She would love to see an angel. They joined the whispering, waiting crowd. Men dressed all in black, from their balaclavas and bomber jackets to their steel-capped boots, eyed and corralled the crowd. They entered through enormous, rusted metal doors and joined one of the many queues that had been organised. As each person reached the head of their queue, they handed over cash. They then had to open their mouth. A small, blue tablet was placed on the tongue. This rapidly melted, the process closely observed by one of the balaclava-wearing men. They then drank a large mouthful of water. No chance was allowed to palm the tablet. They were then directed into a cage. Once two hundred or so people were crammed in, the doors to the cage were locked and chained, and a large digital clock was set. Five minutes started to count down; five minutes until they were freed from the cage.

The girl squeezed closer to the young man. She started to feel a slow turning in her stomach. Four minutes. Her feet felt soft and leaden. Three minutes. Her breathing slowed as a feeling of warmth flowed like heavy honey through her veins. She looked at her fingertips, and they glowed. Two minutes. She looked around her, and everything was shiny. The people were all smiling. They were beautiful, children of stars. One minute. And then she saw it, rising slowly just beyond the cage... a tall figure with the face of perfect beauty, trailing long wings of light. The girl reached out. She was part of heaven. She could see an angel.... She glanced at her companion. He wasn't smiling.

RILEY WAS IN A ROOM. The walls and floor were lined with dirty and cracked white tiles. On a small table stood a large, dark-purple box, which rattled occasionally. It was as if something within listened keenly to the outside world and batted at the walls, impatient to get out and join in the fun. A thin and wrinkled old man sat, slumped, in a cheap plastic chair. His hands were cable-tied behind his back, and his bald scalp reflected the harsh glow of the single strip light that flickered above them. Riley sniffed. He suddenly smelled smoke. A man walked into view. Riley couldn't see where he had appeared from; there were no doors or windows in the room. The man was of late middle age but remained very handsome. He was dressed in a dark grey suit, white shirt, and a long coat. If Riley had known about such things, he would have recognised cashmere. He didn't know about such things; all he knew was he was scared. Where were the angels?

The older man spoke, his smooth voice echoing off the cold grubby surfaces. "Not very inspiring, is it, Riley?" He gestured around him. "But you don't have the most vivid of a subconscious. This is all I had to work with; your school changing rooms." He placed a hand on the shoulder of the old man, who flinched. "And your next-door neighbour." He looked at Riley, and his blue eyes sparkled with amusement. "Life, Riley. Life is full of decisions. Left or right? Cherry or apple? Revenge? Or Justice? But most of the time, our decisions are not made for ourselves. We make them for others. We fear what others will think. We try to deny the black mark that is human nature. We are ashamed by the naked human soul."

Riley's face crumpled. He had no idea what this posh git was talking about. The man sighed. "Goodness is a cult, Riley. Badness, the true spirit of humanity, is a multitude. But we must choose it." He produced a large black gun and placed it on the table. It clunked with heavy solidity. "I offer you the chance to make that choice. To choose your true nature. To feel the power that this gives you." He laid his hand on the box, which jiggled and vibrated. "Inside here, Riley is the key to all that makes you human: power, strength, will. However, to open it, you must do one small thing, make one small sacrifice. I think you know what that is." He looked down at the old man and then back at Riley.

"I'm going now. No one else is here. No one can see into the secret place that is your subconscious. No one will ever know what decision you make."

Riley was alone again. Just him and the old man. The scent of smoke had also gone. He looked at the box. He looked at the old man. He thought about what had been said. He hated his neighbour. Riley picked up the gun. There was silence, except for the fast wheeze of the old man's shallow breathing and the buzz of the flickering light. Now, how did they do this in the movies? Riley looked over his shoulder. No doors, no windows. No witnesses. Like the anonymous internet chat room where you could say what you honestly thought. Like the voting booth. He could be himself.

"We are a multitude..." he whispered. He raised the gun. He fired the gun. He watched the old man crash to the floor; bony legs pathetically tangled in the fallen chair, mouth slack, eyes unblinking. He felt no pity. Pity, he now realised, merely weakened the soul. Riley grasped the top of the box. It felt warm, like human skin. He opened the box. The eyes of the old man snapped open, his waxy face pulled in a rictus of a triumphant grin. He spoke in the voice of the cashmere-coated, smoke-soaked visitor.

"Welcome to your hindbrain, Riley. Enjoy...."

THE GIRL STARED at Riley as he turned towards her. His lips pulled back from his teeth.

"We got a live one!" one of the balaclava men yelled. There was a flurry of movement as the cell door was flung open. Three men stormed in, pushing aside slack-jawed people who stood, reaching out to visions only they could see. By now, Riley had his hands around the girl's throat. It took all three men to drag him off her.

Two men watched impassively from a metal gantry far above the factory floor.

"It's happening more often, Boss," one of them said in a thick Eastern European accent. "Are you sure there's nothing we can do to the formula?" The Boss grimaced.

"Get him out of here, Fun Boy," he said. "As far away as possible. Then he's not our problem anymore." Fun Boy shrugged and moved off to do whatever the Boss wanted. He was too scared of him to do anything else.

The Boss moved off the gantry and approached a thick metal door in the brick wall. He keyed a code into the security lock and pushed the door open. He stepped through the door, which swung closed behind him, abruptly silencing all the noises from the vibrating, pulsating factory floor below. The Boss was now in a large, dimly lit room. The strains of classical music flowed through the air, and there was a smell of expensive cologne and smoke. Long metal trollies lined the brick walls, each trolley laden with metal suitcases containing neatly packed bundles of cash. A handsome middle-aged man with blond hair was sitting at a large wooden desk, carefully counting money. His face was half obscured in the dim light that emanated from the naked, swinging bulb above. He didn't look up.

There's been another one," the Boss announced, his voice harsh in the cavernous brick-lined space.

"There's been another one, what?" the blond man replied, not pausing in his careful counting.

"There's been another idiot kicking off after taking the Code Bl...." The Boss abruptly stopped as he felt his tongue swell and start to block his own throat. His tongue suddenly felt as if it didn't belong to him. He gagged on the twisting, follicular mass that now writhed in the cavern of his throat.

"No," said the blond man patiently.

"My Lord," gasped the Boss, his hands clawing at his throat. "My Lord!" He felt his tongue subside, and he clenched his fists in frustrated anger.

"That's better," said the blond man. "Show some respect to your superiors."

"Lord Rosendale," the Boss began again. "We're getting more reactions to the Code Blue." Still, the blond man didn't look up. He ran his hands, almost sensuously, over the money that sat in neat piles before him.

"And what is that to do with me?" he asked lightly. The Boss paused.

"It's your invention. Your formula," he said. "Don't you want to–?"

"Are they still turning up? Are they still paying?" interrupted Rosendale. The Boss nodded angrily. "Then we keep selling," continued Rosendale. "We still have thirty thousand doses of Code Blue in its present formulation to shift. That's three million pounds once we put the price up again. And I need those three million pounds."

There was the sound of a shoe softly brushing over the concrete floor. The Boss looked to his right and saw a tall man in a black suit. He, too, was half-cloaked in shadow. He was thin and long-limbed. Despite the dimness of the factory, he wore small, oval, dark-lensed glasses, so his eyes were hidden. The cuffs of his shirt and jacket were slightly too short for him, and his pallid wrists, thick with dark, curling hair, protruded from the ends. His hands were folded in front of his waist in an almost monastic fashion. The Boss frowned at the familiar sight of this silent shadow; he was always present with Rosendale, but the Boss had never heard him utter a word.

"Pay no attention to Mr Ketch," said Rosendale mildly. The Boss dragged his eyes back to the blond man at the desk. The blond man finally looked up at the Boss. "I await word of our next shipment of raw materials," said Rosendale. "The raw materials to make Code Blue. Once we have that, then I might think about tweaking the formula." His handsome mouth pulled up in a small smile. "But until then, it is so delightful to see the choices people make. Giving in to their true selves once they know no one is watching." He giggled slightly.

The phone on the desk vibrated. Rosendale picked it up with a languid hand. "Speak of the Devil," he said with another small smile. He answered the phone and sat listening to the high-pitched voice at the other end of the line. Rosendale then abruptly stood up. "What do you mean, a diplomatic mission? What sort of diplomatic mission?" He began to pace. "Who's leading this mission? Give me their name," he insisted. Rosendale then stopped stock still. "What did you say? Who?" There was a long silence. Rosendale then continued speaking. "Yes. Yes, I know Tristan Beaulouf. It is my misfortune to know him very well. And his entire, stinking family."

Rosendale's expression twisted as if there was a foul taste in his mouth. "Now, listen very carefully. I am going to tell you what to do. You are going to arrest this diplomat, Tristan Beaulouf, and anyone who is with him. And you will lock him up in your deepest, darkest prison. And then you will throw away the key until I tell you otherwise!" Rosendale listened impatiently as the voice on the other end of the line rose in panic. "And I'm telling you," snarled

Rosendale. "That it has been me and my money, buying up your shrivelled little plants, from your shrivelled little province, in the back end of nowhere in the Middle East, that has been keeping the wolf from your door. You will do as you are told. Make them disappear. I know for a fact that you do this all the time. Make them disappear like you do all the others and await my orders." Rosendale cut off the call and stood, thinking. "Damn that family," he muttered.

Rosendale glanced over at the Boss. "Someone is sneaking around trying to uncover my secrets," he said angrily. "Are your men watching every dose? Is every tablet accounted for?" Rosendale demanded, growing more agitated. The Boss nodded his head. "No one. No one but me knows the formula," declared Rosendale. Rosendale marched over to his desk and fished a set of keys out of his pocket. He glanced around the dim room, eyes peering with suspicion into the shadowed corners. "It is my work. Mine! Years in the making. I don't trust computers or phones. I destroyed all paper copies. There is only one copy left. One." He inserted the key into the thin metal top drawer and rattled it impatiently. "It's in two halves. Like the key to a bitcoin. Two halves, two halves of hologrammed paper. One here and one hidden at my...." Rosendale's voice rose as he patted his hand around the open drawer, desperately searching for the piece of paper. "Two halves. I had them made—a thing of beauty. I must have beauty. One half in here...!" But the small space was empty.

Rosendale pulled the metal drawer out of the desk and hurled it across the room to slam into the brickwork and fall, broken, to the concrete floor. He advanced on the Boss, who again felt his throat close. "No one. No one except you and I have access to this room! No one except you knows my name; no one knows I am here." Rosendale's face was now ugly with rage; his skin flushed a deep red. The Boss's eye flicked sideways towards Mr Ketch. "I told you to ignore Ketch!" screamed Rosendale.

"Samples," was all the Boss managed to say before all air was choked from his lungs.

The Boss felt the pressure on his throat abruptly relax. There was silence in the room except for the harsh, ragged breathing of the Boss. Rosendale looked coldly at the Boss.

"Well?" he said. "What about the samples?" The Boss swallowed, his throat painful and throbbing.

"You wanted ten tablets sent across to Manchester. Samples for the gangs over there. You said you were thinking about expanding business."

"And?" said Rosendale.

"I brought the Courier up here. The man who was going to supervise the tablets. He would make sure they were all consumed, not stolen. I brought him up here to give him the goods. You know you have all tablets counted in and out of this room." Rosedale didn't react. "He must have scoped out the desk," continued the Boss. "He must have thought he'd come back and see what he could help himself to. It's the only explanation."

"And where is he now?" demanded Rosendale. "This Courier." The Boss shrugged. Rosendale walked close to the Boss, who could smell cologne and incense and ashes. "You will find him. And find my formula. Do you understand? Or I will crucify you," said Rosendale quietly. The Boss looked him in the eye and saw that he meant it. The Boss nodded. "And if he's betrayed me in this, he could betray me in everything," said Rosendale, abruptly turning and slamming shut the metal cash-filled cases. “I’m leaving. I can’t afford to be caught here.”

“You’re safe. No one knows about you. And I have people on the inside...” the Boss began. Rosendale ignored him and continued his preparations to flee.

“You will continue to run the Sheffield operation. You will continue to let everyone think you are in charge. And you will find this courier and retrieve the missing half of my formula. Do you understand? And if anyone, and I mean anyone, gets in your way, you are to kill them. Show them the same measure of mercy that I would show you.” Rosendale turned to the Boss, a suitcase of cash in each hand. “I will be keeping a close eye on you. You know what I can do to you, don’t you?” The Boss nodded again. There was only one person in the world of whom the Boss was scared. And he was looking right at him.

CHAPTER EIGHT

Mac pulled up outside his apartment block and then sat in the driver's seat, looking at the homeless man crouched nearby. He was a boy, really. Probably no more than eighteen. Already looked thirty. His pale face was pinched and blank. Was he going up or coming down? Either way, no good state to be in on a night as cold as tonight; sitting in a dirty doorway with a ragged sleeping bag pulled around his skinny knees.

It was one in the morning in Sheffield city centre, and Mac wanted his own bed. He might not sleep, but he still wanted his bed. The boy was now pulling a piece of cardboard around himself. Mac could see him shivering from where he sat. He sighed and opened the car door. He walked over to the boy. The boy looked up at him and ran the back of his grubby hand under his nose, sniffing wearily. For some reason, Mac was reminded of the small, blonde doctor he had reluctantly helped.

"I don't do tricks, so piss off," the boy said. His voice was harsh, but his face was fearful. Mac dug his hands deep into the pockets of his jacket.

"If I gave you twenty quid, would you go and get some food?" asked Mac. The boy's face was blank. Calculating. He then nodded eagerly. He pointed to a takeaway open at the junction of Devonshire Green and West Street.

"I'll get a kebab!" he exclaimed. Mac watched as the boy's eyes then slid away towards the figure that circled on a low BMX bike around the graffitied basketball pitch on the other side of the road.

What this boy needed was not to have had the violent or neglected, or indifferent childhood that he had had. What this boy wanted was drugs. Lots of drugs. To take the cold away. To take the pain away. To take himself away from a world that hated him. At what point, Mac reflected, did the world stop feeling sorry for the poor, abused little child, and decide that the adult should be hanged?

"So, not twenty quid then," said Mac. The boy looked affronted. "I'm not stupid." Mac looked at the circling figure on the bike. He looked at the squalid doorway and the broken human being in front of him. He unzipped his expensive down jacket and dropped it onto the boy's knees. "This is for you, not for selling," he said sternly. "Stay warm, son." Mac walked back to the car. He'd done all he could do.

Mac's phone buzzed. He answered the call. "Sinclair," he said. "Why are you awake?

"I was going to ask you the same thing," came a low voice with a Scottish accent. "Did the date with the lovely Martina not work out then?"

"The date with the lovely Martina went as well as could be expected. We both got what we wanted, and now I'm home again," said Mac.

"And will there be a third date?' asked Sinclair.

"No," said Mac brusquely, slamming the door to his car and locking the vehicle.

"Ah well, two dates, that's more than most," said Sinclair philosophically. "You'll find someone in the end." Mac frowned.

"As you know, Sinclair. I don't want anyone. I don't need anyone. I'm glad to be exactly as I am."

"Glad to be unhappy?" asked Sinclair brightly. Far too brightly for one in the morning, thought Mac darkly. "Well, at least you'll be warm," said Sinclair. "If not with love, then in that new jacket of yours. You'll need it tonight." Mac said nothing.

There was another long pause. Mac looked over at the basketball court. The young homeless man was offering Mac's jacket to the man on the bike. They were arguing. He closed his eyes.

"You're near Devonshire Green. Where the druggies hang out. You just gave your jacket away, didn't you?" said Sinclair. She sounded deeply frustrated. Mac said nothing but started heading into the apartment building. "For the love of God, Mac, what is it with you and homeless people?" declared Sinclair. "Toddy and Hafez saved for weeks to get you that jacket for your birthday..." she stopped herself from saying any more. "You're going to have to buy yourself another just like it. Before they realise you're not wearing it." There was silence.

Mac opened the front security door of the apartment building and looked over at the basketball court again. The drug dealer was now riding in big lazy circles, wearing Mac's coat. The young homeless man was nowhere to be seen. Mac shook his head. He'd made yet another poor decision. He closed his eyes and felt his heart speed up. Just breathe, he thought. But he couldn't stop it, couldn't stop remembering. Afghanistan. Nox Section. Mac heard his father's voice echoing from the past.

"There's something I need to tell you, son." He heard the ghost of a single gunshot from behind a locked door. Mac's palms became moist, and his chest felt tight. *Just breathe*, he thought. *I'm a man of the North, I can do this...*

"Was that all, Sinclair?" he asked, his voice heavy.

"I'm sorry, Mac," replied Sinclair quietly. "You don't need any more grief. I just want you to know that we're here. Waiting."

"Waiting for what?" said Mac, but then cursed himself because he knew the answer.

"Waiting for you. To come back to us," said Sinclair.

"Sinclair..." Mac objected.

"We need you...." Mac broke the call and then turned his phone off. He wearily made his way up to his flat and, after washing, threw himself into bed and fell into a deep and fitful sleep.

MAC AWOKE WITH A CRY. He looked at the clock. It was now four in the morning. He was so, so familiar with four in the morning. Mac sat on the edge of the bed and ran his hands over the tightly bunched muscles in his neck. What had that dream been about? He was used to bad dreams, but this nightmare had been different and not one he'd had before. He'd been home on the estate, running barefoot through Druids wood, up towards the Watchtower. And something had been chasing him. He hadn't seen it, but had sensed it. He'd been terrified.

Mac's heart gradually slowed. He stood and walked into the front room. The lights of the city spread below him, harsh in the curtainless window. He sat and pulled his phone towards him. Sinclair's news when he had left Sally's house and returned to base had not been good. However, they had been unable to do anything about the problem. He had tried to distract himself, but now he needed to talk to someone. But who?

Mac turned the phone on and scrolled his contacts. Mother? He knew that she, too, would be awake. But he would never disturb her at this hour. He shook his head as, once again, his father's voice echoed from four years ago.

"I have something to tell you, son...." The vision of a closed door and the remembrance of a terrible sound shook him again.

"One, two, three, four...." He began counting slowly, trying to breathe, trying to empty his mind of the past. But then he thought of the present....

Mac continued to scroll down his contacts. George? He smiled at the thought of his steady and sensible younger brother. He'd be asleep, preparing for his early shift at St James's Hospital, Leeds. Mac couldn't possibly disturb the newly appointed consultant anaesthetist. James? His youngest brother. God only knew what Jim would be up to, but it was best not to disturb him at it. Jess? Mac sighed. Jess Pendle-Howard? The only member of his family who was more messed up than he was. She was probably either dead drunk or preaching somewhere. Or both, knowing Jess. Mac lowered his head. He wished he could pray. He wished he could forget. He felt the push inside his chest; the rising panic. What should he do? When would he be able to make a decision again? Make a decision without feeling as if he was going to die.

Mac's phone buzzed. He looked down in surprise—incoming call.

"Sinclair? Again?" he said. He slumped back in his chair. "Once again, how do you know I'm not asleep?" Sinclair's low, calm voice sounded vaguely amused.

"I figured if I couldn't sleep, then neither could you," she replied. "And that you'd need someone to talk to. And I wanted to apologise for having a go earlier." Mac sighed deeply. Now it came to it; he didn't know what to say.

There was a long silence. "Mac," said Sinclair quietly. "I think we may have missed a trick. With this Code Blue drug that's appeared in Sheffield." Mac lifted his head.

"Where's this come from, Sinclair?" he asked.

"No sleep," she said. "And from what you told me about Maya. And what you saw at the hospital. I started thinking about Jordan's last phone message to me." Mac frowned. Sinclair was talking about Jordan Linton, her dead fiancé. He'd died from a roadside bomb four years ago when they had all been serving in the same British Army company in Afghanistan. "Jordan said he'd seen a guy with weird blue eyes," continued Sinclair. "I thought he meant a man with eyes that were blue. Who wouldn't? But now I'm wondering...."

Mac groaned and closed his eyes again. What Sinclair was saying made sense. Terrible sense. Sinclair's voice hardened. "I should have killed him while I had the chance, Mac," she said. "Not...not...I should have chosen Revenge." He heard her anger echo down the line. "We should have killed them all. We should have taken down Nox Section."

• • •

After she'd put the phone down, Maddie Sinclair lay on her side in the quiet darkness of her room. She again listened to the four-year-old recording of Jordan Linton's voice. She didn't cry. She'd cried every tear she'd had on the day he'd died. On the recording, Sinclair could hear the busy sounds of the army camp. The voices of service men and women in the background of the hasty message.

"Hey Bruiser!" came Jordan's voice. Sinclair smiled, as she always did, at the nickname he'd given her. "It's me. We're just off on patrol. Listen, I didn't catch you this morning, but I saw this guy with weird blue eyes last night." She heard him turn from the phone and yell, "Jacko, I'll be right there!" he moved back to the phone. "Really freaked me out. Anyhows, see you later. We'll talk...." His voice lowered to a whisper. "Love you. Always." And he was gone.

CHAPTER NINE

It was early morning. Charlie stood in the doorway of Sally's room, gazing at Ben and Sally. She took in Ben's boots and fully clothed state and relaxed slightly but was still startled to see him there. She knocked lightly on the open door, and both Sally and Ben started awake. Sally did a double take at Ben, who sleepily removed his hand from her head and sat up, looking around the room as if trying to remember how he had arrived there. Sally frowned slightly and gazed at Ben.

"You do know I really don't fancy blokes?" she stated firmly, the word "blokes" unexpectedly emerging with a soft, northern accent. However, she didn't ask him to leave, Charlie noticed. Ben ran a hand over his eyes and stubbled chin.

"You're a Leeds lass, aren't you, Sal?" he said. He grinned widely at her and seemed immensely pleased with his deduction.

Charlie shivered in the doorway as a draught blew across the wooden floor. She was wearing guest pyjamas, the hems of which pooled on the floor. She was also wrapped in a satin bedspread of a shade somewhere between grey and violet, but her bare feet felt like blocks of ice. Charlie sidled closer to the empty corner of the enormous bed and eyed the thick duvet. Ben knew the look, having seen it on his son's face many times. "Hop in, lass," he said. Sally looked horrified, but Charlie didn't need to be asked twice. She slid under the far corner of the duvet and grinned like a Cheshire cat at the sudden warmth on her small feet. Sally looked between the two of them, and her mouth opened slightly but then snapped shut. She leaned back on the expanse of pillows behind her, lifted her hands as if in weak protest, and then let them fall back onto the white, crisp bedding.

"Are there a few passing squirrels who might want to join us?" she grumbled.

"I'm sorry we've spoiled your privacy," said Charlie, looking apologetic but also a little wistful. "But I'm glad you let us stay. This house is one of the most beautiful places I've ever seen. It feels so... loved." Sally stared at Charlie and was horrified to feel her eyes prickle with the start of tears. Someone else felt it too. Maya had always been so angry and resentful. It had felt as if Maya and the house had hated each other. The place felt so much quieter and more content now that Maya was gone.

Charlie's face lit up. "Breakfast!" she exclaimed, but then her face fell. "No eggs!" she muttered. "You can't have a proper breakfast without eggs! I'll have to manage...". She pointed at Sally. "Now, I know you have no allergies". Despite herself, Sally grinned back at Charlie's warm smile. "But you...". Charlie pointed to Ben. "Any allergies, food fads, or preferences?"

"You put it on a plate, lass, and I'll put it away," declared

Ben confidently. Charlie grinned again and exploded out of the bed, and scampered away. They heard her bare feet on the wide, wooden stairs heading down to the kitchen, and they both relaxed.

Sally turned her body to face Ben and drew her knees towards her chest. He lay back down and turned to her. They regarded each other for a long time.

"I'm sorry," said Ben, eventually. Sally shook her head.

"There's no need. I'm a grown woman. I could have kicked you out." There was another long silence. "Why did you come into my room?" asked Sally. Ben didn't look embarrassed, just sad.

"I heard you," he said. "Crying. In your sleep. Do you have bad dreams every night?" he asked.

"Do you?" replied Sally. Ben looked startled and then thoughtful.

"No," he said, not looking at her. She waited. He eventually met her patient gaze. "Maybe," he admitted.

They continued to look at each other. Sally reached out and touched a strand of Ben's hair where it lay on the pillow. She then hesitantly ran a finger over the healing cut on Ben's open left hand. Ben didn't move.

"Left-handed. Like me," she said. There was another long silence. "Do you know what the opposite of an explosion is?" asked Sally. Ben said nothing but shook his head slightly. "It's an implosion," continued Sally, "And that's what happened to my family when my brother died." Ben continued looking at her, a tiny line between his brows the only sign that he had understood what she'd said. "We were twins," Sally continued quietly. "I was the unexpected one, the younger one. The unwanted one." Again, she waited for a response that didn't come. "Peter. I love... I loved him so much." *Where is this coming from?* Something inside her screamed. *You have never said this, never told anyone this!* But the words just kept coming. They flooded from her like long-dammed water, finally released. Ben listened; a man who knew the precise cost of loss. "He had dark auburn hair, just like yours. You... You remind me of him."

Sally now felt exposed in Ben's steady and open gaze. She pulled the bedding tight against her chest and throat. However, she couldn't stop talking. "But, Peter. Peter had brown eyes. Big brown eyes. And freckles. But they never teased him at school. Everyone loved him; his massive smile, his kindness. He could make anything, mend anything. And for some reason, he loved me. His gawky sister with her bad teeth and stutter." Ben just listened, calmly drinking in the flow of her grief. "My Mother. She'd always tolerated me. She never liked other women, never trusted them. And when it happened... she blamed me. She threw me out as soon as I reached 16. My grandparents were dead, my Dad was long gone. I made... compromises." Sally paused, her face fierce and pensive. "I eventually escaped to University and worked; all day at my business degree, all night at the takeaway. I graduated first in my year—a first in academic skills but a definite third in social ability. I got a job in an IT company. I found I was rather brilliant at it. So, now, I can get whatever I want, including this place. And I always make sure I owe nothing to anyone."

"Has it made you happy, lass?" asked Ben softly.

"We're not here to be happy, Ben," said Sally. "We're here to be rich, and that's the best chance we have to avoid pain. Life is just one big competition."

"Is that what you really think, Sal?" said Ben. "What about friendship? Family?"

"Friends?" said Sally, pronouncing the word as if it was profoundly unfamiliar. Ben nodded.

"Friends," he repeated. "People in whom you put your faith." They regarded each other. Ben shook his head. "You must be so lonely, Sal." Sally hesitated and then edged slightly closer to him.

"I think you are, too," she said quietly.

Ben reached out and gently lifted a lock of Sally's dark brown hair from her forehead.

"It must have been so difficult for you. Losing your other half," he murmured. He went to say something but stopped. He sighed. "You'll be glad to know that you look nothing like my older brother," he said, a thoughtful look on his face. "He was competitive too. And lonely. By the end, I think he was very lonely."

"How do you do it?" asked Sally.

"Do what?"

"Remain so unrelentingly kind?" Ben looked at her for a while.

"It's easy," he said, eventually. "I wake up each morning and decide who I am. And each morning, I decide I'm not going to be like my brother." They were quiet again. It was a strangely comfortable silence.

Ben glanced over at Sally's dressing table and frowned. He pushed back the covers, walked over to the surface, and picked up the applewood log. The carved face had been turned towards the wall. "Is that what you think of my work?" he said, half joking, half indignant. Sally didn't know what to say. She felt herself flushing.

"It's not me," she said. "You're trying to flatter me. You don't need to. It's skill I'm looking for, not compliments." Ben returned to the bed and lay down again, crossing his ankles. He ran his long, calloused fingers reverently over the carving. He looked serious.

"This is no flattery, Sal," he objected softly. He turned his head to look at her again. "I told you. I carve what I see. You're beautiful, Sal." Sally said nothing. Ben looked around the room. "In fact, you're magnificent. Look at what you've done, what you've achieved. You've dragged yourself up by your bootstraps and come through. You create; you survive." Sally was looking down at her hands, sensing the familiar fear that came with her feeling too much. Ben nudged her shoulder gently with the carving. "You were brave and beautiful last night when Maya went for you with that big knife. Magnificent. Just remember that. Just hold on to that." Sally had no answer. *That's just the sort of thing Peter used to say*, a small part of her mind whispered. She looked, wide-eyed, at Ben. He was studying the carving of her face again and didn't see her expression. "You've terrible taste in women, mind you," continued Ben, shaking his head mournfully. "Just awful." Sally now looked offended.

"I haven't offered you a job yet!" she declared.

"Then that means you're not my boss yet," said Ben, briskly leaping off the bed. "I can say what I like. But, for now, I think we have... breakfast?" They smiled tentatively at each other as the scent of coffee and what smelled like kippers, croissants, and butter wafted up the ancient stairs.

"Well then," said Sally. "As I'm so competitive, I'll race you. Last one to the table is a big fat loser...."

He was out of the door faster than she ever would have suspected. And she could never have anticipated the cry of,

"Yeee Haaww!" as he slid down the broad banister, reckless of harm or pain in the shafts of warm spring sun that melted through the glowing halls on that magical morning. *Just like Peter would have done,* came the tiny whisper.

Ben was right. There was coffee and croissants. And tinned kippers in butter and pepper on toasted ciabatta left over from the night before. And peaches in brandy. Charlie sat them at the island and fussed around them, handing out warm plates, pouring coffee, and ensuring they had everything they needed. Then Charlie quickly inspected Sally's wounds with gentle and efficient hands. She seemed pleased with their progress. Instead of feeling resentful at the intrusion of her home, Sally found the feeling of being cared for comforting. She allowed herself an edge of croissant and a thin slice of buttered ciabatta with the hot, smoked fish.

Sally looked around her kitchen. It looked like a different room. There was the detritus of a lovingly made breakfast on the work surfaces, the kitchen door was ajar, and the scent of the wild peaks crept into the room. Charlie had placed some primroses in a small glass. The flowers glowed in the spring sunshine, warming the room.

"I can't believe you have two ovens, Sal," enthused Charlie. "And plate warmers and two ice makers!"

"I have?" said Sally, feeling slightly hunted. She'd never got the hang of cooking and had never felt the need. Charlie nodded happily.

"And that Italian coffee machine is amazing." She pointed to a large chrome device crouched sleekly on one of the long work surfaces.

"Can't say I've ever used it," said Sally, slightly defensively. "I like instant. At least I did until now." She held out her cup. "Now that you've figured out how to use it... any chance of another?" Charlie beamed, jumped from her chair, and headed for the glistening device.

"What shall we do? It's a beautiful day!" said Charlie over her shoulder. She stopped in her tracks and turned towards Sally, looking apologetic and crestfallen.

"Sorry, you'll want us out of here. You must have hundreds of things you need to get on with...."

Sally had thousands of things to be getting on with. However, she still couldn't bear the thought of the house being empty again.

"Why don't we go for a drive?" she suggested.

"Where's your car?" asked Ben. "I couldn't see a garage yesterday."

"You'll see," replied Sally mysteriously. She was enjoying the anticipation of finally showing off some of her most prized possessions. "Shall we get ready for the day? Then I'll show you."

It seemed that Maya had taken the idea of an accommodating country house seriously. There were toiletries and clothing basics in all the guest bedrooms for people who had never been welcome to stay before now. Ben found himself in another luxurious, en-suite bathroom, with underfloor heating warming the smooth, expensive tiles beneath his feet. He showered and shaved and used a toothbrush fresh from its box. All the toiletries exuded the same exotic perfume Charlie had noticed the day before. He shook his head. Charlie was right. Rowans Holt was one of the most beautiful places he'd ever been in, and he had worked in some of the wealthiest areas in Sheffield and the North. He remembered Sally's mournful gaze from this morning;

her insistence on being ugly. All this wealth, and still so unhappy. He hated to see anything suffer.

"Magnificent," he murmured.

THEY MET IN THE KITCHEN, and Charlie started to clear up. "Ok," said Sally briskly. "One thing you have to know about this area is that it used to be mined and worked—coal, gritstone, minerals. There are caves and tunnels everywhere. Most of them have been unused, sometimes for hundreds of years. We're sitting on a gritstone edge. It's called Bellych Edge, but it was originally Belle Wyche or Beautiful Witch Edge. There was a loud clatter. A tray had slipped from Charlie's grasp and landed on the floor. She bent to pick it up, her face hidden.

"Butterfingers," they heard her murmur. "Carry on, Sal."

"During the War, Rowans Holt was used by the Military," continued Sally. "Mainly to care for wounded officers, but also for top-secret meetings. If the Germans ever did invade, Rowans Holt would be a site for planning and carrying out the resistance of the North. This house has some unusual additions and hidden places...." She led them to the hallway, took out a swipe card and pressed it against an ordinary-looking part of the ancient panelling. An entire section slid back to reveal a small lift door. Sally looked at them. "This takes you down to the base of the cliff. Deep under the house, there are caves. That's where my cars are."

CHAPTER TEN

Ben felt the hair on the back of his neck rise slightly. The way Sally had said 'cars'. Ben loved cars in the way Charlie loved food; the look, the feel, the anticipation. He just couldn't afford them. Sally was speaking again.

"Shall we go see them?" She pressed the card against the lift console, and the door quietly slid open. She stepped inside and smiled at them. "Come on." Charlie and Ben looked at each other, and then both stepped into the tiny lift. "Close your mouth, Ben," Sally whispered. The door slid shut. Ben did as he was instructed.

After a brief ride, the lift doors opened, and they stepped out into a cavernous space, their footsteps and voices echoing. It had been carved from gritstone, and the roughly hewn walls glimmered in the powerful lights that flicked on. Large hangar-like doors sat ahead of them, with small windows studded along the top. The mouth of a low, dark tunnel was set in the long wall to their right. It led away from the cavern, burrowing deep into the primordial stone. Ben's eyes roamed over four large, covered objects. Metal workbenches, crowded with neatly ordered car maintenance tools, stood against the stone walls. They were in the space of someone who meant business when it came to cars. Sally saw his face, and a wide grin broke over hers.

"Do you want a tour?" she said, already knowing the answer. She pulled off the first cover.

"You have an Aston Martin Vantage?" breathed Ben.

"My first proper bonus," replied Sally, looking at the car with something close to affection. "I always wanted to be James Bond."

"Is it as much fun to drive as they say?" asked Ben, his eyes drinking in the smooth, low lines of the vehicle.

"Way more than they say..." grinned Sally. She took hold of the next cover and pulled it away like a magician, revealing her greatest trick. Another sleek and gleaming car emerged. "My second bonus," Sally announced. Ben's face fell.

"A Ferrari 488?" he said faintly.

"You certainly like black," observed Charlie, who had no interest in cars at all. Her battered 13-year-old VW Polo, which had never been washed by anything other than rain, stood as a testament to this. Ben shot her a comic, fierce glance.

"They're not black, Charlotte," he growled. "The Aston's a special edition Ceramic Grey, and the Ferrari's a... Blue Pozzi?" Ben glanced at Sally for confirmation, and she raised her left eyebrow slowly.

"Well, well! So, the boy does like cars," she said. "In that case...". She walked to a secure-looking silver cabinet on the cave wall and pressed her card against one side. The door swung open to reveal a set of high tec. keys. "Which one do you want first? Aston or Ferrari?" Ben hesitated.

"Neither..." he eventually said. "I want to see what's under the other two covers. He pointed. "First bonus, second bonus. What did you do with your third and fourth?"

Ben indicated the third covered vehicle. Sally said nothing and crossed her arms. Ben strode over and pulled the cover off with a dramatic flourish.

"A Dodge Demon?" He began laughing. "An American muscle car?" Sally shrugged, grinning.

"Did you pay the extra dollar?" said Ben excitedly. "Get the box of extras? I bet you did...." Charlie felt totally out of her depth.

"It's another black car," she said, shrugging. Sally and Ben both turned to her and said in unison;

"Not black, Maximum Steel."

"One of only thirty in the world," added Ben, running his hands in wonder over the gleaming bonnet of the beast of a car.

"Yes, I paid the dollar," said Sally. "But I've only taken her out once." She indicated with her head toward a large black box sitting against the cave wall. Ben and Sally walked over and opened the box to reveal a deep-red interior filled with equipment. The image of a demon hovered menacingly on the inside of the lid. They began discussing the contents enthusiastically, Ben lifting out obscure bits of equipment which seemed, to Charlie, to resemble parts of a jet plane, not a car.

"If you put this in, they say you can do 0-60 in 2.3," enthused Ben.

"None of this is solving the egg problem," commented Charlie, but neither of them seemed to hear. They were caught up in discussing something called an octane button and an ECU.

Charlie drifted over to the mouth of the tunnel. The light shone only a foot or so into the tunnel mouth; it then seemed to be consumed by the darkness. "I'm in the dark," Charlie whispered. "I am the dark...." She felt a soft breath of air push against her, almost like a deep sigh emanating from the tunnel. Inside her head, something turned and shifted.

CHARLIE WOKE UP. Without realising it, she had walked into the tunnel. She now stood enveloped in the darkness. She looked back and saw a rough circle of daylight approximately twenty feet behind her. Again, the soft push of air stirred against her hair and skin. Charlie seemed to hear a voice echoing from her past.

You must always look towards the light, Charlie Bear. Charlie nodded as if in a dream, but then she felt a smooth slither that seemed to pulsate deep within her brain.

"I'm sorry, Briddie," she whispered. Charlie lifted her foot to walk on into the darkness. She then hesitated. Part of her yearned to continue into the comfort of nothingness, but then she heard Sally and Ben's voices echo, as if from another world. Sally was laughing; she sounded surprised. Ben's voice rumbled good-naturedly. And Charlie realised she wanted to be with them. She wanted to go back to the house, to the waiting garden. To warm wood, to good food, and the smell of sweet parchment. To friendship, to loving-kindness. So, Charlie turned her back on the dark. She forgot.

. . .

Sally looked up. Charlie was standing by the fourth covered vehicle. She was about to pull the cover away. Sally nudged Ben, who now had smudges of oil on his hands and face. She nodded towards the large hulking mass that lay under the fourth cover.

"What do you think of this?" she said. The cover slipped away.

"A Range Rover Autobiography?" exclaimed Ben. "Oh, Sal, I can die happy now."

They were soon comfortably seated in the Range Rover, Sally and Ben in front and Charlie in the back. Sally pressed a button on her key fob, and the hangar doors silently slid open. They sailed through the doors and then were on a smooth, narrow tarmac-covered track that skirted the base of the cliff. Trees grew on their right-hand side, and thick ferns and lush undergrowth cast a cool, green shade over them. The path led up towards the main road. They saw a heavy, solid-looking barred gate ahead. Sally pushed a button on the dashboard, and the gate slowly rolled open. They saw cars hurling past on the main Manchester Road. Sally pulled out and accelerated, and Charlie felt the powerful pull of the V8 engine. Sally asked Ben to pass her a pair of sunglasses from the glove compartment, and she settled down with obvious enjoyment to drive through the emerging beauty of the moorland surrounding the north-west of Sheffield.

Their pleasure was interrupted by a honking horn. A red VW Golf had pulled close behind them. It was full of young men jeering and gesticulating for Sally to get out of their way. The car veered dangerously across the white central line, trying to overtake on the busy road. A gap in the traffic emerged, and they zipped arrogantly past Sally and disappeared around a bend in the road. Sally's mouth hardened into a straight line.

"Sod that!" she muttered. She stamped her foot down on the accelerator, and three tonnes of car leapt, like a wayward thoroughbred from its starting gate and sped down the road in pursuit. They quickly caught up with the vehicle, and Sally pushed right up against its rear. A frightened face peered from the rear window, and, with a lightning-quick manoeuvre, Sally overtook the small car with contemptuous ease. As the Golf disappeared in their rear-view mirror, Ben eased his window down and made a leisurely rude gesture.

"It's the small pleasures in life..." he sighed. Ben glanced at Sally, who was now easing off the accelerator. "Nice driving," he said, nodding appreciatively. "Where did you learn that?" Sally briefly glanced back at him.

"There's a racing track near York. I took lessons for a while and then spent a lot of time there. Doing laps." Ben craned his head round to look at Charlie.

"Letting off steam, I'll bet," he said. Charlie nodded.

"All that frustrated energy," she added.

"Erm, I'm right here..." interjected Sally indignantly. "And insulting me isn't going to solve our egg problem."

THEY MADE their way to the Lodge Moor area of Sheffield. Green fields and dry-stone walls surrounded them. Charlie saw a bright sign by the narrow roadside, *Plantation Farm Shop and Cafe*. They turned up a long, straight track that led to a well-kept farm and pulled into the large car park. It was full of 4x4 cars and well-heeled yummy mummies, availing themselves enthusiastically of organic produce and confectionary. Charlie shrank back in her seat. She was suddenly aware of her dishevelled appearance in borrowed track pants and stained work trainers and felt out of her comfort zone. She realised she had no cash or card and looked apologetically to Sally, who was observing her shrewdly from the front of the Range Rover.

"Sorry, Sal, I've come out with no money. Maybe you should go in...." Sally reached into the glove compartment again and brought out a large roll of cash.

Ben did a double take.

"Cash? But you've got an app..." he said. Sally had the grace to look embarrassed.

"Just because I invented the algorithm doesn't mean I want to become part of it," she muttered. "I prefer to be anonymous. I deal in cash when I can." Ben shrugged and smiled.

"Makes sense to me," he said. Sally grinned back at them both.

"Let's all go in. This place is owned by a woman named Georgia. She's the person Maya found to stock the freezer and cupboards. She'll be very pleased to see me, and..." she waved the large bundle of money. "All of my friends."

Sally strode into the farm shop with her head held high. It was filled with well-groomed women, chatting and eyeing up the wares. Prices were high, and a wide range of luxurious items was piled expertly on gingham-covered tables designed to catch the eye. Local cheeses, cooked meats and handmade pies jostled for space in the large fridge displays. The shop led to a light, airy stone-flagged café buzzing with customers and chatter. A bevvy of fresh-faced young girls in gingham aprons with *Plantation Farm* logos embroidered tastefully over the bibs busily served the customers. A middle-aged woman in jodhpurs and an expensive body warmer stood overseeing things, her ear glued to a mobile phone. On seeing Sally, however, staring imperiously over the heads of the crowd, she hurriedly ended her phone conversation.

"Miss Marshall, how nice to see you!" the woman announced, striding towards them. "We don't usually see you here. How are your home supplies? Does anything need topping up?" Her eyes beadily took in Charlie and Ben, who were staring around them at all the delicious-looking items. Ben's stomach audibly rumbled. He held it apologetically. Sally kept her face straight and nodded toward Charlie.

"Thank you, Georgia. My friend here is the chef. She needs some eggs. Can I leave her in your expert hands?"

"Of course, anything for my special customers," gushed Georgia, taking Charlie's arm and whisking her towards a vertiginous pile of boxed eggs. "Now, was it hen, duck, quail?" Georgia artfully led the hungry Charlie past a display of biscuits and homemade cakes, slowing down to take in the cheery but sophisticated packaging. Charlie's hand stretched out to touch the honey and ginger cookies, and Georgia knew she had her. "I'll get a basket," she said smoothly. Sally approached Charlie and handed the thick roll of cash to her.

"Enjoy yourself, and let's have a killer lunch," she said, smiling. Georgia's eyes bulged as she saw the exchange. She hurried across the room with a large wicker basket clutched in her be-ringed hand. She barged one of the smiling shop-girls who had been approaching Charlie to offer help.

"No, Leticia, I have this customer," she hissed. The girl's friendly smile faltered, and she backed off. "Have you ever tried white anchovies?" asked Georgia to Charlie with a coy smile. "And we have fresh sourdough just delivered... and would you like a sample of our handmade sausages?" Charlie sniffed the delicious scent of herbed sausage, and a little smile escaped onto her face.

"What sort of sourdough?" she couldn't resist asking. "And we may need just a tiny bit of cheese," she said, starting to enjoy herself. Ben and Sally melted out of the shop and back to the car.

They stood by the vehicle in companionable silence, both thinking how strange it was to feel so comfortable with someone they barely knew. They gazed out over the fields, and Ben marvelled at the vast and restless sky looming over the city's lush edges.

"I love living in Sheffield," he said quietly. "Thanks for bringing me here." He touched the muddy but sleek car appreciatively.

"Are you talking to me or the car?" asked Sally wryly. Ben made a puzzled face.

"You know, lass, I'm really not sure...."

Their relaxed banter was interrupted by a loud rumble as a dirty van slouched its way up the entrance track. It was grubby, with a thick layer of dust on its tired, black paint-work. The windows were blacked out, so whoever was inside could not be seen, and rust caked the wheel arches. It groaned to a halt, the driver's door was flung open, and a tall, skinny young man clambered out. He was dressed all in black with a long black coat that flapped around chunky biker-style boots. Long, dark, unwashed hair fell around his pale face, which was drawn into a deep frown. The passenger and rear doors opened, and two more young men emerged. They were dressed similarly, booted and all in black. They walked purposefully towards the shop and entered, the leader pushing the door open forcefully. A slight movement caught Ben's eye, and he was sure someone was left in the van, watching them. They looked at each other. Ben drew himself up, all amusement gone, as did Sally. They walked swiftly back to the shop.

A tense sight met their eyes. Georgia, looking very annoyed and red-faced, was arguing with the driver of the van.

"Well, I don't care what anyone said!" Georgia huffed. "I haven't seen Lucy. She didn't turn up to work yesterday or today. No phone call, no explanation, nothing." The driver spoke angrily, his face pale and waxy.

"Well, you were one of the last to see her. Did she say anything to you about where she was going, who she was seeing?" He gazed around at the shop assistants standing frozen, watching the scene. "Well?" He shouted. "One of you bitches must know something!" Ben spotted Charlie, pressed against a table, her face pale and pinched. She looked very distressed. Georgia puffed up like an indignant bullfrog.

"How dare you come into my shop and speak to my employees like that!" The man in black nodded to his two companions, who, in unison, each pushed over one of the display tables. There was an enormous crash and screams from the gathered customers and staff.

Ben and Sally stepped forward. "Stand down!" Ben shouted at the men, who looked as if they were ready for more affray. The leader spun round to face Ben and Sally, who both squared up to him, prepared to defend themselves. Sally may have had issues with her personality-disordered ex-girlfriend, but she was never willing to let any man intimidate or bully her. She looked him in the eye, and he saw she was not afraid. He spread his arms and feinted towards her, expecting her to flinch back. Instead, Sally threw an unexpected (and, in Ben's view, splendid) right hook that caught him square on the jaw. His head cracked back, and he staggered sideways with a distressed cry. Sally squared up again.

"Do you want some more? Punk?" she growled. From the corner of her eye, she saw the two other young men approach her, one from either side. Ben stepped up and stood with his back against Sally's. They circled warily. Sally could see at least four mobile phones out and the police being rung.

"They're on their way! The Police are on their way!" Georgia called stridently. "Get out of my shop!" The leader just shook his head and, from his coat, drew an enormous hunting knife, which he handled with practiced animosity. He looked Sally in the eye.

"You want to play, bitch?"

CHAPTER ELEVEN

Ben heard Sally gasp at the sight of the knife, and he sensed her sudden fear. He stepped in front of her.

"Bring it on," Ben said, quietly and fiercely, half hoping the young man would attack. With his former soldier's eye, Ben measured the space between them. He planned at least three ways to disarm him when he made his move. He wondered how many bones he could get away with breaking in the other man's body. They glared at each other. A faint noise of sirens pierced the silence, and one of the young men strode up to the driver.

"Lawrence, we can't do this, not now... we have to go." He grabbed at Lawrence's arm, who angrily twisted away from him and lost his eye contact with Ben.

"Get off me, Bartholomew! You coward." Bartholomew's dark skin flushed.

"I'm no coward, and you know it. But me and Stephen, we don't need this trouble now." He moved closer and hissed at Lawrence. "And what will you do if they search the van?" Lawrence seemed to come to a decision. He made one last half-hearted feint towards Ben and Sally, who refused to flinch. He then hurried towards the door, his henchmen trailing in his wake.

Sally and Ben followed them into the car park. The men flung themselves into the van, and the engine growled to life. They barrelled towards the exit but then screeched to a halt. Sally saw why. A fourth figure in black lounged against the bonnet of her Range Rover. Sally approached the car and, as she drew closer, saw that what she had first assumed was a tall young man in black was, in fact, a woman. She was very thin, not the sort of thinness of anorexia, but someone with too much interest in hard drugs. Her short, feathered hair was platinum white, and her skin was smooth and desperately pale. Her green eyes sat above high cheekbones, and her full mouth had a cigarette clamped in it. As Sally approached, the woman fixed her with a piercing stare.

"Is this your car, or does it belong to your boyfriend?" she asked languidly. She observed the glance that Ben and Sally exchanged and pulled herself up straighter. "Oh, not your boyfriend. And it's your car. Very nice." She pushed herself away from the bonnet and slowly approached Sally. As she got closer, Sally could smell her; a strange mix of fresh sweat and something like spice and sandalwood. Her leather jacket hung open over a tight, black Slipknot T-shirt, and her long legs were clad in tight leather trousers. The woman spoke again. "Got a light?" Sally said nothing and just shook her head. She felt strangely tongue-tied and awkward. The woman smiled. "What's the matter? Cat got your tongue?"

"Agnes!" screamed a voice. Lawrence was leaning out of the van driver's window; his pale face now red with anger. "Get in the bloody van!" Sirens grew louder, carried on the wind blowing up from the Fulwood Road. The woman called

Agnes slouched casually over to the van and opened the back door. She cast one last, piercing glance back at Sally, who again felt a sense of heated dislocation, and then the door slammed and the dirty van, with its cargo of deranged trouble, bounced frenziedly down the track and out of sight.

Sally shook her head. She needed to get out of there, too. She didn't want her name taken by the Police. She'd received enough Police attention. The Company wouldn't like it, and she didn't want the Police in her home again. Sally leant into the car and opened the glove box once more. She grabbed two more rolls of cash and strode towards the shop. She approached the livid Georgia, grabbed her gently but firmly by the arm and looked her in the eye.

"Georgia, I'm sorry about what happened to you, but I have to go." Georgia ignored her and carried on exclaiming. Sally held up the bundles of cash, and Georgia suddenly became silent. "I can't afford for the Police to be investigating me. I'd be grateful if you didn't mention me by name."

"But you hit him," said Georgia, her eyes still fixed on the bundles of 50-pound notes Sally was discreetly holding.

"I know, but he deserved it, don't you think?" replied Sally. She waved the cash once more, and Georgia reached out and grasped it.

"I won't use your name," she snapped and turned towards the wreckage of her displays.

Sally and Ben scooped up the pale and frightened-looking Charlie, who hugged her shopping as if her life depended on it, and they hurried back to the car. Sally grimaced as her stitches pulled painfully at her arm. Blood had leaked through her sleeve again. Without a word, she threw her car keys to Ben, who silently caught them and hopped into the driver's seat to start the engine. Sally bundled Charlie into the back of the Range Rover and then slipped into the passenger seat. Ben skilfully guided the car onto the road.

"Are you alright, Little One?" Ben asked gently. He looked at Charlie in the rear-view mirror. She nodded.

"I'm sorry," she said in a small voice. "I just hate aggression. I... I had a lot when I was growing up, and it sort of takes me back. And after last night...." They drove in silence, all three reflecting on similar issues in their own past. After a while, Ben broke the silence.

"Sally. Punk? Really?" The car filled with much-needed laughter.

THEY WERE SOON BACK at Rowans Holt. They sailed through the cool, green, hidden path, and the cavern's enormous doors slid open as if by magic. Ben reversed the car into the vast space, and they silently sat for a moment.

"What was that all about?" asked Ben, to no one in particular. Sally shrugged, vague thoughts of a pair of green eyes echoing at the back of her mind. Charlie leaned in to the front of the car.

"I'm sorry I'm such a wuss. I don't mind blood, brains... but I hate violence. I always scurry off to Minors when it kicks off in A and E. Poor Georgia." Sally smiled grimly.

"Georgia will pull through, believe me. How many tins of white anchovies did she manage to sell you?" Charlie smiled back.

"You really don't want to know. Ooh, let's try some. I'll do a salad niçoise. I've got all the ingredients, including..."

she waggled a bulging hessian tote-bag, complete with *Plantation Farm* logo. "Eggie-weggies!"

Sally and Ben looked at each other and then at Charlie. "Did you really just say eggie-weggie?" asked Sally slowly. Charlie paused, gazing out of the windscreen, her brow wrinkling.

"Yeees," she said, equally slowly. "Consider that a brief lapse of...."

"Sanity?" finished Ben. Charlie began giggling, and Ben shook his head.

"So, it's eggie-weggies all round," he said, and Charlie snorted with laughter. Ben looked at Sally again. "And then we'll get out of your hair, Sal." Charlie's merriment abruptly stopped. "It's been great fun, but I'm sure you need your place back to yourself," Ben continued. Sally looked at him and, after a pause, nodded tersely. They all got out of the car in somewhat gloomy silence. They each avoided looking at the other's faces, so they didn't see the disappointment there.

CHARLIE, however, was soon back in her element, busily poking around the beautiful kitchen, boiling eggs and chopping sweet spring onions and black olives. She had two cans of very expensive, line-caught tuna, fresh butter, a beautifully crusted French-flour sourdough baton and a large, moist, glazed carrot cake crying out to be eaten. The only delay was waiting for the tiny, fresh potatoes to come to the boil. She turned to ask Sally if she liked green beans but found she was alone. She heard a faint murmur of voices at the end of the vast lounge and Charlie wandered towards the sound, her bare feet sinking into the velvet pile of deep rugs.

Charlie walked down a dark corridor and entered the library. Sally and Ben stood just beyond the entrance.

"Are you sure?" Ben was saying. "You said you never want to owe anything to anyone. I can see you're a proud woman, Sal, but I still have a few dregs of self-respect myself." Ben looked a bit fierce. "I don't want you to offer me work just because you feel you have to. You owe me nothing." Sally crossed her arms, lifted her chin and glared back at him.

"The work you did on the applewood yesterday is why I'm asking you to restore my library," she said.

"The applewood carving you say doesn't look like you?" replied Ben curtly. "Well, if that's the case, I'm obviously not that much of a craftsman." Sally paused, caught off guard.

"Well..." she said, lost for words.

"Well, what?" said Ben, a tiny smile now appearing on his mouth. "I'll do it. If you say the carving looks like you. If you say, my carving looks magnificent." Sally looked at him and said nothing. She then looked around at the torn and gaping wood and grimaced with frustration.

"Alright!" she exclaimed.

"Alright, what?"

"That carving might look a bit like me," managed Sally. Ben's smile widened.

"Might look a bit what?" he insisted. There was a pause.

"Magnificent," muttered Sally.

"Yes!" crowed Ben, clapping his hands together. He happily moved towards the damaged panelling and ran his hands over it again. His fingers lingered on the torn baby rabbit, and his face fell slightly.

"It's a lot of work and research, Sal. I'll have to source

woods, make resins," he said. "You'll have to put up with me for a while." Sally nodded.

"I'd do anything for this house. Even put up with you," she said, still annoyed at being blackmailed. "I pay very well, but I expect results." Ben continued to examine the small, damaged rabbit.

"Don't worry," he said. "This'll be a labour of love. I won't let you down."

Sally turned to Charlie. "And will you come and keep us company when you can? I enjoyed today, and I could do with feeding up." She ran her hand over her right upper arm where the stitches were. "And if Maya ever turns up again, I may need your skills."

"Oh my God, don't say that!" exclaimed Charlie. But then she did a little dance of joy and enthusiastically hugged Sally, who stiffened at the unaccustomed display of physical affection.

"Personal space," muttered Sally.

"Sorry," said Charlie, stepping away. "But I was hoping you'd ask. I felt so sad at the thought of never seeing you, the house, the garden again." She did another little victory dance but then looked panicked. "The potatoes!" she cried and headed back towards the kitchen.

As Charlie passed the trifold window, she saw large, dark clouds rolling in from the peaks and obscuring the sun. A few fat raindrops fell against the glass. Charlie lifted the lid of the simmering potatoes and speared one with a knife. She turned back towards the window, blowing on the hot, steaming globe, only to drop the blade with a small scream. A man was pulling himself over the cliff edge beyond the courtyard wall. Sally came running from the library, closely followed by Ben. Sally looked in the direction of Charlie's pointing hand. She relaxed.

"Oh, it's Mac," she said.

"Who?" exclaimed Charlie.

"My security adviser. Mac. You saw him at the hospital," said Sally calmly.

"I don't remember! What's he doing?" said Charlie, still shaken. Sally shrugged.

"He's an obsessive climber. He hates enclosed spaces, so he put pegs in the cliff face. He climbs up from the cavern. He can't stand the lift."

Mac was now walking across the courtyard. The rain had drenched the stone, but he seemed oblivious to it. He opened the kitchen door, running a hand over his face to clear the moisture away. Mac looked surprised when he saw Ben and Charlie standing next to Sally. He slowed and stopped. Charlie studied him, struggling to remember him from the hospital. It was just an exhausted blur after the terrible Friday night shift. She remembered his serious, well-spoken voice and furrowed forehead. *I thought he was going to deliver a eulogy,* she remembered.

Mac regarded the three of them. He nodded to Ben and looked back at Sally. He barely glanced at Charlie.

"Your phone signal is gone again," Mac said. "I came to make sure you were ok." Sally folded her arms.

"I'm fine," she said. "No thanks to you." Mac shifted his stance. He, too, folded his arms.

"What do you mean?" he said. "What's happened?" His eyes flicked between Ben and Charlie. "Why are they still here?"

"Without these two, I could be dead," said Sally. Mac unfolded his arms and placed his hands on his hips, craning his head to one side as if he was having difficulty understanding what Sally was saying.

"What?" he said intently.

"Maya," said Sally. "She came back." Mac was shaking his head. Sally continued. "She thought taking a knife to me again might help us kiss and make up."

"But they detained her," said Mac. "At the hospital. I saw her detained." Sally just looked at him.

Mac felt the heavy weight build within his chest again, but it took his breath this time. He had left Sally. He was employed to keep her safe, to advise her on safety. And he'd failed. He'd failed in his duty. Again. Maya had come back. He had made the wrong judgement. Again. Echoes of his failures beat against his mind. *There's something I need to tell you, son... I'll keep you safe, Pinks, I promise... Madeleine. I know the temptation is for Revenge...* He was incapable of keeping anyone safe. Incapable of making a correct decision.

The weight in his chest grew heavier and tighter. He couldn't pull air into his lungs. His breathing rate increased, but still, he couldn't get enough oxygen.

"Mac? Mac! Are you all right?" He heard Sally's voice as if it were coming from a different room. He felt Ben's hand on his shoulder and saw his face, creased with concern. His mouth was moving, but Mac couldn't hear what he was saying.

There's something I need to tell you, son. He heard the memory of his father's voice speaking down a long-dead phone line. The memory of a single gunshot. He now heard Ben's voice.

"Are you alright, Captain?" Mac tore his shoulder away from Ben's grasp.

"I'm nobody's Captain!" he shouted, chest heaving,

backing away. His arm swung out, and he felt it contact with something. A small glass spun to the red-tiled floor and shattered—yellow primroses scattered through the glistening splinters. *I break everything,* Mac thought. *I destroy everything I touch*. And now he couldn't breathe. His throat had clamped shut. It felt narrow like a straw. He couldn't breathe. He was going to die. He backed away, turned, and staggered into the storm.

CHAPTER TWELVE

Sally and Ben looked at each other, aghast. "I didn't know the Cap had asthma!" exclaimed Ben. "When did he get asthma?" Ben made to follow Mac, but Charlie stopped him, grabbing his arm firmly.

"I'll go," she said. "It's not asthma." Ben went to protest, but Charlie pulled rank. "I'm the doctor," she said decisively, shaking her head. "It's not asthma. I'll deal with it!"

Charlie ran, barefoot, into the rain. It was bitterly cold, and this took her breath away. She looked around, hoping Mac hadn't approached the cliff edge, but there was no sign of him. Charlie ran down the path, wiping her eyes and squinting against the deluge. She glimpsed a figure leaning, head down, right arm braced against the weathered brick wall of the enclosed garden. She went to him and touched his shoulder. He span, eyes wide, chest heaving and backed away from her until he was pressed tightly against the wall. She moved closer to him.

"It's OK!" Charlie shouted over the rain and his rapid, gulping breaths. "You're having a panic attack. It's probably your first one. You feel like you're going to die!" Mac just stared at her. "Are your fingers cramping and tingling?' shouted Charlie. Mac nodded. He looked down at his right hand. It had closed into the shape of a claw. He looked up, horrified, at Charlie.

"It's alright!" she repeated. "It's because of your breathing. Your calcium levels have fallen, making your muscles spasm. You're hyperventilating. You have to slow down your breathing." She put out her hand and gently placed it on his chest. "Look at me," she ordered. He gazed at her. He remembered her sitting by the bedside of the dying, gasping woman. She had helped her, Lily. The old woman's lungs had been filled with cancer. Is that what had happened to his chest? Had it slowly filled with a poisonous growth, pushing against his heaving heart?

Charlie gently continued to speak to him. "Just look at me. Breathe slowly, like me. Deep, slow breaths." He looked into her eyes, which were dark, almost navy blue. Blue and calm. He watched her breathing and tried to match his breathing to hers. Mac pulled in a deep breath and held it. He felt her small hand lying over his chest. He placed his hand over hers. The rain pelted down, drenching them further. He closed his eyes and concentrated on the cold. The tingling in his hands gradually faded, and the cramping of his fingers relaxed. He opened his eyes. She was looking at him, her wide gaze full of compassion. "You have things going on in your life causing you real, massive pain," she said. "You feel overwhelmed. That's okay. Come inside; let's talk about it. I'm sure we can help...."

Mac felt her small hand over his pounding heart. He started to feel his heart slow down. Her hand felt warm. He then felt a loosening in the tight, bitter knot he carried constantly curled inside his chest and stomach. Mac pulled in a sharp breath. He remembered Charlie in the hospital; her face furrowed in concentration as she seemed to pull the pain from the dying woman and draw it into herself.

"Stop it!" Mac shouted. He flung Charlie's hand roughly away from him. "Get off me!" Mac pushed past Charlie, the rain now hammering hard around them. He strode back across the courtyard, Charlie running after him.

"I didn't do anything," cried Charlie. "But you can't walk around with that much pain and not let someone help you!". Mac swung around again, furious.

"Just don't!" he exclaimed, advancing on the small woman. Charlie backed away, her face now distressed, but Mac could not contain himself. "Don't you try and take away the only emotion I have. The one thing that makes me feel as if I exist!" He turned and leapt over the low wall.

"No!" she cried. "You can't climb down again. Not in that state." Mac ignored her. He swung his body over the cliff edge and disappeared from view without another word or glance.

Charlie returned to the kitchen and stood, shivering, and looking out of the window into the storm. She turned to Sally.

"What is the matter with him?" she asked, bewildered. Sally shook her head, looking equally bemused.

"I've known him for over three years, and I've never seen him like this," she said. Ben had brought warm towels from the downstairs bathroom. He draped one around Charlie's shoulders and handed her another. Charlie began drying her hair.

Sally marched to her laptop and activated an alert. The

icon of Sinclair lit up. "Sinclair?" said Sally urgently. There was silence for a few moments before she got a reply.

"Miss Marshall? Sinclair here. Have you seen Mac?"

"Yes, he was just here."

"Thank goodness," said Sinclair, sounding relieved.

"Not really," replied Sally. "He's in a complete state. Sinclair, as your employer, I think I have a right to know what's going on. I appreciate you have other contracts, but if it's impacting your ability to work for me...." There was a long pause.

"He wouldn't like me to talk," said Sinclair.

"Sinclair, I'm worried about him," insisted Sally. Sinclair sighed deeply.

"I'm worried too," she said. She paused again but then spoke. "You know what happened to Mac's father?" Sally shook her head.

"No, we usually only discuss business," Sally said.

"His father committed suicide," said Sinclair flatly. "Two days after Mac was dishonourably discharged from the army. He shot himself. Mac has always insisted it wasn't suicide, but his father was found in a locked room. Suicide note and everything."

Sinclair sighed again. "It was all to do with illegal drugs in the Army." Ben flinched. "We now think it might be connected to Code Blue. And we think that we might have missed an opportunity to stop it. Mac's eaten up with guilt about it and about his father's death. And now..." Sinclair paused. Sally, Ben and Charlie looked at each other.

"Carry on," said Sally.

"His father's brother, his uncle, has been like a father to Mac and Mac's brothers since his father died," said Sinclair. "He's a senior diplomat. He's used to travelling to dangerous places, but his uncle left on a secret diplomatic mission a week ago, and yesterday, instead of returning, he disappeared. Completely."

"And you're sure he's not simply out of phone range?" said Ben. There was a long pause.

"Who the hell is that speaking?" said Sinclair, sounding angry. Sally looked at Ben.

"It's OK, Sinclair; he's here on the recommendation of Mac."

"I said, who the hell is it?" repeated Sinclair, slightly louder.

"It's Morton, Ben Morton," said Ben, leaning towards the laptop. "We've never met, but I've heard about you." Sinclair's avatar abruptly went dark.

"She's gone!" said Sally.

MADELEINE SINCLAIR PUSHED her chair away from her laptop as if it was on fire. She sat for a long time, looking at the blank screen. She hadn't seen that one coming. Sinclair knew damn well why Mac hadn't told her that Ben Morton was around. Mac was definitely falling apart.

CHARLIE, Ben, and Sally looked at each other. "What just happened? Again," said Ben, slowly. Sally shook her head. She went and sat at the kitchen island and was joined by the other two.

"Why would Sinclair cut off like that?" said Sally. "She refuses to be seen on screen, which is odd, but she's normally completely calm and efficient." Ben shifted uneasily in his chair.

"It's me," he said. "Or rather, my brother, most like." The women waited. Ben looked at his hands. "When I was in the army, I served in a different military company to Sinclair and Mac. My older brother was in Mac's company. And he was trouble. Big trouble"

"What do you mean?" asked Sally coolly. Ben didn't look up.

"He was always difficult," continued Ben, his voice quiet. "But then he had encephalitis when he was young. The psychiatric doctors said the two halves of his brain stopped talking to each other. He didn't have to listen to restraint, to his conscience, anymore." Ben took a deep sigh. "And then, when he joined up, he got a head injury, which made him worse. He was useful to the army. There are always things to do for a man who's happy... to kill."

Ben paused. He closed his eyes. "Mac. I met Mac during my basic training. He comes from an old West Yorkshire family. They've always served in the army, going back hundreds of years. He was one of the best Captains I've ever met. In the Yorkshire regiment, in the entire army. One hundred per cent there for his soldiers." Ben shook his head and hunched his shoulders slightly. "But when he did a tour of Afghanistan, my brother was allocated to Mac's company. And then my brother formed a section with men just like himself."

"What's a section?" asked Charlie. Ben gave a grim smile.

"Sorry, Charlie. A section is the smallest group of soldiers in the British Army. Anywhere from four to eleven people. My brother managed to form his own section. In his own image. They called themselves Nox Section."

"Nox. Primordial Roman Goddess of the night," said

Sally, automatically recalling information from her vast memory.

"Afghanistan is swimming in heroin," continued Ben, unable to look at either Charlie or Sally. "And my brother was happy to swim there too. But no one could prove anything. Mac tried to court martial him, but it came to nothing. After their tour of duty, they returned to England, and Mac gets found with a kilogram of cocaine in his possessions. Wonder how that got there?" Ben's face became grim. "Mac was dishonourably discharged. Only his family name and reputation kept him out of jail. And then, two days later, his father...." Charlie bit her lip, imagining Mac's distress.

"Where's your brother now?" asked Charlie. Ben still wouldn't look at her. His face grew bleaker.

"He's dead," he said. "A bomb under his quad bike"

"In Afghanistan?" asked Charlie.

"No. On his base in England. On the day that Mac got done," said Ben. He finally looked up at them. "But what do you expect if you're a murdering, traitorous bastard?" he said coldly. Ben looked at Sally. "I identified the body. They matched his DNA. He's definitely dead. And, as I said to Mac, I'm glad he's dead."

"And Sinclair?" said Sally. "What do you know about her?" Ben shrugged.

"I just know she and Mac were always thick as thieves. I knew her fiancé, though, Jordan Linton, before he died. Good man." Ben smiled wistfully. "I've never seen a man so in love. But Linton always used to say she was a bit of a handful. Bad temper. He said she had this twitchy mouth thing going on when she got angry. But he always said it's when the twitching stopped that you had to worry." Ben pushed himself away from the island. "She got into a bar fight in

Croatia once. I heard a man lost a hand, and she almost lost an eye." Ben shrugged. "Like I said, a bit of a handful. But I've never met her."

"Neither have I," mused Sally. "I don't even know what she looks like."

"How can you work with someone for over three years and not know what they look like?" asked Charlie, bemused. Sally shrugged.

"I live online most of the time. You get used to not seeing what people look like."

The storm had passed as quickly as it arrived, and the sun again poured over Rowans Holt. Tendrils of steam rose from the evaporating pools of water in the courtyard.

"Shall we sit out?" said Charlie hesitantly. Sally nodded in agreement.

"I could do with some fresh air," she said, indicating where an old wooden table and chairs stood, covered, in the stone-flagged courtyard. "And then we can talk some more. I need to think."

There was a chill in the air, so Sally slipped on a Moncler gilet. Ben dug out his shabby Barbour, and Charlie, having poked around a cupboard in the hallway, found an old Belstaff, waxed biker jacket. Charlie pulled the coat on and dug her hands in the pockets. She frowned as she found something there. She drew out an old, dog-eared photograph but couldn't see it properly in the dim cupboard. Charlie absentmindedly slipped the photo onto a shelf and hurried back to the kitchen. Ben and Sally seemed very amused by the jacket, as it looked enormous on Charlie. The coat smelled faintly of lemon cologne and Charlie couldn't place where she had smelled it before. She carried out her salad niçoise with great pride in a large, copper rondeau pan.

She cut up the bread and plonked a small jug of garlicky, balsamic dressing onto the silvered wooden tabletop. They tucked in, hungry after the adrenaline-packed morning.

Sally only put a small amount onto her plate, but once again, she enjoyed the taste of the food. She automatically looked up, expecting to see someone glaring at her, judging her each bite, and calculating how many forbidden calories she was consuming. However, all Sally saw was Ben nodding appreciatively and giving Charlie a thumbs-up sign, as his mouth was too full for talking. And she saw Charlie slathering butter onto yet another slice of sourdough bread and using it to mop up the last trace of syrupy, brown, herb-drenched dressing.

"Any chance of a drink, Sal?" asked Ben, leaning back in his chair and rubbing his stubbled chin. "It's been a hell of a day so far." Sally checked her watch. It was already three o'clock, a bit early, but this was no ordinary day.

"I'll see what I can do," she said, standing and looking at the dirty plates. Charlie held up her hands.

"Cook doesn't have to tidy up," she said smugly. The women looked at Ben, who shrugged, and started clearing up with an air of reluctance.

"I don't have to do this at home," he muttered, only half-jokingly.

"Ahhh, does mummy do your plates for you?" asked Charlie teasingly.

"Now then," said Ben sternly. "No comments about one of the finest women to walk this earth." He pointed a butter-smeared knife at Charlie's nose and waggled it theatrically. He piled up the dirty dishes and slouched off towards the kitchen, still grumbling. Sally had disappeared, presumably off to the wine cellar.

Charlie stretched out and lifted her face, eyes closed, towards the sun. Something primal within her rejoiced in the light and warmth. She felt... content, welcome... loved. She relaxed and listened to the whispering breeze as it caught the surrounding trees, the sigh of dust as it drifted across the aged, grey-yellow gritstone flags and the creak of the old house as it eased its worn, wooden bones in the spring sun. And two small butterflies, this time with blue wings, appeared and danced across the sunny space.

Ben eventually emerged, blinking in the sunlight like a sleepy mole. "You don't half make a mess when you cook, Charlie," he grumbled.

"I am an artist," said Charlie loftily. "Little people must put up with inconvenience as the price of perfection." Ben lobbed a crust of sourdough at her in disgust. Sally appeared a little later with a large tray. There was a dusty bottle of red and of white wine and some exquisite crystal glasses that glinted in the sun. They sat, drinking extraordinary wine, in the Spring warmth.

"So, what happened to the library, Sal?" asked Ben, already suspecting the answer.

CHAPTER THIRTEEN

Sally was quiet for a while, staring into her glass. "When I met Maya, I was at a party," she began. "I wasn't meant to be there. My boss wouldn't answer his phone, and I needed to run an idea past him. The logical thing seemed to be to see him in his home. I walked up to him and started talking. He started laughing at me, and I realised it was almost midnight and he had lots of people standing around him. They were all looking at me. He put his arm around me, which I hated, and told them I was going to make him millions." Sally was gazing into the distance, deep in remembrance, her wine glass held loosely in her left hand. "Maya was one of those people. She seemed so confident and glamorous and decadent; all the things I wasn't. I was swept off my feet; for a short while at least." Sally shifted in her chair. "She has her own place in town, but she insisted on moving in here. Eventually, it came to feel as if she wanted to watch me constantly. To own me."

"It got worse after she got lost in the caves," continued Sally. "She was always edgy, obsessive, temperamental." Ben and Charlie exchanged glances; Sally's description of Maya was probably being kind. "One day, she decided she wanted to *know* all of Rowans Holt. She didn't like the house, she said it didn't like her. Maya resented how I felt about it, the time I'd spent here without her. She started in the attic, looking into all the rooms, tapping on the walls, looking for hidden cupboards or tunnels. She found a few as well." Sally grimaced, remembering Maya's childish triumph. As if she had somehow outwitted a house. "She worked her way down, into the cellars and lower, into the cavern and then the tunnel. She wouldn't stop. She insisted on going in alone with a torch and wouldn't let me go with her. Said she was 'going to find all the secrets.'"

Sally paused, lost in thought. "All the secrets," she repeated quietly. "Hours passed, and I got worried. I took my own torch and chalk to mark the walls and followed her in. I walked for what seemed like miles. There are lots of old rooms down there from the War, filled with old bunks, empty filing cabinets and bits of metal, mostly junk. I could see where Maya had gone into some of them, see her footprints in the dust. I marked the walls every few paces, I called and called, but nothing. The tunnels eventually turned into what looked like mine workings. There were carvings on the walls, old graffiti by the looks of it, but also some other marks. Odd looking, like some religious cult had been down there long ago. I got scared and came back. It was night by this time. I sat in the cave all night, waiting. But nothing."

Sally didn't tell them she had called Mac as dawn broke. It had taken him and his crew a further eight hours to gather and equip themselves. The small squad had headed into the tunnel with climbing ropes, powerful head torches, and all the survival gear needed for a cave rescue. It had still taken them over a day to find her. Maya had been alone for almost two days. In the dark. "It took two days before she came out," said Sally. She didn't describe the dusty, cadaverous figure Mac had brought up in the lift from the cavern. Maya had still been clutching her torch that had run out of battery after only a few hours. She had squirmed away from Mac's grip as if it burned her and, to Sally's horror, had tried to run back into the lift, desperate to return to the cave. "And Maya was never the same," said Sally. "Wouldn't talk about what had happened, how she'd felt. Just at night, sometimes, she'd cry out in her sleep. 'I'm in the dark! I am the dark!'."

Charlie and Ben looked at each other and shifted in their seats. Sally took a large sip of wine and then continued. "She took to spending time in the library, looking for goodness knows what in the books there. She became more and more angry when she couldn't find what she was looking for. Blaming me, the house, but never saying what for. One night, she came home with a crowbar and took it to the wood, trying to prise it off the wall, trying to take the desk apart. I eventually managed to stop her. She never apologised. She'd hurt the house, so I finally found the courage to tell her to leave."

She glanced up at Ben and Charlie, who looked both concerned and sympathetic at the same time. "She moved back to her flat two months ago," continued Sally. "She's bombarded me with calls and messages that Mac has mostly fielded. Then she called me in the early hours of Saturday morning. Said she needed to see me. I asked Mac to come with me. She didn't realise he was there." Sally reached for the white wine bottle and emptied what was left of the alcohol into her glass. "I owe Mac my life," she said simply.

"I was very harsh on him earlier." She nodded, looking thoughtful. "Yes, I owe him. I owe him a lot," she said. Sally did not look happy. "And I make a point in life of owing nothing to anyone." She was quiet for a moment, lost in thought. "Do you think finding a lost uncle would pay him back?" She mused.

"Without a doubt," said Ben. He looked at the near-empty red wine bottle. "But we'd probably best not start right now."

"We?" said Sally. Ben looked embarrassed.

"Well, after all the pain my brother's caused him. I think I owe him too...."

"Anyone fancy a swim?" Sally said abruptly. The other two stared at her.

"If you think I'm going skinny dipping in that river down there, you are so wrong!" huffed Charlie.

"Oh no, something much better. Come with me," said Sally, with an enigmatic smile. "I'll get some more wine...."

SALLY LED them down the dark corridor towards the library but turned right just before the library entrance and opened another large, dark, heavy door. A broad stairwell lay before them, lights automatically flicking on. They went down one floor and emerged into a grey-carpeted corridor. On their left, they could see, through a smoked glass wall, a large gym filled with top-of-the-range equipment.

"Do you spend a lot of time in there, Sal?" Ben asked, knowing full well what the answer would be. Sally scowled.

"That was Maya's thing." Sally opened a door to her right and looked at them, a new expression of suppressed excitement on her thin face. "This is my thing."

They walked through the door, and a blast of warm, moist air hit them. They were in a room with vaulted ceilings. In front of them lay a large swimming pool. Almost every inch of the space was covered in a stunning mosaic. Animals frolicked around the walls; brightly shaded birds soared. Olive and cypress trees seemed to wave gently, and a sly, vulpine head peered from shady green ferns. The sun, moon and stars glowed, and Charlie thought she recognised Adam and Eve, heads lovingly bowed together, and the Serpent coiled tightly around the Tree of Life. The pool stretched before them, and the underwater walls glowed as squid and octopi waved their legs languidly, and brightly coloured fish chased across the gleaming shades of blue.

"Maya hated this room. Wouldn't come in it," said Sally. "I think this was designed and made by a prisoner of War. There was an enormous camp on the outskirts of Sheffield during the War. Near to Georgia's farm, in fact. He was a brilliant artist, whoever he was."

"And probably an Italian missing home," said Ben, nodding towards the olive trees.

"Anyone up for a swim?" asked Sally again. "There are some cubicles over there and some swimming costumes in the cabinet. Again, for guests who never arrived." Sally looked rueful. "They're in a 1940s knitted design, so they will probably fit anyone. Maya became obsessed with the 1940s for some reason..." she trailed off. Ben had disappeared. There was a sudden whoop, and he ran from the cubicle where he had hurriedly changed and leapt into the water, causing an enormous splash.

"Come on in!" he shouted gleefully, shaking his head like a damp but enthusiastic puppy. "The water's great!"

Sally smiled. "One last thing," she said. She walked

across to the far wall beyond the pool, where mosaic ended in a plain stone wall. She pushed a lever, and the entire wall slid silently to one side, leaving an infinity-pool effect as the sky appeared. The sun hung in the blue afternoon sky, and light poured through the massive space. The distant moors and gritstone edges glowed misty purple, and a sweet breeze carried in the green smell of trees and warming earth. Charlie gasped.

"Perfection, "she breathed.

Of course, there were inflatables. Sally and Charlie bullied Ben into using the electric pump stored in the cabinet to inflate three loungers, and they floated in the pool, watching the sun as it lowered, gleaming like a copper disc, in the sky. They drank more wine and teased each other gently.

"You need to watch that Charlie," said Ben to Sally. "She'll sink quietly to the bottom if she drinks any more of that red."

"S'Okay," said Sally, with the slightest of slurs. She gestured vaguely. "I've gotta thing... alarm. Goes off if anything goes into the water and stays at the bottom of the pool. Had to turn it off, though, kept alarming even with no one in the room. I'll turn it back on." She pulled herself to the side and went to the control panel in a dark corner of the room. "It may be the automated pool cleaner setting it off," she said over her shoulder. "But he's fast asleep in his little pen most of the time." She returned to the pool and the comfort of her floating lounger. "There you go, lovely Charlie. Have as much red wine as you like."

Sally did now think of Charlie as lovely. She was touched by Charlie's compassion at the hospital, admired her attitude to life and food and, as someone who genuinely dreaded hospitals and anything medical, found herself pathetically grateful for the way Charlie had stitched her arm up. She worked in a world of computers and finance, and the waters there were full of nothing but sharks.

"What shall we do tomorrow?" she asked suddenly. Charlie's eyes widened.

"Tomorrow? Can we stay again tonight? Are you sure, Sal?" Sally nodded.

"I haven't taken a day off in..." Sally's lips moved. "Two years," she said. "Let's do something!"

"Cars!" said Ben decisively. "And more cars." Charlie's face fell.

"If you don't mind, can I stay here? Explore the house... and the bath?" Sally looked at Ben. He grinned.

"Circuit near York?" he asked. Sally nodded and grinned back.

"Then massive, huge roast dinner," said Charlie firmly. Sally beamed at Charlie and raised her glass.

"Here's to new friends," said Sally. An odd feeling of lightness slowly exploded inside her, and she realised she felt happy. She hadn't felt this way in a very, very long time. In fact, not since the bad thing had happened; since Peter had died. Ben lifted his glass, too.

"Here's looking at you, kid," he said, toasting both women.

"This could be the beginning of a beautiful friendship!" cried Charlie, laughing. Ben smiled.

"I don't get it," said Sally uneasily.

"They're lines from the film Casablanca," said Charlie. "It's an oldie, but it's one of my favourites."

"Oh. I think I've seen that one in the cinema," said Sally slowly.

"I didn't realise they still showed it in cinemas," replied Charlie, frowning.

"No, I've seen it sitting, available to be shown, in my cinema," Sally replied. There was silence for about a minute while Ben and Charlie's drunken brains deciphered Sally's last comment.

"You have a cinema?" Ben said, eventually. Sally nodded.

"Only a small one."

"You have a cinema?" said Charlie.

"Yes," said Sally testily.

"With Casablanca?" said Charlie. Sally threw up her hands in mock frustration.

"How many more times? Yes!"

Ben wanted to see Aliens but, in the end, they watched Casablanca. The seats were big and plush and covered in crimson velvet. Ben fell asleep, but Sally and Charlie watched right to the end, and, of course, Charlie cried.

On Monday, Ben and Sally got up early and went to the racing track near York. They took turns to drive the Dodge Demon, and Ben spent an insanely happy morning burning rubber, egged on by the equally speed-crazy Sally. Charlie took the longest, deepest, most luxurious bath of her life and then drifted round the beautiful house and garden in a fluffy, white, velvety bathrobe, trailing vastly expensive scent. She sang quietly in the gently luminous kitchen as she prepared a full roast dinner for them all. She felt at complete peace: as if the warm, wooden soul of the house was gently wrapping itself around her bruised heart. The evening was spent in a pleasant, unreal daze of food, wine, and more films. But then Tuesday morning came.

The three sat around the kitchen island with a sense of sadness. Sally needed to catch up after her unprecedented amount of time off. Ben needed to finish the job he was doing in the Dore area of Sheffield, and Charlie, with a sinking feeling, knew that she had to go home.

"I can give you a lift," said Sally. "I need to go into Sheffield. To my office."

"Thanks," replied Charlie with a weak smile. There was a pause. "Sal," said Charlie quietly. "Would it be okay if I revisit this Saturday?"

"You can come on Friday night if you like," replied Sally tentatively. "Bring a weekend bag?" Charlie's face lit up like a Christmas tree. At last, something to look forward to. She wouldn't take those locum weekend shifts after all

"I'm on a late shift, but I can come over after if that's OK?" she said. Sally nodded

"I keep odd hours, so I'll be up," Sally said. "Late is fine."

"I'll cook," said Charlie, clapping her hands. "Slow-cooked tagine on Saturday, and chicken with all the trimmings on Sunday. And I can have a proper look around the walled garden. Ohhh, I can't wait!" Charlie started making a shopping list in her head and then drifted off into the pantry to check for preserved lemons.

Ben drove away, and Charlie and Sally left shortly after. Sally drove the Aston Martin this time, as there were just the two of them, and they were soon at Crookes. They drove up Mulehouse Road, turned right onto Stannington View Road and came to a halt. They sat in silence for a moment, Charlie looking bleakly at her house. She shook herself and smiled at Sally.

"Thanks for everything, Sal. Are you sure you don't mind me coming back on Friday?"

"I want you to come back," said Sally firmly. Charlie opened the car door. With one last warm grin, she slipped onto the pavement and walked towards her house. As she walked, Charlie pulled the Belstaff jacket, which she still wore, tightly around her. Sally smiled, thinking how big the jacket looked on Charlie. She wondered briefly how the jacket had found its way into her hallway cupboard and where Charlie's own coat might be. She then started the car.

Charlie felt a sinking feeling in her stomach. *Silly Charlie!* she heard, echoing in her mind. She flinched as she remembered her childhood and the blood on the walls. And, more recently, a pair of pale, bare, unmoving feet. *Onions, rice, tomatoes.* She tried to think of a recipe for tagine. *Apricots, almonds, harissa.* It was no good. The memories came, as they did every hour of every day.

CHAPTER FOURTEEN

Sally glanced at the back seat as she reversed the car. She braked abruptly. Charlie had left her backpack slumped there. Sally stopped the car, grabbed the bag, and opened the car door. She made her way down the narrow gennel she'd seen Charlie walk down. Seen from the back, the houses of Charlie's street were painted in pretty pastel shades and looked out over the beautiful Rivelin valley. Charlie's house, however, remained unpainted and seemed bleak in comparison. The back yard was covered in cracked concrete, tufts of weak grass and weeds pushing tiredly through, and the grimy windows were covered in grey net curtains. Sally frowned. Was she at the right house? But it was the right number.... She gently knocked on the kitchen door but there was no answer. Sally pushed the door open, stepped into the dark, cold kitchen and looked around. A small pile of unwashed dishes stood by a grimy sink, and a can of baked beans sat with a fork sticking out of its congealed centre. There was no trace of anyone's personality in the kitchen, no sign of anyone who loved cooking or food.

Sally's foot kicked at dusty rubbish on the greasy floor. She glimpsed, at the base of a yellowing Formica cupboard, a long spray of brown rusty spots that looked almost like old blood, and her frown deepened. Ahead of her, a door led to a cellar. The door was slowly closing as if someone had just gone through it. Sally walked over and pulled the door open. A broken lock sagged from the shabby wood. She peered down the narrow stone steps. A single lightbulb swung above her head, casting ghostly shadows, and she smelled a curious blend of incense and cleaning fluid. The air temperature dropped abruptly, and from the inky black stairs Sally thought she heard a slow harsh indrawn breath which stopped abruptly; as if life had been extinguished. Sally listened, horrified, but there was no further sound.

"Charlie?" Sally called softly. There was no reply.

Sally now stepped towards the dark stairwell that led upwards from the kitchen. The floor had been cleaned at the base of the stairs. A large circle of bleached linoleum gleamed in the half-light. As Sally stepped onto the first stair, she looked back towards the cellar and shuddered. She slowly climbed the threadbare stair and gently pushed at the half-open door to her left. The door was splintered and torn where it had been forced open, and another lock hung, useless, on the outside. She looked in.

Charlie sat in the semi-dark on a single bed pushed against the far wall. A tattered book was held in her arms. Sally could make out the word *Azkaban* and wondered what that meant. Charlie's face curled in distress as she saw Sally at the doorway, and she stood rapidly.

"Sal!" she exclaimed. "What are you doing here?" In reply, Sally held up Charlie's backpack. She was mystified.

"But, you're a doctor," Sally said simply. "Why are you

living like this?" Charlie's face became bleaker. She hugged her book tightly to her chest and sat back on the bed.

"I lived with my sister until a few weeks ago," she said quietly. "Emily. She had issues. She was an addict." Sally felt a wave of pity for Charlie. She understood obsession, having lived with Maya. And she'd now experienced the havoc that adding drugs to this type of personality could wreak. Charlie spoke again. "All my money went on her debts, to terrible people. Or on rehab, trying to get her clean. It never worked. She never stayed." Sally waited, and Charlie pushed words into the aching void. "And six weeks ago, I eventually had enough. I told her to leave. We both knew that I meant it this time. And then I came home... and I found, she'd taken too much. I found..." Charlie didn't need to explain. Sally had already sensed what terrible thing Charlie had found in the cellar.

"Didn't your family help?" asked Sally. Charlie flinched.

"My mother is not a very nice person," she said, lifting the book to cover her mouth as she spoke, as if ashamed of her words or scared that they would be heard. "We don't speak." Sally again felt the stream of sympathy washing from her towards Charlie. "And now," said Charlie, her voice drenched in fatigue. "And now, just getting out of bed in the morning is a real effort."

"But you were so happy...," said Sally. Charlie looked up quickly.

"I was. I can't remember when I felt so happy. With you and Ben and, and the house. I can't wait to come on Friday." Sally shook her head, frowning.

"No, Charlie, you're not coming to my house on Friday." Charlie's face fell, but she tried to smile. Sally recognised the pulling in of her chin as if someone had aimed a blow at it. Charlie nodded, her eyes glistening.

"That's okay. I wouldn't want me there, either."

"No, Charlie," said Sally impatiently. "You're coming to the house now. I won't leave you here."

Sally marched to a low chest of drawers and pulled it open. She stopped in surprise and pulled open another drawer. She turned to Charlie.

"Where are your clothes?" she demanded. She pointed at the drawer. "There are no clothes in here." Charlie looked at her.

"She sold them," she said in a small voice. "Emily. Sold my clothes. That's why I finally told her to leave." Charlie hugged the old book to her chest again. "Twenty pounds. That's what she got for them." She looked towards the open door and the dark stairwell. Her eyes widened in horror. "Twenty pounds," she whispered.

Sally continued hunting. She discovered two worn pairs of scrubs and some misshapen underwear. She opened the bag and stuffed them in. Sally went and sat next to the defeated Charlie. They looked at each other.

"Charlie," said Sally. "I've been told that friends are people you have faith in. And I have faith in you. Let me be your friend, Charlie." Charlie looked at her, unspeaking. "I've never had friends. I've certainly never had a proper female friend," continued Sally. "And I think you need one, too." Charlie nodded, her eyes filling with tears. "Come and live with me," said Sally.

"But what if that leads to trouble?" asked Charlie, holding her book up against her mouth again, overwhelmed. Sally shook her head.

"What sort of trouble could we possibly get each other into, Charlie?" asked Sally. Charlie looked at her wide-eyed.

"I'm scared to find out, Sal," she said quietly. "And, I think maybe you should be too."

"Do you have faith in me, Charlie?" asked Sally. Charlie nodded. "Well, I have faith in you. Let's just have faith in each other, shall we? Come and live with me for a while. Leave this awful place behind." Charlie slowly lowered her book, and a smile broke across her face like a small sunrise. "But, if we're going to spend more time together, we really need to discuss the concept of personal space," continued Sally in a firm tone. Charlie nodded; her mouth now compressed in a fierce little line. She then dropped her book and embraced Sally hard. "Oh dear," said Sally.

Sally dropped a tearful but elated Charlie at Rowans Holt and again headed for town. She parked in a discreet underground car park under a tall glass, brick and steel building at the top of Ecclesall Road. After submitting to fingerprint and retinal analysis, she took a lift to the upper floors. Sally braced herself as the lift doors opened. A wave of sensory overload threatened to overwhelm her. Bold colours glowed on white walls with The Company's world-renowned logo repeated in varying fonts and sizes. Smiling, casually dressed employees sat around large, open-plan office spaces. There were beanbags and free snacks, and table hockey. Sally flinched at the brash sound of arcade-style games and narrowly avoided an employee who sailed past her on an electric scooter. She scowled at the cats, which were, for some reason, allowed to roam around the building. Sally was obliged to attend the office at least one day in the week. She always found it a trial.

"Seven more months," Sally muttered, making her way towards her own small room. "Only seven more months." She closed the door and pressed her back against it. She looked in relief at the plain, clean surfaces of her desk; the calm, empty walls. She was in control again. She sat and opened her laptop. "Now, what can I find out about Mac's uncle?" she mused.

A few minutes later, there was a knock at the door of Sally's office. Sally opened it and was utterly unprepared for the loud exclamations from the crowd of employees who had gathered outside.

"Sally!" The crowd started cheering, clapping, and whooping. Sally stared at them, her face expressionless. She had never spoken to most of them. A figure stepped from the crowd. Randall. It figured. Randall Paige was the second in command of the British branch of The Company. He had arrived from Silicon Valley, California, around six months ago. He wore designer jeans, a black linen shirt, and large black glasses. His feet were bare, and multi-coloured love beads looped around his scrawny neck. He nodded enthusiastically in Sally's direction and lifted his hands, clapping and encouraging the crowd to applaud even harder.

"Sally! The Company's own little warrior!" Randall shouted, and the crowd roared their appreciation. "She survived the Code Blue madness!" Randall announced. He slipped an arm around Sally, who tried to shrink away, but Randall merely pulled her closer. He waved to the crowd for silence. "Sally Marshall is a true The Company employee," Randall enthused. "Diligent, determined, defined!" There was scattered applause. "She survived the Code Blue chaos of Friday night. And I want to assure everyone here that The Company puts the safety of every employee right up there." Randall waved his finger towards the ceiling. "People above profit!" he announced. "And if this city is not safe for The Company's people, then The Company will move you on out!" There was a pause as people looked at each other, uncertain. "All expenses paid!" yelled Randall. The applause started again.

Randall again pulled Sally close and moved down the corridor towards his large glass-walled office. "Me and Sally are going to debrief," he announced. "Back to work, people! And remember, if you're having a good time, you're not playing; you're working for The Company!" He pulled open the tall glass door and led Sally inside the room. All sound abruptly stopped as the door closed on the soundproofed room. Sally and Randall looked at each other. Randall's broad smile dropped away. He moved behind his wide, jet-black desk. It was completely clear, except for a bronze statue of a cat, over which Randall stroked his long-fingered hand. Sally recognised the tall, slim effigy as a depiction of the Egyptian goddess, Bastet.

"God, I hate this city," he muttered. "Investing in the North is like investing in barbarians." He glared at Sally. "You had a head injury. Are you sure you're safe to work?" he demanded. Randall had always bitterly resented Sally and her reputation. He hated England, he hated Sheffield, but, most of all, he hated Sally.

"I had a head C.T–" began Sally. Randall waved his hand impatiently.

"Yeah yeah, I saw it. No bleeding. No skull fracture."

"You saw my head C.T.?" said Sally, incredulous.

"Yeah. I wanted to reassure myself your brain wasn't as

big as Richie seems to think it is," replied Randall, with a hint of malice.

Sally paused. Richie Kassel was the CEO of The Company. He'd employed Sally six years ago and had watched her progress with satisfaction; partly because of the money she'd made for him, but also because he admired her intellect and attention to detail. He'd even moved The Company up North hoping to find more raw talent like hers.

"Where is Richie?" Sally said slowly. Randall was usually more discrete with his dislike of her.

"Oh, did Richie not confide in his little Golden Girl?" asked Randall, a grin re-emerging on his face. "He's gone on retreat for the next seven months." Sally shook her head. Randall continued. "Yeah. You see, Richie finally knocked up his...." Randall held up his hands and made quotation marks with his middle fingers. "'Life Partner' Zenobia-Rosebud. They've decided to spend the pregnancy as far from the toxic modern world as they can." Randall smirked. "Yeah. Right now, they're halfway up a mountain in Tibet. Or Bhutan. Whatever. Either way, there are no mobile phones, no internet. Just slurping on Yak milk and focussing on their super-foetus." He looked at Sally, his eyes glittering. "Which puts me in charge."

Randall sat in his high-backed, black, vegan-friendly swivel chair. He put his hands behind his head and his smile widened. "And I say, if this city is full of murdering, drug-addled freaks, then we up and out!" Sally shook her head.

"You can't pull all these people away from their homes. "

"I run The Company now. I can do what I like," said Randall. "Yeah. Let's say six weeks. And if this Code Blue is still on the streets, then we are out of here. Hasta la vista, Sheffield."

"London?" said Sally. She could tolerate travelling down to London one day a week. Randall shook his head.

"Oh, no. Back to California." Sally shrugged and turned to leave.

"I won't be going with you, Randall," she said.

"Pity," replied Randall. "We'll have to sell Rowans Holt to help fund the move. So, you'll be homeless and jobless." Sally stopped. She turned back to Randall, and it was her turn to smile.

"Rowans Holt no longer belongs to The Company, Randall. It's mine. Richie gave it to me in return for the BanKin App. I signed a contract. I have a contract. All I had to do was serve out two more years with The Company, and then I was free. The house is mine." Randall opened a drawer and removed a sheaf of papers.

"Do you mean this contract?" he asked casually. He waved the papers languidly with his right hand as if fanning himself. Sally froze.

"It's watertight," Sally said. "I spend one day a week in the office. I give work of value to the Company for two years. I have seven months of my two years left to work, and then I can leave if I wish."

"Yeah. Except, you haven't been giving work of value to The Company, have you?" said Randall. "You spend one day hanging around, not joining in, not being a Team Player. What have you actually done since your over-hyped, over-paid little app, huh? And where's that ground-breaking new A.I. project you promised Richie?" Sally said nothing. "Let's look at what you've done this morning, shall we?" said Randall, throwing the papers down and picking up an iPad. "Hmm. You investigated some guy called Tristan, by the looks of things. A British civil servant, a diplomat." He put down the iPad and glared at Sally. "As usual, you engaged in your own little projects; *not* doing work of value to The Company."

Randall stood up. He picked up the contract and crushed it in his hand. "Well, I'll give you a little project, Missy," he said. "You might have failed in your A.I. mission, but I won't fail in mine. The Company will move fully into Artificial Intelligence research as a priority. This Code Blue has massive potential for cybernetics with its particular psychotropic effects. Get me some."

"What?" exclaimed Sally. Randall moved from behind the desk and walked towards her, he came close and whispered in her ear.

"I've heard that Code Blue lets some special people see the thoughts of others. Can you imagine the potential of that? I could know all the secrets. *All* the secrets." Sally glared back at Randall. He stepped back and held up her contract. Sally could see her name scrawled confidently over the pages. She remembered her fierce joy as she had signed it.

"I am in charge now. You're the amazing Sally Marshall. You can do anything. Well, get me some Code Blue within the next six weeks. And if you don't, you will not be fulfilling the terms of your contract." He moved closer again. "I will take back Rowans Holt." Sally shook her head.

"You can't do that. I'll sue you; I'll run rings around you in court," she said defiantly.

"And I will bulldoze your home to the ground before you serve your first paper. You know I will. You can fight all you like in the wreckage," Randall hissed. "You have six weeks. Get me some Code Blue. And if you mention this to anyone, I will deny it. And then, I will fire you."

Sally felt a burning in her chest. It was rage. She looked at Randall and saw his small eyes, deep within the black frames of his glasses. They gleamed with pleasure and spite. She realised he meant every word. That he planned to hurt her. Sally then became calm. She needed to think, to plan. She turned for the door. Randall spoke again.

"You know, I liked Maya," he said in a low voice. "She's a classy lady. Yeah. You should have kept hold of that one."

A FEW MINUTES LATER, Sally sat in the dim car park, breathing heavily. Her hands clamped on the steering wheel of her Aston Martin, and her eyes gazed ahead of her, unseeing. After a while, she spoke.

"Sod that!" she exclaimed. Sally fired up the engine and headed for home.

CHAPTER FIFTEEN

Sally pulled up to the front of Rowans Holt. Ben was parked up, leaning against his Volvo, looking relaxed. His job in Dore was finished. He was chatting with Mac, who stood, arms folded, in his usual combative stance. They both looked at Sally as she got out of the Aston Martin. Ben grinned, a stark contrast to Mac's glower.

"Back already? Are these I.T. hours? I'm in the wrong job!" he called. Sally ignored both men and strode past them and into the house. Ben and Mac looked at each other and then followed her in.

Sally threw her briefcase onto the desk and then paced up and down, her hands clenching and unclenching.

"Sally?" said Mac. "Sally, what's wrong?" Sally shook her head and carried on striding around the room. Charlie emerged from the library. Mac frowned. He hadn't realised she was still there. Charlie approached Sally.

"Sal," she said gently. She reached out and touched Sally's arm. Sally stopped.

"Personal space, Charlie," she said firmly.

"Friends, Sally," replied Charlie, not backing down. "If we're to be friends, then that means we help each other. Tell us what's wrong."

Sally let out an exclamation of frustration. "My new boss wants to bulldoze Rowans Holt into the ground!" she exclaimed. Both Charlie and Ben took a step toward her.

"No way!" declared Ben, glancing protectively towards the library.

"Sal!" said Charlie, her face creased with distress. Sally quickly related what had happened. Charlie shook her head.

"He wouldn't do that, Sally." Sally looked at her.

"But he would, Charlie. Randall Paige would do just that. Small village standing on land The Company wants in California? Handy chemical fire clears all the families out with no compensation. Accusations of bullying? The whole department closed down and fired. Why do you think I want out?" Sally shook her head. "I should have known it wouldn't be this easy." She walked to the sweeping window and placed her hand against it as if she could touch the distant, gleaming peaks. "You can't love something so much and not have someone want to take it all away from you," she said quietly.

"What are you going to do?" asked Mac. "You rang and asked me to meet you here. What do you need?" Sally turned from the window.

"I need some Code Blue, of course," she said. Ben snorted.

"Just like that? Get hold of some illegal drug that the whole of the Police force can't find?" Sally looked at him.

"And why not?" she said archly. "I am Sally Marshall. I am magnificent." Ben looked taken aback, but then his face broke into a slow, delighted smile, and he nodded. Sally then regarded Mac. "But it means that I need my Head of Security at his best."

Sally and Mac stood facing each other in front of her desk. Charlie noticed how different Sally was around Mac. She seemed to close down and become sharper, less emotional than when she was alone with Charlie and Ben.

"I'm sorry," said Sally and Mac at the same time. They both sounded a little angry, but Mac unfolded his arms, his tension seeming to ease a little.

"I shouldn't have left you the other day," said Mac. He looked both frustrated and awkward. "And I'm sorry about yesterday." Sally shook her head.

"No. We couldn't have known Maya would escape from the secure psychiatric unit. It was unfair of me to take it out on you, Mac. You saved my life when Maya attacked me the first time; and now I need you to help save me again. I need you to help save Rowans Holt." Sally paused. "It's the same thing; saving me and saving the house. So, if I help you, you can help me."

Sally flipped open her laptop but then stopped. Randall had known what she'd been looking at on the internet. He had told her he admired Maya. Sally groaned. She lowered the lid of her laptop. She turned to the others. Holding her finger up to her lips, she indicated that Mac, Ben, and Charlie follow her. Sally led them to the library and closed the door.

"I'm completely compromised," she said. "Maya must have put spyware on my computer. She's involved with Randall somehow, and he's been watching me. I'll need new hardware. I'll need to redo everything." Mac nodded sharply.

"I'll take it all with me to Sinclair. She'll set you up. Do you want her to run a diagnostic, find out what it is?" Sally nodded, looking gloomy. "But what about your passwords, account numbers?" asked Mac. Sally tapped her head.

"Don't worry; everything's up here." She sighed. "But this is going to delay things."

Sally looked at Mac. "In the meantime. What have you discovered? About the whereabouts of your uncle?" Mac's mouth hardened in frustration. His arms returned to their crossed position, and he glared out of the library window. Grey clouds gathered over the distant peaks, and the tall rowan trees around the house moved uneasily in the gathering storm. "I see," said Sally. "Well, I've discovered that your uncle is Tristan Beaulouf, second son of George and Oonagh Beaulouf. Red hair, green eyes, age fifty-four. Weight one hundred and eighty pounds, shoe size eleven." Mac didn't react. Sally continued. "Favourite colour, emerald green. Favourite book, *To Kill a Mockingbird*. Apparently works for the Diplomatic Service, but more likely, it's the Secret Service. Trouble-shooter. Missing and whereabouts unknown." Mac was now staring at Sally, his face unreadable. Sally looked at him. "There must be someone you know, high in government," said Sally. "You're old money. Old gentry. You're Lord Beaulouf." Mac looked at Sally, expressionless.

"Don't call me that," he said flatly.

There was silence. Mac shook his head. "No one will say anything about where my uncle is because no one knows," he said. "It was a closed mission. All I know is that he was sent to a place in the Middle East. A place called Perda."

"Purdah?" isn't that something to do with elections? said Charlie. Mac didn't answer or look at her.

"No, Perda. It means lost," said Sally. "Some Victorian civil servant was probably being sarcastic."

"It's a small province between Iran and Afghanistan. So barren and inhospitable neither country wants to lay claim to it. My uncle went there with a small crew of soldiers," said Mac. He paused and looked at Sally. "From what I gathered, when I spoke to him last, he was trying to talk to tribal leaders. About drugs being smuggled into England." Sally looked at him, wide-eyed.

"Middle East. Drugs. Sinclair said you came across a new drug when you were in Afghanistan. That it might have been Code Blue." Mac looked at her, his face angry and hopeless.

"Code Blue, heroin, whatever. It doesn't matter now. It doesn't help me get my uncle back if he's been kidnapped a thousand miles away." Sally waited. Mac sighed. He glanced at Ben. "Jude Morton. We think he got hold of an experimental drug. The army had resurrected some old research but quickly closed it down when it got out of hand. They wanted super-aggressive soldiers. I imagine it got very messy." It was Ben's turn now to look distressed.

"What happened?" said Sally. "I need to know."

CHAPTER SIXTEEN

AFGHANISTAN FEBRUARY 2012

Mac sat awkwardly at his desk in the burning heat of the Command tent. Lieutenant Sinclair stood before him. She was weeping. Heaving sobs tore at her, and with each exhalation came a low cry as if she were in physical pain. Sinclair kept trying to stand to attention; her fists clenched, but her shoulders shook too much. He sat, back rigid, looking at a point to the right of her head. The last week had been like Hell on Earth for him and his company of soldiers. Mac had testified against Jude Morton and his men, but the court martial had come to nothing. He had spent eight roasting, sweaty hours in what had felt like a kangaroo court rather than the legal arm of the British Army. The head of the board who had found Morton not guilty, Major Marcus Rosendale, had approached Mac after the hearing.

"Beaulouf, I'm so sorry. I argued your case as strongly as I could, but it was a majority ruling."

"It's alright, Major Rosendale," Mac had replied stiffly. "Thank you for trying."

"We need to stamp out this vile poison of drugs in our army," muttered Rosendale, shaking his head, his handsome face troubled. He'd looked up at Mac. "I know our families have not always seen eye to eye, Beaulouf. But I'm glad we can agree on this at least." He'd held out his hand, and Mac had reluctantly taken it. Rosendale's hand had been hot and dry. Rosendale had smiled, and Mac felt as though tiny insects had suddenly started crawling over his spine. "Give my regards to your father, Beaulouf," Rosendale had said. "We were friends at Oxford, you know?" His smile had then become hungry. He pulled Mac slightly closer, his hot grip on Mac's hand tightening. "And send my love to your mother. As always. Send Laura my love."

'Nox' Section, as they had come to be known, were now being abruptly shipped out in two days. The four remaining members of the Section, Jude Morton, Mike Quigley, Jake Fawkes, and Billy Ronson, paced, like relaxed jackals, around the compound. Quigley, Fawkes, and Ronson were bullish thugs, Morton was different. He was tall and remarkably assured, with short blond hair and restless, light blue eyes that were never still. The rest of the company watched them with fear and hostility. And today, there had been another IED and another three dead British soldiers. They had been on the way to investigate an opium warlord—three more fallen comrades. Among them had been Sinclair's fiancé, corporal Jordan Linton.

Sinclair's sobs had quietened. She finally stood to attention. "Permission to speak freely, Sir," she said, her voice tight and harsh.

"Granted," snapped Mac, now looking at a place above her head.

"They're going. Nox. They're letting them go. We know

what they've done. And why." Mac said nothing. He merely gave one sharp nod. "You know I'm a physicist. My degree was in physics," she said. His eyes drifted down to meet her gaze. It was as hard as ice. As bitter as winter. "I'm a comms and science geek. And geeks talk to each other. I know about one of the British Army's experimental developments. They were trying to resurrect some old research project. They were trying to make a drug—a drug to give you super strength and aggression at will. My contact says it went horribly wrong. Men died. They closed it down permanently last year. But a few months ago, some of the drug got stolen."

There was a long pause. Mac stood and walked over to Sinclair. He crossed his arms and leaned closer to her. He could see the tracks of her bitter tears through the dust that coated her face. Dust covered every surface in the heated hell-hole that was the Camp.

"Continue," he said quietly. Her reddened eyes flicked to the tent's entrance, then back to him. She whispered.

"I think Nox have found a way to make it into a recreational drug: mixed it with pure heroin or something. That would figure, given their local links. Morton's always filming. He films everything. I bet he's filmed them at it, either high or experimenting with it." Mac raised an eyebrow.

"And?"

"What if I can get access to Morton's computer?" There was another pause.

"Get access.... How?" Asked Mac. "He's never alone. He's completely paranoid. We'd never get within ten feet of his tent. And they leave in two days." Sinclair said nothing but looked ahead in stony silence. Mac sighed. "What do you propose to do, Sinclair? Torture a password out of him? And if we steal the laptop, A; it's bound to self-destruct if we access it, and B; Nox will come after us and kill us." Sinclair said nothing; her mouth turned down in a grim line. Mac continued. "Plus, if we steal it, any evidence we get from it will probably be inadmissible in court." Mac sighed again and pulled gently at his right ear.

"I can get the password," said Sinclair quietly. "At least let me try." Mac looked at her. Her face was now neutral. She looked straight ahead of her.

"How?" repeated Mac. Sinclair shrugged.

"I'll think of something," she said vaguely. Mac frowned.

"Madeleine," he said quietly. "I know the temptation is for Revenge. But we can't do that. We have to be better than that. We have to seek Justice. Or everything falls apart." Sinclair slowly turned her gaze to him, and he shivered internally.

"Really? Sir?" she said. "And have you ever lost the thing you loved most in the world? What will you say when they're taken from you? When they're murdered?" Mac straightened his back. He remembered his schooling, his training, his duty.

"It would be difficult, Madeleine. I'm not denying that. But it would have to be Justice. Otherwise, we're no better than the killer. We're no better than animals." Sinclair looked at him for a long moment, then returned to eyes front.

"I'll get the password," she repeated.

JUDE MORTON WAS WALKING DOWN one of the broad, sand-filled avenues that were called roads on the base. Quigley and Fawkes, heads down, arms hanging like corded shovels, walked either side of him. He looked to his left and saw the briefest flash of a booted ankle. He stopped in his tracks. The ankle and the boot had now gone. His eyes narrowed. Jude Morton knew that ankle. He had covertly filmed it, studied it, watched it as it moved and ran. He knew the beautiful body to which it was attached almost as well as his own. A jeep was parked down a blind alley. It was listing slightly. He would bet the back right wheel was sunk deep in sand, spinning, unable to move. He motioned for the others to go on. They looked at each other and reluctantly left their leader.

Jude Morton stood for a moment, observing, but the ankle did not reappear. He saw a flash of sand from behind the vehicle. Someone was digging frantically, by the look of it. He pulled open the door of the long, tented building that made up the righthand side of the blind alley. It was an old medical facility that now stood empty, billowing and ghostly in the constant desert wind. He walked through the empty space, quiet and lithe, looking through the grubby windows, his eyes fixed on the alley outside. He came level with the jeep. No one sat within it or stood beside it. He slipped out of the back of the long building and pulled himself up onto the roof of a box-like, empty structure. He walked across the roof, lowered himself onto the white, scoured, burning surface, and peered over the edge and down into the alley. He'd been right; it was Sinclair. She was alone, digging around the back right wheel of the jeep, clearly angry and frustrated. She was on all fours. Sweat soaked the back of the khaki shirt that she wore, and it clung to her skin. Her long lustrous hair had worked loose from its tightly restrained style and rippled over her left shoulder like a darkly glimmering waterfall to brush against the hot sand. The smooth skin of her neck glistened. From where he lay, he could hear the occasional angry grunt and muttered curse. He smiled. She was definitely alone, separated from the bunch of losers she usually associated with. And she was in distress.

SINCLAIR LOOKED UP, squinting in the sun. She had removed her shirt, and her sweat-drenched vest moulded to her. She couldn't see who stood above her, only make out broad shoulders and muscled legs. It was Jude Morton. He said nothing to her. He bent his knees and grabbed the rear edge of the jeep. Morton slowly lifted, and the wheel eased gradually out of the sand. Sinclair quickly slipped the traction matting under the wheel, and, without a sound, Morton released the jeep. He stood looking at Sinclair, who stared back at him, her face dripping and flushed. She looked Morton slowly up and down. Sinclair said nothing but grabbed her shirt, stood, and walked to her jeep. She got into the passenger seat. Morton smiled. He hopped into the driver's seat and turned to face Sinclair. She held out the vehicle keys.

"Your place. Or mine?" was all she said. Morton started the jeep and, with casual skill, eased the firm wheel out of the soft, clinging sand.

CHAPTER
SEVENTEEN
AFGHANISTAN FEBRUARY 2012

Sinclair walked into the Command Tent, rubbing her hair dry with a towel in quick, efficient movements. She had returned an hour ago, pulling up in the jeep, grim-faced but quietly triumphant. She had written a nine-letter password on a piece of paper and handed it to Mac.

"It's a dollar or a percentage sign as the last figure. I'm sure of it, Sir," she had said. "And he suspects nothing. I made sure of that too." Mac had stood and looked at the paper. He then looked at Sinclair, at her flushed face and unbuttoned uniform. Realisation broke over him like a slow and terrible wave.

"Madeleine..." he began. "What have you done?"

"I told you. He films everything," Sinclair said, raising her chin and not dropping her gaze. "He needed to open his laptop." Mac shook his head and began to object.

"But Jordan... Morton actually thought...."

"He's a man," snapped Sinclair. "And a narcissist. He saw what he wanted to see. He believed what he wanted to believe."

"But Madeleine..."

"Don't!" she had said, raising her hand and pointing an angry finger at him. "Don't you dare say one more thing. You are my commanding officer. Don't make the mistake of thinking you're either my father or my conscience. I've watched your back at every moment. So now, you watch mine." She nodded towards the piece of paper. "There's the Justice you wanted!" she said. "Every sordid, dirty, necessary piece of it. Don't worry; I'll wait for my Revenge. At least that will be clean." She'd left the room without another word. It had taken her a long time to shower and change.

"She's found out what?" exclaimed Sergeant Todmorden, glaring at Mac. Mac had called in the rest of his most trusted soldiers from the Company. Chris Todmorden stood six foot three, and his tattooed arms and neck bulged like a veined oak tree. There were plenty of gyms on base, and body-building had become an obsession for some soldiers, bored and restless on their unrelenting six-month tour.

"Give the lass a break. We need to listen to her and Mac," reasoned Warrant Officer Arthur Wetherby calmly. He was the eldest of the group. A quiet, lean, seasoned soldier of the Yorkshire regiment. He'd served with Mac's father, and his family had worked on Mac's family estate for generations. Mac had known him all his life.

"This is ridiculously dangerous!" snapped Corporal Hafez. His slim, restless figure paced around the tent. "We could face serious consequences." Rumi Hafez had joined the army as a way out of a Manchester sink-estate. His highly educated but fragile mother had found herself there, a single-parent asylum seeker. She had fled Iran with her husband and two young children after her brother had been shot through the heart for questioning the local militia. Only she and Hafez had made it. She still spent her days in mourning, her sleepless nights waiting for the long-lost loved ones to knock softly at her door. Hafez had been bullied incessantly at school for his appearance and accent (which he'd soon lost). He probably had an underlying ADHD diagnosis, too. He'd left school with few qualifications, but in the army, he had shone. In Afghanistan, he had been invaluable with his intelligence, bravery and bilingual skills in Farsi and Pashto. Fiercely proud of his Persian heritage and totally loyal to his new country, he was combative and the group's questioner. He constantly looked for both sides of a situation; problems, and solutions. He had struck up a firm and unexpected friendship with the towering Todmorden.

"I notice you didn't tell us not to do it, Hafez," observed Mac shrewdly. Hafez shrugged.

"They're a bunch of murdering thugs with friends in high places," he said. "Hack the bastards. I'm in. I'll do it." Mac nodded.

"Then we're all agreed," Mac said. "As soon as they leave their tent, Hafez will access Morton's computer and lift whatever he can about the drugs they're messing around with." They all nodded.

Mac handed a memory stick to Hafez and then looked around him. "Where on earth is Pinks?" asked Mac. Sergeant Tim Pinks, a thin and nervous man, was the last member of the group of six, or The Crew, as they thought of themselves. With thinning, strawberry-blond hair, he burned terribly in the Afghan sun. He was pathetically devoted to Mac but struggled to impose discipline on the men under his watch. Pinks appeared at the tent door and slid through.

"Sorry!" he breathed. He brought out a blue asthma inhaler, shook it, activated a dose into his moist, red mouth, and breathed it in deeply. "What's going on?" He managed after he finally expelled his breath.

"I don't have time to explain now. You should have been here earlier," said Mac firmly but gently. Pinks looked mortified. "We've managed to get hold of Jude Morton's password," Mac continued. "We're going to access his computer. Find evidence of Nox's drug crimes. Don't worry; we'll be safe."

"When were you thinking of d..d..doing it?" Pinks stuttered.

"Right now," said Sinclair. "It's mess time. The entire Company are in the Canteen. Nox always take the same table." She pulled a face in frustration at their bullying behaviour. "We'll check they're there, and then we move."

"Let's go," said Mac.

"But, wait, wait! How did you get it?" called Pinks. His wavering voice rose urgently high.

"Should have been here, Pinks," muttered Hafez as he swept past him.

They headed for the Canteen. Their Company were, indeed, eating. The Crew stood at the entrance and watched the scene. Nox section already had their meals and sat solidly at their usual table. This table was right in the middle of the mess hall. No other soldier dared sit at it, at least not more than once. Quigley, Ronson and Fawkes bent over their food, shovelling methodically into their grim mouths. Like Todmorden, they spent most of their spare time at the gym. Their necks were thick and bullish, much like their personalities. Jude Morton was not eating. His cold, blue eyes in his handsome, square-jawed face roamed around the room, searching for patterns and changes, monitoring all entrances and exits. He spotted The Crew standing, watching him. Morton smiled and fixed Sinclair with his gaze. He raised his glass to her and took a slow sip of water. *Enjoy the taste of freedom while you can, you murdering bastard*, thought Sinclair.

Mac nodded slightly, and Hafez quietly slipped out of the messroom. The Crew moved to join the line of servicemen and women waiting for their evening meal. Mac nodded casually at the salutes that came his way. His chin lifted, and The Crew felt their spirits soar at his calm confidence. Sinclair noticed Pinks' hands were trembling as they clutched his tray. Mac had seen too. He spoke quietly.

"Don't worry, Pinks," he said reassuringly. "Nox won't know we've been in their tent." Mac helped himself to bread and glanced again at the jittering Pinks. "There'll be no repercussions. I'll keep you safe, Pinks, I promise." Pinks swallowed, Adam's apple jerking in his scrawny neck.

They sat at a table in clear view of Nox Section. Morton continued his scrutiny of Sinclair, who studiously ignored him. Morton leaned close to Fawkes and Ronson and spoke quietly. Fawkes and Ronson craned their necks round and looked towards Sinclair, leering.

"Oi, Todmorden!" grated Quigley, grinning in gap-toothed delight. "Where's yer husband?" Todmorden ignored him, hunching over his meal. Weatherby sat, elbow to elbow, with Todmorden and matched him, slow mouthful for slow mouthful.

Pinks seemed unable to catch his breath. He squirmed in his seat, panting in slight, shallow huffs. Mac frowned.

"Are you alright, Pinks?" he said. "Do you need to go to the Medical Tent?" Pinks dropped his fork with a loud, clumsy clatter. He pushed himself up abruptly from the table, clearly distressed.

"I think... I think I just need to...." The Crew watched him. Mac threw his serviette down and stood in anxious concern.

"Pinks," Mac said, holding out his hand. Pinks backed away, his face contorting and his mouth pinched.

"No!" announced Pinks. "No! I'm not broken. I don't need fixing, for God's sake. Why do you always think I need your help? I just need to...." He turned and lurched away.

The Crew watched in horror as Pinks staggered over to the table occupied by Nox Section. Morton looked up at Pinks but didn't motion him to go away as he would to any regular grunt. That was odd. Pinks stood with his thin back to the Crew. He was leaning sideways, clearly speaking to Morton. Morton slowly turned his head and looked at the Crew. At Sinclair and then at Mac. His face became blank and unreadable. He leaned over and spoke to his men, who leapt up and rushed from the mess tent. Mac felt the blood drain from his face as he realised what this meant. This was the reason Nox had always been one step ahead. A viper had been at the heart of all The Crew had done and said. Mac stood and charged out of the tent, swiftly followed by Todmorden and Weatherby. Mac raised his walkie-talkie to his mouth and hissed;

"Hafez, they're on to us. Get out, get out now!"

Sinclair was left standing, looking at Morton, who watched her, expressionless. But then he smiled and slowly raised his hands to his face and breathed in deeply of their scent. She realised that, although she had scrubbed her entire body, trying to clean away all traces of what she had done, his body still reeked with the redolence of her. He wore it like his wreath of laurels, like her chain of ashes. Sinclair leaned over and spat on the ground between them.

THEY RETURNED to the Command Tent and looked between themselves with shock and disbelief.

"Pinks!" declared Todmorden. "The lying, stinking, traitorous...." He turned abruptly, went to the tent window, and stared out, clenching his fists." Rumi, where's Rumi? If he's hurt, I'll tear Pinks apart with my own hands!" Todmorden looked more distressed than Mac had ever seen him.

"We can't go after Nox," Mac said firmly. He looked at Sinclair's mutinous face. "It's one thing to steal information. Without Pinks, they would never have known we'd been in there. Not until they were arrested. It's another thing to steal a laptop that they will inevitably come after. We'd have open violence on the base, and we know what they're capable of. I won't put your lives at risk." There was silence. "I've made my decision as your commanding officer," Mac said loudly. "Do you understand me?"

"Sir," came the reluctant answer from what was left of The Crew.

They turned as a figure limped through the curtained door. It was Hafez, his face was bruised and bleeding. Todmorden grabbed him, pulling him into a rough hug, and Hafez coughed and choked. Todmorden released him and thumped him on the back. Hafez winced and spat an object into his hand.

"Calm down, big guy!" he objected, slipping into a Mancunian drawl. Hafez handed over the memory stick that he had hidden in his mouth. He looked at Mac apologetically. "I did what I could," he said. "But I only had a few minutes. Barely enough to get booted up. But I got a few video files." Sinclair winced. Mac nodded.

"Thank you, Hafez. You're a brave man."

Mac turned to The Crew. "Weatherby, Toddy, Hafez, mount a guard. Sinclair and I will see what we've got." The men moved into position by the windows. Sinclair sat before Mac's laptop. As night fell, she watched images of Nox section as they milled, clearly under the influence of some substance. But there was no sign of manufacture, of sale, of anything that would lead to prosecution or warrant a formal investigation."

"Nox are here," murmured Weatherby as night fell over the camp. There was the quiet sound of weapons being drawn. The tent was silent and dim as Sinclair continued scanning the images Hafez had retrieved. However, in the end, she had to admit defeat. She turned to Mac.

"There's nothing here of any use that I can see, Sir," she said. Mac looked at her sadly.

"It was worth a try, Sinclair. Thank you." Sinclair nodded but didn't meet his eye. She felt drained and empty. "Nox will be gone tomorrow," said Mac. "We'll see you back to your tent. We'll stand guard for each other tonight."

Sinclair approached Hafez as they prepared to leave the Command Tent. She spoke quietly.

"I don't suppose you... saw a video of Morton's? A personal–"

"I deleted it," said Hafez shortly. He looked down as he adjusted the strapping on his jacket.

"You didn't... watch?" said Sinclair. Hafez's face curled in disgust.

"No, Sinclair!" he exclaimed. "That would be like looking at my sister!" Hafez's expression grew bleak. The brief memory of a black wave breaking over a tiny boat filled with terrified, huddled strangers threatened to engulf him. He saw his older sister, aged only eight, pale-faced as she was plucked, like a baby sparrow, into the arms of the turbid sea. He saw his father, unthinking, as he had launched himself after his little girl. Hafez remembered the dark, long-fingered hands of the Sierra Leonean school teacher who had grimly held on to Hafez's screaming mother to stop her from throwing herself after the two of them. Hafez shook his head and looked at Sinclair. "No," he repeated. "I didn't look. And neither will he. Ever again." Sinclair looked down.

"Thanks, Hafez," she said.

PINKS HAD BEEN FOUND dead the following day, just as Nox Section left the base. He had, apparently, shot himself. In a sealed room. Suicide note and everything.

CHAPTER
EIGHTEEN
ROWANS HOLT 2016

Mac sighed. The memories had flashed across his mind in mere seconds. "We obtained the password to Jude Morton's computer and tried to look for evidence," he said wearily. "We were betrayed. We failed. We found no evidence of any new drug. But we knew Nox Section were knee-deep in it." Mac looked at the others. "And that's it," he said. "But Jude Morton's dead. Fawkes, Ronson and Quigley were dangerous but incapable. It's not them running the Code Blue operation. It will be some new thug with a brain and a loyal following." Mac shrugged. "But it's Sheffield's problem now. The Police's problem, not mine."

"Well, it's now my problem too," said Sally. She paced. "New drug, Middle East," she muttered. She stopped. "I'll bet that's what your uncle was doing." Mac frowned.

"I assumed he was talking to the tribal leaders about heroin. It's always about heroin," he objected. Sally shook her head.

"Why send a senior diplomat for something that's always been a problem? But if there's a new drug, Code Blue, for example, causing chaos and bad publicity for the government and the Police? You'd send your top man then."

Mac looked thoughtful and pulled gently at his right ear. He opened his mouth to say something, but there was a sudden blaring noise that repeated, again and again. Mac looked around for the source of the noise. Ben pulled himself upright. Charlie looked at Ben, who suddenly seemed like a different person, all easy-going slouch gone. Ben looked enquiringly at Mac, who nodded back at him. Mac smoothly drew a gun from the hidden holster under his left arm. He then drew a knife from the sheath at the base of his back. He threw the large blade to Ben, who caught and curled it expertly into position. Ready to kill, Charlie realised. She shrank back. *No, not more violence.*

Sally surprised her by putting an arm around her shoulders. Sally called loudly to Mac.

"It's OK! It's the pool alarm. Saying someone's in the water. It's defective, remember." Mac looked at her.

"But we had it fixed!" he called back. "And can you be sure it's not Maya? With a knife, or someone else worse? One hundred per cent?" He shouted. Sally looked at him, then shook her head. Mac nodded sharply. He indicated that Ben follow him and headed towards the dark corridor that led to the stairs.

"Hang on!" called Sally after Mac. "I pay you for this. Not him." She jerked her head towards Ben, who smiled.

"It's alright, lass. I'm not letting him have all the fun. This one's on me." He turned and followed Mac.

The two men quickly made their way down the stairwell.

Mac led and occasionally glanced back at Ben. The alarm continued to blare. Mac cautiously eased the door open and scanned the corridor. It was empty. They emerged into the corridor, Ben automatically covering the rear. Mac approached the entrance to the poolroom. He eased this open, too and peered into the dimly lit space. Despite himself, he gasped when he saw two dark figures, deep in the water, clearly struggling with each other. Their limbs thrashed and twisted, caught and distorted by the low light. Ben's eyes widened as he saw them, too. The alarm screamed right above their heads now.

"Drowning... drowning... someone's drowning...." it seemed to exclaim.

Mac slammed his hand onto the main light switch. It flicked the overhead lights to full brightness and illuminated — an empty pool. Mac and Ben ran to the pool's edge and stared into the water. It was definitely empty. The alarm continued to scream. Ben walked across to the switch box and flicked the alarm off. The noise abruptly stopped, but their ears continued to ring. Their nerves also jangled, adrenaline causing their hearts to pound. They looked at each other.

"You saw them, didn't you, Yorkie?" demanded Mac. Ben nodded, breathing heavily, his fitness considerably worse than Mac's.

"Two men. In the water. Looked like they were fighting," agreed Ben. Mac waded into the pool until the warm water was halfway up his thighs. He raised the gun in his right hand. With his left hand, he reached into the water and waved it, trying to part the water and pierce its mysteries. There was nothing. The images of sea creatures waved gently back, languid in their colourful elegance.

The men looked at each other. "A trick of the light," said Ben. "Must have been a trick of the light." Mac nodded slowly. There was no other explanation. He didn't believe in ghosts or magic or spirits. He believed in nothing other than life and death and duty. Mac shivered, however, as an image flickered into his mind. Of Maya, when they had found her, squatting in the moist, noisome dark of the caves. For one second, on the edge of the light, he thought he'd seen a hand on her right shoulder. A long-nailed, yellow-skinned hand; fingers like bones wrapped in rotting gossamer, gripping her possessively. He had looked again, and the hand had gone. There was no one else in the cave. And then Maya had started screaming, and he'd forgotten all about it. Except in his dreams. Except in his nightmares.

THEY RETURNED UPSTAIRS IN SILENCE. Neither man met the other's eye. Sally and Charlie greeted them warily.

"Well?" said Sally.

"You were right. It was the defective alarm," said Mac. Sally looked between him and Ben. Something was not quite right.

"You saw them," she said slowly. "You saw them too...." The men looked at each other, deeply uncomfortable now.

"Saw who?" enquired Charlie, looking at the three troubled faces.

"An optical illusion. In the pool," replied Mac. "Before you turn the main light on, the mosaic animals look like...." He paused.

"Two men. In the water. Fighting to the death," finished Sally. There was a moment of silence.

Charlie spoke brightly, trying to lighten the atmosphere. "How exciting. I didn't know you had ghosts, Sal!"

"Don't be ridiculous," snapped Mac, still highly discomforted by what he'd seen. "There's no such thing as ghosts. Are you some sort of child?" Charlie's face slowly flushed.

"Child or not, at least I can keep a civil tongue in my head!" she announced angrily.

"Can you really?" said Mac. "And is this before or after you start crying?"

Ben's eyes widened in a mixture of surprise and horror. He backed away from the two angry figures; his hands held up, palms outwards.

"Woah there, you two! When did we land back in the playground?"

"He started it!" exclaimed Charlie, realising, too late, how childish she still sounded. Charlie turned to walk away, but Mac spoke again. "My coat!" Charlie turned back to him.

"What?"

"My coat." He held out his hand. "You appear to be wearing my coat." Charlie looked down at the old Belstaff jacket that she still wore.

"This is yours? But it's ancient–"

"It belonged to my father. And he gave it to me. Please, give it back." He held out his hand. Charlie slowly removed the jacket. She caught the scent of lemons again and felt slightly heady. She briefly thought of dropping it on the ground but baulked at such petulance. Charlie held the jacket out to the Insufferable Man (as she now thought of him). He took the coat, and she turned and walked away. Sally and Ben looked at each other. Ben shrugged, mystified by the ill-tempered exchange.

• • •

It was two hours later. Ben was sitting happily in the library. He had a pad and paper and was meticulously mapping and photographing the damaged wood panels. He hummed to himself as he planned his restoration project, and the wood seemed to glow and turn in delight beneath his reverent touch.

"We'll get you sorted. Don't worry," he whispered.

We know... We trust you.... the house seemed to whisper back. The sun streamed through the ancient window, and the scent of applewood crept into his peaceful mind. A different, delicious scent floated through the open library door. Charlie had raided the cavernous freezer and store cupboards again. She was making something with clams, white wine and spaghetti. Ben hadn't felt this happy in a long time. He hummed again...

Charlie, however, was not happy. The Insufferable Man was still there. He and Sally were sitting, heads together, at Sally's desk. Charlie called across the kitchen.

"Lunch is almost done. I'll get Ben." Sally and Mac barely looked up. Charlie wandered into the library. She leaned casually against the desk where Ben sat.

"So, who exactly is your rude acquaintance?" she asked. Ben glanced up, his sleepy blue eyes twinkling.

"You asking for a friend?" he said. Charlie batted at his shoulder.

"Is he really a lord, like Sally said?" she asked, curious. Ben stopped teasing her and became serious.

"I don't think he'd want me to say any more than I already have." Ben peered down the corridor and reassured himself that Mac was out of earshot. "Aye, he's a Lord. And his mum's an American heiress or something." Ben paused as Charlie reached into her pocket and retrieved a dog-eared photograph. She placed it on the desk in front of them, and they both leaned closer to look at it.

"I found this in his jacket pocket," said Charlie quietly. "I put it on a shelf and just remembered it now. But I don't want to get my head bitten off by giving it back." The photograph was of what looked like a large oil painting. An elegant, Black woman was sitting in a high-backed chair, surrounded by men. A group of three young men stood to her left as you looked at the photograph. Two older men stood behind the chair, and a handsome man with greying hair stood close to her right. Charlie recognised Mac as one of the group of three. He was smiling and looked happy and carefree.

"Who are all these people?" asked Charlie. Ben pointed to the woman.

"That's Mac's mother, Lady Laura, the American heiress, and that will be his dad." Ben pointed to the handsome man with greying hair. They could both see his resemblance to Mac. His eyes were bright blue, and he looked happy and confident. Certainly not what you'd expect from someone who would go on to take their own life. Ben pointed to the two young men standing next to Mac. "This one will be his younger brother, George. He's a doctor, apparently." Charlie looked at the serious young man, who was slightly taller than Mac. He certainly looked intelligent and studious. In contrast, the other brother looked like he'd just carried out a practical joke: his face was brimming with contained amusement. "That's James, his youngest brother," said Ben. "James runs the estate with Mac's mum now, apparently," said Ben.

They looked at the figures standing behind Laura's chair.

"This man looks just like Mac's dad, except with red

hair," said Charlie. Ben nodded, looking at the kindly-faced, smiling man.

"I bet that's his uncle Tris," he agreed. Ben looked sad. "Mac had it all figured out before his dad died. Spend a few years in the army, then go back to run the estate, like all his ancestors before him. Somewhere up in the Yorkshire Dales, the estate is, in the old West Riding, just West of the Pennines. After a few drinks one night, I remember he told us he genuinely believed it was God's Own Country. The most beautiful place on Planet Earth." Ben shook his head.

"So, why is he here?" asked Charlie. "Doing security work?" Ben shrugged.

"I don't know. But I guess he can't face going back after what happened to his father. He probably blames himself."

"I almost feel sorry for him," said Charlie.

"Well, don't tell him that!" exclaimed Ben. "Unless you really do want your head bitten off."

"I said almost," smiled Charlie, patting Ben's shoulder warmly and slipping the photograph back into her pocket. She'd try to return it to Mac's coat when she could. "In the meantime, it's lunch. I hope you like clams and spaghetti."

"You put it on a plate, lass and I'll put it away!" said Ben confidently. They ambled back towards the kitchen.

When Charlie walked towards the library, Mac looked at Sally. "I can understand why you'd want Yorkie around," he said. "Who wouldn't? He's a good man. But why have you brought weeping Rapunzel back here?"

Sally didn't look up from the page on which was making notes, now she had no computer.

"Leave her alone, Mac. She's been a friend. A good one."

Sally now looked at Mac, her face serious. "The two of them also probably saved my life. I'm grateful. And she's an excellent cook; I'm rediscovering food. Her sister died recently. Drug addict. It looks like she's had a bit of a nightmare life. I think she goes to work because she has nowhere else to go." Mac shook his head.

"You had enough drama with Maya, Sally." Sally looked back down at her notes.

"Look in that bag, Mac," she said, jerking her head towards Charlie's rucksack, which sat by the kitchen island. Mac walked over, picked it up and undid the zip. He looked at the contents. There were some worn out scrubs, a slim volume of Walt Whitman poetry, and a Harry Potter book with yellowed pages.

"What am I looking at?" he asked, mystified.

"Charlie Hart's worldly possessions," said Sally, still looking at the page. "Her sister sold anything nice or new. Eventually, she sold Charlie's clothes for a fix. Her last fix, as it turned out. And Charlie can't forgive herself for standing up to her."

Mac closed the bag and dropped it back to the floor, his face expressionless.

"You're not a home for the lost and the lonely, Sally," he said.

"I couldn't leave her where she was. In fact, I'm sick of rattling around this place on my own, Mac," she said quietly. "Those two, they just feel...." She struggled to find a word in her vast vocabulary. What did Ben and Charlie feel like to her? "Nice." She said simply. "Who knows? This could be the beginning of a beautiful friendship."

"Things must be bad if you're quoting Casablanca at

me," said Mac grumpily. The ghost of a grin floated across Sally's face.

"It's one of my favourite films, don't you know? Just give the Doc a break. For me?"

Charlie and Ben came back to the kitchen. Charlie had laid four places on the kitchen island. She added olive oil to the cooked spaghetti, then poured the clams, white wine, garlic and butter sauce into the large pan and stirred. Charlie then tasted a little of the sauce and, after a moment's thought, added a pinch more of chilli flakes and a kiss of lemon juice. She cut thick slices of ciabatta (with another silent thank you to Georgia and her well-stocked freezer) and called to Sally and Mac.

"Time to eat, you two." Sally stood and walked over enthusiastically. Mac remained seated. "I've cooked," said Charlie.

"I know," he said, not looking up. "I don't like seafood."

"I didn't know!" exclaimed Charlie.

"You didn't ask," replied Mac, finally looking at her. "Poorly planned..." he glanced at the steaming plates, "... adequately executed. No. Thank you." Charlie spluttered.

"And I suppose you don't like lemon drizzle cake either?" She waved at the still-warm golden mound of cake that she had drawn from the oven just an hour ago.

"I like it well enough," was Mac's clipped reply. "Just..." *when made by my mother* flashed across his mind, but he couldn't possibly say that. Instead, "Just not made by you," came out of his mouth.

Mac realised, too late, how rude and abrasive this was. The three of them looked at him in silence. Mac stood. "I'm sorry," he said. There was a long pause. "Your culinary skills are beyond doubt. It's my manners that are defective." He nodded to Sally. "Sinclair will sort out new hardware. I'll be back as soon as it's ready." Mac walked across the kitchen and out of the door. They watched him as he marched, straight-backed, across the courtyard. He leapt over the low wall and lowered himself over the cliff edge. Charlie looked panicked.

"I hate it when he does that!" she said.

"No wonder he always has the women after him," grumbled Ben.

"Only the suitably grown-up ones, we hope," muttered Charlie sourly.

MAC BEAULOUF WAS a man of considerable pride. However, he didn't want to be seen as a boor, and he realised he had been exceptionally rude to Charlie. This rudeness was one reason why, twelve hours later, Mac walked into the Northern General Hospital at three in the morning. He thought if he couldn't sleep, he might as well make amends. The security guard looked up blearily from his desk. All he saw was what looked like an on-call anaesthetist in a very expensive cycling jacket and helmet, flashing what looked like his ID card in his direction.

"Bloody anaesthetists!" the guard muttered bitterly to himself. "All on their bloody bikes and in their £300 bloody jackets." Perfect camouflage. Fifteen minutes after this, Mac was standing in the corridor outside Trauma Theatre 3. He was looking at a trolley piled with blue surgical scrubs. He'd changed into scrubs himself. Now, did he take the extra small size to flatter her? Or get the medium that would actually fit?

A voice cut through the air behind him. "If you've come

in for the trauma case, it's cancelled. Didn't they tell you? The idiot died." Mac slowly turned. A very tall, slim woman stood behind him with her arms crossed. She, too, was in scrubs. Blood-stained, oversized white crocs contained her perfectly formed feet.

"No," replied Mac. "I was unaware." His smooth, deep voice echoed in the empty corridor.

"Having your arse pass through your brain at ninety miles an hour tends to do that to a person," she drawled. "Fool should have worn a seat belt." She looked him up and down. "I haven't met you before. I thought I knew all the new blood."

"Just arrived. Fresh from Leeds," Mac replied carefully.

"Jimmy's or LGI?" she snapped

"Jimmy's."

"Then you'll know Nikolai."

"Of course."

"How's he finding life, running ITU these days?"

"Next time I play a round of golf, I'll ask him," said Mac. "He retired six months ago. Or did you already know that?"

"I knew. Just checking that you did," replied the woman. Not for the first time, Mac was grateful for his beloved younger brother, who was a consultant anaesthetist. In Leeds.

The woman's beautiful, haughty face relaxed. Dark brown, glossy hair accented with opulent, honeyed highlights peeked from under her theatre cap. Her skin was a delicate olive shade, smooth, with the faintest scent of expensive body lotion. She looked him up and down slowly.

"Welcome to Sheffield. I look forward to working closely with you." She paused, then asked coyly. "What's your sport?" He grinned, a slow, wide, charming smile. He was practised in this particular game.

"Rugby," he lied. Polo had always been his sport, back when he'd the time or heart to play.

"With those shoulders? Prop, I'll be bound." She smiled back at him, her head tilted to one side. Her large brown eyes widened, and her soft, pink tongue emerged and briefly touched the corner of her upper lip. He shook his head shyly and looked at her from under his long eyelashes.

"Believe it or not, Centre."

"Ooh! a great all-rounder. Good with your brain... and with your hands." She chuckled, a warm and sensual noise.

The moment was broken by the loud screech of her bleep. She made a face and marched to the nearest phone. She glanced down at the extension number as she moved.

"Sara Hadid," she snapped. There was a pause. "I am your Surgical Registrar, not your cannula-buddy. What's your name again? Well, Max Khan, F2, it's not my problem if your patient has 'gone off.' Get on with it...." She paused, listening impatiently. "I don't care if you've failed three times. Ward six is not 'just round the corner.' I'm about to go back into theatres. A critical RTC victim. When you've failed at a femoral stab, then you may call me back!" Sara Hadid slammed the phone down. She turned back to the handsome anaesthetist, only to find the corridor empty. Cursing under her breath, she slouched into the nearby coffee room and picked up a copy of Hello magazine. She had no patient. He was dead—the idiot.

Mac watched her from his vantage point in the shadows and then silently moved off. He'd been doing some research of his own and had come to the hospital hoping to find a lead. He hadn't expected to find one so quickly. *Sara Hadid? Interesting*, he thought.

Charlie awoke in the early hours to prepare for her A and E shift. She found, neatly folded at the end of her bed, three pairs of brand-new scrubs—size medium.

CHAPTER
NINETEEN

In an old steelworks two miles away, The Boss bent intently over his task: a tricky root canal, posterior molar. Difficult to access. Deep, deep, thick nerves. He considered his next choice of instrument and decided on the drill again. Just a slightly wider aperture, and he should be able to access those evasive tissues. The diamond-tipped drill snarled to life. His client looked up at him, wide-eyed over the green hygiene dam. Blood trickled from his mouth. His head was tied firmly with a thick, dirty rope. There was no anaesthetic. The Boss didn't care if the client was ready to speak. He would finish his root canal, and then they could chat. About the importance of loyalty. About the whereabouts of a certain ten tablets of Code Blue. About the whereabouts of half of a Formula. *I'm getting sick of being the one intelligent man in a world of fools*, thought the Boss.

He looked around as the faint scent of smoke wafted around him. He could see no evidence of a fire. The Boss walked to the edge of the gantry and looked down at the factory below. Dim lights outlined long benches. The dark, heavy heads of lab workers, gowned and masked, hung, attentive to their tasks. There was the faintest of sounds from the metal gantry floor. The Boss looked to his right and saw the tall, thin figure of Mr Ketch. Ketch held up his hand. There was a mobile phone in it. Ketch held the phone out to the Boss, who took it with slight trepidation. He held the phone to his ear.

"Is that how you see it?" came the voice of Marcus Rosendale, cold down the line. "That you are the one intelligent man?" The Boss closed his eyes briefly. He had never got used to the fact that Rosendale could sometimes see into his thoughts. "Well, has the one intelligent man figured it out yet? Where is my Formula?"

The Boss was aware that Ketch had silently made his way to the client and was staring down at his contorted, captive face. The Boss watched as the thin man ran a long, bony finger along the client's cheek, scooping up a mess of blood and nervous tissue. Ketch then delicately licked his finger. His tongue was long and pale, and the Boss frowned, squinting to see in the half-light. He could have sworn that the tongue had two ends. The thin man slowly inserted his bloodied digit into his mouth, right up to the knuckle, and sucked with eager pleasure. He looked hungry. "Pay no attention to Mr Ketch," the Boss heard Rosendale snarl in his ear. "You must learn to ignore his particular tastes."

The client's eyes were now even wider as they stared in horror at Ketch. His chest rose and fell with terrible rapidity.

"I'm questioning a friend of the Courier as we speak," said the Boss. "He's agreed to be my latest Client." He walked over to a stainless-steel tray and angrily sorted through the dental implements. One by one, he held them up to the light to assess their suitability for what he had planned. "But the

Courier seems to have disappeared without a trace." He heard Rosendale exclaim in frustration, but the Boss cut him off. "We'll find him!" the Boss snapped. "This city is the largest village in England. We'll find him. And we'll find your half of the Formula. It's just a matter of time."

"I don't have time!" Rosendale's voice exploded with anger. "Ten tablets are missing. Ten opportunities for my enemies to discover my work, to bring me down. And you have no idea how long it's taken me to develop that Formula."

"We'll find him," repeated the Boss soothingly.

"And anyone, anyone who might have seen the Formula. You must kill them!" Insisted Rosendale.

"It will be my pleasure," said the Boss. "Playtime. My favourite time." The drill buzzed hungrily and the Boss bent once again to his task. "Let me just finish this root canal."

CHAPTER TWENTY

Dressed in her unexpected, fresh scrubs, Charlie trudged up the gentle slope that led to the rear of the A and E department. The sun was just creeping over the houses slouched on Barnsley Road. For once, there were no ambulances or Police cars parked in the yellow-hatched ambulance bay. Could this be a good sign?

"Please be quiet today," whispered Charlie to herself. "Please don't let anything horrible come in." She smiled wryly. *Fat chance*!

There was a sullen roar behind Charlie, and an old black van coughed its rapid way up the road. *Big fat chance*! Charlie sped up; her eyes fixed on the rear of the truck that had now slewed to a halt. A slim figure dressed in black stumbled awkwardly from the driver's side and started tugging at the rear doors. He looked back at Charlie and cried out,

"Doc, Doc, come quick! They're not breathing!" Charlie recognised the young man from the farm shop. Stephen? Had that been his name? Another figure joined Stephen in fumbling at the van doors. It was a thin young woman with bright blonde hair. She looked at Charlie as she approached. Charlie could see her pupils were dilated fully wide, their blackness almost obscuring her green irises. *Meth*? Thought Charlie *or MDMA*?

The two had now thrown the back doors wide. The dirty, blacked-out windows made the interior opaque, but the slender, early morning light slid inside. Charlie could make out two still figures, supine, side by side on a filthy mattress that lined the rusted floor of the vehicle.

"They're not breathing, do something, Doc!" shouted Stephen, his hands running in distress through his matted hair. Without thinking, Charlie scrambled into the back of the smoke-smeared van.

"God help me if I step on a needle," she muttered.

Charlie looked down at two emaciated male figures and again recognised them from Georgia's farm shop. Stephen was right; neither of the men was breathing, and their lips were blue. She pulled back the eyelid of the nearest unmoving figure and saw his pupil was contracted tightly. Pinpoint pupils. *Heroin overdose* thought Charlie grimly. She said nothing but flung herself from the back of the van and hit the ground at a sprint. She ran into the empty A and E department and looked around wildly. Where was everyone? A familiar figure walked into view from the resuscitation bay, whistling quietly. It was Matt.

"Matt!" Charlie shouted. "Heroin O.D., outside, get the crash trolley!" She grabbed at an airway, bag and mask from the nearest resuscitation bay and returned to the van at a run. She hopped inside and heard the rumble of the crash trolley being wheeled up to the van by the ever-efficient Matt.

Charlie slid a rigid plastic airway into the mouth of the

man known as Lawrence. With a twist, it was in place. She then firmly placed the mask over his face and, with practised pressure from her small and ring fingers, hooked under his jawbone and opened up his slack airway. She firmly squeezed the bag, shooting air into his unmoving chest, and was gratified to see his blue lips quickly becoming pink. By now, Matt was next to her, doing the same with the unconscious Bartholomew.

"Smackheads," muttered Matt in disgust. "Where did they get the money for this little party, I wonder? I hate smackheads. We'll never get a needle in," he added sourly. Charlie looked up at him and smiled.

"Is that a challenge?" she asked, continuing to push air into Lawrence.

"Ten quid says you'll never do it," said Matt, smiling back confidently.

Charlie rifled through the emergency trolley and grabbed what she needed, including two yellow and white syringes pre-filled with the opiate-blocking drug Narcan. She hopped back into the van where Matt was managing the airways of both moribund young men. Charlie reflected that this was one of the few times you actually and definitely got to save a life. Now, was he right or left-handed? she thought, remembering the knife he had wielded in the farm shop. The arm opposite his dominant hand would be completely messed up. She rolled up Lawrence's right sleeve and ran her practised hands up his pallid forearm. Where would be difficult for him to reach? she mused. Charlie moved up to his mid-arm. She knew the cephalic and basilic veins were lurking, hidden by reedy muscle.

"No chance!" chuckled Matt; however, his face fell as Charlie, with an intent look of concentration, worked a slim, pink cannula into Lawrence's mid-arm and got a flashback of fresh blood.

"That'll be ten pounds, please!" grinned Charlie, fixing the cannula in place and flushing it with saline. She was inordinately pleased with herself. Charlie picked up one of the syringes and started injecting the Narcan into the muscle of Bartholomew's upper arm.

Matt looked disgusted and shook his head. He grabbed the nearest syringe of Narcan and attached it to Lawrence's new cannula.

"Don't give it too quick!" cried Charlie. "You know what happens if you...." But it was too late. Matt had injected the Narcan straight into Lawrence's cannula.

"Wakey wakey, sleeping beauty," he said grumpily. Lawrence jerked and then drew in a deep, shuddering breath. He batted aside the mask and sat bolt upright, choking on his plastic airway and spitting it out. He then proceeded to vomit, loudly and noisily, all over the back of the van. Charlie and Matt scrambled out of the cramped and stinking space and watched as Lawrence looked around him in a frenzy.

"Who did that?" he howled. "I was sleeping. I was high!"

"You were dead, mate," observed Matt. Beside Lawrence, Bartholomew was stirring, his overdose reversal a gentler process. Charlie looked at Matt.

"You knew that would happen!" she said accusingly. "I've got vomit on me, and I haven't even started my shift yet!" Matt shrugged.

"Makes up for losing a tenner," he said.

They both looked up as the doors to the van were slammed shut. Matt walked towards the truck; his hand held up authoritatively. "Now then," he declared loudly. "You're going nowhere. That Narcan'll wear off, and you might need more." Lawrence stared wildly from the back of the van.

"Just drive!" he yelled at Stephen, who looked between him and Matt, uncertain. Charlie realised he was going to leave. She grabbed two more Narcan syringes from the crash trolley and flung them through the driver's window just as the van lurched away. She could see Lawrence looking in wonder at his cannula. Her heart sank as she realised she'd just provided him with a way of injecting himself efficiently and easily.

"You're going to die!" Charlie yelled after the disappearing van. "You are going to die!"

Charlie looked around to see Matt staring at her and shaking his head.

"What?" she said.

"Melli's right. You're just a disaster magnet, Charlie," said Matt. "How can someone so nice attract so much chaos?"

"What do you mean?" asked Charlie, bewildered.

"You've got a reputation, you know?" sighed Matt, starting to wheel the resuscitation trolley towards the A and E department. "If it's all kicking off, Charlie Hart's bound to be on shift."

CHARLIE'S DAY seemed to go downhill from there. Fergus Eaton was the Consultant in charge. He made no reference to his outburst on Saturday morning and certainly showed no remorse. Charlie was sure he was adjusting the order of the waiting notes, so she got the difficult or complex cases. She looked up from a particularly tragic history sheet to see Inspector Decker standing nearby, watching her. He smiled, and his brown eyes twinkled in his prematurely lined face.

"Hello again, Dr Hart. Y'alright?" he said. He was holding two disposable cups. He raised one cup. "I got you a coffee. Do you have a moment?" Charlie looked down at the set of notes she held. This person was going nowhere. She nodded and smiled wearily at the policeman.

"I'd love a coffee, thanks. If we go to the mess room, there might be a chocolate biscuit," she said, slotting the notes back into the bulging stack of waiting cases and accepting the proffered cup.

Charlie led the way through the busy department and typed in the code to access the staff mess room. A couple of paramedics sat, feet up on a low table, watching the cricket on the television on the wall. They nodded to Charlie, who always made a point of chatting with her ambulance colleagues. Charlie looked disappointedly at the empty chocolate digestives packet that lay near the paramedics' feet. Decker and Charlie sat at a small table.

"How are you and Dr Eaton getting on today?" asked Decker, shaking a sugar packet before emptying it into his drink. Charlie felt embarrassed that Decker had seen her telling-off at the hands of her superior. She said nothing, shaking her head slightly. "We show people what we want them to see, Charlie," said Decker gently. "I'm sure Dr Eaton didn't mean to show you his darker side." He blew on the hot coffee and sipped it, only to pull a face. "Should have stuck to tea," he grimaced, making Charlie smile. "That's better," he said. "You have a face that's made for smiling, Charlie." He paused. "And are you managing not to give too much of yourself away?" Charlie looked at him in surprise; she'd forgotten this part of their conversation on

Saturday morning. She shook her head and smiled wistfully.

"I'm afraid that's easier said than done for me," she said. Decker smiled back, but his face then became serious.

"Are you ready for Friday night?" he asked. Charlie hadn't thought about it, but her stomach lurched when she realised what he meant. Friday night, Code Blue night. Ten thousand doses. Ten thousand chances someone would turn.

"I think nothing can prepare us for that," she said. "I'll just keep my fingers crossed. Hope for the best."

"Hope for the best, prepare for the worst," said Decker, nodding. "Listen, Charlie. I'll be around on Friday night, but I need your help."

"Me?" said Charlie, surprised. Decker glanced around him, making sure they weren't being overheard. He nodded.

"I'm sure you're aware we aren't having much luck finding the people making this stuff." Charlie nodded and took a sip of her coffee, wincing at the foul taste. "The truth is, Charlie. It's becoming obvious that they have people on the inside. Including in the hospital." Charlie's eyes widened.

"No!" she exclaimed. Decker held his finger to his lips as a paramedic glanced over at them. Charlie put her hand to her mouth. "Sorry," she said in a quieter voice. Decker nodded.

"It looks that way. And, listen, Charlie, I wasn't joking when I said the gang leader, the Boss man, is utterly ruthless. So, there's liable to be trouble." Charlie's eyes widened. Decker patted her hand. "Don't worry, Dr Hart, I'm not going to appoint you deputy Sherriff. I just want you to keep your eyes open. I want you to let me know if you see anyone acting suspiciously. Would that be okay?" Charlie looked at Decker's creased face and thought he looked exhausted. He must be under enormous pressure with the deaths and mayhem this drug was causing.

"Of course," she said. "Anything to help"

"And we'll do likewise," said Decker. "Anything to help our medical colleagues." They smiled at each other, and Charlie felt her spirits lift.

Decker slid his card across the table. "Put this number in your phone, Charlie. If you see anything, if you need anything, call me." Charlie nodded. She picked up her phone and started keying in Decker's number. "Just don't trust anyone, Charlie," said Decker quietly. "I know that goes against your sweet nature, but it's important not to trust anyone until we've got on top of this situation. It's destroying my city." Decker looked down, and Charlie saw his hands clench and a look of deep frustration suffuse his face.

"I hope not trusting anyone doesn't include you, Inspector Decker?" said Charlie lightly, trying to relieve his sudden distress. Decker looked up and smiled wryly.

"Yes, it includes me, Dr Hart," he growled. He held up his plastic coffee cup. "But it especially, undoubtedly, includes the jokers who made this coffee. I'll give them "Bangin' Baristas, Best Coffee in Sheffield!'"

Charlie eventually found herself driving back to where she now unconsciously thought of as *Home*. She debated taking a quick nap in her new room's enormous, warm, soft bed. Or maybe she'd take a hot, deep bubble bath. Or perhaps she'd make scones again. All the options were good ones. She pulled up outside Rowans Holt, and her heart lifted. Sally had given her a key and explained how to turn off the alarm, but Charlie knew Sally and Ben would be in all day. She opened the door and walked into the softly shining hallway.

"Hellooo?" she called.

"In here!" came Sally's voice. Sally was sitting at her desk with Mac standing beside her. Charlie's heart sank. It was the Insufferable Man. She caught the faint, familiar scent of lemony cologne and her stomach clenched slightly. Why did he have to be here again? A new laptop lay open on Sally's desk. Sinclair's icon was lit. Sally was shaking her head.

"I don't know where to start with getting hold of some Code Blue. I've accessed Police records, and they're at a loss too. Places pop up at random on Friday nights. The Gang are using word of mouth and intimidation. Old school. And it seems they supervise every single dose. It has to be swallowed there and then."

"If we knew the formula, then I could make you some," said Sinclair's voice. There was a shocked silence.

"What?" exclaimed Sally. Sinclair sounded like she was smiling.

"I'm a physicist, but I'm a pretty good biochemist too. If I had the formula, I could make you some."

"If we had the formula. If we knew what was in it...." Sally was deep in thought again. "New Drug, Middle East," she said. "What if it's made from something that only grows in harsh conditions, in a specific place?"

"Of course," said Sinclair. "That's why the experimental drug was resurrected again in Afghanistan. They realised they could source the substance."

"And now in Perda. Same conditions," said Sally. She looked up at Mac. "If we know what's in it, maybe we can narrow down where it can be grown. Get closer to where your uncle might be?" Charlie watched Mac's face as it softened momentarily. She glimpsed the briefest flash of hope before it settled back into its familiar frown. He shook his head.

"Hope is dangerous, Sally," he said. "If we can't get hold of a tablet, all this is just dangerous speculation."

There was silence.

"However," said Sinclair. They looked at her icon, which glowed softly on the dark screen. "What if we got hold of the blood of someone who had recently taken Code Blue?" Mac and Sally looked at each other. There was a long pause. They then turned to look at Charlie.

"What?" she said. "What's wrong? Have I got something on my face...?" She touched her lip guiltily, thinking of the Twix she'd eaten on the way home. Her last patient had been a particularly sad suicide attempt. Chocolate had been essential.

"Charlie," said Sally. Mac said nothing but stared at Charlie with his arms folded. "Sinclair's right. If we can't access the drug, we can try to access some blood from someone who's taken it. Recently taken it." said Sally.

"How are you going to do that?" asked Charlie. Mac and Sally just regarded her. Charlie slowly realised what they were proposing she do. "Oh!" she said. "And you want me to...?" Mac and Sally nodded.

CHAPTER TWENTY-ONE

Charlie put down her bag. "Well, you're the second request for help I've had today," she said. Mac frowned. "Inspector Decker at the hospital says that there's probably someone working on the inside," said Charlie. "For the gang making Code Blue. He asked me to keep an eye open for anyone acting suspiciously." Mac and Sally looked at each other.

"It makes sense," said Mac to Sally. "To have people on the inside." Sally frowned.

"Well, doesn't that make it dangerous for Charlie, then? If one of her colleagues is working for the gang, and if the man running it is ruthless, we could put her in danger."

Mac looked at Charlie. "You don't have to help," he said simply. He didn't smile or attempt to apologise for his outburst the other day. Nor did he try to charm or persuade her. Charlie ran her hand absently over her new, stained scrubs, suddenly realising that it hadn't been Sally who had sourced them for her but Mac. He had a strange way of communicating, she thought ruefully.

"It's okay," Charlie said, nodding slowly. "It's okay. I'd do anything to help you, Sally." She looked at Mac, who stared back at her, and she faltered. "Anything to help...." Charlie glanced down at the blood and vomit stains on her new scrubs. "I'm sure we'll get people who've taken Code Blue in on Friday night." She winced slightly. "It's been a long day, I'm tired." She wearily picked up her bag and headed for the door. "I'll get blood," she said, not turning round. "If I can. I'll give you blood." Sally looked up at Mac. "Why are you always so angry with her?" she asked. Mac shrugged but said nothing.

Ben emerged from the library. "You free, Sal?" he said. "I've got the plan for the first panel. I just want to run it by you. Part of the scene is so badly damaged, it's almost obliterated. You have a chance to put something else in there." Sally pulled a face. The thought of changing the panels made her deeply uncomfortable. She stood and followed Ben. Mac stood for a moment, gazing at the hallway door where Charlie had exited the kitchen. He was tired too. He kept having the recurring dream where something was pursuing him through Druids wood. It was waking him in the early hours, and he could not sleep again, worried by the dream and his fears about his uncle. Mac sighed and headed for the library, too.

Some time later, there was a knock at the door to Charlie's room. "Hello?" Charlie called. Sally put her head around the door. She looked worried.

"May I come in?" she asked, rather formally.

"Sal!" said Charlie with weary delight. Charlie had gone to bed, exhausted and fully clothed, for a snooze. She patted the bed next to her. Sally came and stood at the bedside, looking perplexed.

"Get in!" said Charlie. "We can talk better then." Sally felt out of her depth. She pulled the duvet back and then hesitated. Charlie nodded and smiled in encouragement. "It's okay. We'll have a girlie chat." Sally got under the covers and sat, with her hands holding the duvet tightly to her chest. She felt mildly terrified. Sally had never had a 'Girlie Chat' in her entire life. Sally gingerly lay back.

Charlie turned on her side and faced Sal. "How are you?" she said and looked at Sally. Sally didn't know how to respond. A social chasm had opened under her feet, and she teetered, not knowing how or where to step next.

"I'm fine..." she ventured.

"Are you?" said Charlie, her eyes wide and a slight furrow on her brow. Sally panicked.

"Now, that's not fair!" she replied hotly. "I gave you an answer, and you didn't take it at face value." Charlie's face broke into a gentle smile.

"I'm sorry, Sal. You're right; I'm not being fair. We've only known each other for a few days. But we've already had so much emotional water under the bridge. It can't be easy for you, with your Asperger's and everything."

"My what?" exclaimed Sally, sitting up suddenly. "My what?" Charlie looked stricken.

"Oh Sally, I'm so sorry. It's just, with me doing Psychiatry and working in an ASD clinic in Paeds... I thought you knew. ASD means..."

"I know what ASD is!" exclaimed Sally. "I know what EVERYTHING is!" She paused, thinking. She did know what everything was. "And why can't it just be a traumatic childhood...?" She trailed off.... She knew. She remembered. Sally remembered everything, kept it all stacked in boxes in her beautiful mind. Ordered and stable. Filed and labelled. She slumped back on the pillows. She looked at Charlie.

"I keep all the cars in name and date order," she said. "Or I feel they won't work for me. ASD?" she whispered. Charlie lay down on her pillow again. Her face, like a sunflower, followed the brilliance of Sally's burning light.

"I'm here," was all she said.

DOWNSTAIRS, the two men had stayed in the library. Ben had lit a fire, and the two shared a bottle of red wine from Sally's magnificent cellar.

"How's things?" ventured Ben. Mac sighed deeply. He gazed into the crackling fire, his dark, handsome face assuming its default, brooding aspect.

"Fine," he replied brusquely.

"Are you? Really?" said Ben. Mac looked up.

"What is this? A girly chat? It's not like you to dig, Morton." Ben looked down.

"Well, I'm not that man anymore. Death does that to a person." Mac looked ashamed.

"I'm sorry, Morton." He looked Ben in the eye and raised his glass. "To little Ben." Ben nodded and raised his glass.

"And here's to your Father." They drank to those who had gone before them. And then they drank again.

SALLY LAY LOOKING up at the ceiling of Charlie's room. It was covered in plaster roses and vines.

"Who am I?" she said. Charlie made a face.

"Er, the magnificent Sally Marshall!" she exclaimed. Sally

looked at her. She looked as if she was in genuine pain. It hurt Charlie. She reached out and grabbed Sally's right hand, automatically trying to ease her hurt. "Genuinely, Sally. You are one of the kindest, cleverest, most amazing people I've ever met. If I have to leave tomorrow, I will have had the best time in my life with you and Ben. The face of that bloke when you hit him!"

"I don't want you to go," said Sally. "Don't go. I'm learning about friendship. I think I like it."

"I like it too," said Charlie. She then hesitated. "Thank you, Sal. It's all I've ever wanted. To have somewhere that I feel safe. To be with people who want me there."

"Then stay," said Sally. She looked down at Charlie's small hand grasped in hers. "And don't feel you need to give anything. You don't need to give me anything; you don't need to hand over any part of yourself. You just being you is enough." Charlie didn't reply. Sally now looked intently at Charlie. "So, I know most things, but not about this. What exactly is a Girlie Chat?"

"So..." said Ben, warming to his subject. "Then the power goes out, and they can see on radar that the spooks are bearing down on them. The spooks then come PAST the walls; should be all over them. But they're nowhere to be seen. That's when they look up, and BAM! they're coming through the roof." Mac shook his head.

"Nope, don't remember it."

"Oh, man, you were there!" said Ben in disgust. "That cinema they rigged up in Camp Bastion! You have seen Aliens. Best film, ever." Mac shook his head again.

"If it's the cinema I'm thinking of. I ducked out. Had

other business." They looked at each other, and a moment of understanding passed between them.

CHARLIE HAD STOLEN DOWN and retrieved two bottles of white wine from the cellar. She had heard the low, confidential tones from the Library. She and Sally were now in the third room of Sally's closet. Sally's closet consisted of three separate rooms, one leading from the other. The first was for work clothes, bags, and shoes. The outfits were hung on velvet hangers. They hung in colour order, then designer order, then material order. Most of the colours were black, cream, navy and charcoal. The shoes were low-heel and mainly Jimmy Choos. The next room was casual wear; neatly piled and hung jeans, jumpers and sweat-shirts, elegant silk dresses and crisp silk and linen shirts. Once again, all items were colour-coordinated and sorted by material and designer. Shoes, boots and handbags lined an entire wall, floor to ceiling. The last room was supposedly for formal wear, but Sally clearly didn't go out much. Two long silk dresses were hanging in plastic covers—one in dove grey, the other in black. There were a few pairs of Christian Louboutin shoes and a beautiful, grey silk stole that Charlie stroked and asked if she could try on. One entire wall was a mirror. Sally didn't think she'd ever tried a dress on in here.

By now, they had both drunk a bottle of wine each. Charlie had insisted on painting Sally's toenails light pink whilst sitting in the middle room. They now knew which Disney film the other liked best; Sally, the Aristocats (Peter had loved it. Charlie knew all about Peter now) and Charlie, Frozen (that dress, that song!). Charlie lay on the floor of the third room, staring up at the ceiling, a Miu Miu, jewelled, high-heel shoe on each hand. She had also found Sally's collection of something called a Birkin bag. Three of these bags, in various discreet shades, lay around her head.

"I had a really bad day today," she intoned, turning the slippers so they caught the light. "First, those goths we saw at the farm shop turned up, not breathing. And then, at the end of the day, I had to deal with a man who'd slashed at his neck repeatedly with a scalpel. He really wanted to die. I got covered in his blood," she said conversationally. Sally screwed up her face.

"No, don't tell me. I've got this... That must have been awful for you?" She looked hopefully at Charlie.

"Well done!" exclaimed Charlie. “You're a natural at active listening."

"However!" said Sally. "However! That type of situation... is precisely why I work in I.T.... Don't let the bastards grind you down!" Charlie snorted with laughter and tried to put one of the jewelled, extravagant shoes onto her small foot.

"WHERE DO you think your uncle is, then?" asked Ben. Mac sighed deeply and ran a hand over his face.

"God only knows, Morton," replied Mac. "My only hope seems to be isolating some Code Blue. Sinclair can put it through the spectrometer and try to pinpoint the area he may have been visiting. Let's hope Hart gets some blood on Friday."

"Oh, call her Charlie, like everyone else, " Ben sighed.

"She annoys me," replied Mac tersely. "I can't abide drama. She seems to drag it with her like a ball and chain."

"We can't choose our families. It's not her fault," replied Ben. He looked down at his empty glass. "She's one of the kindest people I've ever met. Kind to the dying, the pathetic. You and Sal saw her in action in the hospital. Give her a break." Mac merely frowned. "If I didn't know better," said Ben slyly. "I'd say you fancied each other."

"You should concentrate on your own love life, Morton," Mac retorted.

"Nah, there was only ever one woman for me. My wife, Becky," Ben replied with a resigned grimace. He stood up and waved his empty glass. "Fancy another?"

"We need to get a blood sample," said Sally thoughtfully. "But I don't want you to be in danger." She looked towards Charlie, who was lying on the carpet, dreamily waving her legs in the air. The Miu Miu shoes were on but on the wrong feet. Charlie airily waved her hand in the air.

"I'll be fine," she said confidently. "Everyone always underestimates me. Silly Charlie..."

"Well, I don't think you're silly at all," said Sally. There was a comfortable silence. "Do you want to see some jewels?" Sally asked. Charlie's head whipped round.

"Do you have a crown? Tell me you've got a crown, Sal!" she exclaimed. Sally crawled towards the mirror.

"Only a few tiaras, I think."

"Oh, my God. That is a crown as far as I'm concerned," said Charlie as she followed Sally across the deep-pile, almond-coloured wool carpet.

Sally pulled at one side of the mirrored wall. It slid open noiselessly. A brightly coloured portrait of a beautiful, dark-haired, smiling Chinese woman hung on a wall. Below it, a large, black safe squatted in the wide space behind the mirror. Sally pulled herself up on it and gestured extravagantly.

"Charlie, meet my grandmother, Isabella. Unfortunately, deceased." Charlie bowed her head towards the portrait.

"Delighted to meet you, Grandma Isabella," she said seriously.

"And this!" Sally patted the secure box. "Is my big safe. I have a few little ones, but this is my safe-safe. Safe from Maya's prying eyes. So safe, in fact, that I haven't looked in here for years now. Just in case.... Now, what are the dates of the battles of Cannae and Carthage? Oh, I know! I know everything!" she declared.

With a satisfied air, Sally dialled a six-digit number into the keyboard on the front of the vast safe. The door clicked discreetly, and Sally pulled it open. The ample space was full of jewellery boxes of various sizes. It also contained a large, black lacquered box with Chinese writing over the seals. Sally eyed it drunkenly. "Ohhh. What's in here? I sent Mac, in person, to bring it back from a Zurich safe box for me. Three years ago."

As she spoke, Sally was lifting boxes out of the safe. She placed them, neatly and evenly spaced, on the carpet. She then lifted out the black lacquered box. “I paid two million dollars for the liquid assets of a man whose company folded; Felix Qing. Had him over a barrel, with his fingers right in the Chinese State cookie jar. He was terrified. He always said he was a direct descendant of the last Chinese Empress, Cixi. I didn't have a clue what the assets were, but a contact said it was worth it."

"Well, if it's a crown... it's definitely worth it!" said Charlie.

Half an hour later, Charlie sat happily wearing a very

large tiara, three diamond bracelets, and emerald earrings the size of pigeon eggs. And they still hadn't opened the Chinese box. "What do you think Fergus Eaton would say if I turned up to work in these?" She giggled, looking in the mirror and turning her head from side to side, making the jewels flash and sparkle. Sally furrowed her brow.

"Doctor Hart is an adequate doctor, but her choice of work-wear is an abomination!" she intoned. They started giggling even more. But then Charlie became thoughtful. She looked down at her worn jeans and then at the haute couture all around her.

"My clothes are an abomination, aren't they?" She murmured self-consciously.

"Well then, let's go shopping," said Sally decisively. "Here's to a new wardrobe!" She raised her glass and looked surprised to find it empty.

"I'm going to get one more bottle," said Sally. "And then let's open Felix Qing's treasure chest."

"How long have you known Sal, then?" asked Ben, starting in on a third bottle of red.

"Around three years," replied Mac, holding out his glass. He didn't usually drink, but this conversation felt good, and he didn't want the evening to end. He'd always liked Corporal Morton. It was a pity Sinclair had reacted so angrily to Mac contacting him again. "We have various clients, but she pays the best, and the work is never boring. Are you sure you two haven't met before? You seem to have known each other for far longer than a few days." Ben squinted as he furrowed his brow.

"I know. It's weird, that. But it feels like I've known Sal

and this place forever. I just feel really comfortable around her." Ben shrugged. "Like you don't even need to talk." They sat in comfortable silence. They, too, didn't always need to speak.

"And another thing...," said Charlie. They were now lying on inflatable loungers in the pool, side by side. Charlie's left and Sally's right arms almost touched. The wall was open, and the moon and stars cast soft shadows over the dark moors. The lights were on in the water only. They were surrounded by a warm, blue and jewel-like iridescence. The alarm was most definitely off. "What is it with that climbing up and down cliff faces? What sort of person DOES that? Is he showing off? Is he insane?"

"Now, if I didn't know better, I'd say you fancied each other," said Sally, intoxicated by wine and her newfound fluency in Girlie. She waved a knowing finger in the air but then squealed loudly as Charlie tipped her lounger over.

CHAPTER TWENTY-TWO

It was Friday night. Charlie was on a late shift in A and E. The entire department was on edge, the memory of last Friday still burning in their minds. Charlie, however, was experiencing a rare, happy moment. Matt had presented her with a crisp, ten-pound note.

"This is only because I'd never hear the end of it if I didn't pay up," he grumbled. Charlie held up the note and grinned. Most of her wages were still going to pay for Emily's debts. Charlie wondered about looking at lipsticks when she went shopping with Sally. Her happiness, however, was short-lived. The ten pounds was twitched out of her hand by Carmella, who sailed down the corridor, waving the money.

"This will pay for what you owe the tea fund, Charlie."

"Melli!" exclaimed Charlie.

"If you didn't eat so many chocolate digestives, the fund wouldn't cost so much," came Melli's disapproving reply.

"It's not me; it's the paramedics!" objected Charlie.

"That's not what the paramedics say!" sang Melli, disappearing into the Mess room.

Charlie sighed in resignation. She was going to have words with the paramedics. She grabbed a set of notes, only to drop them when the ambulance bay doors crashed open. A young man staggered through. He was crying and holding up another young man who weaved and stumbled as if his legs were made of rubber. The two collapsed onto the hard floor. Staff descended around them.

"Help him, help me brother!" cried the first young man. His companion slumped to the ground. Charlie saw his face was a mess of bruises and blood. "It's our neighbour, Mason Donovan. He's gone mad. Not a word to us for five years, then he goes mad." He looked up at them, his face drawn and shocked. "He went for Grandad and then Jamie. Grandad, I think he's killed Grandad...." By now, the staff had manoeuvred the unconscious Jamie onto a gurney and were wheeling him into resus, Fergus Eaton performing a brisk assessment as he walked beside the trolley.

"He's bleeding from the ears, likely base of skull fracture," Eaton announced crisply. "Alert radiology and the neurosurgical on call. Let's stabilise this C Spine." The team moved into action. The young man stood at the door to resus, wringing his hands.

"He kept screaming he was a multitude. What does that even mean?" he said.

Where's this Mason? thought Charlie with a shiver. She soon found out.

The ambulance bay doors again burst open, and four police officers barged through into the department. They were struggling to contain a writhing form that screamed and heaved. Each held a limb, clearly unable to immobilise the figure.

"He burst the cable ties!" exclaimed one of the red-faced officers. "He needs sedating!"

"Here we go again," muttered a grim-faced Matt as he pushed past Charlie. Charlie could see the blue tinge in the whites of the young man's eyes. Jamie's brother pointed at him.

"That's him! Mason Donovan!"

Mason grinned at the officers around him and gnashed his teeth, miming biting them. They heaved him onto a trolley.

"I am a multitude!" he screamed. Matt edged closer with a syringe full of powerful sedative. Matt shook his head in frustration; he couldn't get a clear space to inject the medication safely. Mason whipped his head around and saw Charlie looking on. He grinned widely.

"It's the Parasite!" he announced gleefully. Charlie felt a jolt run through her. That was what Maya had said. "Silly Charlie!" yelled Mason. Charlie felt the blood drain from her face. This is what her mother and Emily had called her. "What's in your head, Charlie?" Mason called, straining towards her. Charlie felt her heart pounding like a sledge-hammer against her chest. Was this a dream? A nightmare? Mason was repeating what her family had said to her all through her teenage years, from the age of eleven. "Come over here, Charlie," panted Mason. "I'll crack your head open, and we can all have a look!"

As Charlie backed away, she felt something turn and move within her mind. Something opened a sleepy eye, dark and cunning. Without realising what she was doing, she pushed it down and away. Years of choices, years of practice.

She unconsciously turned towards the Light. The eye closed and returned to its uneasy sleep. She forgot.

Fergus Eaton elbowed past her. "If you can't help, get out," he said brusquely to Charlie. "I'll prepare the anaesthetic. Matt, get ready to manage the airway. I know just how to shut him up!" Disturbed and bewildered, Charlie backed out of the Resus Bay. There was no way she was getting blood from Mason Donovan.

WHEN CHARLIE, at last, returned to Rowans Holt, at one in the morning, Sally, Ben and Mac were waiting for her. Mac glared at her, but it was Sally who asked the question.

"Did you get any blood?" Charlie shook her head. "I'm sorry, but no." She suddenly felt foolish. Sally and Mac looked at each other.

"Were there no Code Blue patients? None?" demanded Mac. Charlie looked at him. How could she describe the night's events to him; the blood, the shouting, the fear?

"I wasn't able to," said Charlie quietly, looking away. Mac said nothing but silently left the room. They heard the front door close, and his car start up.

Ben patted her on the shoulder.

"You look like you had a rough night, Little One," he said. Hot Chocolate?" Charlie smiled weakly and nodded.

"Thanks, Ben. That's just what I need." Charlie sat at the kitchen island and put her head in her hands. Ben moved around the kitchen, arranging cups and filling a pan with milk. Charlie heard a chair being pulled up next to her. It was Sally. Charlie felt a warm hand gently stroke her hair.

"It's okay, Charlie. I'm here," Sally said.

. . .

Wednesday soon arrived. Charlie was coming to the end of another early shift. She was due to meet Sally and Ben in town and do some clothes shopping. She looked down at the old man who lay on the trolley. He had a fractured neck of femur and would need an operation. He looked scared and a little confused. Out of the corner of her eye, she recognised the figure of Sara Hadid bearing down on her. Hadid was the trauma surgeon on call for the day and would deal with Mr Peterson's broken hip. Charlie was surprised when Hadid let out a slight squeak, abruptly turned on her heel and rushed back down the corridor. Hadid didn't usually do squeaks.

"Hart!" came an angry voice. She looked up, and her heart sank. Mac stood in the middle of A and E with his arms folded, glaring at her. He looked at his watch. "You were supposed to be outside. Twenty minutes ago!" She'd been so busy sorting out Mr Peterson, she'd lost track of time again. Matt approached Mac.

"Excuse me, sir, but you can't be here." Mac glared at him, but Matt, a veteran of A and E and angry glares, didn't back down.

"It's okay, Matt," called Charlie. "He's with me. I'll be one minute." She bent over her notes, hurriedly making sure the patient had enough IV fluids, and painkillers prescribed.

Mac stood watching Charlie, carefully out of the line of sight of the CCTV camera. There was a flurry of cream silk, and suddenly Sara Hadid stood at Charlie's side. She'd changed from her usual scrubs into her day clothes; an expensive silk blouse and slim, expertly cut, ankle-grazer chinos. A discreet glint of pearls glowed at her neck, complementing her beautiful skin. She took Mr Peterson's hand and held it almost tenderly.

"I'm Miss Hadid, the trauma surgeon on call today. You must be very scared, Mr Patterson."

"Peterson," corrected Charlie. Sara ignored her.

"I just want to assure you that you will be in the safest of hands, Mr Peterson. I am an expert trauma surgeon." Mr Peterson gazed up at her as if an angel had appeared at his bedside. Sara reached up to adjust one of the pins that held back the luxurious mass of her glossy brown hair. Her hand must have slipped because her hair escaped and cascaded down her shoulders like a waterfall of glistening satin. She laughed, pearl-white teeth flashing, and threw her head back to move the hair away from her face. As she did so, she caught sight of the glowering Mac. She looked surprised. "Oh, my goodness! I didn't see you standing there," she exclaimed. She dropped Mr Peterson's hand like a hot stone and advanced on Mac. "You must remember me from the other night. I certainly remember you." Charlie was amazed to see a broad smile break out over the face of the ordinarily aloof Mac. He looked totally different.

Sara Hadid craned her neck to look out of the ambulance bay doors and to the gleaming Aston Martin parked nearby. "Is that yours?" she asked admiringly.

"Would you like to see it?" smiled Mac. He took her arm, and they moved towards the doors. Mac looked at Charlie over his shoulder, and the glower was back in place. "Get ready now!" he mouthed angrily. Charlie pulled a face. She'd give anything to do what Sara Hadid did... or at least be able to look like that in a silk shirt.

WHEN CHARLIE finally joined them outside, Sara and Mac looked like old friends. Sara was leaning on the Aston Martin and looked very impressed by both the car and Mac. She was not impressed by Charlie's arrival.

"So, how do you two know each other?" she asked beadily. She looked between Charlie in her shabby jeans and cheap t-shirt and Mac in his pristine black jeans and Canali leather bomber jacket.

"We have a friend in common," said Mac smoothly. "And are you two friends?"

"We've known each other since medical school," said Charlie quietly. "But Sara tended to sit on the back row."

"We used to count the holes in the back of your jumpers, you know, Charlie?" smiled Sara waspishly. "Tony Faveringham once spent the whole of a cardiology lecture using you as target practice; the holes were so big!"

"I know," said Charlie. "I had to throw that top away. With all those paper and spit balls on it."

"Faveringham. Of Harrogate?" asked Mac.

"Yes! Do you know him?" said Sara, hopefully.

"No. But I know his father." In his mind's eye, Mac saw a new recruit being bawled out by a red-faced Major. The recruit had been reduced to tears. He guessed Tony was just like his father, the Major.

"You missed out on so much fun on the back row, Charlie," continued Sara.

"Maybe. But at least I didn't miss out on a First-class degree," replied Charlie, calmly. Sara's eyes narrowed angrily. She was savagely competitive, so this hit home. Hard.

Mac looked at his watch. "I'm afraid we have to go." Charlie again looked in wonder at the warm, charming smile that broke over his face. Sara's face, however, fell.

"But I didn't catch your name!" she pouted. Mac opened the car door.

"You're right," he said. "You didn't." Charlie hopped in, and the Aston Martin glided towards the Barnsley Road exit of the Northern General Hospital.

Sara Hadid watched the car go. She smiled. The game was on. He was definitely interested. Humming to herself, she marched back through A and E. Mr Peterson was being wheeled towards one of the Orthopaedic Wards. He called out to her.

"Miss Hadid, oh, Miss Hadid...." She didn't turn around.

"Whatever!" she said. And went to get changed back into her scrubs.

"WHY ARE YOU HERE?" asked Charlie as Mac drove. "I thought Ben was picking me up. We're meant to be visiting his mum after we finish shopping." Mac didn't look at her.

"I don't want Sally to be alone," he said. "And this case isn't the only one I'm working on."

"Sara Hadid? You're spying on her?" gasped Charlie.

"I'm not spying on anyone," snapped Mac. "This isn't James Bond, Hart. Grow up." Charlie bit her lip and slid down in her seat. Mac sighed heavily. "I'm sorry, Hart. That was unfair of me. Again." He drove in silence towards the town centre. "I didn't know you got a First," he said. Charlie glanced at him.

"I have a very good memory." She now looked at her hands. "It's a mixed blessing. And there's a lot of things you don't know about me," she replied.

"I know you like the poetry of Walt Whitman," Mac commented. Charlie looked at him in surprise.

"Do you like poetry?" she asked. Mac didn't reply but continued to study the road ahead.

There was a long pause. "Thank you," Charlie said finally. "For the scrubs. I assumed it was you." Mac still didn't reply; he just continued to drive. "I'm sorry about the blood," Charlie said. She looked down at her hands again and her bitten nails. "The man. He was so violent. The things he was saying. I just couldn't...." Mac still didn't speak. "I'll do better this Friday," said Charlie, glancing at his closed face. Her chin pulled down as if Mac's silence were a secret blow. Mac eventually spoke.

"I understand," he said. The car drew to a halt outside the large John Lewis store at Barkers Pool in the town centre. Mac looked at Charlie. "We all get scared sometimes," he said, his face without expression. "And I respect that." He spoke without a trace of anger or sarcasm.

"What will you do with the blood if I get it for you?" asked Charlie.

"Take it to Sinclair, at our base, as soon as possible," Mac replied. Charlie thought about what she had heard about Sinclair; the temper, the bar fight.

"And you trust her?" she asked. Mac frowned.

"With my life."

CHAPTER
TWENTY-THREE

BEAULOUF MANOR, NORTH YORKSHIRE, OCTOBER 2012

Sinclair had saved his life. Mac knew this. Sinclair had saved him from himself, in his darkest days. It had been two months after his Court Martial. Two months after the subsequent death of his father. Eight months after the failed attempt to access Jude Morton's computer. There was a smart knock at the large door of Beaulouf Manor. Lady Laura Beaulouf opened the door. Standing at the bottom of the ancient stone steps was a group of four people. At their head was a tall, imposing woman who was heavily pregnant. A plump, bespectacled, middle-aged woman hurried up behind Lady Beaulouf.

"My lady, I'm so sorry. You shouldn't be answering...." She peered round the door at the group. "Warrant-Officer Wetherby! What are you doing here?"

"That would be Mr Wetherby now, Mrs Douglas," Wetherby replied calmly. "May we see Lord Beaulouf?" Wetherby paused, uncomfortable. "The new Lord Beaulouf, that is."

"Lord Beaulouf is indisposed!" snapped Mrs Douglas. Her face flushing as she leaned around the Lady of the house.

Lady Beaulouf looked at the group calmly. They were clearly all military.

"Why do you wish to see my son?" She asked quietly, in a soft, American accent. The four looked at each other. The slim man with the dark beard and sharp, brown eyes spoke first.

"He's turned off his phone. He won't return our calls." Lady Beaulouf sighed heavily.

"He won't return anyone's calls, I'm afraid. I think you've made a wasted journey. My son truly is indisposed." The tall woman lifted her chin and looked Lady Beaulouf in the eye with an expression that was both determined and deeply sad.

"Would it make any difference if I told you, it was regarding this?" She laid a hand protectively over her heavily swollen abdomen.

"Oh," said Lady Beaulouf.

"Oh!" said Mrs Douglas, holding a trembling hand to her chest. "Oh, No!" The tall woman raised one eyebrow.

"I'm sorry you see it that way," she said. "I see it completely differently." Lady Beaulouf opened the door slightly wider.

"Wetherby. Are you here in the best interests of my son?" She looked down again at the large bump. "And of... the child?"

"Absolutely, Ma'am," said Wetherby, looking her in the eye with an unwavering regard.

"Then you'd better come in," said Lady Beaulouf.

. . .

MAC HADN'T DRAWN the curtains back for two weeks. He sat, surrounded by empty bottles and unwashed clothes—the jetsam of a sea of misery. A bottle of pills sat, waiting, on the small table next to his leather chair. He watched the same film again and again. And again. High Noon. It had been one of his father's favourites. They had watched it together, alone. For once, James and George, his younger brothers, had been elsewhere that day. Mac remembered leaning into his father's warm shoulder. He had felt his strong arm sliding around him and pulling him close. He had felt completely safe, completely loved.

"They're making me run. I've never run from anybody before," said Gary Cooper to Grace Kelly. Mac spoke along with the dialogue. Tears streamed down his face. "They'll just come after us. Four of them..."

The door to his room burst open without a knock, and four people strode into the room. The tall figure leading them marched straight to the wide, heavy tapestry curtains and pulled them open. Mac cried out as sunlight exploded into his vision. His alcohol-fuddled brain struggled to understand what was happening. The tall figure came and stood, hands on hips, glaring down at him.

"I'll tell you this for nothing. If I have to hear Todmorden say, 'This isn't how The Captain used to do it,' just once more, then I will go insane." He recognised Sinclair's Scottish accent. Her voice was like a whip on his ears. "Wetherby is pining for you like an incontinent old Labrador..."

"Now then!" exclaimed Wetherby indignantly.

"And as for Hafez..." continued Sinclair, "he's completely out of control!" Hafez lifted one of the many dirty glasses in the room to his nose and made a face.

• • •

"*Whatever he poured into our cup, we drank,*
Whether it is of the Wine of Paradise
Or the drunkard's brew,"

HE MUTTERED SADLY.

"See?" exclaimed Sinclair. "A constant stream of mournful Persian poetry. I'm going to go mad." Mac leaned forward in his seat and covered his face with his hands.

"Go away, Sinclair!" he moaned. "All of you. Leave me alone. Go back to the army, where you belong."

"Well, that's just too little, too late, Sir!" snapped Sinclair. "We're all out now. Out of the Army. And we need work." Still, Mac covered his face, refusing their presence. He felt one of his hands being firmly grabbed. It was placed on a tense, swollen belly. He felt something kick and turn and move beneath his imprisoned fingers. With a cry, he pulled his hand away. He finally looked up at Sinclair.

"What?" was all he managed. He looked in dazed panic at her abdomen and sat back in his chair.

"Yes!" Snapped Sinclair. "It has been a while, hasn't it?" Meet Linton Junior. It's a boy. I found out I was pregnant the day after I found out his father was dead." She jabbed an angry finger at Mac. "You. You got to spend time with your father. I need to support this child. And then figure out a way to explain to him how we went after his father's killers."

Sinclair looked at the tablets on the table next to Mac. Her top lip twitched, and she made a tutting sound. "For God's sake!" She grabbed the bottle, and he heard her flushing the tablets away in the en-suite bathroom. A glass of water was then slammed down onto the table. "Drink that. Now!" He picked up the glass, his hand trembling pathetically. Sinclair continued. "I've got an offer of work—a woman near Sheffield. I've been doing covert IT business for her. She's good. She pays well, but she expects results. She's an app developer, but she also specialises in taking over weak and corrupt businesses. Gives them enough rope to hang themselves, and then she moves in. She now wants a company checking out in the field. And someone to go to Switzerland for her. We need you, Captain."

Mac looked blearily around the room. Wetherby was watching him sadly, leaning against one of the intricately carved poles of Mac's four-poster bed. Hafez and Todmorden were going through the contents of Mac's wardrobe. Todmorden had found his Oxford University Polo-Club tie. He was wearing it, Rambo-like, around his head. Hafez was holding up his dress kilt.

"Honestly. Do you think I'd look fat in this?" he asked. Todmorden ignored him and looked over. He beamed widely and said;

"Alright, Cap?" Mac shook his head, feeling dazed. "This is crazy. I haven't even got any guns," he said faintly, the dialogue of High Noon still imprinted on his grieving mind. The four looked at him, concerned.

"Don't worry, Cap. It'll all become clear. Once you sober up," said Todmorden, reassuringly. "And we've got more than enough guns for all of us." Mac stood unsteadily.

"I guess I'd better have a shower," he said and slowly headed for the bathroom. He turned at the door and looked once more at Sinclair.

"She goes after the bad guys?" he asked. Sinclair nodded.

"We'll all go after the bad guys," she said.

. . .

MAC FROWNED at the painful memory. He glared at Charlie. "I trust Sinclair with my life," he repeated.

"I'm sorry, that was a stupid question," said Charlie. She gave Mac a small smile. "I'll do better this week." Mac didn't return her smile. He nodded once but then turned his head to stare forwards out of the windscreen, waiting for her to leave.

BEN AND SALLY were waiting for her in the John Lewis store café. Ben was looking at a large scone with suspicion. He poked at it with his knife.

"Nowt compared to me Mam's," he announced sourly. "Or yours, Charlie." Charlie beamed.

"I do my best," she said brightly. "So, shall we shop? I need a new pair of jeans and some t-shirts. Shouldn't take long."

"You need an entirely new wardrobe," announced Sally briskly. She looked at her watch. "Our appointment is due. With the Personal Shopper."

"What?" cried Ben and Charlie at the same time, both sounding alarmed.

"This is going to take as long as it takes," said Sally pointing sternly to the two of them. "Style is important."

"What's a Personal Shopper?" asked Charlie. "And why would I need one?" Sally looked her up and down.

"You don't like shopping for clothes, do you?" she stated. Charlie shook her head slowly. "You need clothes," continued Sally. "Nice ones. So, let's introduce you to someone who loves clothes shopping."

. . .

Christophe did, indeed, love his job as a Personal Shopper. The best bit was seeing people's faces when they (often for the first time) put on something that both fitted and suited them. He was tall and slim with gingery blond hair and a perfectly groomed beard. He wore a waistcoat, jeans and highly polished, oxblood-red Doctor Martens. Sally took him to one side.

"Right. Dr Hart hates shopping, but she needs a completely new wardrobe. Get her measured up and do her colours. There's no budget limit, so whatever she fancies, she gets. And whatever you know she'll look good in, put that on the bill too. I'm paying. She'll need completely new underwear and a fancy set for, you know, special dates." Christophe pulled away slightly and looked a little awkward.

"You're paying? And you're asking about underwear? There's not... anything funny going on, is there? With the greatest of respect." Sally's face screwed up in distaste.

"No! There is nothing 'funny' going on. She's a good friend who's lost all her belongings in unfortunate circumstances. And if no one intervenes, she'll carry on wearing that..." Sally indicated Charlie's shabby attire with a disdainful finger. "Until it rots. This is an act of mercy. On behalf of the people of Sheffield."

"Still standing right here!" said Charlie indignantly.

"Well, that's all right then!" said Christophe. He turned enthusiastically towards Charlie. "Let's get started!" He whipped out his tape measure and advanced on her. "I can see you're a Summer, so soft, rosy colours. Size eight to ten waist," he muttered. "Oh...a bit bigger on top. Where shall we start?"

"Can I look at a silk blouse, please?" sighed Charlie. Sally leaned toward Christophe and whispered.

"Get her one in every colour that suits. And you may as well open a bottle of Champagne. This may take a while."

"Fabulous!" breathed Christophe. He had longed for this moment his entire career. Pretty Woman! It was finally happening.

SALLY AND BEN sat watching Charlie being flattered and spoiled outrageously. They smiled at her happiness when she looked in the mirror and saw herself wearing something that made her look like the beautiful woman she was. Ben casually looked towards the other side of the store and froze as he saw a familiar figure.

"Give me a minute, Sal," he muttered. Sally watched as Ben approached a slim woman in jeans and an old Barbour quilted jacket. She had shoulder-length dark, glossy hair and looked vaguely familiar. Ben put his hands in the pockets of his jeans and hunched his shoulders defensively as he approached the woman. Sally realised who it was; she'd seen the woman in the photos on Ben's phone. It was Ben's ex-wife, Becky.

"Hi Becks," muttered Ben quietly. The woman spun round in surprise at his voice. Ben noticed that the first thing she did was to look over her left shoulder. She seemed nervous, and he saw that she'd lost weight, weight which she could ill-afford to lose, as she was slim at the best of times. "How's things?" He asked. He felt like a man as parched and dry as a desert. Ben drank in the sight of her face. Her brown, soft skin, her brown eyes, the long line of her neck. He hadn't realised how completely he longed for her. They'd known each other since the age of seven and had been together since the age of twelve. Inseparable. 'Till death do us part,' they'd both vowed on their wedding day. Well, death had indeed parted them. But it hadn't been the death of either of them.

A man approached them. He was heavily muscled, with tattoos of a bulldog and a union jack on both his forearms. His face was handsome, but his blue eyes were too close together, and his mouth seemed pulled into a slight, permanent sneer. He smiled down at Becky and put a protective arm around her waist. He pulled her close and then smiled heartily at Ben.

"I can't leave you alone for one moment, can I?" he said cheerily to Becky. "Turn my back for one minute, and you're at it. With your little ways." Becky looked at the ground.

"He came up to me, Steve," she murmured. Steve's mouth widened until it seemed he wore a rictus rather than a smile.

"Do you always approach strange women in shops?" he asked Ben conversationally, his arm tightening on Becky's waist. "Do you like coming on to other people's women?" Ben's eyes flicked in disbelief between Becky and the grinning Steve. Since when did Becky take any messing from anyone, let alone a fool like this man?

"Actually, she's my ex-wife... Steve. So, if I want to say hello, that's what I'll do!" he snapped. He was taken aback by the terrified glance that Becky shot him from under her lowered brows. Something dark flashed in Steve's eyes, too.

"How convenient," he said softly. He looked down at Becky's lowered head. "The first time we're in town for months, and you two just happen to meet up." Ben felt his fists tighten, and a dark mist crept into the corners of his vision.

Ben suddenly felt a cool hand on his shoulder, and Sally twisted herself against him.

"Darling!" She sighed. "I was getting lonely, sitting over there all on my own. You promised us lunch at the Fitzwarren. And then we'd go ring shopping." Sally looked up at Ben adoringly. She appeared to notice Becky and Steve for the first time. "Oh, hello!" she gasped. "Do you know my fiancée? Darling, introduce us." Steve looked bewildered at the appearance of a sophisticated, beautiful woman. Becky looked up and, for a moment, Sally glimpsed what must have been the old Becky as Becky's jaw tightened, and her eyes flashed angrily at Ben.

"No!" snapped Steve. "We don't know him. Do we, Becky?" He shook Becky slightly. Becky kept looking down, shaking her head and saying nothing. With a sharp tug, Steve pulled Becky towards the escalator. Sally's hand tightened warningly around Ben's arm as she felt him strain to go after the couple.

"Leave it," she hissed. Ben's head shot round to face her, his eyes full of rage.

"You will cause a scene; she will suffer," said Sally, quietly but clearly. "Believe me, I know." Ben hesitated, and understanding grew in his eyes. He nodded sharply. "Come on, said Sally, let's sit and talk."

They returned to an excited Charlie. "You know what we need now?" said Sally heartily.

"Shoes!" Christophe exclaimed. He was in full sartorial swing. He looked at Charlie and said enthusiastically, "and bags!" Charlie's face fell slightly.

"I've never had a handbag. I'm more of a rucksack girl." Christophe looked her up and down.

"Yes. I'm afraid you are, Darling. But I'm the man who can change all that." He looked at Sally, who nodded permission for them to go downstairs to the shoe and bag section. She stopped Christophe briefly.

"Look at the online Mulberry bags while you're down there, please, Christophe. Get her a few in different colours. And one more thing... What's that over there?" Sally pointed to a creation on display in an exclusive-looking part of the store.

"Oh, that's our only one," exclaimed Christophe. "All silk, a display piece. But it would fit her perfectly, with the lacework." Sally nodded.

"Put it in with the rest of the order, but don't tell her. It'll be a nice surprise." Christophe positively glowed.

"Absolutely. Oh, I'm having the best time!"

CHAPTER
TWENTY-FOUR

Sally smiled as she watched Charlie, Christophe, and the champagne disappear downstairs. She turned to Ben, who slumped in a chair, head in hands. Her smile fell and she sat down opposite him.

"It's called Coercive Control," she said quietly. Ben looked up. "It starts with little things," she continued. "Criticising what you wear, how you eat, your size. The way you walk. The way you speak. They gradually get you to give up your independence, cut you off from family and friends. Make you hate yourself. Make you forget your magnificence. It's what Maya spent years doing to me," Sally ended simply. Ben just looked at her.

"What do I do, Sal?" he said hopelessly. Sally sighed.

"We have two options."

"What?"

"You support her quietly to build her confidence. Offer her options to leave, get her family and friends to help you. But they often just go straight back to their abuser."

"And the other option?" asked Ben, hopefully.

"As soon as we find Mac's uncle and get my Code Blue, we stalk Steve on the internet, find out everything we can about him, and then take him out," she said. Ben's mouth fell open.

"You'd take him out, Sal?"

"No soft arse! But we can do the stalking and the planning; anything that's the legal side of murder. I promise you. We'll sort the creep out." They looked at each other. Ben nodded. He believed her. They'd sort it out.

THEY ENDED up at Ben's mum's for tea. Meggie Morton (she hated the name Margaret) was a rounded, bright-eyed woman who exuded affection to all those around her. She lived in a little stone terraced house on Bradley Street, Crookes. Meggie had a grumpy moggy inside and an original red Mini parked in pride of place outside. She welcomed them warmly into her pristine home, and Meggie's sharp eyes took in Ben's dejected air. She guessed straight away that it was something to do with Becky. It had always been about Becky. Meggie had heard rumours about Becky's new man, and none of them was good.

Charlie looked at all the photos lining the walls. They were a timeline of Ben's life, with many pictures of Becky and little Ben taking pride of place. There was no sign of any older brother. Ben and Sally sat next to each other on the sofa, sharing the same footstool. Each took turns kicking the other's feet off the furniture. Charlie helped Meggie carry through the tea things, and then she sat close to Sally.

Meggie observed the three of them carefully; the way they gently teased each other, the way Charlie fussed over the other two, making sure they were kept topped up with cake and tea. She saw how Sally kept covertly checking on Ben. *So, she knows about Becky too,* thought Meggie. She saw the deep and gentle friendship that clearly existed between them all. She nodded to herself approvingly. *He'll be reyt,* she thought. *With these two, he'll be reyt.*

FRIDAY NIGHT APPROACHED FRIGHTENINGLY QUICKLY for Charlie. However, staying with Sally at Rowans Holt felt like healing, not just for Charlie but for all of them. The three were easy in each other's company, and Charlie explored the house and gardens with childlike wonder and constant delight. They heard Ben gently singing as he worked in the library, and Sally felt that her beloved house resonated with deep content, happy to be restored by his loving hands.

Charlie hummed as she stood in the kitchen, making a large cheese and tomato sandwich to take to work. Should she also take the remains of the lemon drizzle or the carrot cake? *Decisions, decisions,* she thought. The door in the kitchen swung gently open with a creak, like a warm sigh. She could have sworn she'd closed it firmly and heard it click shut. Nevertheless, the sun was streaming in.... Maybe one more quick look at the walled garden? Charlie wiped up quickly and then walked out into the courtyard. Her hands caressed the worn wooden door frame as she went through it and her fingers caught at the whispering leaves of the ancient bay tree.

Charlie waved to Ben and Sally. They were at the far end of the courtyard, messing around with a football. Ben had found the old ball in the back of his Volvo. He'd challenged Sally to a game of Keepie Uppie, not expecting her to accept. She was proving annoyingly adept.

"I used to play football with Peter," she said, watching the ball intently as she bounced it from foot to knee to foot again. She was now at thirty hits and no drops. Ben was glad that she could now mention Peter's name without hesitation. "We used to do this all the time in our backyard," she added.

A fierce look appeared on Sally's face. "I wonder..." she said. She kicked the ball slightly higher and then gracefully slid under the ball, bending down, her arms spread on either side of her. The ball came down on the back of her neck where it met her shoulders and balanced there for a brief second.

"Oooh!" exclaimed Ben, and then "aaah!" as the ball fell to the ground. He clapped his hands in delight. "Almost!"

Sally looked at him, grinning. She stood tall and relaxed, with her hands on her hips. Her expression was one of delight and triumph. The breeze caught in her dark shiny hair, her previously sallow face was flushed with warmth, and her hazel eyes sparkled with happiness and health.

"God, I love you, Sal," said Ben, without thinking. Sally's face fell.

"Ben. I don't—" she said, shaking her head. Ben held up his hands.

"I know, I know," he said. "I didn't mean it like that. And Becky's the only woman I'll ever love like that. But... there are lots of different types of love, Sal." Sally nodded,

"Agape, Eros, and Philia," she said, retrieving information effortlessly again from her beautiful mind. Ben's face creased.

"You just lost me."

"Agape; the Love of Mankind and God. Eros; a sexual,

obsessive love. And Philia; the love of friends," she said. Ben nodded.

"Then it's the last one," he said. Sally regarded him and then glanced over at Charlie, who was walking across the far end of the courtyard, waving at them. Proper understanding of what he meant hit her for the first time in her life.

"Friends," she said. Ben nodded.

"Friends," he agreed. He gazed at her. "People in whom you have faith. You can have faith in us. Keep the faith in us, Sal." There was a pause. He picked up the ball. "I counted twenty-five," he said assertively. And that just started an argument.

Charlie, meanwhile, skipped down the stone steps and pushed at the door to the walled garden. It opened willingly at her wondering touch. She seemed drawn to the well cover once more, and she sat on it, cross-legged. In her mind, she started planning the planting—beans there, pumpkins here, and rows of fragrant herbs with bright nasturtiums tumbling between. The well cover seemed warm beneath her. She wondered what lay beneath... she looked down.

There was a sudden, loud slam. Charlie's head shot up. A tiny window, almost hidden by the eaves, was high at the top of the house. It drifted slowly open and slammed closed again as if caught in an invisible draught. Charlie stood up and walked towards the building. A vehicle had drawn up by the front entrance. A figure stood beside a muddied old Land Rover, carrying a box.

"Georgia?" called Charlie. The figure turned. It was, indeed, Georgia.

"Oh," she said, looking Charlie up and down and sounding disappointed. "Is Sally not in?"

"Yes," replied Charlie. "But can I help?"

"I'd rather speak to the organ grinder, to tell the truth," said Georgia brusquely. Georgia's Hermes scarf was tied rather tightly around her neck. Her already-ruddy face flushed worryingly as she struggled to hold on to the heavy box in her arms.

"Let me help you!" said Charlie, walking towards her, arms outstretched. Georgia whisked the box out of reach with a high-pitched,

"No!... it's fine."

The front door opened, and Sally stood regarding them.

"Sally!" exclaimed Georgia heartily. "I have a box of documents that your partner requested. Old records that I found at Plantation Farm. They relate to Rowans Holt in the Second World War." Sally frowned, clearly unhappy at the mention of Maya.

"Maya's not here, Georgia. We're no longer together, and she won't be coming back. I'm sorry, you've wasted your time," replied Sally starting to close the door.

"Well, I've gone to considerable expense and effort locating these bits of paper... family heirlooms... priceless antiques!" declared Georgia assertively. Sally sighed and pulled the door open again.

"Come in, Georgia. Let's negotiate." As Georgia stalked into the house, Sally raised her eyebrows in amused exasperation at Charlie, who grinned back.

Charlie remained outside, holding her face up to the sun again. She concentrated on drinking in the light before she plunged into the darkness of her twelve-hour shift.

"Well, what have we here?" sighed an unexpected male voice. Charlie jumped. She opened her eyes and saw a man standing near her, far too close for comfort. His eyes were a burning blue in an intensely tanned face. He had a half-smile that showed white, painfully straight teeth, but didn't reach his eyes. His overly-snug, ocean-blue shirt was expensive, but smelled like it had been worn more than once, and his suspiciously luxuriant hair was a barely believable shade of solid, dark brown. *Aiming for thirty. With Botox, could be forty. Probably the wrong side of fifty,* thought Charlie.

"Who are you?" she asked. "Does Sally know you're here?" Charlie went to walk towards the front door but stopped when she felt his damp, firm hand on her forearm. "Get off!" She exclaimed, pulling her arm away from him forcefully. The man stepped back as if someone had slapped him; both hands held up defensively.

"Hey, pretty lady!" he said in an overly cheery, public-school tone. "No harm done. You surprised me, that's all.'

"I surprised you?" exclaimed Charlie.

"Baz!" snapped a voice behind them. Charlie turned to see Georgia slipping a roll of money into her Purdey Gilet. "I told you to stay in the car. What are you doing, sneaking around again?" She brushed past Charlie and walked close to the man.

"So help me, Basil! If you weren't my brother, I'd let you hang!" She hissed. "I can't let you out of my sight for one minute, can I?"

"Have you seen this place, Georgie?" he whined. "Amazing real estate! The real deal!"

"This is my client, my turf!" snapped Georgia. "Hands off my clients, hands off my money, hands off my girls. I'm watching you, Baz." Georgia shooed the man into the car and, ignoring Charlie, angrily reversed and roared off in a cloud of diesel. Charlie could see the man, still goggling at Rowans Holt, through the rear window.

• • •

LATER THAT AFTERNOON, Charlie walked into the A and E department for her shift. Out of the corner of her eye, she saw someone in the shadows around the side of the entrance. It was Fergus Eaton. He hunched over a mobile phone, talking intently.

"I have given you everything you asked for!" he retorted. "You have no idea how difficult this is for me." He listened intently for a moment. "I don't care what threats you make to my family and me," he said. "I need more time." Eaton looked up to see Charlie watching him. He flushed angrily and stared at her, his hand tightening around his phone. Charlie moved on, wondering who he was speaking to and why he looked so afraid. Her heart sank when she saw the Agency Staff Nurse Lianne barge into the department. Matt and Melli didn't look too happy, either. They were all in for a long shift.

CHAPTER TWENTY-FIVE

Detective Inspector Decker felt his heart speed up. He spoke quietly into his radio.

"Is everyone in place?"

"In place, Sir," came the reply.

"And can you see people gathering?" he asked.

"Roger that, Sir," was the answer. He sensed the excitement in Detective Sergeant Aziz's voice. This was it. At last, they'd received a tip-off about where the illegal Friday night gathering was taking place, where the elusive gang were holding their latest Code Blue issue. Decker saw a group of people dressed in dark clothing making their silent way towards the disused warehouse that the Police were covertly watching in the Attercliffe area of Sheffield. Just give them enough time, enough rope to hang themselves. Decker's hand tightened on the steering wheel of the darkened Police Vehicle.

"As soon as you see lights, then it's party time. We move in," ordered Decker.

"Just say the word, Sir," replied Aziz with quiet excitement.

Five minutes later, a rippling, bright light streamed from inside the warehouse, glowing behind the boards and bars that covered the broken windows.

"Move, now." was all Decker said. Men and women emerged from cars and rapidly moved into place around the building. They had planned this meticulously all afternoon and were wary but confident. The doors were locked but quickly broken down by officers in riot gear. Armed Police streamed into the building, expecting trouble from the vicious gang. Cries echoed from the cavernous space. Decker ran towards the building. *No gunshots. Thank God*! They'd taken the place without violence.

Decker strode through the doorway, metal doors hanging, broken off their hinges. His pace faltered as he saw a group of around fifty shabbily dressed men milling around in the vast area, clearly outnumbered by police officers. But there should have been hundreds, thousands. And where was the gang? The drugs, the guns? He sensed, rather than saw, Inspector Christian Blanchflower, beloved of the Chief Inspector, bearing down on him. He felt his arm being grabbed and a voice hissed in his ear.

"What is this, Decker? Because if it's the proverbial in a brewery, you have just proved that you can't organise even that." Decker looked up at the angry man who stood over him. A clean-shaven, career copper in a second-rate suit with a third-rate mind. He pulled his arm roughly away.

"I take full responsibility, Sir." Decker said. He would not drop Aziz and his contact in it. "We had a tip-off from a reliable source. It was worth the chance."

'Was it worth your career, Decker?" sneered Blanchflower. "Was it?" He stalked away, motioning for the operation to stand down. The Police melted away.

One of the mob that had clearly been hired for the occasion jeered over at Decker.

"Oi Decker! Constable Decker!" Decker recognised the man from back in the day when he had walked the beat in Upperthorpe. Back when the Police still had a beat. Fat Barry; notorious low-level drug dealer and troublemaker. He sighed.

"Spare any change?" laughed Barry. "Oh, no. I think you'll need it for when you get the sack." The men roared riotously. Decker closed his eyes. God only knew what would happen now. He'd best get to the hospital.

TWO MILES AWAY, in a disused building on an industrial estate in the Parkwood part of the city, the actual party was taking place. The buyers were placed in cages for the five minutes it took for them to come up. To make sure none of them went loco. And then they were free to continue their experience. The girl had paid her money. The cost for one tablet of Code Blue was now £100. It was minute three.

SUDDENLY, Chloe was no longer standing excitedly next to her friends. She was standing in an empty beauty salon. The walls and chairs were a bubble-gum pink, the fluffy towels violet and green. She felt slightly nauseated by the colour scheme. A woman of late middle age was sitting tied to one of the pink chairs, her head slumped down, a line of grey peeking through the parting of her garishly-dyed red hair. She seemed vaguely familiar. The windows were blacked out. Music played on multiple speakers scattered through the salon. Rihanna.

A man walked into view, and Chloe started. She could see no doors. How had he got in here? The man looked old to Chloe but sleekly handsome. His dark-blond hair was thick and shone in the salon lights. He came and stood uncomfortably close to her. He looked deep into her eyes and smiled.

"Chloe," he said gently. "Your time has come." She took a small step back. He smelled of smoke and aftershave but also of... what? She couldn't place the smell. An image of rotting wood and rat poison flashed into Chloe's mind; the cartoon image of rat poison, with the big black bottle, red skull and crossbones flashing on it. The man was speaking again. "Have you seen your present?" he asked softly. Chloe looked at the salon reception desk where he was pointing. A box stood on it. It was covered in gold foil with a big black velvet ribbon tied in a bow. The box seemed to pulsate gently as if quietly breathing. As she watched, the box jerked and moved closer to the edge of the desk.

"That box contains all your hopes and dreams, Chloe," said the man. "You can be who you want, when you want, and how you want. Film star, millionaire, goddess? All you need to do to release your inner self is one tiny thing." Chloe looked at the man. She didn't like his smile or his expensive suit. Or his smell. The man placed a small silver gun on the chair that stood next to Chloe. It had a mother-of-pearl handle. "You know you want to do it, Chloe," he said. "Allow yourself to do it. After all, if you cannot obey yourself... you will be commanded."

The woman groaned and raised her head. With a start, Chloe recognised Miss Rogers, her English teacher, from year seven to year eleven. The woman who had mercilessly picked on her for five long years, had refused to let Chloe leave class when she had bled through her pad. Had read her essays out in class with contempt, encouraging sniggers and derision. Miss Rogers, who had made Chloe feel sick every day of having lessons with her. "I'm going now, Chloe," said the man. "Don't worry; nobody will ever know what decision you make. Nobody but you and your subconscious." He disappeared.

Chloe knew what she was supposed to do. She picked up the gun. She thought about being a goddess. She thought of rat poison. Her step-father had liked poisoning rats. Chloe made a decision. She walked to the bin and tossed the gun in. Chloe was not a frightened girl anymore. She was a young woman. She headed for the wall. If this was a dream, then she could pass through walls. As she walked, she said clearly and confidently,

"I'm already a goddess, and I forgive you. That makes me the stronger one. Goodbye, Miss Rogers." She marched to the wall and pushed at it, but it was cold and hard beneath her touch. She turned round. Miss Rogers had left her chair and loomed right behind Chloe. Chloe screamed. The woman had moved so fast, so silently.

"Wrong answer, Chloe!" announced Miss Rogers, her badly dyed red hair hanging over her waxy face. Her small, black, piggish eyes were almost invisible in the pale folds of flesh that sagged on her face. But she spoke with the voice of the man who smelled like smoke and rat poison—the man who reminded her of her step-father. The box shuddered.

"Just shut up and use the gun, Chloe," said Miss Rogers. Chloe shook her head. She clung to her waning confidence.

"I'm a goddess," she muttered.

"Wrong answer, Chloe!" shouted Miss Rogers, louder

now. "You don't know your own mind. You have no idea what is right or wrong, Chloe. So, do as you're told and use the gun." Chloe shook her head. Her mouth was now too dry to talk. Miss Rogers screamed.

"Not sad? Not mad? Well, bad then. Witch! Burn the witch!"

The box burst open like a deranged jack-in-the-box. Dark creatures with leathery wings flew up and out. Claws span and fangs clamped. Chloe screamed and screamed. It was Pandora's box, she realised; a poisoned gift of the Gods. All the world's Evils crammed into one small space, just waiting to spill out and eat their fill. And as she fought and bled and cried, she remembered Hope. Hope had been the last thing in Pandora's box. She staggered over to the remains of the container and, with desperate hands, sifted through the shards of skin and squared bone. Miss Rogers started laughing, a rich gleeful sound. And she spoke, still with the voice of the rat-poison man.

"Are you looking for Hope, Chloe? Don't you know? Hope is dead! Just like God. Hope is dead, Chloe!" Chloe felt a rising wave of heat that started in her feet and flowed up to her head. Her eyes throbbed, and a terrible headache smashed like a sledgehammer into the back of her skull. Her fingers closed on a small, soft object at the bottom of the box. It was still. It was lifeless. She knew no more.

"Charlie, get into Resus!" shouted Fergus Eaton as he marched past the bay where Charlie was inserting a cannula into the fragile veins of a ninety-year-old woman. She smiled at the woman's tearful daughter.

"I'll be back in a moment," she said. "Don't worry; we'll

get that hip fixed as soon as possible." The daughter nodded, sniffing. Charlie removed her gloves and washed her hands hurriedly. She put new gloves on and a clean apron while moving towards the resus bay. She saw the body of a young woman, still, on the Ambulance gurney. A paramedic was making a half-hearted attempt at resuscitation. The young paramedic looked like he was about to cry. She heard his colleague start the handover.

"Twenty-one-year-old female, Chloe Hoyland. Found collapsed and unresponsive in a backstreet in the town centre. Suspected malignant hypertension. Both pupils blown. GCS 3. No cardiac output for at least ten minutes prior to us arriving. Looks like Code Blue related." Eaton stepped forward. He examined both of the young woman's eyes with an ophthalmoscope. They still showed a slight blue tinge.

"Back of the eyes a total mess," he muttered. "She's coned. Call it!" announced Eaton.

"But she's only twenty-one!" objected Charlie. Eaton looked at her with barely hidden contempt.

"If you want to waste your time on a corpse, help yourself, Charlie," he sneered before disappearing through the curtains.

The young paramedic stopped his cardiac compressions. An even younger-looking police officer appeared in the cubicle. He looked highly distressed.

"Is she? Is she?" he asked. Charlie nodded.

"Yes, she's dead," she said. She needed to say the word 'dead'. Not 'passed' or 'gone'. Those words were so easily misunderstood. The word dead has a terrible certainty.

"Did you find her?" asked Charlie. The young police officer swallowed and nodded. "Is it your first time?" said

Charlie gently. She imagined him frantically pressing on the young woman's unmoving chest in the dark, dingy back street, trying to restart a heart that was forever broken. The young man nodded again.

"Her parents..." was all he said. Charlie sighed.

"We can tell them together," she said, patting him on the shoulder. "I'll meet you at the nurses' station." The police officer, with one last remorseful glance at the young woman, left. Charlie was on her own.

She turned to the body of the young woman. Charlie smoothed the hair from the young woman's face. She was so young. Her right hand was still gripped tightly over something. Charlie gently opened the hand. A small object fell through the slack, pale fingers. It was a tiny baby rabbit with soft, pure-white fur. It wasn't moving. It was dead too. Charlie looked at the blood-taking equipment. There was no one around. She grabbed a syringe. The paramedics had inserted a small cannula in the dead Chloe's right arm. Her heart was no longer beating, so Charlie might not get any blood from the cannula. She opened the hub and attached the syringe. Slowly drawing back on the syringe, her heart leapt as a few millilitres of dark blood reluctantly seeped into the plastic container. She popped open the top of a yellow-topped blood bottle and squirted the precious liquid in. She stroked Chloe's hair.

"Sorry, Chloe," she whispered.

Charlie turned to the curtain and jumped when she saw Lianne glaring in at her.

"What are you doing?" Lianne demanded. Charlie didn't answer but pushed through the curtains. Charlie slipped the precious bottle into the pocket of her scrubs. She would need to call Mac immediately so he could pick up the sample. Out of the corner of her eye, she saw Inspector Decker sitting with his hand on the shoulder of the young policeman. Melli sat on the policeman's other side; her head bent towards him in kind sympathy. Melli nodded at Charlie and indicated towards the phone.

"Thanks, Melli," mouthed Charlie. It seemed that Decker and Melli were going to inform Chloe's family. Charlie reached for her mobile phone but stopped when she felt a hand on her arm. It was Lianne.

"I said, what are you doing?" announced Lianne loudly. Matt wondered over.

"What's going on?" he asked, looking between Lianne and Charlie.

"This doctor's taken blood from that dead woman," said Lianne. "That's not allowed!" Matt looked Charlie up and down, frowning.

"I'll deal with this, Lianne," he said. Lianne glared again at Charlie but then backed away, muttering.

Matt walked closer to Charlie. "What are you up to, Charlie?" he said quietly. Charlie shook her head.

"Nothing," she replied. Her hand closed over the precious bottle. Matt's eyes slid down to look at her scrub pocket. He frowned again.

Charlie backed away, went into an empty cubicle, and closed the curtains firmly. She fumbled with her phone, trying to message Mac. The curtain was pulled abruptly open and Fergus Eaton stood looking at Charlie, Matt hovering at his shoulder.

"Have you taken blood from the woman I just pronounced dead?" he demanded. Charlie said nothing, terrified of both being caught and of Fergus Eaton. With one smooth move, Eaton reached into Charlie's scrub pocket and twitched the bottle out. His mouth tightened as he looked at it. He glared accusingly at Charlie and held up the bottle.

"You have just given me all the reason I need to sack you, Dr Hart," he said. However, he then looked around the rapidly filling department, and practicality clearly got the better of him. Eaton didn't need to be down yet another member of staff. He turned back to Charlie and waved the bottle threateningly at her.

"Just one more slip-up. And you are gone. Do you understand?"

CHAPTER TWENTY-SIX

Charlie stood by the large pile of notes. There were lots of people waiting to be seen. She was furious. She'd had the blood in her hands, had held the thing that might save Rowans Holt for Sally, might help Mac find his uncle. *Stop Mac being so angry with me all the time,* a small part of her thought. Charlie was aware of Matt, Eaton, and Lianne as they moved around the department. She remembered what Decker had said about the gang having someone working within the department. She couldn't believe Matt would ever do anything like that. But Eaton, with his furtive phone calls? Lianne? She was going to have to be more creative.

Charlie grabbed the top set of notes and set off towards cubicle eight. She read the details as she walked. Unknown male found in Brightside, badly broken right ankle and left calcaneal foot fracture. Charlie grimaced. This man would be a dodgy character. That sort of injury classically came from jumping out of a high window, normally with someone else's property in your pockets. She flung open the curtains and took in a sharp gasp. This wasn't a young, troubled, drug taker. This was a middle-aged man who was clearly very unwell. He lay on the trolley, eyes closed, face grey, breathing heavily. He was dishevelled, and blood caked around his mouth. His lips were cracked and dry, and he had lost a lot of weight rapidly and recently. She moved towards him, pulling on a pair of gloves.

The paramedics hadn't cannulated him. Charlie tutted. Had they thought the same thing she had; this man was up to no good and deserved everything he got? She pulled a phlebotomy trolley from the corridor and gently touched the man's grimy forearm. His eyes flew open, and he pulled away from her, his face vivid with terror. Charlie looked at him and smiled gently.

"It's OK. I'm Dr Hart. What's your name, sir?" The man shook his head and his hands gripped the sides of the trolley. His lips pulled back from his teeth in a grimace, and Charlie was shocked to see holes had been drilled into them. She backed away from the traumatised man. She held up her hands, trying to show him she meant no harm. "You're in A and E. You're safe," Charlie said calmly. By now, the man was sitting upright; his body backed tightly against the wall behind him. He spoke, his voice muffled by the pain of his wounded mouth.

"I escaped," he gasped. "But the Boss. the Boss will find me." Charlie wondered if he was paranoid. Was he mentally unwell? "I told him I didn't know where they were. The tablets, the formula. He wouldn't believe me." Charlie was horrified to see his face crumple. Tears flowed from his clenched eyes. "He hurt me," the man sobbed, holding a hand across his bleeding lips.

Tablets? the Boss? Charlie remembered what Decker had

said about the man in charge of the Code Blue gang being ruthless. Charlie approached him.

"Are you talking about Code Blue?" she whispered. The man looked at her and nodded. He then groaned in pain and rocked with distress, covering his mouth again. Charlie felt so sorry for him. She took hold of his shoulder and pulled in a deep breath. She flinched as she physically felt the deep pain that bored into every part of his skull, into his ears and behind his eyeballs. Without thought, Charlie pushed part of her well self into the man and pulled part of his suffering into herself. She frowned as the usual headache clamped across the front of her head. The man looked up at her, his eyes filling with tears as he felt his pain ease.

"How did you do that?" he whispered. "Why would you do that? For someone, you don't know?" Charlie shook her head.

"I've done nothing. But I need to get you some proper painkillers. Paracetamol, morphine. You need fluids, and you need to go to theatres to get those feet, and that mouth, looked at."

The man grabbed Charlie's hand and pulled her close. Charlie was horrified by the man's ruined mouth and staring, maddened eyes.

"I didn't tell him. I didn't tell him." The man said in a hoarse whisper. "Because I knew that if I told him, the Boss would kill me. Kenny, it was Kenny. Kenny stole it. He stole half of the formula for Code Blue. And ten tablets." Charlie just stared back at him, not understanding what he was saying. "But Kenny's dead," said the man. "He called me, said he was sick. Said his lucky charm had gone bad, and he'd lost the lot." The man started to laugh, a high laugh with no amusement. "I asked around. He was brought in here. Dead. A few weeks ago. He'd gone to the Fitzwarren. He'd gone to Lau. Lost the lot...."

The curtain behind Charlie suddenly pulled back, and Fergus Eaton pushed through.

"Charlie," he snapped. "V.E. needed in cubicle one." Charlie barely glanced at him. One of the disadvantages of being a female doctor was that you were expected to do all the vaginal examinations.

"I'll do it when I'm finished here," she said, all her attention focused on the man before her.

"No, now!" insisted Eaton. He didn't move but stood staring at her, his arms folded.

"OK," sighed Charlie. Eaton stalked off.

Charlie looked at the man. "Listen," she said. "I'll be back in a few minutes. I'll ask the nurses to get you some painkillers." The man nodded pathetically. "I think you need some fluids, and we can put the pain killers in through the drip. You won't have to swallow. Let me pop a cannula in and take some blood," she said. The man's eyes widened in fear at the mention of a needle. "I'll be gentle," assured Charlie. "Then we can get you some proper, strong painkillers." The man nodded reluctantly.

Charlie reached into the phlebotomy trolley and found what she needed. She leant over him, inspecting his arm's faint, collapsed veins. He stank of sweat and fear. She cleaned his skin and, as gently as she could, inserted the cannula, efficiently drawing off blood as she did so. As an afterthought, she pulled some blood into a blood gas syringe. This would give her a quick idea of just how dehydrated he was, she thought.

"What's your name?" she asked, but the man just shook his head. Charlie sighed. "I'll leave the blood here for a moment then," she said, writing 'Mr X' and the date and time on the bottles. "We'll talk when I get back," she whispered.

Charlie left the cubicle and entered the locked clinical room where the blood gas machine was stored. Slipping the thin blood gas syringe into the fragile port, she gathered what she needed for the gynaecological exam. Charlie heard the chatter of the device as it printed the report of Mr X's blood chemical balance. Juggling the packets she held, she slipped the paper into her pocket and disposed of the syringe.

Charlie walked towards cubicle one. Matt and Lianne were at the open drugs cupboard, heads bent over the controlled drug book. Charlie avoided them and sought out Melli.

"Melli, can you give some IV paracetamol to the man in cubicle eight please?" said Charlie, "He won't give me his name, so I'll write it up when I finish in cubicle one." Melli nodded.

Charlie had just finished the examination when she heard the emergency buzzer sound. She rushed towards the resuscitation bay. To her horror, she recognised her patient with the fractured ankle. He was lying unconscious, with Matt performing CPR on his chest. He'd been rigged up to a cardiac monitor, and, even from where Charlie stood, she recognised the severity of his condition; the electrical activity of his heart showed a severe problem. Melli looked up at Charlie, her face anguished.

"I'd just put up his paracetamol. I went back to check on him and found him like this!" she exclaimed, her hands busy with oxygen tubing and a face mask.

Fergus Eaton stood at the end of the bed, coordinating the resuscitation team.

"Where's Eddie Lam with that blood gas?" he demanded. A doctor rushed in from the clinical room, a piece of paper clutched in his hand. He pushed his straight, dark hair away from his eyes.

"His potassium's off the scale!" declared Eddie, waving the paper. "Severe dehydration, by the looks of it. Or renal failure." Eaton nodded.

"God only knows what he was up to," he said. "Have you seen his calcaneal fracture?" Eddie Lam nodded.

"We all know what that means," said Eddie, knowingly.

They worked on the unfortunate man for over half an hour, but his heart could not be restarted. Eaton eventually declared the man dead, and the team stopped, despondent at their second death of the evening.

"Where's Hart?" demanded Eaton, looking around the bay. Matt shrugged.

"The trouble magnet? Haven't seen her since we started working on the arrest," he replied.

Charlie Hart was sitting in a locked toilet cubicle near the mess room. She held her blood gas report of Mr X in her hand. The blood gas that she had taken minutes before his collapse. His potassium had been normal. Someone had used her cannula to administer a fatal dose of the chemical to him, a chemical that was kept under lock and key in the controlled drug cupboard or on the resuscitation trolley. The blood samples that would have proved his potassium had been normal had disappeared. Charlie was afraid, very afraid.

. . .

Charlie returned to Rowans Holt to find Mac, Sally and Ben waiting again for her. She dropped her bag and walked up to Sally, desperate for human warmth and contact. Sally stiffened up, as she usually did.

"Personal space," she muttered automatically. Ben frowned and walked over to Charlie.

"Sal," he said quietly. "The lass is upset." He drew Charlie to him and held her in his arms. She smelled him; cotton, wood oil and washing powder and the musky scent of man. He rocked her slowly as if she was a scared child. She buried her head gratefully against his shoulder and felt hot tears on her face. The kitchen was quiet.

Charlie eventually pulled away, wiping her eyes. She saw Mac had turned and was staring out at the night, his arms folded tightly across his chest. He looked at her, and she thought he seemed upset rather than angry. The moment didn't last.

"Well?" he demanded, his face assuming its usual frown.

"I got some blood," she said. She heard Sally gasp softly. A look of hope blossomed on Mac's face, only for Charlie to dash it when she said, "And then it got taken off me." She sat on one of the high chairs. "But I learned something else," said Charlie. And she recounted the events of her shift.

CHAPTER TWENTY-SEVEN

When Charlie had finished, there was silence for a moment, and then everyone began talking.

"The formula's been stolen? Half of the Code Blue formula is out there?" exclaimed Mac.

"There's ten tablets of Code Blue available?" said Ben.

"That poor, poor man," said Charlie sadly.

"Charlie's in danger!" Sally's voice cut through the mix of voices. There was silence.

Sally moved towards her computers. "What time was your man brought in tonight, Charlie?" demanded Sally, throwing herself into her desk chair.

"About half an hour after poor Chloe, so around ten o'clock at night," replied Charlie. "He must have taken the opportunity of Code Blue night to escape, but he broke his ankle and foot doing it."

"Let's have a look then," said Sally.

"How?" said Charlie. "You can't access NHS CCTV." Charlie looked over Sally's shoulder. "Oh. You're accessing NHS CCTV," she said in a small voice.

They watched grainy footage of ambulances drawing up outside A and E earlier that evening. Sally sped the footage up, but Charlie could still recognise a slumped, pathetic figure when it arrived.

"There," she pointed. "That's him!"

"OK," said Sally. "And moving inside..." she accessed footage from the department. "That's odd," she muttered.

Sally moved from camera to camera. It soon became apparent that all the cameras were filming the same view; the long corridor that led to the Clinical Decisions Unit. Nowhere on the department floor was visible. They would never know who had entered Mr X's cubicle to poison him. There was an uncomfortable silence. Sally looked up at Charlie, reached out and took her hand.

"The Boss has someone deep inside the department, Charlie. You must watch your back."

"Tell us again exactly what Mr X said," demanded Mac intently, looking at Charlie. She felt awkward in his gaze and found herself blushing slightly. She pushed her hair behind her ear and pulled her chin down. Charlie then closed her eyes, concentrating. She was exhausted.

"He said, 'I didn't tell the Boss because I knew, if I did, he'd kill me.' And then he said, 'Kenny, Kenny stole it. Half the formula for Code Blue and ten tablets.'" She could sense the others looking at each other, but she didn't open her eyes. She kept them tight shut, trying her best to remember the dead man's exact words. "Then he said, 'But Kenny's dead. He called me and said he was sick.'" Charlie paused. "He said that this Kenny had been brought into the Northern General Hospital, dead. That his lucky charm had gone off, gone wrong?" Charlie opened her eyes. "I can't remember the exact words, but he definitely said that a lucky charm had gone wrong. And he said that this Kenny had died two weeks ago. And that he had gone to the Fitzwarren, and something called Lo."

"Lau," said Sally firmly. "The Fitzwarren hotel is one of a major chain, and they are all owned by one man, Wellington Lau."

Sally's hands had continued to dance across her keyboard.

"Two weeks ago." She was muttering. "He was inside the Fitzwarren hotel." Sally's face creased with irritation. "The Fitzwarren have an internal security system. I'm going to struggle to access it quickly."

"Well, what about the emergency services? Someone must have called them. Maybe we can access that call?" said Charlie. Sally turned to Charlie, a big grin on her face.

"So, I'm not the only genius in the room," she observed.

Within moments, Sally had accessed the Emergency Services call log. She then narrowed down her search to calls from the city centre and screened for the word Fitzwarren.

"Emergency. Which service do you require?" They heard a woman's voice snap. There was a pause, then,

"Er, er, ambulance?" It was a female voice. A girl, by the sound of it. She was local, and she sounded very scared.

"Is the patient breathing?" said a new, male voice.

"Oh. Er, yes, I think so." The girl replied, her voice changing volume as she seemed to look away from the phone.

"Is the patient conscious?" The call handler asked, calmly but firmly.

"I'm not sure; his eyes are closed...."

"What is the nature of your emergency?"

"I, I think he's having a heart attack. The man's having a

heart attack. Come quick." There was the sound of a phone receiver being dropped onto a hard surface.

"Are you with the patient?...." there was no answer from the girl. "Hello? Hello?" The Call Handler raised their voice. In the background, there was the sound of a man groaning loudly. The phone was picked up again, and a hurried voice said.

"He's in the Fitzwarren, room 1503. Come quick!" The phone was thrown down again, and they heard a door open and close.

Sally could not access cameras inside the Fitzwarren, but she could access some of the traffic cameras outside the large hotel. They watched the footage from the time shortly after the emergency call. A figure emerged from the Fitzwarren, wearing a baseball cap jabbed tight and low. It seemed to be female in tight black jeans and a shapeless black jacket. Her hands were covered in what looked like lace gloves. The figure didn't look up. Clenched in her left hand was what could easily have been a wallet. She walked swiftly down Arundel Gate and then broke into a run. She was soon lost in the dark, narrow streets. An ambulance, lights flashing, sped past her towards the hotel and the doomed man in room 1503.

Sally then matched the time and date to the hospital and accessed the CCTV pictures from A and E again. They watched as the unfortunate Kenny was wheeled, unresponsive, into the resuscitation bay, a paramedic busily performing CPR on his chest. A small figure with blonde hair walked into view. She bent over his arm, looking for somewhere to insert another cannula and get blood. It was Charlie.

"Him?" said Charlie softly. "But, I worked on him. It was

a Thursday night, absolute chaos. He was brought in, unconscious." They watched the images and saw Charlie pick up the wall-mounted phone and start dialling. "I was trying to reach the cardiac catheter lab," said Charlie quietly. "I remember because it was so serious. He was tombstoning." Sally raised a quizzical eyebrow. "He was having a massive heart attack," Charlie explained. "Your ECG, the electrical trace of your heart, basically looks like a massive tombstone. And that's what happens. Most of the time, you end up under a tombstone. Just like him." Charlie sighed. "We couldn't save him. It was too late. Not a flicker from his heart. We called it after forty minutes."

There was a moment of silence. "Sorry, Charlie, but did you see anything? Did he have any possessions with him?" asked Sally. Charlie shook her head.

"Nothing. Normally, the paramedics grab what they can, but he had nothing. No name, no wallet. We had no name to write on his notes. It was so busy and chaotic that I just moved on to the next patient and the next." She paused. "The only other thing I remember about him is a strong smell of cheap, musk perfume."

There was another long silence. "So, what do we do now?" said Ben.

"I think Charlie has done enough," said Sally slowly. "There's a killer on the loose in A and E, and Charlie mustn't do anything else that might put her at risk." Everyone nodded. "However, we now know there might be not just ten tablets of Code Blue out there, but part of the formula to this drug itself." Sally sounded excited.

"Now hang on, Sal," said Ben, his voice uncertain. "This is all getting a bit real and a bit too dangerous. The guy running this is clearly an evil piece of work."

"But the fact remains that I could lose my home, Ben," replied Sally. "Because of someone's greed for Code Blue. I almost lost my life because of Maya taking Code Blue. Charlie and her colleagues are being forced to see terrible things and deal with terrible things because of this Code Blue. Our city is being terrorised." Sally looked at Mac. "And Mac's uncle is missing, most likely because someone wants to protect this Code Blue." She looked at Ben, and a small line appeared between Sally's brows. "Don't you think we should at least try to close it down? If I promise not to put myself in danger. Won't you help me?" Ben sighed.

"You promise no danger?" he said. Sally just smiled at him.

Sally turned back to her screens. "The Fitzwarren is Chinese," announced Sally. Ben shook his head.

"No way," he said indignantly. "It's British. I know a stack of people who work there. It makes a point of taking on local workers. They do High Tea and Medieval banquets and everything. It's more English than barm cakes."

"Chinese," replied Sally firmly. "All your mates will work in low-level jobs. Waiting-on, chamber-maid work. The senior staff, the high-paying customers, Chinese. Lock, stock and barrel, Chinese money." She hit the return button. The image of a slim, high cheek-boned East Asian man appeared on the screen. "And this is the owner. Wellington Lau," Sally declared. "Chinese. Flits between here, Singapore and Shanghai. Owns all the Fitzwarren hotels"."

"But why on earth would he base himself in Sheffield?" asked Ben. "Don't get me wrong, I love the place. But it's the biggest village in England."

"Hiding in plain sight, I suppose," shrugged Sally. "There's too much noise in other cities."

"Lone Wolves," said Charlie quietly. They looked at her. Her eyes seemed a little unfocused. "Sheffield is full of Lone Wolves. And Big Fish. It's such a small pond. Such a small pool." The other three looked at each other uncomfortably. They each remembered the image they had seen in the pool downstairs.

"Time for a cuppa, I think," said Ben briskly, breaking the moment. "And a chocolate digestive. Someone had the good sense to go out and buy biscuits this morning," he said, looking darkly at Sally.

Mac stood and started pacing the room, his arms folded in front of him.

"So, this Boss who's running it all *is* the ruthless killer Decker implied he was," said Mac. "And this Kenny stole ten tablets from him. And part of the Code Blue formula. But what format is this formula in? Is it a hard drive? A disc? Surely not a piece of paper? We don't know what we're looking for. And why would Kenny take them to Lau?" Mac stopped pacing. "And does this mean the tablets are still in Sheffield?" Ben gently put a steaming cup on the island next to Charlie, along with a biscuit. He ruffled her hair and patted her shoulder. Charlie beamed up at him. From the corner of her eye, she thought she saw Mac's face fall again, but when she looked up, he merely looked his normal detached and introspected self.

Sally's hands had been busy on her keyboard again, her eyes scanning her screens.

"Lau seems like the real deal," she murmured. "Property developer, he's no drugs baron. Hang on, though…." They looked at Sally. "There was a son. Only son. Died in a heroin-related incident."

"Not so clean then?" said Mac. Sally shook her head.

"Lau's paid a lot of people a lot of money to scrape his child off the internet. Completely. There's no sign of him."

"It must be a great shame to the family, having your son involved in drugs," Mac said. His face fell. He turned away and started pacing the long lounge once more. He found it difficult to sit still, Charlie reflected.

"Should I tell Inspector Decker what's happened?" Charlie asked.

"No," said Sally firmly. Mac turned and looked at Charlie.

"Sally's right. If we let the authorities in, they'll be all over it. And you've seen how incompetent they can be." Charlie shivered at the memory of the escaped Maya. "We may lose our only chance of getting hold of some Code Blue. But, more importantly, you don't know who the gang contact is in A and E. If you let Decker know Mr X spoke to you, and he starts questioning people, you reveal your hand. You're then putting yourself in real danger." Charlie nodded but felt bad at the thought of not telling the truth, especially when Decker had specifically asked for her help.

"Tomorrow, I'll go and speak with some people I know who work at the Fitzwarren," said Ben. He glanced at the kitchen clock and smiled ruefully. "Later today, I mean," he added. Mac nodded.

"I'll see if I can get to meet Lau himself," Mac said confidently. "And take a look around the hotel."

"And I'll see what I can dig up online," said Sally. "I think I know how to access some new facial-recognition software. The Russians will never miss it," she added quietly. Sally looked at the others. "Then let's meet back here and come up with a plan." She smiled. "We're going to get hold of some Code Blue. We're going to save Rowans Holt. I can feel it.

CHAPTER TWENTY-EIGHT

Later that morning, Ben reached Crookes and popped in to see his Mum, Meggie. She hugged and kissed him soundly and then pretended to cuff him gently.

"Where have you been? La-di-dah with your new woman," she said. Ben smiled and helped himself to a fig roll biscuit from her well-stocked cupboard.

"It's not like that, Ma. Me and Sal are just friends. She's pushed some great work my way." Meggie looked closely at her son as he put the kettle on, whistling quietly to himself. He seemed happier than she'd seen him in years.

"Sorry, I haven't called more," he added, getting two cups down from the sideboard. "Phone signal's terrible out by Strines Moor, and Sal's got this massive firewall on her computers so no Wi-Fi."

"Just as long as you're all right, son," Meggie said. Ben put his arm around his mum's waist and applied a firm kiss to the top of her head.

"And it's new women, not woman," said Ben, smiling. "You've met Charlie too." Meggie frowned.

"What are you up to, Benedict Morton?" she demanded. He ignored her question.

"Do you have Danny Bramall's number?" he asked.

"No, but I have his dad's," replied an indignant Meggie. "But you're getting nothing until you tell me what's going on..." Ben helped himself to another fig roll. He carried on smiling. He loved it when he wound his mum up.

Mac stood and regarded the shabby alleyway at the back of the imposing building that was the Fitzwarren Hotel. A wall of polite silence had met him at the Fitzwarren, a silence that had become less polite the more he'd tried to gain information regarding Wellington Lau. An assistant manager had been called, and Sally had been correct. Senior positions seemed to be held by non-English staff. The charming but firm Miss Leung had rebuffed any enquiries. She'd then offered him the assistance of three rather large gentlemen to find his way back to the front entrance.

The decrepit buildings lining the alley were shabby and boarded up. Amateurish graffiti covered some of the cheap wooden panels. Rubbish and black, oil-slicked puddles filled the cobbled gutters. One building, however, seemed to be in occasional use. He approached it. Black, peeling paint covered what looked like a Victorian warehouse. The front entrance had a rusting, metal grille which was padlocked closed. In contrast to the grille, the heavy padlock was new and expensive, but there was no other sign of activity. Mac shook his head. He hoped Morton was having more luck than him.

. . .

The plan was to meet back at Rowans Holt. Mac had first gone to the Crew's base and had tried to persuade Sinclair to join them. Sinclair, however, had adamantly refused to be in the same room as Ben. She had then tried to convince Mac to let The Crew take charge of looking for the Code Blue.

"We could find them and the formula in five minutes if you'd let us," said Sinclair. Mac had shaken his head.

"This is a professional outfit we're dealing with, Sinclair, willing to kill. And the Police are everywhere. We've always been below the radar, and I want to keep it that way. I'll deal with it."

"But Mac," objected Sinclair. "Hafez is bored, and that's just dangerous. Toddy's shoulder's better. And Wetherby; Wetherby's just... Wetherby. We've all spent months on the firing ranges. We're sick of running security. We can take this gang out.

"No."

"Yes, we can, Captain." insisted Sinclair. Mac scowled at her.

"I am nobody's captain," he retorted.

"You're my Captain," she said, her mouth fixed in a straight, stubborn line.

"I am nobody's captain," repeated Mac, looking equally obstinate. "I'm a civilian. We're all civilians. We are a security outfit."

"We're The Crew!"

"We are a security outfit. Security. And that's what I will give you. No one else will die under my watch."

Sinclair let out a sigh of frustration. "It wasn't your fault!" she exclaimed, shaking her head.

"But they died, Sinclair," replied Mac, his face drawn with keenly remembered pain. "They died! Under my watch.

Linton and Haworth and Sale. And Pinks! Damn him." Mac started pacing; his eyes fixed on the floor. "Pinks turned traitor for a reason. But I didn't see it. Why didn't I see it? Pinks stood there, every day, next to me. And I didn't see it. And... and...." He paused, frowning, lost in thought.

"Your father?" said Sinclair gently. Mac's head swung round to look at her.

"Who?" he demanded.

"Your father," repeated Sinclair. Her face creased with sympathy at Mac's agitated distress.

"What about my father? What do you know about my father?" Mac started pacing again.

"I know that he's dead," said Sinclair gently. "And it wasn't your fault."

"Linton and Haworth and Sale and Pinks." Mac paced in time to the names of the dead. "I had one thing to do," he whispered. "One thing. Keep my people and my family safe. And I just wasn't good enough."

"Mac..."

"One, two, three, four," Sinclair heard Mac quietly recite.

"Mac..."

"One, two, three, four."

"Why are you counting?" asked Sinclair. Mac shook his head in frustration.

"You know, I saw a therapist, Sinclair. In session one, she said there is no tomorrow. There is just the moment. And if you can get through the moment, count to four, and get through the moment. You can get through the next."

"And what was session two?" asked Sinclair, trying to keep Mac talking, trying to pull his mind away from the past. Mac stared at her in disbelief.

"Session two? Do you think I went back after session

one? I'm not an idiot. I can count to four. That's all I needed to know."

Sinclair sighed deeply. "I see," she said.

"What do you mean, 'I see'?" demanded Mac angrily.

"I see. You still need time," she said.

"I need to keep my people safe, Sinclair!"

"You need time," she repeated. "And you are my Captain. Whatever you believe. You're our Captain. Even if you don't remember it. You will."

"Sinclair..."

"You will. We need you. I don't want to lead The Crew. If you decide you don't, or can't, lead us, there's no point. We'll end it. Go our separate ways."

"Sinclair. Enough. You will stand down," said Mac firmly. "You will not engage with the Code Blue gang. This is my job. No one is to risk themselves."

"Except the little doctor?" demanded Sinclair. "Except Charlie Hart? It's OK for her to be at risk?"

"She's in the middle of a packed A and E department. She's safe."

"And who have you said that to before?" said Sinclair, unable to stop herself. Her top lip twitched slightly. "We're ready. The Crew are ready." Mac and Sinclair glared at each other.

"You will stand down. Until I give the word," he repeated firmly. There was a long pause. "And will you come to Rowans Holt?" asked Mac. Sinclair shook her head.

"Not if he's there. Morton."

"You can't judge him for the sins of his brother," Mac said in frustration.

"It's like Hafez says," replied a stony-faced Sinclair. "Blood will always be thicker than water. No thanks."

. . .

WHEN MAC ARRIVED at Rowans Holt, he found Charlie had cooked lemon chicken stew with dumplings.

"You do eat chicken?" she'd asked Mac, in a nervous voice, when he'd arrived, climbing up from the base of the cliff as usual. He'd nodded sharply. However, he had to admit that she was an excellent cook.

"It's all that vitamin L she puts in it!" observed Ben after his third helping, grinning over at Charlie. Sally was certainly blooming with all the home cooking. Charlie thought she looked remarkably fresh-faced that afternoon.

"I've sourced that new facial recognition software," said Sally. "Let's hope the Russians don't miss it, after all," she muttered. "I've fed in the details of this Kenny that I lifted from the hospital camera. He's a low-level gang member from Manchester and adept at avoiding security cameras. Usually wears a hat as a matter of course." Charlie stopped clearing the lunch things and drifted over to where Mac, Ben, and Sally were intently watching CCTV footage on Sally's computer. "But there's no hat-wearing here in the Fitzwarren two weeks ago," said Sally. "However, this is the only footage that I got." They watched as Kenny mingled with well-dressed guests in the vast lobby bar of the Fitzwarren hotel. He furtively looked over his shoulder as he was allowed past two burly security guards. They were standing at the entrance to somewhere called the Hanover Suite. It seemed an event was taking place that was invite only. "Interestingly," said Sally. "He goes in, but he doesn't come out again." They watched as speeded-up footage showed people coming and going but no sign of Kenny. The doors were thrown open at three in the morning, and cleaning staff marched into the empty room.

"That'll be one of Lau's gala nights," said Ben. They turned to look at him. "I tracked down Danny, who works at the Fitzwarren," said Ben. "Danny says the hotel's a good place to work, very fair. But Lau's impossible to get hold of, a bit of a recluse. He lives in a suite on the top floor, and nothing gets past his management team."

"And what are these Gala Nights?" asked Mac.

"It sounds like a bit of a circus," said Ben, scratching his head. "Once a month, Lau holds a Gala night for the great and the good of Sheffield and the North. If you turn up and you are someone, you get invited in; celebrity, millionaire, football manager. Or, if you have a good business proposition, you can get in too. But there's no guarantee he'll speak with you. He sits and watches everyone; if you're lucky, you get summoned for a few minutes of his time."

"Sounds more like a medieval court," said Charlie.

"And no jesters allowed," added Ben.

"Well, I'm no jester," announced Sally. "Mr X said Kenny went to Lau, and we have him on camera doing just that. And he then disappears, and the tablets disappear. It's our best lead. I'll attend the next Gala night. With Lord Beaulouf." Mac frowned with irritation at the mention of his title. Sally continued confidently. "Miss Sally Marshall, IT entrepreneur, and Lord Beaulouf, landowner and aristocrat. Between the two of us, we'll get to talk with Wellington Lau.

CHAPTER TWENTY-NINE

The Boss was standing, arms folded, supervising the burial. Fun Boy and a nameless grunt were pouring cement from a mixer into a hole in the factory floor. The cement slopped and splashed noisily over the still figure lying in the hastily dug hole, its arms still outstretched as if begging for mercy. It was the body of the guard who had been on duty when the Client had escaped. Failure was not tolerated.

"You're right," said a voice behind him. "Failure is not to be tolerated." A figure stepped up to his right-hand side; another stepped up to his left. The Boss recognised Marcus Rosendale and his skeletal companion, Ketch. Rosendale gave a tight little smile as he looked into the hole in the floor. "You allowed the Client to escape," he said. He laid a hot, dry hand on The Boss's right shoulder. The Boss felt a firm, vice-like grip. "I wonder if we have the right man in this grave?" continued Rosendale, lightly. "What do you think, Mr Ketch?" The Boss squinted sideways at Ketch, who was staring at the hand that still rose from the rapidly drying cement, fingers bent as if in a corruption of blessing. Ketch licked his lips, his oddly shaped tongue flicking over his pallid mouth. He still looked hungry.

The Boss gestured angrily to Fun Boy to continue pouring cement. Fun Boy looked terrified and dropped his gaze to his grisly task. He had never seen this well-dressed stranger, but he knew enough to be scared. Fun Boy smelled ashes and was reminded of his grandmother's tales of demons and hellfire.

"The Burning man," Fun Boy muttered and secretly made the sign of the evil eye.

Rosendale's phone buzzed and he looked down at it, dropping his hand from the Boss's shoulder as he did so. It was a call from abroad, from Perda. He pulled a face, stepped away from the grave, and walked into the shadows of the factory. However, the Boss could still hear his smooth arrogant voice echoing around the cold space.

"What do you mean the prisoners are causing trouble? Deal with them. Beat them, torture them, do whatever it is you people do, but they are not to die until I say so. Do you understand?" Rosendale returned to the graveside, his face grim.

"Don't you have enough on your plate without organising kidnap and torture in a foreign country?" asked the Boss, unable to help himself needling his employer. Rosendale glared at him.

"It's personal," he snapped. "When it comes to Tristan Beaulouf, it's very, very personal. And at least I have control over my prisoners." Rosendale stepped closer to the Boss, who took a step backwards. Rosendale smiled slightly. "Do you have control? I heard your prisoner, your Client, ended up in the Emergency Department at the Hospital," he said softly.

"Then you'll have heard I had him dealt with," said the Boss, his voice harsh. "He's dead." Rosendale smiled again and leaned closer to the Boss, who had to fight the urge to cringe away from the heat and smell of smoke that emanated from him. Rosendale gripped his shoulder again with his hot hand and pulled him close.

"But who did he speak to?" Rosendale whispered. "Have you dealt with them?"

"He couldn't speak," announced the Boss, with more confidence than he felt.

"Are you sure about that?" hissed Rosendale. "Perhaps he couldn't speak, but he could sing. Sing like a little birdie, says Mr Ketch." Ketch now turned towards the Boss, his dark oval lenses hiding his eyes, his thin, pale lips cracked and unsmiling. He nodded slowly. The Boss, used to seeing fear in the eyes of others, not feeling it in himself, swallowed.

"I'll deal with it," he said. He felt the grip on his shoulder tighten, and the heat began to sear his skin.

"Yes, you will," whispered Rosendale. "Or I will deal with you."

The Boss had endured enough. He pulled his shoulder roughly out of Rosendale's grasp.

"Kill me, and then who'll do your dirty work?" he demanded, backing away. Rosendale's smile widened.

"My plans won't fall apart if you aren't here, believe it or not," he said. He glanced at Fun Boy, who studiously averted his gaze. "There's always some poor little sap ready to step up and take your place." He put his head to one side. "Your Client disclosed some interesting information before his unfortunate demise. So, whoever your Client spoke to at the hospital must die. Whoever they, in turn, might have spoken to must die as well. Do you understand?" The Boss nodded. "And you're right, again," continued Rosendale. "Ketch is hungry. He's simply ravenous."

CHAPTER THIRTY

It was Wednesday, and Charlie was working in the walled garden. She'd left Sally and Ben in the lounge area; they were both taking a break from their work and playing backgammon. Ben had taught Sally the rules, and now she was obsessed. Charlie had cleared a space in one of the plant beds. It was full of weeds, but the soil was warm and rich beneath. She reached for a large dandelion, but as she pulled, she felt something slice across her palm into the soft flesh beneath her right thumb.

"Ow!" she declared, pulling her hand back. Blood oozed from a long, deep cut. There must have been a shard of glass hidden in the soil. Pain blossomed. "Ow ow ow!" The gate to the garden opened, and Mac stood, framed in the doorway, frowning as usual.

"Hart! What's the matter?" he demanded. Charlie's face fell and, with the fearful gesture Mac remembered from the hospital, she hid her hand behind her back. Irritated, he strode over to her. "Show me," he said curtly. Charlie drew her hand out and looked distressed by the blood dripping through her fingers and across her palm.

"It's nothing," she said, not looking at him. She squeezed at the wound with her left hand. Looking annoyed, Mac drew a handkerchief from his pocket, took Charlie's hand, and wrapped the material firmly around the cut. It was a large square of navy silk which quickly darkened with her blood. Charlie noted initials embroidered onto the edge of the handkerchief in red silk; W C W B.

"On, no! It's your handkerchief; I'm ruining it!" She started to unwrap the material, but Mac stopped her.

"I have plenty," he said. "My grandmother insists my brothers and I always carry one." Charlie looked up at him. She couldn't imagine Mac having a grandmother. As if reading her mind, Mac added, "She's a rather formidable woman."

"You have brothers?" Charlie couldn't help herself asking, even though she knew he did. Mac nodded.

"Two," he said.

"No sisters?" asked Charlie. Mac paused.

"No," he said. "No sisters. And don't..." he stopped. He'd been about to say, "And don't mention it to mother when you meet her." Mac frowned. The strain and lack of sleep were affecting him more than he realised. Charlie Hart would never meet his mother.

Mac looked down at the path and the overgrown beds and was surprised to see no trace of blood. All he could see was mossy bricks and earth where Charlie had cleared around the little primroses to let them greet the light. A cloud passed over the sun, and a cool breeze shook the tops of the trees, scented with the promise of rain.

"They were your primroses in the glass," he said slowly,

remembering when they had last been alone together. "I spilled your primroses." Charlie looked up at him, remembering that day, too. She nodded.

"That's okay," she said quietly. "Everything I touch eventually gets broken."

The gate pushed open again. It was Ben. "Charlie, Sal says to come in before it rains..." he stopped when he saw Mac. He took in Charlie's hand and the blood. "What have you done now, Charlie?" he said, walking over to them. Ben nodded to Mac and quickly looked at Charlie's hand. He snapped into medic mode. "Soil and a deep wound? We need to get that cleaned up and quick. You know that, Charlie." Charlie nodded, and with a last glance at Mac, she followed Ben to the kitchen. Ben turned on the tap and took Charlie's hand. He swiftly unwrapped the silk handkerchief and dropped it onto the sideboard.

"Charlie's cut her hand!" he called over to Sally, who was lying on her front on a large blue and grey rug in the lounge. "I'll just get it cleaned up." Sally glanced up from the backgammon board, which she was studying intently. She nodded and looked down again. Ben shook his head. "I've never met anyone so competitive in all my life," he said, smiling. He sounded proud, thought Charlie.

Ben held Charlie's hand under the running water, looking keenly for pieces of soil or glass. Charlie found herself looking at his large, gentle hands and then up his muscled craftsman's forearms. She remembered leaning against his firm shoulder. She studied his face, remembering his smell as she did so. He really was very handsome, she thought. She suddenly realised how long it had been since anyone had touched her in any meaningful way. She'd spent years so drowned in the dysfunction of her sister that a physical or romantic relationship had been impossible. Now, at Rowans Holt, she felt safe and loved. Finally, home. And her body felt it too.

Charlie sensed her cheeks flushing. Ben looked up and saw her regarding him. His face fell, and he dropped her hand, taking a step back, away from her.

"Charlie, no. I'm sorry... If I've ever made you think...." Charlie was shaking her head, mortified.

"No, Ben, no," Charlie looked down. "It's just been a long time..." she said quietly. She looked up to see Ben's face, creased with sympathy.

"I know what it means to be lonely, Little One," he said gently. He moved forward and, with his hand, lifted her chin. "But, I'm taken. It will always be Becky." Charlie looked up at him and smiled, her face still flushed.

"I know, Ben."

There was a soft click as the kitchen door closed. Charlie and Ben looked up to see Mac, shoulders and back straight, heading away from them, towards the wall. He hopped over it and lowered himself over the cliff edge.

"What's up with him?" said Ben. "He didn't even say hello." Charlie shook her head.

"I never know what's up with Mac," she replied. It wasn't until later, when she went into the courtyard, her hand paper-stitched and dressed by Ben, that she saw the handful of primroses scattered there. As if someone had picked them as an offering, only to change their mind and cast them away.

Mac drove away from Rowans Holt, angry and frustrated, but unsure just why. It was only natural that Morton and

Hart would develop feelings for each other; at least, that's how it looked. They certainly spent enough time together. But then, why would Morton go on about his ex being the only woman for him? Mac was hemmed in by uncertainty; driven to fury by it. And all he could do was wait. Or was it? Mac hesitated. He could always try his cousin, Jess Pendle-Howard in Manchester. Maybe she would know something about Uncle Tris? He could pretend he was just saying hello, keep it casual.

Once he was sure he had a clear signal on the outskirts of Sheffield, Mac made the call.

"Jess," said Mac.

"What do you want, Beaulouf?" replied Jess, her voice slightly distorting on the phone line. "Make it quick. I've got to lead the church alcohol support group."

"You can't do that!" exclaimed Mac.

"Why not?" said Jess.

"Because you only have two states of being, Jess; drunk or hungover. All the time. Neither of which makes you suitable to run an alcohol support group!"

"Well, there's only Gramps or me," replied Jess. "And he's already doing five things for the Parish at the same time." She paused. 'And you've forgotten that beautiful state where I've had just two drinks, and I'm not quite drunk, and not quite sober."

"And how long does that last, Jess?" asked Mac.

"Until the third drink," said Jess. Mac could tell she was smiling.

There was another pause. "And then there's my state of being in the Other Place," she murmured.

"I'm not a believer, Jess," said Mac emphatically.

"Really, Beaulouf? So, you're not ringing about Uncle

Tris?" asked Jess. Mac said nothing. "You don't want to ask me if he's dead?" Mac still didn't reply. "So, not a believer, but you want to know if Uncle Tris is dead?" continued Jess. Mac sighed again.

"Jess.... Please," he said. There was the click of a cigarette lighter, and Jess inhaled deeply.

"I don't think he'd dead, Beaulouf," she said quietly. "Or, if he is, he hasn't come to see me, like the rest of the family always have done when they pass over." Mac said nothing but felt a bitter mix of relief and profound sorrow.

"Do you want me to see if I can find him? In the Other Place?" said Jess, her usually confident voice hesitant and tinged with fear.

"No!" replied Mac urgently. "No, Jess. I'd never do that to you. But have you seen or felt anything else?"

Mac felt as if he was failing by asking this of Jess. Like his mother, he was a staunch non-believer in the metaphysical, but his crazy, wild cousin seemed like an unexpected beacon in his sea of despair. Jess sighed.

"If I tell you, will you tell me you are penitent, Beaulouf?" she asked. Mac frowned. This again?

"Jess, none of us knows what that means. You don't; We don't. The Beaulouf Family doesn't know what we have to be sorry for. Or why your Great grandma was so obsessed with our so-called Penance at the end of her life." He heard Jess sigh again.

"I suppose it was worth asking," she said. "And you want to know if I've seen anything else? Like I always say, Beaulouf, it's random what the Old Bag and the Universe put into my head. I can't control it. No, nothing else. Except..."

"What, Jess?"

"You should have given her the flowers."

"Who?" demanded Mac.

"I don't know!" groused Jess. "The Old Bat says you should have given her the little yellow flowers."

When the call ended, Jess stood, looking down at her phone. She'd had a feeling someone would call her today asking for information. However, she'd thought it would be Miss Whelan asking, yet again, if her dead Great Grandmother had given her any clues to the whereabouts of the Belle Witch. Jess shook her head. There had been no hint of anything like that. But Mac had sounded strange. Should she go and visit him, perhaps? Jess shook her head again. No. He was in Sheffield; on the wrong side of the Pennines. She'd wait for him to come to Manchester. A faint whisper pulled at the edges of her mind.

"Should have given her the little yellow flowers, Beaulouf," Jess murmured.

Charlie approached A and E with her usual feeling of trepidation. Five days had passed since she'd cut her hand. She'd missed the chaos of another Friday night, but her wound was healing well, and she was back on duty. She knew Sunday was usually quieter. Sally had been immersed in preparing for the Gala night she planned to attend on Thursday. Charlie had heard her practising speaking mandarin hour after hour.

Charlie looked at the enormous pile of waiting notes and sighed. So much for being quiet.

"Charlie!" declared a voice behind her. It was Fergus Eaton. *What now*? Thought Charlie mutinously. She turned around, notes still in hand. "Did that man with the calcaneal fracture, the one who died, say anything to you last week?" demanded Eaton. Charlie was taken off guard.

"Why do you want to know?" she asked weakly.

"I don't. The Coroner does," said Eaton, his face angry and pinched. "She has an unidentified body in the morgue, and she's not happy." Charlie saw Matt leaning against the nurses' station, arms folded, listening intently. Lianne was at the drugs cupboard, but she, too, had turned round and watched the exchange. Charlie felt trapped. She called out to a passing figure.

"Eddie!" Eddie Lam stopped mid-stride and came over to Charlie and Eaton.

"Make it quick, Hart. I'm busy," he said. Charlie glanced over at Matt. She and Matt had a running joke that Eddie Lam would tell anyone who would listen how busy he was, but he actually saw the least patients. Matt, however, wouldn't meet her eye. He frowned at the floor.

"Eddie, did that man with the calcaneal fracture say anything to you last week?" asked Charlie. Eddie's face creased.

"No, Hart. He was dead!" Eddie strode off, shaking his head. Eaton carried on, glaring at Charlie.

"I asked you, Charlie," he said accusingly. "Well?" Charlie felt herself blush. She was a terrible liar.

"No," she said in a small voice. "He said nothing." She looked down at the notes in her hand, then glanced up to see Matt, Lianne, and Eaton staring at her. As if they didn't believe her. Charlie backed away, feeling suddenly very exposed. Her mouth was dry, and she felt a rising tide of fear. "I'm just going to..." she gestured vaguely. Charlie put the notes back in the waiting pile and hurried to the ambulance entrance.

Once outside, Charlie breathed a deep breath of air and felt her heart slow down. She glanced at a nearby parked Police car and recognised Inspector Decker. He was slumped in the driver's seat. He had a hand over his eyes and looked tired and disconsolate. The local papers had been savage in their coverage of South Yorkshire Police, and the national press had now picked up on the story with equal brutality. She felt a stab of sympathy for the man. Decker looked up and smiled wearily at Charlie. He lowered his window and greeted her gently.

"Dr Hart! I'll pass on coffee. I might not survive drinking it." Charlie smiled back at him.

"Hello, Inspector." She crouched down and peered through the car window.

"Out for a breath of fresh air?" asked Decker. "That's not like you, Dr Hart." His face creased with concern. "Have you had another difficult case?" Charlie shook her head.

"No, it's Dr Eaton again," Charlie replied. "Asking if I spoke with a patient last week. A patient who died." Decker said nothing. Charlie felt herself blush again.

"He spoke to you," said Decker quietly. Charlie looked up, her face anxious. Decker smiled.

"It's OK, Charlie. You don't have to tell me anything. Although it would be a help if you did." Charlie looked at him and still said nothing. Decker sighed.

"Nothing about this Code Blue business is easy," he muttered, shaking his head. "And it was me who told you to trust nobody. Good girl." He started the car. "You have my number, Charlie. Call it any time."

Charlie watched as Decker drove down the slip road.

Behind her, she heard Eaton's voice speaking quietly and urgently.

"I don't know what she knows, and I'm not going to get it out of her. I'll deal with it in my own time." She realised Eaton could not see her where she stood behind a concrete post. Who was Eaton speaking with? She peered around the pillar and saw Eaton hunched over his mobile phone, his face pale and scared. *Trust no one,* she thought. *No one.*

CHAPTER THIRTY-ONE

Ben was distracted and thoughtful. He'd spent many long hours in the library working on the renovation. The lack of phone signal, and Sally's security restrictions on internet access, meant he couldn't trawl for information about Steve. He'd thrown himself into his work instead. Ben recreated oak trees and meadows and small humble churches. He made plans for the walls of an abbey splintered and torn, almost beyond recognition. Where carvings had been destroyed, he had created, in loving detail, landscapes surrounded by roses and rich vines. The flowers seemed to unfurl like living things within the oak and the vines sprang, triumphantly crowned with corpulent grapes. Becky's favourite flowers had been roses. They had grown them, along with a vine, around the front door of their tiny first house in Walkley.

"Because these are our days of wine and roses, and don't you forget it!" Becky used to say primly before swiping a cloth at Ben for dropping one tiny piece of dirt in her pristine home. And a close observer of Ben's carvings would have seen a small rabbit, crouched and downy-round, sheltered and secure within a wooden shield of rose thorns and sturdy stems.

Sally was distracted and restless, too. She had prepared for the hoped-for meeting with Wellington Lau with her usual fierce intellectual rigour. As well as brushing up her Mandarin, she had chased any details regarding Lau and his business associates. She even found out all she could about his mistress, Annie Wei. When Charlie returned from work on Sunday night, she heard Sally at her desk muttering;

"She loves Scarlet Heart and the Kardashians,"

"Scarlet Heart?" asked Charlie, dropping her bag on the floor and flicking the kettle on.

"A Chinese television series," said Sally, not looking up. "Beautiful girl time-travels back to the beginning of the Qing Dynasty. Falls in love with royal princes, etcetera, etcetera..." she tailed off.

"So, not your thing," said Charlie. "Would you like me to watch some of it for you? For research?" Sally tore herself away from the screen and grinned knowingly at Charlie.

"But very much your thing, Hart."

"Don't call me that!" said Charlie. "You sound like the Insufferable Man!"

A deep frown suddenly transformed Sally's face. She hissed loudly and held her left side.

"Ow!" she exclaimed.

"What's wrong?" asked Charlie, walking over to her. She'd been slightly uneasy about Sally for a few days now. She'd seemed more pale than usual. Charlie had pulled out all the stops when cooking, but Sally had often pushed her food around the plate, distracted. Charlie thought the threat of losing Rowans Holt was getting to Sally. She also worried that the presence of her and Ben might be proving more stressful than Sally had expected.

"I'm fine. Fine," said Sally and stood up. She smiled brightly at Charlie. "Really. It's all okay. I think I'll just have a lie-down." Charlie felt uncomfortable now. Sally did not do 'lying down'.

"I'll bring you a glass of water," she said. Sally nodded vaguely as she headed for the door, holding her left side.

A LITTLE LATER, Charlie sat at Sally's bedside, looking down at her. Charlie had changed into her new navy satin pyjamas, ready for bed, but she'd brought her work rucksack up with her. She felt Sally's forehead. No fever. She slipped the thermometer into Sally's ear and confirmed this; temperature 36.9. She felt her pulse, and it was a steady 80. A little fast, but not concerning. Her oxygen levels were perfect at 99. Sally looked up at her, her eyes very wide.

"Any pain when you pee?" asked Charlie.

"No," grumbled Sally. "But I have got a bit of a gippy stomach. I probably just ate something."

"Any vomiting? Any blood when you poo?" continued Charlie. "Any pain here?" Charlie dramatically indicated the right lower abdomen where the treacherous appendix lurks.

"No! Stop it!" said Sally. "You don't need to... I'm fine."

"Can I just feel your stomach?" said Charlie. "I'm worried about you. Are your periods regular?" Sally picked up a pillow and threw it weakly at Charlie.

"My periods are all over the place, thank you. They had stopped for months. But thanks to you and your force-feeding, they've just restarted again. Today, if you must know." Charlie smoothed some hair from Sally's forehead.

"Then that's probably it," she said. She went to ask the question she always asked at times like this but hesitated. She bit her lip. No, she wouldn't ask that. Not that question. There was no need.

"So that's a 'no' to the abdominal exam?" said Charlie.

"No!" said Sally. "I just need to sleep." Charlie went to leave. She looked back once more. Sally smiled at her.

"I'm feeling much better now. Go!"

IN HER DREAM, Charlie was running down a cobbled street. They were just behind her, but she mustn't let them catch her again. The needle. She was so scared of the needle. Charlie turned a corner, the cobbles cold and slick beneath her bare feet. She reached the steps. She needed to climb the steps. She might be safe if only she reached the top of the steps. But then she heard it... Charlie cried out. Her cry grew into a scream. A high, howling, shrill shriek...

"Drowning...Drowning... Someone's Drowning!"

CHARLIE SAT UP, sweating and terrified in the dark. It took her moments to realise where she was.

Silly Charlie! The thought vibrated in her head—the pool alarm. The pool alarm was sounding! Who'd been stupid enough to turn that on? Charlie staggered across the room and pulled open the door. The noise was deafening. She ran down the stairs and fled across the front room. The door to the stairs was just closing. Ben or Sally must be moments ahead of her. Charlie flung herself down the stairs. An awful thought occurred to her. What if someone had tried to take a late-night swim and had decided to drink? Had slipped, quietly and yieldingly, beneath the warm waters, forgetting what it was to breathe?

Charlie burst into the poolroom, and, sure enough, there was Ben. His hand was raised to the alarm. But he didn't touch it. He didn't need to; the sound went off abruptly and completely. Ben slowly turned to face Charlie.

"It wasn't turned on..." he whispered. "I swear. The alarm wasn't turned on." They looked at each other. Charlie's stomach pitched sickeningly. She knew something was terribly, terribly wrong.

"Where's Sally?" she said. She looked into the pool as if she might see Sally's still body floating there, but the pool was empty.

"Sal?" called Charlie. "Sal?" She ran to the door and tore it open.

WHENEVER SHE LOOKED BACK at the terrible events of that evening, Charlie could never recall how she got up to Sally's room. All she remembered was seeing Sally's prone figure lying halfway across the bathroom entrance. The illumination from the dim mirror light showed the dark stain of blood that flowed down her legs and soaked the carpet. Charlie turned her friend over and shook her frantically, terrified at her pallor and unresponsiveness. She laid a hand on Sally's abdomen, something she should have done four hours ago, she raged to herself. It was swollen and terribly, terrifyingly hard.

Charlie flung herself into the bathroom. She emptied the small chrome bin onto the floor and pawed through the detritus until she found what she hoped for. Found what she dreaded: a pregnancy test. It was positive.

"NO!" howled Charlie. She crawled back to Sally. By now, Ben was there. He turned on the main light. This allowed Charlie merely to see how deeply unwell Sally was. A horrible thought had occurred to her. She looked Ben in the eye.

"Did you two have sex? Did you?" Ben looked as if he had just been slapped. But then he closed his eyes and nodded. They had. Charlie realised they had. On the first night they'd all met.

"You bastard!" shouted Charlie. Ben recoiled. Charlie never swore.

"Charlie, it wasn't like that," exclaimed Ben angrily.

"Just shut up, Ben. Let me think!"

Charlie, pale and angry and desperate, pursed her lips. Medicine was all about decision-making. They never taught you that in Medical School. Funny that. It was all lectures, practical skills, and self-directed learning. Reflections on the art of Medicine; the pursuit of intellectual perfection. But then you qualified and hit the wards, and a tidal wave of chaos met you there. That was when you realised it was all about do or do not. Test or watch. Treat or not treat. Live. Or die. A tiny embryo had formed. Not in Sally's womb, where it should be, but somewhere else in her pelvis. Most likely in one of her fallopian tubes.

The womb has a massive blood supply. Blood is required to grow life, to feed this terrible magic. Lots and lots of blood to feed something that would take over your body. Something that would strip you of all oxygen and nutrients if it had to. Kill you, if it had to; mindless and ruthless in its squirming urgency to grow at all costs. The blossoming embryo had eroded into one of Sally's arteries. This artery had suddenly burst, causing a catastrophic torrent of blood to fill her pelvis. There was now not enough blood to carry oxygen to her brain or her failing heart.

Charlie felt for a pulse at Sally's wrist. Nothing. At her neck? Charlie felt a faint flutter, terribly fast, terrifyingly weak. Call an ambulance? Thought Charlie. No signal. She also had no idea what Sally's postcode was. In addition, the last ambulance Charlie had called had taken forty minutes at least to arrive. And that had been for a case of chest pain, something that should take eight minutes. Sally could be dead in fifteen minutes. Or less. But the bleed could have stabilised. If they move her now, they could dislodge a clot, and the bleeding could restart. Could drain the life from her.

Charlie made a decision. "We move. Now. We have to get her to hospital. Where's her key card?" Ben had recovered from his shock. He, too, was now tight-lipped. Ben moved decisively, accepting Charlie's leadership. He opened Sally's bedside drawer and withdrew the card and lanyard. With one smooth movement, he threw it to Charlie.

"Pick her up. As gently as you can," ordered Charlie. "No pressure on her abdomen." Ben picked up Sally's light, limp body and cradled it gently against him. She seemed to weigh hardly anything. Her head flopped, like a rag doll, against his chest. He wasn't sure if she was even breathing. He refused to think. *Move*! he thought. *Just keep moving*. As he headed down the stairs, Charlie ran back up to her room. She retrieved her work bag and rushed after Ben. She met him at the lift door and opened it for him. As the lift sank, they avoided each other's gaze.

In the cavern, Ben gently laid Sally on the floor. She was ashen, her breathing shallow and rapid. Charlie unslung her bag from her shoulders and flung herself down next to Sally.

"Get the Dodge Demon ready," she snapped. "We're going. Just as soon as I do this."

"The Demon?" said Ben, "Not the Range Rover?"

"The Demon's only got one front seat. We put her in the front well. I can manage her airway from the back. And it's faster. Get it damn well ready!" Ben went to get the keys.

Charlie emptied her work bag onto the floor of the cave. Two green cannulas and a three-way tap. She remembered the first night they had spent together. "A-negative. Sally said her blood group was A-negative," Charlie muttered. She grabbed the first of the green cannulas. "Get me a glove!" she shouted at Ben. He pulled a vinyl glove from a box on one of the workbenches. Charlie quickly tied the glove around Sally's right upper arm. She'd spotted the prominent median vein in Sally's arm as they had lain, side by side, in the pool. People who cannulate for a living tend to do that. You won't realise it, but they'll be eyeing your veins as they speak to you. Just in case. It's a professional thing.

Charlie could no longer see the vein, but she knew it was there. She pierced the skin with the large needle, cursing that she didn't have an even larger Grey cannula. She withdrew the guide needle, removed the hub, and threw the needle recklessly to one side, not caring where it fell. A weak flow of dilute blood trickled slowly back down the plastic tube of the cannula. The cannula was in, but Sally was critically hypovolaemic. Charlie secured the cannula with tape, as she had no dressings. She attached the three-way tap and primed it with Sally's blood, as she had no flush. She now had seconds before the blood clotted in the cannula, and it became useless.

Charlie looked up at Ben. "Cannulate me. Now," she ordered. He sank to his knees and, with shaking hands, tied the glove around Charlie's left upper arm. He shook the second green cannula out of its packet. With practised skill, Ben eased the needle into her arm. Charlie barely flinched at the sharp bite on her flesh; her eyes fixed on Sally's unmoving face. Blood flashed back. With his index finger, Ben advanced the plastic cannula over the still needle and into the vein. Ben unscrewed the hub end of the cannula needle and gently screwed it onto the cannula poking from Charlie's arm to stop blood from flowing out. He then rapidly taped it into place. He looked around for somewhere to put the long needle. Charlie angrily grabbed it from him and threw it after the first.

Charlie ripped open the fifty-ml syringe. She flipped the port at the top of her cannula, fitted the fifty ml syringe into the port and then pulled back. Warm, dark-red blood filled the cannula. She just drew back 10mls at first. Charlie needed to flush Sally's cannula and stop the blood clotting. She inserted the cannula into the three-way tap, tuned the port to open, and pushed her blood into Sally. There was a slight, sickening resistance, and then the blood flowed in.

"Let's go! We've got less than a minute before it clots again," she snapped.

Ben gently lifted Sally. He laid her in the well next to the Dodge Demon driver's seat. Charlie hopped in and lay next to Sally. Ben closed the door and threw himself behind the wheel, pressing the fob to activate the hangar-like doors. As they slipped open, he looked at Charlie.

"I thought you were going in the back," he said.

"I will, but she needs blood." Charlie looked up at Ben, her eyes dark pools in her paper-white face. "She's dying, Ben. Drive."

CHAPTER THIRTY-TWO

As the engine roared into life, Charlie attached the three-way tap to the end of her cannula and Sally's. They lay, side by side, as close as could be. By turning the port, she could guide fluid flow between the cannulas. She pulled fifty whole mls from her vein and then, turning the port, pushed the blood into Sally. She felt her body press back as Ben drove the throbbing hulk of metal down the narrow path. He looked down at Charlie.

"I thought it killed you to have someone else's blood if you're not a match?" He said above the engine's roar.

"She told me she was A-negative when I stitched her up," said Charlie. "I'm A-negative too. I'm sure she said she was A-negative...." Charlie had made her decision. She pulled another fifty mls of her lifeblood from her vein and pushed it into the limp arm of her friend. And another, and another, and another. By now, Ben had reached the Manchester Road. Charlie looked up at him. "Go. As fast as you can," she said. Ben put his foot down.

• • •

POLICE OFFICERS PETE LOXLEY and Kylie Porter sat in a dark layby just off the Manchester Road. The two young, single officers were supposed to be on patrol, but they had ended up just talking for the last hour. Pete looked at Kylie's round, dark brown eyes and soft, brown, tightly curled hair tied back in a neat, regulation bun. He realised that she was the prettiest woman he'd ever seen.

"Go on," he said. "What happened next?"

"Well, then they had this report about a squirrel running in circles on Crabtree lane," said Kylie, smiling. "The man was worried it were sick or dangerous. So, they send Heavygate and Toyne." Pete pulled a face.

"Oh, God. What happened?"

"They only arrived and ran the squirrel over by accident!" They both started laughing. "Case closed!" giggled Kylie. Pete saw Kylie had dimples when she laughed.

There was a sound like thunder. They looked up, only to see an eight hundred and forty horse-power blur that was gone before they even registered it. They looked up the road and a tiny smudge of taillights winked before smartly disappearing round a corner. Pete grabbed at the radio, ready to report the speeding vehicle. Kylie gently touched his hand.

"We'll never catch that, Pete. And then we'll have to go back. Just tell me about that man with the gun, the toilet brush, and the bag of chips again." Pete put the walkie talkie down. She was right; nothing could catch that car.

CHARLIE WAS PRESSED against the back seat of the growling vehicle, cradling Sally. Sally's breathing had slowed marginally, but her pulse was still too faint and far too rapid. Charlie had given Sally six hundred mls of her blood and was feeling dizzy herself. She fumbled for her phone. They had a signal! She dialled the Jessop maternity hospital.

"Switchboard," came a bored voice. It was three in the morning. The Witching Hour. The time when the human body was at its lowest ebb, the time when you were most likely to slip into death.

"Hi, my name's Dr Charlie Hart. Can you put me through to the Consultant on call, please?"

"And where are you calling from?" asked the voice.

"I'm approaching Sheffield now with a patient," said Charlie.

"The Consultant only takes calls from their Registrar or another Consultant," said the bored voice. "I'll put you through to the Registrar."

"No!" shouted Charlie. She lowered her tone and spoke with what she thought of as her 'doctor voice'. "I insist on speaking to the Consultant. I have a critically ill patient. I must speak to them!" There was a pause that seemed to last a lifetime.

"Putting you through," said the laconic voice.

Please answer, please answer! pleaded Charlie silently.

"Fletcher," snapped a voice. Charlie felt tears of relief sting her eyes.

"Oh, Miss Fletcher! It's Charlie, Dr Charlie Hart."

"Charlie? Are you calling from A and E? You know you should discuss patients with my Registrar. Or book them direct with the Early Pregnancy Unit."

"No!" Charlie interrupted. I'm in the back of a car with my friend. She's moribund, burst ectopic. I... she's dying, Miss Fletcher!"

"You need to get her to the Northern General Hospital,"

said Miss Fletcher crisply. "They can stabilise her. They have full resuscitation facilities. You know that, Charlie!"

"She's bleeding, Miss Fletcher. Bleeding out! We have to drive past the Jessop to get to the Northern. We have to stop the bleed." There was another long pause.

"I was just on my way home. Complicated Caesarean." Charlie heard Miss Fletcher turn from the phone and have a muffled discussion with someone else in the room. Her voice came back to the line. "OK, Charlie. You're sure it's an ectopic?"

"Yes! Positive pregnancy test. PV loss, pelvic signs. Moribund...".

"How far out are you?" Charlie looked up at Ben, who put his foot down even harder on the accelerator.

"Five minutes," she breathed.

"Bring her straight down to Theatre Three. We'll be ready. I'm scrubbing in now." The phone went dead.

THE DODGE DEMON screeched to a halt, with a stench of burning rubber, outside the ambulance bay of the Jessop Wing. A porter was waiting with a trolley. Ben gently lifted the unconscious Sally onto the gurney. They fled to the lift that took them down to the hospital's basement and the Theatre Department. The doors to Theatre Three were open wide, and they wheeled Sally straight in. Miss Fletcher stood in a full, fresh surgical gown and mask, curly, brown hair caught in a theatre cap. She held her sterile, gloved hands folded at her waist to ensure she touched nothing that could contaminate her. She nodded brusquely to Charlie. Fletcher's eyes took in the cannula in Charlie's arm and Charlie's glassy-eyed pallor.

"You. Sit there." She jerked her chin towards a low stool next to the Anaesthetist.

Ben was sent out to wait on a hard plastic seat outside the department. Charlie glimpsed his terrified face as the theatre doors closed. The theatre staff had swung into action, covering Sally with a heating blanket, covering her hair and cleansing her bulging abdomen with brown, anti-septic liquid. A sticky see-through plastic layer was laid on Sally's skin over the area to be operated on. There would be no scar-sparing, delicate cuts across the bikini line, no keyhole procedures. This was going to be raw, bloody, life-saving surgery.

At the head end, the Anaesthetist was busy doing their work. Charlie recognised Saanvi Ray, who regularly worked with Miss Fletcher. They bickered like an old married couple.

"Name?" demanded Saanvi as she ran her hands over Sally's veins, looking for access.

"Er, Emily, Emily Foster," said Charlie. She felt compelled not to give Sally's real name. Lying did not come naturally to Charlie, and she stumbled on her words. Saanvi noted the name, date of birth, and address that Charlie gave her. She tutted.

"She's really shut down, Juliette!" she called to Miss Fletcher. "I may have to put a neck line in!"

"Just get her under!" snapped Fletcher as the scrub nurse busily opened packs and loaded trollies around her.

The scrub nurse started loudly counting swabs, and the diathermy snapped and hissed as the ODA ensured all the equipment was in working order.

"What the Hell have you been doing, Hart?" said Saanvi. When Charlie hesitantly told her, she shook her head in disbelief. "You fool! She could be having a transfusion reaction right now!" Saanvi coaxed the green cannula into a semblance of order, drawing pallid blood and clots from the port. She then drew off blood for cross-matching, clotting, full blood count and other necessary tests. She flushed the cannula with saline and applied a proper dressing. Saanvi then held Sally's jaw with practised ease and started injecting the first bolus of general anaesthetic and then muscle relaxant.

"She's going under, Juliette, "called Saanvi. She skilfully intubated Sally, passing a long plastic tube into her trachea and then inflating a cuff that would protect the airway from fluids.

Charlie looked up at the monitor. Sally's blood-oxygen level had been 86% when they had come in, her heart rate was 160, and her blood pressure was barely detectable at 60/30. Sally was deeply shocked. Like the conductor of an orchestra, Saanvi marshalled her skills to ensure each complex part of the human body's symphony was played out in order. Replace lost blood, but not so fast as to dislodge the clots that may have stopped the bleeding. Not too much blood to trigger a cascade of deranged clotting that would mean blood flowing uncontrollably in some areas and clumping in others. Blood products, electrolyte control, temperature, blood pressure, Ph. All needed marshalling by the skilled conductor.

Blood results were rung through from the lab. Saanvi's normally unflappable face creased.

"Her Haemoglobin level was 4 when you got her here, Hart," she said, quietly. "Half of that was probably yours." Saanvi hooked up another bag of O-negative blood.

"And her blood type?" asked Charlie.

"A-negative," said Saanvi. "You saved her life, Hart."

Fletcher made a large, decisive slice down the middle of Sally's abdomen from navel to above the pubic bone. This ensured full access to the abdomen, avoided major nerves and vessels and minimised blood loss. Sally would, however, be left with a large scar. Fletcher paused. It was worse than she thought: massive Haemoperitoneum, with organised clots, obscuring her view. Suctioning was no good. She started removing the liver-like, slippery masses with her hands, using swab after swab to try to clear the area. And then she saw fresh blood pouring from an unknown source. It rapidly filled the pelvis with bright red liquid: arterial blood. The fluid being given had caused Sally's blood pressure to rise. This had pushed away the clot which had sealed the damaged artery. The bleeding had started again. If they didn't identify the ectopic quickly, she would bleed to death. Right before their eyes.

"Blood pressure's going down" said Saanvi, conversationally. Fletcher said nothing. She just worked, her mouth beneath her mask flattened and hard.

The door to Theatre Three pushed open, and the face of a flushed and sour-looking man in his late-fifties made a brief appearance. Julian Foukes, Mr Foukes. He'd been called in to oversee the delivery of one of his more demanding private patients. It had been straightforward in the end. Thank God. At his age, he'd had enough excitement. He was working less and, with quiet desperation, was looking forward to retirement. He'd heard there was some excitement in Theatre Three, though. Juliette Fletcher was up to her eyeballs in it, apparently. So, he'd come for a quick gloat.

He and Fletcher hadn't spoken for two years. She seemed to think his attitudes were 'patriarchal and old-fashioned.'

That he didn't give his female patients enough 'respect'. He sighed inwardly. Julian Foukes had finally come to realise that the only constant in life is change. The days of orderly ward rounds and tea with Matron were long gone. Even his daughter, Portia, was now married to a Sri-Lankan, of all things! Good enough surgeon, but not, you know, what you'd expect. They were expecting their first child next month. A boy.

That weekend, Julian Foulkes had sat in his shed. He'd taken up woodworking in there, to fill the empty hours. He'd caressed and oiled the small cricket bat that he'd made. He had held the tiny blue socks, embroidered with fishes, that he had secretly bought. He had felt the full weight of a hopeless love that had unexpectedly hooked his heart. Love for a little life that had not even been born. Julian Foukes had cried. He had realised he'd never been there for Sheila and the children. He had relentlessly pursued and drowned himself in his career. He would not do the same with his grandson.

Juliette Fletcher looked up at him over a surgical field that looked like an abattoir. That was not like Juliette. She was an excellent surgeon, he grudgingly admitted.

“Julian." Fletcher said, quietly. "Julian. Please?" He regarded her, remembering the animosity of the last two years. He thought again of the tiny socks.

"I'll scrub in," he sighed.

"Do you have your sticky hands on this woman's vagus nerve by any chance, Juliette?" asked Saanvi.

"Nowhere near," replied Fletcher, distractedly.

"Because her heart rate's slowing," said Saanvi. She looked at Charlie. "Is she a good friend of yours?" she asked quietly, her large brown eyes suddenly very serious.

"The best," whispered Charlie. "Why?" Saanvi paused and looked again at the monitor.

"I hate to be dramatic, but... If there's anything you ever wanted to say to her, then say it now. I'll do my damnedest. But she's been too shut down for too long. I think your friend is dying."

CHAPTER THIRTY-THREE

Sally stood deep in the Shambles of York. The medieval, narrow, cobbled streets stretched either side of her. Ancient building fronts leaned close together as if whispering secrets. She was in the most narrow part. She and Peter had come here together when they had been eleven. On the train from Leeds, just the two of them, spending their paper-round money and not thinking of home. It had been one of the best days of their lives, in the sunshine, discovering the ancient, tiny city. Especially when they had found the sweetshops of the Shambles.

Peter now stood on the pavement opposite her, on the other side of the street. If she wanted to, she could almost reach out and touch him. He was smiling at her, and his face was lit up as if he had a thousand candles burning within. And everything around her was clean. So, so pure. It was as if the cobbles themselves were polished.

"I miss you so much," said Sally. "I'm so sorry."

"You've nothing to be sorry for, Daft Lass," said Peter.

Sally laughed as she remembered the name he'd given her. He'd called her that, even as he'd burst with pride at her cleverness.

From the alleyway behind Peter walked a little girl. She was about two years old. She leaned comfortably against Peter's legs, pushed a plump thumb into her mouth, and looked at Sally. Her eyes were hazel, and her hair fell in long ringlets of auburn. Sally felt her heart clench inside her in a way she'd never known. She felt her legs move, ready to take her across the street. To touch, to feel, to hold her child, her flesh and blood. Her little girl.

"Sally!" She heard Charlie's voice by her left ear. Sally stopped and looked to her left, but the street was empty. She looked right. The street down there narrowed and darkened. It seemed to be night-time to the right. A sign swung from a dilapidated building halfway down the darkened street. It moved, even though there was no breeze. It looked like an old-fashioned pub sign. A squeal like rusty hinges echoed with each movement. A large black bird was painted on the sign, a hunched raven, blue eyes glowing in the dimness.

Sally looked back at Peter. The little girl was now in his arms, her head resting in the crook of his neck. She was asleep.

"Sally!" called Charlie. She was crying. "Sally, I'm so sorry. It's all my fault. I should have asked the question. I should have asked if you were pregnant, but I didn't. I'm no doctor. I'm no friend. I've killed you. Sally, please don't go!"

"Charlie?" called Sally, looking for the source of the voice.

Sally looked back at Peter. "Is Gabella here?" she asked. Gabella; Grandma Isabella; beloved Grandma Isabella.

"Of course, she's here," smiled Peter. "She can't wait to

meet this little one." He indicated the child sleeping in his arms. "But she spends most of her time on the Battlements. She's trying to get the Others to come in from the Dark. Some of them are so scared. 'The Empress of Lost Causes.' Do you remember? That's what she called herself?" Peter put on a determined, commanding voice. "There is always hope, Peter Marshall! And it is never, ever too late for salvation!" Sally nodded, smiling, her eyes full of tears.

"There is always hope. There is always salvation," she said. Peter paused. "But some of them like it, Sal. Some of them choose the Dark.

Another child now appeared from the alley behind Peter. This was a bright-eyed, happy-looking little boy of around four years old. He had straight, shiny hair, which was also dark auburn. He reached up with his left hand and gently held onto the foot of the sleeping toddler. In his right hand, he held a bright blue train; Thomas the Tank Engine. Sally recognised the boy, even though, in Ben's photographs, he'd been bald and slightly jaundiced. It was Benjamin Morton.

"I want to come and be with you," whispered Sally. Peter smiled gently.

"That's up to you, Sal."

"Sal!" This time it was Ben's voice that she heard, but this was fainter than Charlie's. "Sal! What have I done?" He was crying as well. Sally wanted to tell him not to cry. "Don't leave me, Sal," Ben pleaded. "Please don't leave me all alone. I don't want to be alone. Not again."

"Time moves differently here," said Peter conversationally. "The blink of an eye can be an entire lifetime where you are." He looked at Sally. "We have Forever. We can wait. There's so much love in the World, Sal. So much love for you to find."

Sally thought of Maya and Nox and the mindless violence of the last months.

"But there's so much hate as well..." she said. "I'm so tired...."

"Evil declares itself from the rooftops, Sal," said Peter. "Remember that. Duty and kindness and care creep quietly home."

"A Poet! I remember!" exclaimed Sally. "You always wanted to be a poet! Like Gabella..."

"Only subject I ever beat you at, English," beamed Peter. His face then became serious. "If you find love and friendship, Sal, you hold on to them. As tight as you can."

The dark sign to the right swung again, harder this time. The squeal of rusty decay grew louder. The little boy pulled urgently at Peter's arm. Peter looked down at him and nodded. He looked back at Sally.

"Ben asks you to keep the faith, Sal," said Peter, serious now. "He asks you to keep the faith, for his Daddy. And for Charlie. They'll need you to keep the faith."

Sally looked at Peter and the small boy who stood at his side. She looked at her little child nestled in Peter's arms. She shook her head.

"The world won't miss one broken woman," she whispered, arms aching to hold her Isabella. Peter shook his head sternly.

"But you're not a broken woman, are you, Sal? You are Sally Marshall, and you are magnificent. It's the World that is broken. And the broken World needs magnificent women.

Sally made her decision. She would not join Peter. Not just yet. She looked at young Ben. The little boy nodded at her, and his face broke into a shy smile.

. . .

SALLY FOUND herself standing on the old metal well cover. She was in her walled garden at Rowans Holt. It was almost teatime. The smell of lavender and herbs washed over her.

"Don't worry, Mac, we'll find the Way," she whispered. She walked towards the house. The air washing in from the peaks was sweet and clean. The trees whispered and sighed. Sally sensed the wooden bones of her home settle more comfortably now she was back. As she approached the kitchen door, it swung open as if welcoming her. Charlie was making a chicken pie by the smell of it. Double crust with carrots and gravy, and spiced apple cake. All Sally's favourites. She stepped through the door. Charlie turned round from the cooker, wiping her hands. Ben looked up from the piece of wood that he was carving. They both smiled at her, their faces warm and glowing with love.

"I'm home," said Sally.

CHAPTER THIRTY-FOUR

Sally opened her eyes briefly. It was dawn. A clean shaft of light streamed through some papery curtains and illuminated the small child who stood looking at her. Dark, curly hair sprang around the child's beautiful, solemn face.

"Isabella?" whispered Sally.

"No," replied a woman's voice. "This is Linton. Linton Sinclair." Sally opened her eyes again. It was an effort; she was so overwhelmingly tired. She saw a woman sitting at her bedside. The woman regarded her with calm, intelligent eyes of a startling, light grey. Her skin was very pale, and her hair was thick, glossy and such a dark brown it was almost black. It tumbled around her shoulders in abundant waves. A thin scar, approximately two inches long, slashed across her right upper cheek.

"You are so beautiful," whispered Sally before falling asleep again.

The woman picked up her phone and dialled.

"She's here, Mac. Alive. I'm with her now."

"Has she woken up, Sinclair? Has she said anything?"

"She has a lot of medication on board. Just mentioned someone called Isabella. That's all."

"Isabella was her grandmother, I believe," said Mac. "Did she say anything else? Anything at all?" There was a pause, and then Sinclair said, with a hint of embarrassment.

"She told me I was beautiful."

"What?" said Mac disbelievingly.

"Beautiful," repeated Sinclair, watching Sally's sleeping face. Mac made a sound. Sinclair had never believed that people harrumphed, except in the wilder type of fiction books. But that is exactly the noise that Mac now made.

"You're right," he said. "She will be on a lot of medication."

"Is Hart there? And Morton?" demanded Mac. Sinclair's mouth pressed into a frown. She looked warily at the man who must be Ben Morton. He was sleeping in an uncomfortable-looking plastic chair on the other side of Sally's hospital bed. He'd slumped forward, over the edge of the bed, his hand reaching for Sally, his fingers grazing her right hand. She regarded his long auburn hair, worn, rough fingers, and shabby clothes. Morton certainly looked very different from his vain, obsessive, dead brother. A petite blonde woman lay curled on the bed at Sally's feet. She was dressed in blood-stained, blue satin pyjamas, but she looked for all the world like a small, faithful dog.

"They're here," Sinclair replied. "Asleep."

A drip stand, ablaze with pumps, bleeped and hummed. Fluid dripped slowly into the cannulas in Sally's arms. A catheter bag hung on the bed. At least her kidneys were working well, thought Sinclair. Sinclair had known plenty of soldiers who had gone into renal failure after hypovolaemic shock. This Marshall woman was made of stern stuff.

"Thanks, Sinclair," said Mac brusquely. "You can go. I'm on my way. I should be there within a couple of hours. Did you manage to get Linton to his grandparents?"

"No," she replied. "But it's okay. He's used to keeping Army hours." She cut the line before Mac started one of his lectures. She made a wry face. Wait until Mac was a single parent. And he was doing a perfect job. Then he could lecture her.

Sinclair stood to leave. She held a sleepy Linton by the hand. She looked again at Sally, so pale and vulnerable in the bed. Sinclair had never been called beautiful. Her father occasionally ruffled her hair and growled that she was his 'bonny lass.' Her mother quietly adored her, but her mother was a woman of few words. And Jordan? Jordan Linton had been her best friend. They had both been athletic and competitive, and loyal. He had been intelligent, with a fierce curiosity that drove him; however, he'd been crippled by the dyslexia that had thwarted his academic progress. He had stumbled, overwhelmed, over the words to describe his feelings for her. 'Reyt fit' had occasionally made it out of his mouth. So, 'beautiful?' Sinclair would take that.

Sinclair walked down the ward corridor towards the exit. The ward was coming to life, ready for another frantic day, and the Night Shift were getting everything in order to hand over to the Day Team. Sinclair passed a short, barrel-shaped, red-haired agency nurse. The woman was looking frantically through a handbag.

. . .

LIANNE FOUND HER MOBILE PHONE. She ignored the cries of the elderly woman in the side ward, who seemed to be bleeding. Lianne jabbed a number into the phone and waited impatiently. The phone was eventually answered.

"That doctor," began Lianne. "That little blonde doctor. The one you wanted watching? She's here. Now. With that other woman. I'm sure it's the woman you were asking about." Lianne peered through the door of Sally's room. "No. She's going under a different name," said Lianne in reply to a question. "She's really ill. She's going nowhere. Do I get my money now?"

IN HER DREAM, Sally was showing her daughter, Isabella, the pond that Ben had built for her in the walled garden of Rowans Holt.

"Big fish!" exclaimed Isabella excitedly, pointing to a flash of gold that twisted in the dark water.

"No, sweet pea, it's not a big fish," said Sally, smiling. "It's a very small pond. Sheffield is full of big fish. Big fish... and lone wolves." Sally looked up. A cloud had just passed over the sun. "Let's go in, darling. There's a storm coming."

THE BOSS WAS COUNTING MONEY. Notes were stacked in neat piles on the long metal trollies, but it wasn't enough for what Rosendale demanded. It was never enough. His phone rang. The Boss peered at it to see who was brave or stupid enough to call him so early. He saw who it was and answered it. He listened.

"You know what to do," he said, eventually. "If you think

they know about the Client. If he spoke to her, then you kill them. Kill them all."

BEN WOKE up to his phone buzzing. It was Mac. "Yeah?" he said blearily. His eyes anxiously roamed over Sally's sleeping face. Her skin looked tissue-thin, stretched over the bones of her skull.

"I'm on my way, Morton. How is she?"

"Stable, I think," replied Ben, shaking his head to clear it. "But, listen," Ben continued. "Charlie said that she thinks some of the staff in A and E are on to her. I'm worried, Mac. If this Boss finds out that man spoke to Charlie, that makes her a witness, doesn't it?" Mac didn't reply. Ben could hear him walking over gravel and opening a car door. "And if he thinks Charlie has told Sal, that puts her in danger, too." Ben lowered his voice. "Someone poisoned that man. Right in the hospital. To shut him up."

"You're in a different hospital, right?" said Mac. Ben heard the car engine starting.

"Yeah, we're in the Jessop Hospital," replied Ben. "And Charlie had the sense to give Sal a false name." Ben took Sally's limp hand and squeezed it tenderly. "I'll push to get her out of here as soon as I can," he said. "But she'll need a couple of days, at least. She almost died, Mac." Ben's voice faltered.

"One of us has to be with them at all times," said Mac. Do you understand, Morton?"

"Yeah," said Ben distractedly.

"I should be with you in ninety minutes," said Mac. The phone went dead.

There was a soft knock at the door. Miss Fletcher and Dr

Saanvi Ray came in. Charlie awoke and guiltily clambered off the bed. Miss Fletcher swiftly inspected the wound and Sally's observation chart. She seemed pleased with what she saw.

"She made a remarkable recovery once we stopped the bleed," she observed. Saanvi nodded, adjusting the pain-relieving infusion pump and IV fluids. She inspected Sally's skin and hands closely, looking for the tell-tale rash that could indicate a potentially fatal clotting derangement.

"I'll add a clotting test to this morning's bloods," Saanvi said. "And I'll hand over to the Day Team to keep a close eye on her." She moved closer to Charlie. "Your friend isn't out of the woods yet," she said quietly.

Miss Fletcher turned to Ben. "Are you Mr Foster?" she asked.

"Er..." said Ben, looking suddenly vulnerable.

"Yes!" piped up Charlie. "He's the father." Miss Fletcher looked uncomfortable.

"Sir, I'm very sorry for your loss," she said. "I'm sorry to tell you this," Fletcher continued. "But the embryo. Your baby. It could never have survived." Ben nodded his head. He understood about ectopic pregnancies. Fletcher continued. "I also have some bad news. We normally always send the embryo for examination. In case there's something wrong. Something that could affect future pregnancies or the mother's health." Ben nodded, wondering where this was going. Fletcher looked sideways at Saanvi. "Unfortunately, we've been unable to locate the sample pot containing the embryo. We'll do everything we can to locate it. Maybe an error was made. It could be lost. In clinical waste. On behalf of the Trust, I offer my apologies."

Behind Miss Fletcher, Ben spotted Charlie. She was

rolling her eyes down to her bag, slouched on the floor by Sally's bed. He thought he understood.

"It's okay!" announced Ben. He held up his hands. "You saved my wife's life. I can never thank you enough. These things happen." Miss Fletcher looked both surprised and relieved.

"Thank you. But if you decide you wish to make a formal complaint, then...."

"No!" said Ben decisively. "That won't happen. And thank you." He looked down at Sally. "From the bottom of our hearts."

Fletcher nodded her head. Dark lines smudged under her eyes. She still had hours to go before her work was done. She turned and walked wearily out.

"What have you done? You took the embryo?" hissed Ben, aghast, to Charlie.

"We don't know what she'll want to do!" whispered Charlie. "And she's here under a false name and address. How can she possibly come back and claim it? I took matters into my own hands." Ben was overwhelmed. A second lost child.

"I need some air!" he said.

Ben stepped out into the corridor and headed to the main ward door. He stepped out into the corridor for a moment. And saw him; dressed in scrubs, with a rucksack over his shoulder, looking at his mobile phone. Steve. Ben's heart felt as if it slowed and crashed in his chest. Steve, the man who had his woman, his wife. Becky would be his wife forever. No piece of paper could ever cancel the vows Ben had made with his heart. Steve, the man who was crushing Becky like an insect beneath his unfeeling heel. Ben ducked back into the ward and hurried to Sally's room. Charlie sat at

Sally's side, smoothing the hair from her forehead and talking to her gently. Ben made a decision.

"Charlie!" he said urgently. "It's Steve." Charlie's face looked puzzled, but then she realised what he meant.

"But, Sally..." Charlie said. Ben shook his head.

"Don't worry. Mac's on his way. He'll be here in an hour. Nothing's going to happen in an hour! I'm going to follow the bastard. It's what Sally would want." Ben didn't give Charlie the chance to reply. He hurried from the room, tucking his phone into his pocket. Charlie was alone.

Charlie slumped into the chair again. They all seemed to have forgotten that Charlie was also two units of blood short. It had been one of the longest nights that she could remember. And she had known some long and terrible nights. Charlie laid her head down on the bed. She held on tightly to Sally's left hand. She slept.

SALLY WAS READING Isabella a bedtime story. Her daughter was snuggled in her arms, smelling warm and clean after her bath. Sally was enjoying herself, doing all the different voices.

"And the little pig said, 'Not by the hair on my chinny chin chin! I will not let you in!'" said Sally. Isabella wriggled in terrified excitement. She turned to her mother.

"Is it to do with the bluebells?" she asked, looking up at Sally.

"What bluebells?" said Sally, stroking Isabella's soft, beautiful, curly hair.

"The ones on your grave," said Isabella conversationally. Sally's hand froze.

“What? What did you say?” she asked, feeling as if she’d been punched in the stomach.

“The bluebells on your grave!” Isabella repeated. She wriggled out of bed and led Sally to the window. The little girl pointed dramatically. “Bluebells! On. Your. Grave!”

Sally looked out of her window into the walled garden. A fresh grave had been dug amongst the tangled beds. There was no gravestone, but the whole of the turned earth was flooded with a mass of bluebells. Except, the nodding heads were not covered in flowers. Where each tiny flower should have been was a small, blue tablet.

“Bluebells,” breathed Sally. “Code Blue. The Boss knows we’re looking for it.”

Isabella spoke again. She looked intently up at Sally.

“Gabella says to tell you. You and Charlie are all, all alone. There is no one. And The Big Bad Wolf is coming.”

CHAPTER THIRTY-FIVE

Sally awoke, gasping. Like a half-drowned woman, she heaved air into her lungs. Her heart was pounding like a sledgehammer against her ribs.

"Isabella? Isabella!" she shouted. Charlie shot awake and grappled for Sally's hand.

"Sally, Sally! I'm here. It's OK! You're in the hospital. You've been really, really sick."

"Isabella? Where's my baby?" cried Sally. Morphine, blood loss and a body pushed to the limits of its endurance pulled her mind to the edge of sanity.

"Oh, God! Sally. The baby's gone. You lost the baby." Sally looked at Charlie as if she didn't recognise her. Charlie stroked Sally's hand and spoke gently to her.

"I'm here, Sally. I'm here. It's all going to be okay." Sally's eyes cleared, but her face remained crowded with fear and anxiety.

"The Big Bad Wolf. He's coming, Charlie. We have to get out of here."

"No. It's okay," said Charlie. "I gave a false name. They don't know you're here." Sally shook her head slowly.

"You don't understand," she whispered. "They do know. I saw bluebells. The Boss knows you spoke to the man. He knows..."

Charlie looked at the call button. Should she call the nurse? She looked at the Drug Chart.

"Are you in pain, Sal? Do you feel sick? I can ask the nurse for something... No, Stop!" Sally had started pulling frantically at the cannula in her left arm, peeling the dressing away, trying to detach it. "Sal!" Charlie cried, scared now. This was clearly post-operative delirium, very common after major surgery. Sally looked up at her. She seemed less dazed now.

"Listen to me, Charlie. It's not just a dream. My grandmother was... special. Gabella was never wrong. You and I are in danger. We have to leave. Now."

Charlie was at a loss. The whole of Sally's world seemed like a bizarre fantasy at the best of times. Charlie felt as though reality was slipping sideways and crazily out of reach.

"What are you going to do, Charlie?" asked Sally intently. Her mouth was set in a hard line. A crease had appeared on her forehead that Charlie recognised. Sally was going to leave, either with her help or without it. What was Charlie going to do? Call the nurse to sedate her, put her under a Section 5(2)? What if Sally was right? But how could Sally know anything? She'd been unconscious for hours.

As Charlie hesitated, Sally briskly pulled the cannula in her left arm completely free. Blood started to flow. With a cry, Charlie pulled up the side of the white sheet and applied pressure to the wound. Sally glared up at her.

"We HAVE to go. Now!" Sally declared. Charlie made up her mind. She would have to play along. For now. And if Sally collapsed or got sick, she would bring her back. But in the back of Charlie's mind, a little voice sang; *Who's afraid of the Big Bad Wolf? tra la la la la...* Sally was pulling at the cannula dressing in her right arm now.

"Stop!" ordered Charlie. "Do not pull that cannula out. I'll get a proper dressing. And a wheelchair." Sally glared at her but then nodded. Sitting up abruptly, Sally pulled off her sheet and swung her legs out of the right side of the bed. Sally's face drained of all colour, as Charlie had known it would. She collapsed back onto the bed, barely conscious.

How on earth are we going to do this? Thought Charlie. Sally clutched the sheets with her right hand and pushed herself upright with her left hand. Her face was paler than Charlie had thought possible, but her eyes gradually cleared. Her breathing was rapid and shallow.

"I think I might be sick," she muttered. Charlie pushed a vomit bowl into Sally's hands. This was not going well.

"I'll be back in a minute," she said.

Charlie walked into the corridor. Shafts of bright, early morning sunlight sliced across the passageway, dissecting it into neat portions of light and dark. The smell of toast wafted from the ward kitchen. The nurses were closeted away in handover and the ward was silent. Charlie walked down the corridor, looking for the clinical room. She needed a small plastic hub so she could detach Sally's remaining drip and leave the cannula in Sally's arm. *For when we need to come back*, Charlie thought darkly. She also needed a dressing. Charlie glanced into the four-room bays as she passed them. The women occupying the beds were a mixture of planned and emergency cases: infections through to cancer.

Most of them still slept; however, some lay, looking up at the ceiling, perhaps engaged in sad contemplation of their own mortality.

There was a persistent buzzing at the ward door. Charlie carried on, looking for the clinical room. She passed the crash trolley. Someone had left a cardboard tray resting on it. It was filled with equipment for cannulation and Charlie triumphantly grabbed a small plastic hub in its sterile packet. A care assistant slowly approached the empty nursing station.

"G1 Ward," she stated flatly into the intercom.

"I'm here for Mrs Foster," came an unfamiliar man's voice. "I'm Mr Foster. Will you let me in?"

OUTSIDE G1, the man waited impatiently for someone to answer the intercom. He frowned at the delay. Where were the stupid bitches? Didn't they know he was in a hurry?

"G1 Ward," came a tired voice. Like an infected faucet springing to fusty life, he turned on his charm.

"I'm here for Mrs Foster," he said smoothly. "I'm Mr Foster. Will you let me in?" He grasped the cheap flowers he had stolen from a sleeping man outside a different ward, holding them before him like a solemn and sacred offering. The buzzer sounded, and he went in. The ward was quiet. He scanned the corridor, trying to grasp the ward layout. He quietly moved to the nurses' station and surveyed the names on the whiteboard. Foster wasn't there. He cursed the incompetence of the night staff. He then started looking for empty spaces in the room allocations. Side rooms four and sixteen seemed to be empty. She was probably in one of those.

. . .

CHARLIE SCRABBLED AROUND, putting the brakes on the cheap wheelchair she had found in the corridor.

"He's here. The Bad Wolf is here!" she whispered to Sally. Charlie's eyes were wide and fearful. Sally heaved herself into the wheelchair, grimacing in pain. Charlie's hands shook as she detached the drip and screwed the hub onto the cannula. She ripped open the package of a 10 ml syringe and lifted back Sally's hospital gown, searching between Sally's legs.

"Sorry, Hon," she breathed. "But this has to come out. Sometimes, there's no dignity to being a woman... and we're travelling light." Charlie drew back 10 mls of water, and Sally hissed as Charlie briskly removed her urinary catheter. Charlie lifted her work bag onto her shoulders. She opened the door and peered out into the corridor. She was too late! There he stood, a man looking up at the name board. His head was hidden by a baseball cap and the cheap bunch of flowers he held up in his right hand. Charlie scanned the room in a panic. Where could they hide?

THE MAN TURNED and approached Room Four with a pace like a cat stalking a wounded bird. He paused outside the room and listened. There was no noise from within. He knocked. No reply. *Little pig, little pig...* he thought, and a thin smile played at his lips. He cautiously pushed the door open. The man slipped round the door, his hand reaching inside his jacket for his gun. He stood regarding the empty room. A window was open and a fresh breeze jostled and pulled at the papery curtains. He listened. He bent smartly and looked under the bed. And then he heard it. The faint, plaintive bleep of an infusion-pump alarm. It was coming from the large cupboard embedded in the wall to the left of the bed. Holding his gun upright in his right hand, he gently touched the cupboard handle with his left. The man paused, savouring the moment. He imagined them, eyes widening as they saw him. He threw the door open; his body turned to the side in case someone tried to aim a weak, defensive blow at him. The cupboard was empty, except for a stand, a flaccid catheter bag and two naked drips, both still leaking their lucent, slow medicinal sap.

The man stalked out of Room Four. He had seen nothing of anyone on the hospital corridors on his way here. They were probably still here. He hurried to the end of the ward and then began methodically working his way back down. He glanced down the fire escape stairs and then into each room as he went, always keeping an eye on the corridor. Side Room Sixteen was empty. The four-bedded rooms were each scanned as he made his efficient progress back towards the Nurses' Station. He looked into the final four-bedded room. An old woman lay, sleeping, her watery mouth hanging slackly open, a high, nasal snore echoing with each indrawn breath. A woman who was clearly a drug addict lay on her side, facing the door, reading. Her thin hair was dyed an unlikely shade of black, and cheap tattoos smeared her wrinkled arms. One of these arms was attached to a drip. The cannula was heavily bandaged. Her veins were so weak and damaged, if that cannula was blocked, they were unlikely to get another one in. A very large South Asian woman lay flat on her back. A black eye mask covered half of her waxy face, and fluffy slippers in the shape of ducklings lay by the bedside. An emaciated cancer patient lay with her back to him, one of the distinctive caps to hide hair loss covering her head. The drug addict looked him up and down without expression.

"If you wanna see any more, you'll have to pay, Luv," she drawled before returning to her magazine.

The man was icy with rage. Where were they? He looked into the room where the nurses were still crammed in handover. They must be hiding in one of the clinical rooms. He slid over to the locked clinical room door. He peered through the small window and squinted at each quadrant as best he could. There was no sign of anyone. Well, he wasn't taking his eye off the front door. They were only getting out of here through him or in a body bag.

CHARLIE CROUCHED on the other side of the clinical room door. She heard the door handle being tried. She held her breath. Could he hear her? She thought of a wolf. Could he smell her? She closed her eyes. The handle stopped turning. She waited for at least a minute and then felt she could breathe again. She slid onto the floor and peered under the door edge. There was no one standing on the other side. He'd moved on. For now. Charlie thanked her lucky stars that the code to the door had still been written in biro down the side of the doorjamb. Just as it had been years ago when she'd worked here on her Obs and Gynae rotation.

Charlie unslung her bag and grabbed her phone. She punched at Ben's name. The phone started ringing, but he didn't answer. Charlie's throat clenched in panic. Mac was still at least an hour away and driving. She called 999. The phone rang, and an answerphone came on.

"We are experiencing a large number of calls at the

moment. If you are experiencing a life-threatening emergency, do not put the phone down." Charlie ended the call. They were all, all alone. Panicking, she scrolled down her contacts list and saw Decker's number. She almost sobbed in relief. She pressed the number and prayed that he would answer. He'd be able to mobilise help.

Outside the clinical room door, in the corridor, she heard a mobile phone start to ring. The phone stopped ringing. A voice answered both on her phone and outside simultaneously.

"Decker..." Charlie couldn't breathe, couldn't speak. There was a long silence. "Is that Doctor Hart?" said Decker. Charlie could hear his voice clearly from outside. "Where are you, love?" said Decker softly. Charlie ended the call. She clutched the phone, her hand dripping with cold sweat. It had been Decker all along, working for the gang. 'Trust no one, Charlie,' he'd said. And now he'd come to kill her. Charlie dried her hands on her pyjamas and looked desperately around the small clinical room. Her eyes fell on the shelves opposite.

Decker remained standing by the Nurses' Station. He slipped his phone back into his pocket. They were still here. Hart and Marshall were still here. He'd arrest both of them and get them alone as soon as possible. As soon as the useless women emerged from the handover, he'd organise a full search of the ward. He saw a doctor in scrubs, and a blue satin headscarf approach the notes trolley and rifle through the paperwork. He approached her.

"Excuse me," he said smoothly.

"No!" snapped the doctor in a broad Yorkshire accent,

not turning round. "I've just come on the ward. No, I don't know any of the patients. And no, I can't get a commode for one of your relatives. Ask a nurse!" She walked off briskly into the side ward, carrying a pile of notes with her. Decker's hands flexed. He imagined what it would feel like to thread his hands around that woman's arrogant little neck and twist...

The druggie woman shuffled out of the side room, pulling her drip stand dismally after her. She disappeared down the corridor, looking for a free bathroom.

He would give it one more minute, and then he would break up the handover. Not wanting too many people to see him was the only thing stopping him. He folded his arms and went to stand against the ward door. They would have to break cover.

A loud alarm sounded, high and urgent. The door to the handover room burst open, and the corridor suddenly boiled with nursing staff.

"Crash alarm, room sixteen!" the nurse in charge cried. They hared down the corridor. Decker smiled. He knew for a fact that room sixteen was empty. They were trying to create a distraction. Any minute now, they'd appear. *Come to Daddy*, he thought.

Suddenly, a skinny, hard hand was pulling at him. He jerked away in disgust and saw the druggie woman next to him.

"Quick, mate!" she said. "You the husband of that woman they brought in overnight? I've found her, collapsed in the toilets! Blood all over her belly. Her mate's there too, in hysterics...." Decker's heart leapt in triumph. He followed Druggie as she scurried to the end of the corridor, pulling her teetering drip stand after her. She occasionally paused to catch her crack-raddled breath. She flung open a door with a flourish. “There!” she said, pointing. The toilet was empty.

Druggie hit herself dramatically on the forehead. “What am I thinking? It’s the other one!” She beetled a little way back up the corridor. “I’m sure it’s this one,” she muttered, glancing slyly over her shoulder at him. A small, knowing smile played around her emaciated lips. And that was when he realised. The doctor had not come out of the sideward. The crash alarm had gone off, but that doctor had not responded—the short doctor with the blue satin head-scarf. Charlie Hart and Sally Marshall had escaped. But not for long. Decker set off at a run.

CHAPTER THIRTY-SIX

Charlie ran. In front of her, Sally was slumped in the wheelchair, her breathing once again rapid and shallow. But they were alive. Charlie knew all about animosity, all about focussed rage. All about violence. You develop a nose for it. You learn when to keep totally and utterly still. And you learn when to run.

When the man had arrived on G1 Ward, Charlie had opened the cupboard in Room Four, only to realise that trying to hide there was ridiculous. She'd instinctively pushed the drip stand into it, along with the now-useless catheter bag. Returning to the door, she peered around it. The man was still at the whiteboard but was now craning round to look at the Nurse handover room. Charlie had taken a deep breath. She slipped out of the door, pushing Sally ahead of her, and slid into the four-bedded ward next door. With her foot, she closed the door gently behind her. The first bed on the right was empty. *Perhaps the best place to hide is in plain sight*, she thought.

A woman with tattoos and nicotine-stained fingers was looking at them curiously.

"Her ex has turned up!" whispered Charlie, nodding towards Sally. "She was pregnant with someone else's kid. If he catches her, he'll kill her!" The tattooed woman nodded sagely. *Wasn't that always the way*? thought Mandy Bradshaw; addict, actor, survivor. *They always got mad when they caught you jigging with someone else.*

"Help yourself," she said, indicating the unmade bed. "She just left. Said if she wasn't going to get any sleep, she might as well get no sleep at home." Mandy lowered her voice dramatically. "Cancer... only weeks to live, they reckon." Charlie nodded but only had limited sympathy. It could be that she and Sally only had minutes to live.

Charlie helped Sally onto the bed. Sally sank down gratefully.

"Turn your back from the door," whispered Charlie. She looked around, desperate for something to disguise her friend. A hat lay on the floor, half concealed by the bed. It was one of the flowery turbans women often wore to disguise their hair loss following chemotherapy. Charlie slipped it onto Sally's head. Sally didn't protest; she felt too weak to do anything except breathe. Charlie crouched down by Mandy's bed.

"If a man comes in, please, don't tell him anything."

"It's alright, Duck," replied Mandy with a wry grin. "Been there, done that, bought the chuffin' t-shirt!" Charlie mustered a smile and then ran quietly to the door.

She edged it open and put her eye to the slim space. Her

heart crashed as she saw a man, head down, peaked cap low on his face, emerge from Room Four and slip, like an agile animal, down the ward. His back was turned. Charlie had to hide, too. She'd finally remembered where the Clinical Room was. If she were lucky, she'd be able to get in. Charlie slipped round the door and scurried up the corridor, expecting a hand to crash down on her shoulder at any moment. Charlie pressed against the door as if she could somehow push herself through the wood and glass. She scanned the doorframe.

"Where is it? Where is it?" she whispered. And there it was, written in black biro to the left of the door frame: cz1815. Charlie pushed the code in with trembling fingers. Behind her, she heard a laconic voice say,

"If you wanna see any more, you'll have to pay, Luv". He was in the room! Charlie crept round the door, closed it as quietly as she could, and then crouched down. Charlie looked around her. On the shelf opposite was a collection of scrubs.

A FEW MINUTES LATER, Charlie confidently strode down the corridor, heading for the notes trolley. After calling Decker and realising his betrayal, she had tremblingly changed into the random scrubs she'd found in the clinical room and, using her satin pyjamas, had fashioned a headscarf to hide her face and hair. From the corner of her eye, Charlie saw the figure of Decker watching her. Inside, she quailed. Charlie turned her back to him and started scanning through the notes. Foster, where was Foster? At last, she spotted them, Foster, E. However, as her hand closed on the buff-coloured documents, she heard his voice right behind her, and she almost jumped in terror.

"Excuse me?" He breathed. He was so close he could touch her, grab her, pull her slowly apart. Charlie's mind plunged and foundered. A tiny part of her remained bobbing above the dark deluge of panic. *What would Sara Hadid say*? Charlie opened her mouth and snapped, as brusquely and assertively as she could, in the broadest Yorkshire accent she could muster;

"No! I've just come on the ward. No, I don't know any of the patients. And no, I can't get a commode for one of your relatives. Ask a nurse!" Without turning round, Charlie grabbed a handful of random notes and stalked, regally, into the side-ward where Sally lay.

Charlie stood with her back against the door, waiting for him to pile after her. She found herself counting. She reached twenty. Maybe she'd bought some time. But now they were trapped in here. How were they going to get out?

"How are you going to get out?" drawled Mandy, as if reading Charlie's mind. She was slowly flicking through a battered copy of Hello magazine. All the featured people were smiling and laughing happily, without a care in the world. Charlie felt as if they were mocking her.

"What's wrong, Luv?" asked a soft voice. Charlie looked over to see that the large woman had removed her eye mask and was looking at her.

"Wife beater on the prowl," said Mandy, still not looking up from her magazine.

"It's a bad man," said Charlie helplessly. "He wants to hurt my friend. I need to get her away. But I need..." her heart sank as she realised what she needed. "I need pain killers. And antibiotics...."

• • •

FATIMA BAIG WAS MARRIED to a very nice man. Her marriage had been arranged, as was traditional and proper, but her mother and Ali's mother had been good friends. The match had been considered a good one, for Ali was kind and clever and gentle. He was a loving father to their two children; he would cook on Saturdays and insist Fatima put her feet up. Ali admired his wife and that she was a respected teacher. He would hold her in his arms at night, and they would whisper, so as not to disturb the little ones, and then they would giggle. Ali would stroke Fatima's skin, which felt as soft and sacred as velvet peach blossom, and he would wonder at the blessings that had given him such a princess of a wife. And then he would tell her each one of these thoughts and feelings.

Fatima Baig's stepfather had not been a nice man. She had watched as he had beaten her mother. Ruthlessly. Without mercy, always avoiding the face and lower arms. He had kept a special stick, which he had stored, oiled and eager, on the top of the china cabinet. He'd called it Kaat. He had treated his stick with far more respect than his wife. And, when Fatima's big sister had become a woman, he had started to visit her room at night, the room that she shared with Fatima. Just to talk, he would whisper softly. Just to sit quietly for a little while. Just to have a little look. Just a tiny touch. Just... here.

Fatima, her mother, and her sister would never talk about his death. His terrible accident. What a sad way to die, everyone at the mosque had said. Alone and cold at the bottom of the stairs. He must have fallen on his stick, everyone at the mosque had said. Heavily. For it was broken into so many, many pieces. No. Fatima Baig's stepfather had not been a nice man.

"Take my medicine!" said Fatima decisively. She heaved herself out of bed and slipped her feet into her duckling slippers. Ali had bought them for her when they had learned she was to have surgery for her fibroids. Fatima marched to her locked metal medicine cabinet and turned the key. "I got a bit of an infection. They gave me antibiotics and painkillers to take home today." She turned to Charlie; her TTO medications held out in her hand. Charlie felt her tired eyes filling with tears at this unexpected kindness. She opened the paper bag. Co-Amoxiclav and Co-Codamol. Perfect. She looked up at Fatima.

"Thank you," she whispered.

"Don't let the bastards grind you down!" Fatima instructed. "I'm a teacher. It's my motto!" Charlie smiled weakly. "I also know what men are capable of," added Fatima grimly. She waddled over to the door and peeked through. "Is it the mean-looking git standing at the ward door?" she asked.

"I suppose doing something sensible like just calling the Police is out of the question?" asked a brisk voice behind them. They looked around. The old woman in the bed opposite Sally was sitting up. She was putting on a neat pair of steel-rimmed glasses. Sally turned her tired head and looked her in the eye.

"It's complicated...." Sally said softly.

"Domestic violence always is, in my experience!" snipped the old woman.

Doctor Phillipa Davies could give Sara Hadid a run for her money when it came to brusqueness. The retired GP had not been known for her bedside manner, but she had been hardworking and efficient. She had carried on working until a few weeks ago, in fact. However, she was now beginning to suspect that her lifelong belief in mind-over-matter was losing out to the ovarian cancer that had so cruelly and silently seeded itself throughout her belly. "I assume she has capacity?" demanded Phillipa of Charlie. Sally became angry and raised her head off her pillow.

"Yes! 'She' has capacity," she replied sharply.

"So. Do we call the Police?" Phillipa repeated impatiently.

"He is the Police," said Sally. There was a long pause as the three women took this information in.

"Well then. Someone is going to have to distract him!" said Phillipa. She looked around her. "Come along, ladies! We need to make a decision. And quickly! I would go...if I could walk. However, I can't. So, it has to be someone else."

"Don't look at me!" laughed Mandy. Her laugh turned into a wheezy cough. "Not for all the tea in China!" she gasped.

Charlie looked down at her right hand. At the beautiful gift Sally had pressed on her when they'd got drunk together all those weeks ago.

"But I'll never wear it!" Sally had laughed. "I've never wanted to look like a Princess." Charlie had been trying it on before she went to bed last night. She had loved the sparkle, so she had kept it on her finger.

"I don't have any tea," she said to Mandy. "But how do you feel about pink-diamond rings?"

AND NOW CHARLIE RAN. In front of her, Sally struggled to keep all the items that Charlie had acquired on her lap. As well as Fatima's medications and Sally's notes, Charlie had ripped open the crash trolley and helped herself to bags of fluid, an intravenous line, and the entire emergency drug box. Sally was hiding the hoard under the blanket that covered her knees. Charlie sped past the big lifts in the central space of the tall building that was the Hallamshire Hospital.

"Charlie!" muttered Sally. "There's no way I can make the stairs."

"Trust me," snapped Charlie.

Charlie scuttered round a corner and headed for the small staff lift hidden away to the rear of the building. It led down, past the Medical library, deep into the hidden basement of the building. She smacked her hand on the call button and stood, sweating and anxious, jigging from foot to foot, and repeatedly looking behind her. The lift was almost there. She then heard a dull boom from the direction of G1 ward. The doors had been flung back with great force. He was coming.

DECKER LOOKED INTENTLY at the main lifts. There was a lift on the eighteenth floor, which was on its way down, and a lift on the ground floor. The women were only seconds ahead of him; they would have had no time to get a lift down. They must have run elsewhere. There was no way the Marshall woman was walking. Decker ran with surprising grace around the area. The door to the laboratories on the back corridor was locked. The ward opposite to G1 was closed for redecoration and also locked firmly. He set off down the staff corridor and pulled up short at the sight of a small lift shaft. The lift was travelling down. As he watched, it reached the basement. It stayed there. Decker smiled. He bet Charlie Hart had wedged the lift door open. Bless her. It seemed almost a pity that he had to kill her. Decker headed for the stairs.

CHARLIE RAN DOWN THE LONG, echoing corridor that linked the Hallamshire hospital to the Medical School. She remembered using this corridor as a spooky shortcut in her student days. The dim lights flickered, and deep booming noises from hidden machinery rose and fell in the gloom. She heard her breath coming in ragged gasps. Far behind her, she again heard a low crash from a door thrown open. She glanced over her shoulder. Down the grey length of the passage, she saw the figure of a man stride after them, his pace lengthening and quickening as he came. Charlie whimpered. She reached the door leading to the Medical School stairwell, turned her back to it, and pushed through, pulling Sally's wheelchair after her. Sally looked dully at the fast-approaching figure and her fingers clutched reflexively at the objects on her knee.

Charlie ran to the lift. Once they were on the ground floor, they stood a chance. People would be around; *witnesses*, she thought. Charlie slowed and looked in disbelief at the lift shaft. Its call light was dark. A piece of tape lay limply across the doors. The lift was out of order. Charlie looked up at the stairs stretching endlessly above her, from the dusty dark lino floor filled with discarded cleaning equipment to the lighter upper levels. She slipped her arm under Sally's shoulder and desperately pulled her up. Sally staggered next to her but collapsed after the first stair. She lay panting, her eyes rolling. Charlie scrabbled desperately through the resuscitation drugs, her hands shaking and trembling. He was coming; the Big Bad Wolf was coming!

CHAPTER THIRTY-SEVEN

Charlie grabbed a syringe of adrenaline. This was only ever given intravenously in a cardiac arrest, to a fatally stalled heart, or by a consultant anaesthetist under carefully supervised conditions. She pulled back her scrubs sleeve to reveal her cannula, which she had forgotten about until now. She injected a small amount of the drug into the vein. Charlie drew a huge breath as her heart crashed and thundered in her chest, and she felt a massive wave of nervous, tremulous energy fill her limbs. She heaved Sally up eight stairs, grunting at the effort. The resuscitation box swung open in Sally's failing hand, and most of the drugs, needles and syringes clattered down the way they had come.

Charlie's drug-induced strength left her as abruptly as it had come, and she felt sick and faint. Her heart pattered, irregular and stuttering. She lay beside Sally on the first narrow landing, exhausted, anaemic, hopeless. Charlie looked at the syringe of adrenaline that lay in her hand. She'd expelled most of it as she had frantically dragged Sally.

There was just enough for one more dose. Charlie looked up at the remaining stairs and shook her head. She would never do it. She could never drag Sally up these stairs in time. Or go down and carry the wheelchair up. Sally looked at her.

"You go, Charlie," she whispered. Her lips were white, and her head lolled on her outstretched arms. Something twisted sinuously inside Charlie's head.

"Turn to me, listen to me," it whispered. "I can help you go, help you survive. She's dying, she's weak. Leave her. You can carry you and me to safety." Without thinking, Charlie once again pushed the thing away and down into the dark. Once again, she forgot.

"I won't leave you here," sobbed Charlie.

"It's OK, Charlie, you can go. Peter's waiting for me," breathed Sally. "And Gabella...." She smiled. "And my Isabella." Sally closed her eyes. Sally felt Charlie's hands close around the neck of her hospital gown.

"Sal!" Charlie called hoarsely. Sally felt her body being shaken with a new sense of desperation. "Sally, no. What if it's Emily waiting for me? What if it's only Emily?"

DECKER PUSHED CAUTIOUSLY at the door. He couldn't see the women through the small square of fire glass, just a spilt wheelchair, a blanket, and scattered syringes. He stepped through the door and looked to his left, up the stairs. Sally Marshal lay, collapsed, on a small landing above him. Charlie Hart sat with her back against the bannister, pale-faced and chest heaving. Decker slowly mounted the stairs, his gun held loosely and confidently in his hand. There would be no surprises. Not taking his eyes from Charlie, he felt the cold neck of the Marshall woman who lay, her hands curled beneath her. Her pulse was barely detectable. She would be dead soon. Charlie looked at him, wide-eyed, like a rabbit in the headlights of an uncaring, unstoppable vehicle. Decker crouched down before her.

"Have you come to kill us?" asked Charlie in a small voice. Decker looked sad.

"I told you, Charlie," he said. "I told you not to trust me. Not to trust anyone." He glanced down at Sally. "You women. It's like you want it to happen. You want us to hurt you." He raised his gun and pointed it at her. "Still giving yourself away to anyone and everyone, Charlie?" Decker shook his head. "See? It only leads to trouble. Now, get up. You're going to come back into the corridor with me. I've found a room. I'll make it quick. Because I like you, Charlie." He smiled. "We're friends."

Charlie didn't get up. She slowly held up her empty hands.

"Have you come to kill us?" she repeated. "I need to hear you say it." Decker leaned closer to Charlie.

"Yes, sweetheart," he said. "I've come to kill you." Decker's grin widened. *No surprises*, he thought.

"In that case, you're right. I'm trouble," said Charlie, her voice low, as if she wanted just him to hear. "More trouble than you could ever imagine." Decker's face fell. "Now!" said Charlie loudly. There was the slightest of movements from Sally's hands. It looked like she was injecting something into the cannula in her arm. She then pulled in a massive sobbing breath and sat up abruptly. Sally had injected herself with the last dregs of adrenaline. In her hand, held like a knife, was a syringe with a large, green needle. She plunged the syringe deep into Decker's neck, and her thumb pushed hard on the plunger. Decker's eyes bulged. Charlie flung herself at his gun hand, and he felt her teeth sink deep into the flesh of his wrist. But that didn't matter. Inside his chest, his heart had come to an abrupt and shuddering halt. The muscles could no longer beat, the electrical signals could no longer pass through the delicate membranes. He had been given a massive dose of potassium.

Decker staggered upright. He tried to pull air into his lungs. His heart muscle started screaming in his chest, crying out for oxygen. He felt a deep, pushing and intense pain in the front of his chest. It spread up his neck and into his left arm. Decker knew no more.

Sally awoke. Her body was jerking rhythmically. Her heels bumped slowly, and she felt a scraping over her back. Charlie had hooked the blanket under her arms and was tugging her, stair by stair, upwards. She couldn't see Charlie but could hear her panting and muttering.

"I won't leave you here. I won't leave you here!" Sally looked back at the stairwell. There was no sign of Decker and no sign of the drug box or its contents. The world went dark again.

Sally awoke again. Charlie had retrieved the wheelchair and was bending close to Sally, trying to pick her up. Sally made all the effort she could to stand, but her limbs refused to work for some reason. Charlie squatted down. She grabbed Sally under her arms and gently lifted her. Sally's head nestled into the crook of Charlie's neck. Charlie smelled of honey and roses and freshly cut grass.

"Personal space," muttered Sally.

"I'll give you personal space, Sally Marshall," growled Charlie, finally getting Sally into the wheelchair. She retrieved the blanket and used it to cover the intravenous line and fluids, which she placed on Sally's knee. Charlie smoothed back her hair and took a deep breath. Charlie rested a hand on Sally's shoulder, and Sally felt Charlie's hands tremble and falter. Sally reached up and gently stroked Charlie's fingers.

"Don't let the bastards grind you down," Sally said.

JOE TOTLEY RUBBED a hand over his tired eyes. It had been a long night, but his shift was almost finished. He'd been a security guard at the Royal Hallamshire Hospital for nearly twenty-five years. Twelve of those years had been spent overseeing the Medical School. The students came and went. He saw them arrive as eager young things and, five years later, with more gravitas, graduate to be doctors. Most of them paid him no heed. He was just an old man to them; no better than a servant. He shook his head. Some of them were so arrogant. And some of them were so kind. Like Dr Hart. Charlie Hart. She'd learned his name almost in her first week at Medical School. She'd asked him the way to the library and, two minutes later, she'd known not just the library's location but the name of his wife, son, daughter, and dogs. And that he was a lifelong Sheffield Wednesday supporter. Well, he lived in Hillsborough. What else was a man to do?

Joe rubbed his eyes again. Speak of the Devil! He stood up. Dr Hart had emerged from the corridor that led to the basement. She was pushing a very unwell-looking patient in a rickety wheelchair. She must have come through the tunnels, past the Mortuary and up into this building.

"Dr Hart!" he exclaimed. She looked dazed, as if she was struggling to focus her eyes. She looked scared. He walked hurriedly from behind his desk and approached the two women.

"Joe?" said Charlie. He saw her lips were pale. What on earth was going on?

"Joe. I have to get this lady home," said Charlie, faintly. "Can you call us a taxi? Joe hesitated.

"Are you all right, Dr Hart?" he asked, gently. He looked down at Sally. "I'm sorry, Dr Hart, but I think this woman looks much too sick to go home." He glanced at Sally's hospital wristband. "Is it G1 ward she's from, Gynaecology? I'll give them a ring for you and ask them to keep her bed."

Joe moved behind his desk and picked up his phone. Joe knew all the ward extension numbers by heart. He dialled. The phone on G1 rang. A hand crashed down on the phone and it went dead. Joe recoiled. Dr Hart: friendly, smiling, gentle Dr Hart stood glaring at him. Her face was like thunder.

"No!" she hissed. There was silence. Joe wondered if he needed to call for backup. His eyes slid to the emergency button. Charlie spoke, low and urgent.

"It's her Ex." Joe looked back at Charlie. Only three words, but he understood what she meant.

Joe's daughter, Tina, had had a rough time a few years ago, back when Mary, his wife, had still been alive. Tina had moved in with a man from Fox Hill. She'd become pale and distant. She'd stopped laughing. And then Joe had seen a bruise on her upper arm. She'd pulled her T-shirt hurriedly down over her skin, made light of it. But he and Mary had known. Joe and some of the lads had gone round there when Tina was out; had brought their pool cues. Asked him if he wanted a game, Sheffield style? That relationship hadn't lasted.

Joe nodded at Charlie but stood his ground. He took his responsibilities to the Hospital and its patients seriously.

"I'll get the lads and lasses to guard the ward. They won't let the joker anywhere near her. But that woman needs to be in a hospital bed," he said firmly. Joe reached for the phone again, keeping his eye on Charlie and raising one warning hand at her.

This was terrible, thought Charlie. What could she say to make him help them? Make him realise how dangerous the men they faced were? She remembered Joe's blue, battered Land Rover Defender. It had always had a sticker on the rear window declaring *I love German Shepherds,* along with a picture of a winsome-looking German Shepherd puppy.

"He killed her dog!" blurted Charlie. Joe paused.

"He did what?" he breathed.

"He killed her dog!" repeated Charlie. "He hanged it. In the dark, outside her house. Her German Shepherd." Joe recoiled in shock. Charlie cringed inside. She had told more lies in the last twelve hours than she had in her entire life. But this was Sally's life at stake.

Charlie could see she needed just a bit more emotional connection. What had the names of Joe's dogs been? She cast around in her memory and was inspired.

"He killed Jarvis in cold blood!" she continued. "And I'm scared he'll bide his time and come for her. We need to get out of here, but we need some help. Please, Joe." Joe looked at her. He thought about poor Jarvis. Jarvis: Joe could see him now, full of fun and lively energy. A bit cheeky, but loyal and a Good Dog. Just like his Turner and Cocker had been.

Good Dogs. What sort of man would hang a dog? Joe drew himself up.

"You go then, Dr Hart. I won't tell anyone." Charlie gave him one beaming, relieved smile.

"Thank you, Joe."

Charlie started pushing the wheelchair towards the Medical School entrance. She turned back and came close to the desk. "And I'm so sorry about your wife, about Mary." Joe nodded and looked down. Dr Hart had always been one of the nice ones. He wouldn't say anything for her sake... and for Jarvis.

IT WASN'T until Charlie got outside that she realised Joe hadn't called a taxi. She walked on, not sure exactly where she was going now. Her legs felt like rubber. Noises sounded as if they were coming from far away. The light seemed too bright. She'd just sit for a moment. She slumped under the Sheffield Medical School motto, written in stone on a wall. *Ars Longa, Vita Brevis*: the acquisition of mastery takes an age, but life is so short. Some lecturer had explained it to them. Tony Faveringham had sniggered on the back row.

"Hart has got a short Ars."

"Vita Brevis," whispered Charlie, as the world seemed to go dark around her. "Life is so short...."

Someone came and stood in front of her, looking down at where she crouched. She looked up but couldn't see who it was. The early sun behind their head blinded her view. By now, she barely cared. She could run no more.

"I didn't call you that taxi, Dr Hart. Where are you going? I'll give you a lift." Charlie squinted up. It was Joe, wearing his raincoat and tweed flat cap, a Sainsbury's carrier bag containing an empty sandwich box swinging at his side.

Joe pushed Sally back up Beech Hill to where he was parked. He still drove the old Land Rover and the German Shepherd sticker was still there, peeled edges and all. He opened the back door and pushed a collection of garden tools towards the bench seats.

"Allotment," he muttered in explanation. Joe laid a few old dog blankets on the floor and gently laid Sally onto them. He shook his head but didn't suggest they return to the Hospital. A Rubicon had clearly been crossed. Charlie clambered in and took Sally's hand. She looked back at Joe.

"Up the Manchester Road and keep going, please," she said. Joe nodded and swung into the driver's seat.

JOE'S EYES widened as they drove down the narrow track to Rowans Holt and over the stone bridge. *You'd certainly need a couple of dogs to protect this lot,* he thought. He looked appreciatively up at the house before carrying Sally in and laying her gently on one of the sofas.

"Well, best of luck!" Joe said. He backed towards the door, waving awkwardly. Charlie followed him. She froze as she saw, in the distance, the gleam of expensive paintwork. An unfamiliar car had turned from the distant road onto the track that led to Rowans Holt. Someone was coming. It could be him, the Boss. She felt the blood drain from her face. She was so stupid. Had she thought that escaping from the Hospital meant that this was over?

CHAPTER THIRTY-EIGHT

The slowly approaching car flashed into view down the hill and then disappeared in a copse of trees. Joe was looking intently at Charlie and his face hardened.

"Is it him?" he demanded. "The dog killer?" Charlie looked back at him, her eyes wide with terror. She didn't reply but nodded slowly. Joe tutted and got out an old mobile phone.

"Well, I'll just call the police," he said. Joe frowned as his phone screen remained blank. No signal.

"Joe," said Charlie, reaching for his arm. "There's no signal. And even if there was...." Joe looked at her.

"Powerful friends?" he said, finally understanding what she had been trying to say earlier. Charlie nodded.

"We're all, all alone, Joe."

Joe looked at his Land Rover.

"Come with me, Duck," he said. He tore off his cap and raincoat, strode over to the rear of the vehicle, tugged the door open, and reached inside. He pulled out a black donkey jacket and threw another over to Charlie. "Put that on," he ordered. As Charlie struggled to get the coat on, Joe jammed a black beanie hat over her head and tucked her long golden hair inside it. He reached down to the ground and grabbed a handful of earth which he rubbed over Charlie's chin and lower face. "Can't have you looking too pretty," he said with a grim wink. Joe lifted a large, sharp-bladed mattock from the pile of tools on the muddy vehicle floor and handed Charlie a pickaxe. He then threw a metal toolbox behind the front wheel and indicated that Charlie stand on it.

"Now, try and look like a bloke, and try to look mean," commanded Joe.

Joe strode out in front of his Land Rover and stood hefting the mattock, his chin jutted and set. Down the path, a large black Ford Raptor slowed to a halt. It sat, engine idling, windows blacked out, so they couldn't see any occupants. Charlie gripped her pickaxe and threw her shoulders back. "Take my phone," muttered Joe from the corner of his mouth.

"There's no signal," hissed Charlie.

"Pretend to call someone! Pretend you're calling for backup," insisted Joe. "Now!" he handed her his phone, not taking his eyes from the sinister vehicle. Charlie pretended to dial and then spoke into the receiver. She also glared at the Jeep. "You want to play?" Joe mouthed at the dark windscreen. "Come on then. Let's play. Sheffield style." A shiver ran down Charlie's spine at the menace that Joe exuded. Joe had a lot of anger and grief, unexpectedly finding a place to ground themselves. The car's occupant felt it, too, for the vehicle suddenly started reversing down the path as if the driver were angry. Charlie and Joe stood their ground, watching as the heavy car finally sped off.

Once she was sure the car had gone, Charlie raced back into the house. She ripped off Joe's black beanie and donkey jacket and scrabbled on the floor where she had thrown the bag of fluids and the giving set.

"Honey, you are so amazing, so brave, so good," she soothed to Sally, who was struggling.

"Get her legs up, Joe," ordered Charlie. Joe was a veteran of a hundred faints in patients who had determinedly wandered outside for a fag mere hours after complex surgery. He swiftly pulled the pillow from under Sally's head and lifted Sally's legs. Charlie ripped open the packaging to the IV giving set and pierced one of the bags of fluid. She primed the line with colloid fluid to drive out any air. The liquid spurted from the end of the line and Charlie attached the giving set to Sally's cannula and instructed Joe to hold the bag high. When the fluid didn't run in as fast as she liked, she grabbed the bag in her hands and squeezed hard. Sally's pallid face twitched, and she opened her eyes blearily.

"Which part of 'personal space' don't you understand, Hart?" she said, faintly but decisively. Charlie found tears streaming down her cheeks.

"Every damn bit of it!" she retorted. She stroked Sally's face and her tears fell harder.

There was the sound of a car tearing up to the house. Brakes squealed. Ben flung himself through the door and into the front room. He stopped to take in the scene before walking over to the sofa and taking Sally's hand.

"Sal..." was all he managed. There was a second screech of brakes, and Mac burst through the door. He didn't pause. He marched straight up to Ben, who rose from Sally's side. Mac punched Ben right in the face. Hard. Ben fell to the ground, his head glancing painfully off a small table. The lamp on the table crashed to the floor, too.

"Now then!" shouted Joe, sensibly holding on to the bag of fluid but, with his other hand, reaching out to the livid Mac. Ben lay on the floor, looking up at Mac. Blood oozed from the corner of his mouth.

"I deserved that," he said quietly.

"One thing!" shouted Mac. "You had one thing to do, and that was protect them!"

"I'm sorry," said Ben. He lifted the back of his hand to his mouth. "But I had an opportunity, and I took it," he said quietly. He looked up at Mac. "I chose my heart over my head. Tell me you don't know what that feels like."

Mac turned and walked into the kitchen. He returned a few moments later with a piece of cord. He pulled a floor lamp across to the sofa. Mac gently removed the bag of fluid from Joe's hand. He looped the cord through the hole at the end of the fluid bag, tied it high on the lamp, and made an improvised IV stand. By now, Charlie was sitting close to Sally. Ben had pulled up a stool and was seated at Sally's side. Their heads, blonde, auburn, and brown, were held close together. Mac jerked his head at Joe. *Let's leave them to it*, he seemed to say. Joe looked down at the three and nodded.

CHARLIE LOOKED between Sally and Ben. "I know you've been through a lot," she said. "But I think I deserve an explanation. An ectopic pregnancy? What happened between you two?" Ben and Sally looked at each other. Sally shook her head, too exhausted to speak.

"That first night, when we met. She'd almost died," Ben

said. He reached out for Sally's hand. She took his hand and held it, her face open and vulnerable. "And I felt like I'd come back to life," he whispered, looking overwhelmed. Ben looked at Charlie. "I told you. I know what it is to be lonely." He looked back at Sally. "We. We know what it is to be lonely."

"Well, I'm lonely too!" exclaimed Charlie. "It doesn't mean I creep around at night! That I spoil..." she gesticulated at the three of them. "This. Whatever 'this' is." Sally looked pained.

"Charlie!" she said. "We were two consenting adults. It just happened. Weird things happen, you know this. You think you're going to die, so you cling to life, to the promise of life, wherever you find it."

MAC AND JOE heard the raised voices. They looked at each other. Joe picked up the kettle and started filling it.

"IT FELT LIKE A DREAM," said Ben awkwardly. "Part of me thought it was." Ben looked mournfully at Sally. "We've never even mentioned it to each other." He sunk his face into his hands. "God, I'm so useless." Sally reached out and stroked Ben's hair.

"You're such a soft arse," she muttered.

Charlie looked at Sally.

"Why didn't you tell me?" she asked. "That you were pregnant? I found a positive test. You knew, but you didn't tell me. I feel..." Charlie cast around for the right word. "Sad. I feel sad. I thought we were friends. I thought we had faith in each other. But now, there are all these secrets. I don't like secrets." *Things unsaid*, Charlie thought. *Lies and dark thoughts. Corrupting everything*. Charlie shivered.

"I'm sorry," said Sally, gently but urgently. "I'd only just found out. And by the time I'd decided what to do, I started bleeding. I thought I was going to miscarry."

"And what had you decided to do?" asked Ben, looking up, his face pained. Sally looked back at him.

"It's OK, you leaving," she said, ignoring his question. "I dreamed. I was with Peter and had to decide whether to join him. Whether to live or die. I heard your voices." Charlie and Ben looked at each other. Sally continued. "I heard you, right next to my ear, Charlie." Charlie nodded.

"I was," she whispered. Her face contorted as she tried to smile and stop herself from crying at the same time. "By your left ear, with the anaesthetist."

"And you wished you'd asked me if I was pregnant," continued Sally. Charlie nodded her head vigorously. Sally looked up at Ben. "I dreamed I saw little Ben too," Ben said nothing. By now, he was almost crying too. "He had a Thomas the Tank Engine. He looked happy. But your son wanted me to keep the faith. For you. I promised I would. So, you did the right thing, following Steve. Me and Charlie can rescue ourselves. Whatever Mac thinks."

"Did you see anything else?" Ben asked softly. Sally's brow furrowed. It all seemed so far away now.

"I can't remember properly, but the wheels were missing from Thomas," she said. Ben swallowed and pulled in a small, tight gasp of air. Benjamin had loved his Thomas the Tank Engine. However, he hadn't been able to play with it properly because he had levered the wheels off using Ben's woodworking tools. He was trying to be like his Dad. Ben had angrily thrown the toy into one of the yellow hospital disposal bags on the night his son had finally given up his long fight. Sally could never have known about the missing wheels.

"You say he looked happy?" he managed. Sally nodded.

"He was with Peter," she whispered. "And..."

"And what?" said Ben, his face tight and sad.

"A little girl. I saw a little girl. She was beautiful, Ben. I was going to have our baby. Please don't doubt that." Ben lowered his head towards Sally. She reached up and stroked his hair. Charlie stood and walked over to the kitchen, leaving them to their moment of shared grief.

Mac was staring at Charlie. He jerked his head towards the courtyard, and Charlie followed him out. She made her way to the low wall and sat on it. She started to tremble and sank her head into her hands.

"What happened, Hart?" demanded Mac. He had arrived at G1 ward to find it in chaos. He'd been told that his friend, Mrs Foster, had disappeared from the ward against medical advice. They also hadn't understood why she had two people claiming to be her husband.

"Decker," said Charlie. She looked up at Mac, her eyes sunk deep in her weary face. "It was Decker working for the Boss all along. He came for us. To kill us. I made sure that was his plan. Before he died."

"What?" said Mac, unfolding his arms and moving closer to Charlie, who flinched away from his looming presence.

"We killed him," said Charlie in a small voice. "Me and Sal. He's dead." Charlie closed her eyes and felt tears start to form. *No! Don't cry again,* she thought fiercely. *Don't let him see you crying again!*

She was aware of Mac sitting down next to her on the wall. He said nothing. Charlie tried to concentrate on the sounds of Rowans Holt, the sighing trees and murmuring water. On the sunshine, warm on her back. She tried not to think of the heavy thudding weight of Decker's body as she had pulled him down the stairs. His sightless cold eyes. She drew a deep halting breath but then felt a soft touch on her clenched fingers. She looked up to see Mac's steady brown eyes gazing at her. His expression was unreadable as usual, but a light blue silk handkerchief was in his hand.

"Would you like to add this to your collection?" he asked with unaccustomed gentleness. Charlie hesitantly took the handkerchief and blew her nose apologetically. This was a second handkerchief Mac would not be getting back.

"I owe your grandmother a debt of thanks," she muttered, and caught the ghost of a grin on Mac's face.

"I dare you to tell her," he murmured ruefully.

"Is she *that* formidable?" asked Charlie, eyes wide, her nose still buried in lemon-scented blue silk.

"Terrifying," said Mac in a confidential tone. "And very, very American." His face broke into an unexpected smile, and his features were transformed; the morning sun glistening over his handsome face. Charlie lowered the handkerchief and smiled back at him. They regarded each other for a long moment, and Mac's face slowly fell. He looked away and then pushed himself abruptly to his feet. "What did you do with the body, Hart?" he growled.

Joe was busy in the kitchen. He'd found a teapot and was making everyone a brew, nodding approvingly at the Yorkshire tea bags. He glanced out at the courtyard. The big man with the powerful arm was pacing up and down, a phone held to his ear. At least he'd managed to get a signal, thought Joe. Joe had been in the army in his younger days and recognised an officer when he saw one. He wondered what the man was saying.

"HAFEZ?" Mac snapped. "Listen, I have a job for you. Round up Toddy and Weatherby. There's a heavy but delicate item to collect." He paused. "Yes, a cold item. Usual drill, but retrieval may be difficult. It's hidden under a stairwell in Sheffield Medical School...."

CHARLIE WANDERED BACK into the kitchen; her arms wrapped miserably around her chest. Joe smiled at Charlie. He lowered his voice and asked;

"Is there really a walled garden?" Charlie looked at him, and her face slowly broke into a tired but warm smile.

"Yes. There's a walled garden," she replied. "Would you like to see it?" Joe nodded, his face lighting up. As if on cue, the kitchen door gently opened with a warm creak. Joe was clearly welcome in Rowans Holt. The two of them stepped into the sunlight where Mac was still speaking intently on the phone. Joe took in the view from the courtyard. The peak of Win hill arose from the purple haze of the surrounding moors and waters. Behind it ran the spine of the path from Lose Hill to Mam Tor; peaks shouldering like slumbering giants from the valleys of Hope and Edale. Joe looked back at the stone house in quiet admiration before they walked, in companionable silence, to the walled garden. Joe frowned at the disused beds and gently ran his hand over the redbrick, weathered wall. *What a waste*, he thought. As if reading his mind, Charlie said;

"I have plans." She pointed to where beds had been cleared against the far wall. Joe smiled.

"That figures," he said. "You always wanted to know what I was up to on the allotment." Charlie's tired face fell.

"It's just, everything takes a lot longer than you think it will," she sighed.

THEY RETURNED to the kitchen and Joe's laden tea tray. He carried the hoard over to the sofa and placed it on a low table. No one spoke as he poured. He scooped two sugars into the first cup and handed it to Sally.

"There you go, Duck." He handed tea and chocolate digestives round, including to Mac, who'd finished his call and now glowered from the side-lines. "You've got a mean right hook there, son," said Joe, grinning. They drank.

CHAPTER
THIRTY-NINE

"I'll be off in a minute, Miss Marshall," said Joe. "Just one thing before I go. That ex of yours, I recognise his type. He'll be back, you know."

"I know," said Sally. She closed her eyes and sighed, exhausted. "But I won't think about that now. I'll think about that tomorrow." She sounded as if she was falling asleep. Her body needed to heal. Charlie grabbed her bag.

"Ben, could you fetch some water, please?" she said. She retrieved the antibiotics and pain killers from her bag. Sally needed to take these before she fell into a deep sleep. Charlie shook Sally gently. She was difficult to rouse, but Charlie was determined; she was going to get her medicine.

Joe picked up his mattock and jacket.

"I'll be off, then," he said. Charlie stood and gave him a big hug.

"Thank you so much. For everything." She smiled at him. He took in her tired face.

"Anytime, Duck. You get that garden sorted. And if you ever need any help...." She nodded.

• • •

Joe settled into his Land Rover. What a morning! But now, he needed his bed. He looked back to the house and to the young people who seemed as close as family. Family was important. His face fell as the thought of his empty home flashed miserably across his mind. But then he remembered the surge of excitement when he'd stood up to that Psycho. That had been one of the longest night shifts ever. But one of the best!

Charlie slumped next to Sally on the sofa. She laid her head against Sally's shoulder. Sally was fast asleep. *At least Sally had managed to take her tablets* was Charlie's last thought before falling into a deep, exhausted sleep. She awoke briefly at the scent of lemons. She was being carried upstairs, Mac holding her easily in his arms. Charlie saw Ben ahead of her carry Sally into her room. He stopped when he saw the pool of dark, dried blood on the carpet.

"Mine. My room," muttered Charlie before laying her head against Mac's firm chest and falling asleep again. She awoke briefly and saw Sally asleep beside her. Sally's face was pale, but her breathing was strong and steady.

Images came in flashes as Charlie briefly surfaced through her exhausted sleep; Ben holding Sally up in his arms, giving her more painkillers and antibiotics. Mac putting up another bag of fluid and adjusting the infusion flow. Ben helping Sally across the room to the bathroom. *She's going to be alright*, whispered a voice in her mind. Sally would be alright.

Charlie awoke once more. It was dark, and a shaft of moonlight fell, shallow, across the room. It would soon be dawn. Ben slept on the silver-velvet chaise longue in the corner of the room. His face was pinched and sad, even in rest. In an armchair by the bedroom door sat Mac. He was awake and alert, his gun drawn and on his lap. Mac's eyes were fixed on Charlie's features, his face expressionless. He saw her eyes open, and, for a moment, she held his gaze, but then his eyes dropped and moved towards the line of moonlight tracing over the thick carpet. Her heart sped up. How long had he been watching her? She turned over, away from him. She slept.

As the dawn poured like molten gold across the blazing peaks, a black motorbike made its slow way down the secret path at the base of the cliff and approached the hangar doors of the Cavern. The doors slid open, and the bike growled smoothly through. Mac sat on one of the metal work benches, arms folded, one leg on the floor, one leg casually swinging. Maddie Sinclair brought the bike to a halt.

Mac walked around the bike, scrutinising it. Sinclair took off her helmet, and a cloud of dark hair emerged and fell around her shoulders. She'd put on a few pounds, Mac thought approvingly. Maybe her deep grief was finally fading.

"So, you replaced the Kawasaki with a Ducati in the end?" he said. "That'll annoy Hafez."

"Panigale 959," replied Sinclair, patting the black leather seat. She shrugged. "He'll get over it. Anyway, he's happy enough with his Ninja 400. Keeps telling me it's better to ride a slow bike fast than a fast bike slow." Mac grimaced.

"That sounds like Hafez," he said.

Mac looked at Sinclair, all joking gone. "Decker, the Detective Inspector, was working for the Boss all along. He came to kill Hart and Sally. They would have been in real trouble if it wasn't for Hart and some random security guard they managed to pick up at the hospital."

"Where was Morton?" asked Sinclair. Mac hesitated.

"He left them." Sinclair snorted and shook her head, throwing her leather gloves into her helmet. She looked up at Mac.

"And you still trust him?" she demanded

"It was personal," said Mac. "Something to do with his ex-wife."

"Of course it was."

"I trust him," Mac said shortly.

"Sir," said Sinclair, her face cold.

"You were going to have to meet him at some point," said Mac. Sinclair wouldn't meet his eye.

"Madeleine," said Mac. She finally looked up. "Madeleine, he's nothing like his older brother. And thank you for coming, anyway. Sally and Hart need our protection." Sinclair sighed.

"It's what we do, isn't it?" she said. "Protect the weak and the vulnerable?" Mac gave a lopsided grin.

"That and provide security for demanding celebrities and spoiled rich kids. You forgot that bit." Sinclair finally relented and gave him a grim smile. Mac visibly relaxed. He depended on his second in command.

Sinclair looked over at the Dodge Demon, which Ben had returned home.

"Did Hart really lie in that and transfuse Sally with her own blood?" she asked. Mac nodded, his face suddenly blank. "Impressive!" said Sinclair. "Maybe she could join The Crew?" Mac scowled.

"Only if you wanted all our vehicles painted pink," he muttered.

"Princess or not, she still deserves respect, don't you think?" said Sinclair. Mac didn't answer. He yawned.

"I'll get some rest," he said. "It's been a long night. Hafez, Toddy and Wetherby dealt with Decker. He'll never be found. Toddy and Hafez will cover tonight, and I'll be back tomorrow." His face became serious. "This Boss is dangerous."

"Well, so am I," said Sinclair. She twitched the key card out of his hand and headed for the lift.

Sally awoke. She had drifted slowly up from a dark and deep dream where she was trying to find Charlie. She could only hear Charlie's voice, floating, faint and half-heard, from a dark tunnel.

"I'm in the dark. I am the dark!" A woman was sitting in a chair near her bed. But it wasn't her bed; it was Charlie's. They were alone. Sally's mouth felt dry as sand, and she ached all over. The woman looked up from the book she was reading. She wore black jeans and a tight black t-shirt. Sally could see the holster for a gun over her shoulders and a pistol snug under her left arm. A black leather jacket and full-face black cycle helmet with an opaque visor lay on the chaise longue.

"Hello again," said the woman. Sally recognised her soft Scottish accent.

"Sinclair?" whispered Sally. "Where is everyone?"

"I haven't seen Morton yet, but Charlie's in the kitchen," replied Sinclair. "She's making you something to eat, I think." The scents of chicken soup and spiced apple cake wafted up the stairs. Sally suddenly realised she was ravenous. She tried to sit up, but her stomach felt like it had been kicked. She groaned quietly.

Sinclair stood and put her arm around her to help her. She adjusted the pillows behind Sally's head. Sally couldn't help but notice Sinclair smelled very clean, of soap and steel and a slight hint of vanilla. "It's time for your tablets," said Sinclair briskly, checking her phone. She pushed out the painkillers and antibiotics from their packets and handed them to Sally with a glass of water. Sally swallowed them slowly. She savoured the cold liquid. She felt very thirsty. Sally realised her drip was down.

There was the sound of a door slamming outside. Sinclair's stance changed almost instantly. She drew her gun and, in one fluid move, was standing by the curtain, body pressed against the wall, surveying the garden. Sally thought she moved with the sleek grace of a cat. She took in the long muscular legs encased in black denim, her slim waist and taut abdomen. Sinclair's pale face wore no makeup, and her eyelashes were long and deepest black. The lower edge of a tiny tattoo glanced from the bottom of her right t-shirt sleeve. Sinclair relaxed. "It's Charlie, in the garden," she murmured. She pushed her gun back into its holster, returned to her seat, and picked up her book. Sally, lying facing her, looked at the title. *When Einstein Walked with Gödel.*

"You look very different in real life," said Sally quietly. Sinclair seemed to be reluctant to meet her eye.

"Don't we all?" Sinclair replied tersely, continuing to read. Sally had a flash of memory.

"You were there! At the hospital..." she said slowly. "There was a child." Sinclair finally looked at her rather sharply.

"Do you remember speaking to me?" she asked. Sally shook her head slowly.

"I just remember you and a child. Linton?" Sinclair nodded.

"My son. Mac had a garbled message from Morton and couldn't call him back. I presume there was no phone signal in the hospital basement," continued Sinclair. "Mac was beside himself. I was closest. He asked me to check out what was going on. Sometimes it's easier to just bring Linton along." Sinclair shrugged. "He's a good boy." She returned to her book. Sally watched her for a while. In real life, she was very beautiful, and the scar on the right side of her face didn't detract from that. Long, clean limbs and that hair! And reading lectures on theoretical physics and maths....

Sinclair looked up unexpectedly, her large, intelligent grey eyes pierced into Sally. "What?" asked Sinclair, rather assertively. Sally cast around for something to say.

"You have a tattoo," she said. It sounded lame, even to her. "What is it?" Sinclair looked at her for a long time. Then she seemed to make a decision.

"I got it a few years ago," she said. "We'd just finished a job in Paris." Sinclair had a half-smile on her face. "Big society wedding. Minor European nobility to famous American film star. They paid very well and covered all expenses. So, we stayed on for a couple of nights." Sinclair settled back into the chair. She was obviously a natural storyteller. "The five of us, The Crew, ended up on Rue St Denis, drinking shots and telling tall tales. The way soldiers do. Wetherby had the bright idea of guessing which Disney character we'd all be."

SINCLAIR'S MIND slipped back to the noisy, crowded bar. They had agreed to have a majority vote on the matter. Wetherby had looked Sinclair up and down.

"With those legs, and that speed, has to be Bambi!" he'd announced. Todmorden and Hafez had crowed in delight.

"Bambi!"

"Don't you think that's rather sexist?" Sinclair had demanded, thinking of the Baby Cham slinky deer.

"Bambi's a bloke. So, no," Todmorden had slurred. "And he's friends with a skunk, so it fits," he'd added, looking at Hafez.

"Oi!" said Hafez indignantly. They'd drunk to Bambi.

They had then agreed that Wetherby, with his faithful ways, was most like Pluto, the dog. Also, no one had forgotten Sinclair's line about him pining for Mac like an incontinent old Labrador. Hafez was considered to be like Mickey Mouse.

"Now you're being racist!" Hafez had huffed.

"No!" insisted Todmorden. "Little bloke, big ears, can talk his way out of any situation? Mickey Mouse!" They had drunk, noisily and enthusiastically, to Mickey Mouse. "Oi! garcon, cinq plus de tequila et cinq cervezas ici!" Todmorden had called to the waiter, mixing languages happily.

By a three-to-one vote, they'd agreed that Todmorden was most like Baloo, the bear.

"Hairy, lazy, and always eating," muttered Hafez.

"I'm not hairy!" Todmorden had replied indignantly. They'd all agreed to get their characters tattooed on their arms that very night. In memory of their friendship and of Paris. Sinclair looked affectionately at the small Disney character on her right upper arm. It had been a good night.

Sally's forehead creased.

"Hang on," she said slowly. "You didn't tell me about Mac. What tattoo did he get? Sinclair grinned widely.

"You're right; I didn't. He's rather sensitive about it. I would tell you, but then I'd have to kill you. Captain's orders."

There was a pause. "You and Mac," said Sally. "Are you...?" Sinclair shook her head and grimaced.

"Ach nei, we got all that silliness over and done with a long time ago!" Sally smiled.

"What?" demanded Sinclair.

"I'm sorry," said Sally. "But you said 'Ach.'" Sinclair glared at her, but then her face softened into a smile.

"You're right; I did. My parents are originally from the Orkney islands. They moved to Edinburgh when I was small. The accent slips out every now and again."

When she smiled, Sally thought that Sinclair's face lit up like a summer's dawn. Sally smiled back at her. She was starting to feel better.

Charlie sailed through the door carrying a big tray. She had bowls of chicken soup, thick slices of bread and butter and a plate piled with oblongs of fragrant apple cake. She fussed around Sally, spreading a large damask napkin over her chest and watching her anxiously as she sipped at the hot, herby liquid. The food felt so good to Sally, but she could only manage a small amount. Charlie was gratified to see a faint flush on her friend's cheeks.

Once Sally was settled, Charlie checked her wound and temperature. Charlie then looked at Maddie Sinclair who was tucking into her bowl of soup with evident pleasure.

"I am such an awful cook," said Sinclair mournfully, shaking her head. She dipped her bread into the amber liquid and scooped up a moist fragment of chicken.

"You and Sally should get along like a house on fire then," said Charlie slyly.

"Your cooking's the only reason I let you hang around, Shorty," replied Sally indignantly.

"It's Linton I feel sorry for," continued Sinclair, eyeing up the apple cake now she'd finished her soup and bread. Charlie handed her the plate. She was pleased by Sinclair's obvious pleasure in her cooking. Sally nibbled slowly at a small piece while Sinclair made short work of her large slice.

"Who's Linton?" asked Charlie, with her usual curiosity about other people's lives and relationships.

Charlie was soon looking at photos of Sinclair's son and asking which books were best for three-year-olds.

"*The Enormous Crocodile* by Roald Dahl," said Sinclair firmly. "With his secret plans and clever tricks."

"Sounds like Mac," said Charlie sourly. Sinclair frowned.

"The two of them can't seem to appreciate the finer sides of the other's character," explained Sally. Sinclair remembered Mac's comments about Charlie this morning. She nodded.

"He takes a bit of getting used to, but he's a good man. He's had a rough time," she said.

"Haven't we all?" muttered Charlie mutinously.

CHAPTER FORTY

The door to the bedroom swung open, and Ben walked through. He went straight to the bed and sat on it, gazing anxiously at Sally. Sinclair stood up abruptly and walked across to one of the windows. She sat on the wide ledge and looked at Ben, her expression closed and hostile. Ben ignored her, all his attention on Sally.

"How are you feeling, Sal?" he said. Sally smiled up at him.

"Exactly the same as the last time you asked."

"I'm working on the next panel, the one with the high hill and the cattle. And I've finally realised who originally made the carvings. It's pretty amazing." He smiled in a self-deprecating way. "But that's just a carpenter thing. Here, I took some photos." He handed Sally his phone, and Sinclair watched Ben's gentle face crease as he waited, anxious and on edge, for Sally's approval.

Sally expanded one of the images, smiled and gently touched the screen.

"It's another baby rabbit," she said.

"It means hope, Sal. Renewal and new starts." He hesitated. "It means keeping the faith." They looked at each other.

"Sal," began Ben, his face anguished. "I've been thinking, and I think it would be better if I go. I'll leave. Someone else can carry on the restoration...." Sally shook her head, suddenly looking equally distressed.

"No. Don't," she interrupted. She touched her chest over her heart. "It's still here, Philia, the love of friends. I have faith, Ben. Please listen. I don't want you to go." Ben nodded and sighed. He then pulled in a deep breath and rubbed his hand over his forehead.

"Shall I carry you down to look later, then?" he asked gently. Sally smiled, relieved.

"I'm walking down those stairs," she said firmly. "But maybe not today."

Ben slowly stood up. He slipped his phone into his back pocket and finally looked over at Sinclair. He smiled weakly at her and held out his hand.

"I'm Ben, Ben Morton," he said. Sinclair folded her arms and didn't take his hand.

"I know who you are," she replied coldly. Ben slowly lowered his hand.

"I assume you knew my brother," he said, his face falling. He shrugged sadly. "That's okay. I understand." As Ben left the room, Sinclair opened the window, and Sally and Charlie watched as she spat out of it.

"Sorry," she said, not looking sorry at all. "Bad taste in my mouth."

Sinclair stood and returned to her seat. She picked up her book and started to read. Charlie and Sally looked at each other, mystified. Sally shrugged. Charlie, the peacemaker, considered what to say next.

"Linton's dad, Jordan. How did you meet?" she asked gently. Sinclair looked up as if annoyed, but then she paused. She hadn't thought about the happy times for a long while.

"At the gym. On Base," she said. "I was struggling with a new bit of equipment, and he tried to help. Of course, I wouldn't let him; I was convinced I could make it work." Sinclair smiled gently at the memory. "Jordan just let me get on with it, making a fool of myself. But he never laughed, like so many other men would. We ended up in a pub somewhere, just talking. They had to kick us out in the end. Then we sat on top of a wall and talked again until the sun came up. He nipped off to make a phone call, came back, and told me he'd just rung his mum. To tell her he'd met the person he would spend the rest of his life with. I went straight home and told my partner, Terry, that it was over. That I'd met someone new, and that was that."

"And how did he take it? Terry?" asked Charlie, entranced by the romance.

"She,' said Sinclair casually. "She didn't take it well at all. But Jordan Linton was a very special man."

THE DAY PASSED QUIETLY. Sally dozed off and on. Sinclair kept watch over her. They would occasionally talk.

"Have you ever killed a man?" asked Sally. Sinclair looked at her.

"Are you thinking about Decker?" she asked. Sally nodded, her hand curling on the edge of her pillow in quiet distress.

"He came to kill you," said Sinclair firmly. "You did what

needed to be done. For you, and for Charlie." Still, Sally looked anguished.

"But he would have had a family," she said quietly. Sinclair gave a lopsided smile.

"Phil Decker had no family, Sally," she said. "Unless you call a divorced and beaten wife a family. Or an estranged and broken son who hadn't seen his father for twenty years, a family."

"How do you know that?" asked Sally, frowning.

"You aren't the only one handy with a keyboard, Miss Marshall," said Sinclair. "Besides," she shrugged. "You meet a few psychopaths, and you get to recognise the signs. I knew where to look."

Sinclair gazed out of the window and pulled gently at her bottom lip. She then looked down at her book.

"Pattern recognition. That's what you do," she said. She looked at Sally. "I like the way you think, Sally. All these years, working together. I've never told you that." Sally said nothing. Sinclair continued. "I admire your logical mind, your ability to create a null hypothesis for every situation."

"You didn't answer my question," said Sally. Sinclair's mouth pulled up at the edges.

"And you're immune to flattery, too," she observed. Her face became serious. "Yes, is the answer. Yes, I've killed my fair share of men. I've killed men who probably should have lived, and I didn't kill men who possibly should have died. Either way, you have to learn to get on with it." There was a long pause as the two women looked at each other. "And you will," said Sinclair softly.

Sally pulled her knees slowly up towards her chest. "Sinclair," she said. "I've been thinking of a new null hypothesis." Maddie Sinclair leaned forwards in her chair, her face intent, one eyebrow rising in query. "But I need your help," added Sally. Sinclair nodded. She looked around for a bookmark but couldn't find one. With a reluctant grimace, she closed the book and dropped it by the side of the chair.

"I hate people who fold down the edges of pages," she commented. "I'll find my place again." She then looked at Sally. "So, tell me. After all, neither of us is going anywhere...."

EVENING CAME. "My shift's almost up," Sinclair said, stretching and shaking out her long hair. Sally felt a pang of disappointment. "Hafez and Todmorden are going to be on watch tonight," continued Sinclair.

"Both of them?" asked Sally. Sinclair pulled a face.

"They tend to be a buy-one get-one-for-free outfit these days," she said.

"It'll be good to put a face to a name after all this time," said Sally.

"Not Todmorden's face," said Sinclair, shaking her head. "Or Hafez's come to think of it...."

When the two men arrived, Hafez launched straight into Sinclair. "You got the Ducati! I told you I was going to get one! You stole my bike!" Sinclair stood, calmly putting on her leather jacket.

"Cry me a river, Hafez," she said. "You've been talking about a new bike for two years. Talking and not doing. It's your M.O." A very tall, large man with short, bright-red hair appeared in the bedroom doorway. He had a piece of apple cake in each hand and was chewing enthusiastically.

"Top notch scran," he said appreciatively. "Any more where this came from?"

"Probably not, but I could do you a sandwich," said Charlie.

"No! Do not start running around after these two!" said Sinclair firmly. "They are more than capable of demolishing your food supplies on their own." Behind Sinclair, Todmorden winked at Charlie in a friendly way. They both knew Charlie would be making sandwiches for anyone who wanted them as soon as Sinclair had gone.

CHARLIE HELPED Sally to the bathroom for the last time of the long, slow day. "I need to get better quickly, in time for Thursday," muttered Sally determinedly. Charlie was horrified. Where did Sally get the idea she'd be able to go to a big, vitally important event in just forty-eight hours? In fact, what were they going to do? She looked out of the bedroom door. Hafez sat just outside the room. He was reading; something in Arabic, his spare, handsome face half-lit in the hall light. Todmorden slept heavily in a camp bed, ready to take over the night watch in a few hours. Charlie felt safe for now. But they couldn't go on like this.

WEDNESDAY DAWNED. Mac returned and took over from a yawning Hafez and Todmorden. Charlie awoke to see him standing, looking out the window of her room. He seemed lost in the view of the dreaming hills. He turned and regarded her.

"How is she?" he asked in a low voice, nodding towards the sleeping Sally.

Charlie slipped out of bed and padded out into the hallway. Mac followed her.

"She had a bit of a rough night. Lots of pain. She's been trying to do too much on her own. But the wound seems to be healing well, and there's no sign of infection." Mac nodded.

"And... how is she? About losing the baby?" he asked. Charlie paused, looking up at Mac's serious face. She had not expected him to be so frank, but he seemed genuinely concerned. She sighed.

"It's too early to say. It's such a different experience for each person. Some people just shrug it off but to others...It's not just the loss of a potential child...." She paused, searching for the right words.

"It's the loss of the person you could have been," finished Mac quietly. Charlie was again surprised. Mac looked away. "Something similar happened to my mother some years ago," he said quietly. "She had desperately hoped for a girl. To be the mother of a little girl." *No sisters* thought Charlie, and she sensed yet another seam of deep sadness in the man.

Mac, however, quickly recovered his usual taciturn manner. "Is she going to be fit for tomorrow?" he demanded.

"Of course not!" whispered Charlie. "She almost died and needed emergency surgery. She's still very anaemic. In my professional opinion, there's no way she can perform the part she needs to." Charlie looked at Mac. "And do you really think we're going to continue with this?"

"What are you whispering about?" came Sally's voice. She sounded imperious, which was a good sign, thought Charlie.

They entered the bedroom. Ben sat up on the chaise longue, where he'd spent a second night, rubbing his eyes and yawning widely.

"That's ruddy uncomfortable," he complained, gesticulating at the chair. He, too, seemed to be getting back to his usual self. Charlie sat on the bed next to Sally.

"Mac's asking if you're going to be fit enough to go to the Fitzwarren tomorrow," she said gently. "I'm telling him probably not." Sally sat up and winced.

"I think I'll decide that!" she announced tartly. Sally looked between Mac and Charlie. "And yes, we will continue looking for Code Blue. And not just to save Rowans Holt. That's the second time I've almost been killed over this drug. I'm furious now." She looked at Mac. "I know I normally ask you to be discreet. But if you get the chance, you grab a handful of tablets, and then you burn the whole damn thing down!" she declared. Mac, his face grim, nodded tightly.

The little crease had appeared on Sally's forehead that Charlie knew meant Sally would not be backing down. Charlie sighed.

"Let's see how we go today, shall we?" said Charlie diplomatically. "Before deciding about tomorrow night. But we're going to need a Plan B." She looked up at Mac, who shrugged.

"If the worst comes to the worst, I'll have to go alone," he said.

"No," said Sally. "One man alone, you'll stand out. You'll seem less threatening if you take a plus one, and if you seem to be enjoying yourself. Why not take Charlie?"

Charlie and Mac looked at each other, and each pulled a face. The thought of an evening in each other's company did not seem appealing.

"I'll take Sinclair," said Mac shortly.

"She's a former soldier," replied Sally.

"I can assure you, Sinclair scrubs up tolerably well," said Mac stiffly.

"No, she looks and acts like a former soldier." continued Sally. "Lau's a businessman. He won't touch two former military with a bargepole. Besides, I don't want any trouble."

"What do you mean? Sinclair's not trouble," objected Mac.

"I mean, I wouldn't want anyone to lose a hand or anything," said Sally coolly.

"What?"

"Sinclair. We were told she was in a bar fight. Someone lost a hand, and she almost lost an eye." Mac shook his head firmly.

"That's not true," he said. Sally relaxed visibly. Mac continued. "The man only lost two fingers. The bit about the eye, that's true." There was a very long pause. Sally regarded Mac, her face unreadable.

"You'll take Charlie," she eventually said.

Sally turned to Charlie. "I can get you up to speed on Chinese culture," she said. "And on Wellington Lau. I'll teach you a few phrases in Mandarin to show respect."

"Not that you'll need to say anything," said Mac. "I'd expect to do the talking." Charlie gritted her teeth. The Insufferable Man was back.

Sally insisted on trying to walk as much as she could. However, she soon wore herself out and spent much of the afternoon in a codeine-induced slumber. Charlie kept encouraging her to drink and tried to press her with food, but Sally's appetite was poor.

"I don't think I will make it tomorrow," she whispered to Charlie, who nodded.

. . .

BY THE EVENING, Sally had recovered enough to get out her laptop. She gave Charlie a whistle-stop tour of Chinese culture and etiquette.

"You don't need to do a deep bow; that's just in the movies," said Sally. "A nod or a handshake will be fine. But not a firm handshake. That's considered rude. And it's 'Ni Hao' to say hello, but 'Nin Hao' to an elder. And always give a gift or present, and receive a gift or present, with two hands...." *Oh, dear,* thought Charlie, *I'm never going to remember this!*

IN THE DARK FACTORY, The Boss paced, his hands behind his back. Fun Boy stood, sweating, his eyes flicking from side to side as he watched the angry, ranging figure. The Boss spun around.

"Well?" he shouted. "Where the hell is he? Where's Decker?" Fun Boy shook his head, his eyes widening.

"Dunno, Boss. No one's seen him since you told him to go to the hospital. To get that doc and her mate." Fun Boy briefly closed his eyes, so he didn't have to endure the Boss's angry glare. "His phone's dead, too," he said in a small voice. "No sign of the tracer you put on him." Fun Boy paused, but there was no point trying to hide things from the Boss. He always found out in the end. "And the doc and her mate are still alive. I saw a couple of blokes with pickaxes guarding the house."

The Boss picked up a pair of pliers from the medical trolly he had assembled for his dental projects. Fun Boy flinched again. With a loud cry, the Boss flung the pliers at the stone wall. They bounced off and fell with a clattering ring to the hard concrete factory floor far below. The Boss looked over his shoulder. He half expected to see Marcus Rosendale and Mr Ketch emerging from the shadows. There was no one, but he remembered the burning hand, the incense-laden breath that had whispered

"I will crucify you...."

The Boss shivered. Decker had been useful; he'd arranged the killing of the client in the Emergency Department and had given Aziz the false tip-off and false intelligence that had misled the Police. But the Boss would have got rid of Decker soon enough. The Boss pulled himself upright. He was going to have to take matters into his own hands. If the client had spoken to the little doctor, as Decker said, she hadn't gone to the Police. What was she up to?

So, in the night, a Lone Wolf came to Rowans Holt. It stood at the shifting tree line and watched the waiting house. The tiny window in the eaves swung and banged its warning until Hafez, sleepy and irritated, pulled it tightly shut. Charlie stirred and drifted in her restless dreams.

"I'm in the dark. I am the dark...," she whispered and wept, unaware.

Sally woke and walked about the room, a half-heard harshness echoing in the scream of waking woodland. Ben sat at the front door, a watcher in the shadow. He felt, once more, the malevolence in the night; but he knew better than to go and greet it. Ben sensed the teeth, the bitter bite of the waiting dark. The Lone Wolf saw a slight movement. He heard the slow, steady breath at the gate. The thin, dark line. He smiled slowly and turned away. He had time.

CHAPTER
FORTY-ONE

It wasn't until the following day, Thursday, that Charlie realised she didn't have a dress to wear. Her shopping trip had supplied lots of lovely clothes, but no dress. Mac arrived mid-morning. He had a Debenhams bag with him, which he placed on the kitchen island. Sally had made it down the stairs on her own, so was feeling very pleased with herself. She had taken up her usual place at her desk and Charlie was glad that things were gradually getting back to normal.

Sally and Charlie eyed up the Debenhams bag. "I got you a dress," said Mac. "For tonight. Something plain and respectable. Something suitable. Sara advised me on it." Charlie felt her throat tighten.

"You asked Sara Hadid for advice on what I should wear?" she said quietly. Mac didn't appear to hear anything wrong in the tone of her voice. He pushed the bag towards her and she opened it, Sally watching her intently. Charlie saw something black. In a polyester mix. Size twelve to fourteen. It had ruffles. Charlie slowly closed the bag. She drew herself up to her entire five foot five and opened her mouth.

"Thank you so much, Mac!" exclaimed Sally before Charlie could say anything. "That's so thoughtful of you. I'm sure you've plenty to do for tonight. What time should we get Charlie to the Fitzwarren?" Mac looked at Charlie. Her face had gone rather red, and he felt disconcerted. Maybe she was somewhat overwhelmed with gratitude for the dress.

"Eight sharp," he said. "Black cab, black dress. No drama."

AT JUST AFTER eight o'clock that night, Charlie approached the Fitzwarren Hotel, which loomed imposingly over Arundel Gate. Her hands felt sweaty, and her throat tight.

"Black cab, black dress, no drama," she muttered to herself. "Black cab, black dress, no drama."

Mac stood waiting at the Hotel entrance. It was now almost five past eight. *Where was she*? He looked towards the line of cars and taxis disgorging the great and the good of Sheffield, but he couldn't see her. There was a low rumble from Arundel Gate, and Mac rolled his eyes. *Some spoiled footballer revving their supercar*, he thought sourly. But then a Ferrari 488 in Blu Pozzi slid into view. The engine roared and throbbed as the car bypassed the slack-jawed onlookers and parked directly on the edge of the red carpet that had been laid out for the monthly Gala night.

The door swung back. A deep brown, oiled, glistening leg emerged from the red leather interior. On the foot was a high-heeled shoe in a complex pattern of delicate straps that encased the ankles. Each part of the shoe was encrusted in tiny crystals that glittered as they caught the light. This was then followed by a stunning woman. Her body was deeply tanned, and her hair was long and hung elegantly over one side of her beautifully made-up face, shimmering in shades of platinum. Her dress was made from individual triangles of silk in shades of teal. They hung from a tightly fitted, halter-neck bodice with a low back and a laced front that plunged deeply, showing a fine slice of bronzed flesh, almost down to the navel. She was wearing Cartier Panthere sunglasses in gold with brown lenses, and a tiny, golden panther loomed out of the top corner of each lens. Her lips shimmered in a red gloss that matched the interior of her car. Mac's eyes widened in disbelief; he swallowed and then felt his mouth go dry.

The woman paused for a moment, hand resting elegantly on the open door of the Ferrari, and looked around her. Cameras on a hundred phones flashed and clicked. She languorously removed her glasses, tossed back her gleaming hair, and threw the glasses onto the passenger seat. The woman confidently threw the car keys to a nearby attendant, without checking to see if he had caught them, and then sinuously approached Mac. A wave of expensive scent enveloped him as she slowly drew closer. He had recovered his composure and was now grinding his teeth.

"Hart!" he hissed, aware that they were being observed from all angles. "I said no drama. And where's the dress I bought?" Charlie looked up at him, her blue eyes darkly kohled. She seemed like a different person. He didn't like it.

"Ah, now, there's a story behind that," she said. "But shall we go in? People are staring. I can't think why...."

• • •

After Mac had left that morning, Sally had half-listened to Charlie shouting. She was thinking. She didn't want to leave anything to chance; there was too much at stake. It could be that Wellington Lau was impressed by Mac's formal Beaulouf credentials, however, it was Sally who had the business acumen that might have interested him enough to exchange information. Mac had confidence, but not leverage, and Wellington Lau was, first and foremost, a businessman. However, he was also a man with an eye for a pretty face, and Wellington Lau was not as discreet about his love life as he was about his finances. Sally had discovered that he juggled not only his wife in Singapore and Annie Wei, his mistress in Europe, but also Augusta Tse, his second mistress in Hong Kong. She knew that if she forced Charlie into the monstrosity of a dress Sara Hadid had engineered, she would shrink into the background and be miserable. And probably argue with Mac even more than usual.

Sally tapped her chin, as she tended to do when thinking.

"You're thinking!" said Charlie accusingly. "You're not listening to what I'm saying!"

"Of course, I'm listening to you," replied Sally soothingly. "You hate Mac and the dress with an equal, terrible passion."

"Yes!" said Charlie, somewhat mollified. Sally picked up her phone and dialled. There was a brief pause before someone answered.

"Georgia," said Sally briskly. "Is your sister available for some private work?" She listened impatiently. "No, not next week. Today. Now, in fact." There was another pause. "Yes, of course, I'm willing to pay, Georgia. Thank you. I'll see you both shortly." Sally looked at Charlie, who seemed a bit scared at the thought of meeting Georgia again. "Cinderella, you shall go to the Ball," she said.

GEORGIA'S SISTER, Deborah, ran a chain of beauty salons in the South Yorkshire area called "Temple of The Golden Goddess, Inc." She wore white from head to toe; tight skinny jeans, white wedge leather boots and a low-cut angora jumper. Her dyed blonde hair was tonged into Farrah-Fawcett waves, and her face was an unlikely shade of brown. Closer inspection revealed skin that had been on intimate terms with many sun beds and had only just lived to tell the tale. Her small, blue eyes were hard as diamonds, and her chin jutted determinedly, just like Georgia's. There was no mistaking them as sisters, but Deborah had always been 'popular'. She dragged a large, wheeled box behind her as she marched into Sally's closet rooms. Her eyes widened as they took in the fashion feast spread before her, but then they landed on Charlie and Deborah winced visibly.

"Do you even know what moisturiser is?" she asked sharply. "And this hair, it's just one big split end!" Deborah turned dramatically to Sally. "She is going to need everything done. I'm talking, everything. How many days do we have?" Sally checked her phone.

"We have six hours," she said briskly. Deborah shook her head.

"Can't be done. If this is what I have to work with." She pointed up and down at Charlie with one gelled, red, talon-like fingernail.

"I'll pay double," said Sally from the chair on which she sat, like a blanketed empress. "Money is not the object," Sally continued. "Perfection is. But, if it's too much for you."

Sally's lip curled. "Well, that's a pity. I was told you were the best. Maybe I'll call Magdalena from *Simply Stunning Babes....*" She picked up her phone.

"Wait!" commanded Deborah. Deborah stalked around Charlie. She grabbed Charlie's trouser leg and pulled it up roughly to inspect her ankle. She shook her head, turned on her wedge heel and stalked towards the door.

"Where are you going?" cried Charlie. Deborah spun around dramatically and hissed.

"I'm going back to the van. To get an entire bucket of wax." Sally sat back.

"Fasten your seatbelts, ladies," she announced. "It looks like it's going to be a bumpy night."

IT TOOK Georgia and Deborah's combined frantic work to exfoliate, spray, cut, bleach, and wax Charlie into a state fit for Sally's high expectations. Deborah paused before starting the make-up phase of renovations.

"What are we going for here?" she mused. Sally looked up from her laptop and put her head to one side.

"A mix of Daenerys Targaryen and Britney Spears, I think," she said.

"*Toxic* Britney or *Oops* Britney?" demanded Deborah

"*Slave 4 U* Britney," said Sally decisively.

"We'll need a bucket of black eyeliner as well then," muttered Deborah.

THEY WERE ALMOST FINISHED. Sally fished under her seat and brought out the Debenhams bag. Charlie's face fell.

"Sal! you can't make me wear that..." she pleaded.

"You never looked in that extra box from our shopping day, did you?" asked Sally.

"Well, I had a quick look," said Charlie. "But I certainly didn't order it, and Christophe never showed it to me, so I thought it was something for you. I put it over there on a shelf." Her eyes widened. "Was that for me?" Sally nodded, smiling. Charlie shrieked and ran to a shelf in room two. She retrieved the large, cream-coloured box and threw it open. There was a collective sigh from the women as she withdrew the silk dress that fluttered and shimmered against her newly bronzed skin. They pulled, coaxed, and tied her into it. She looked at herself in the mirror. "I look beautiful..." sighed Charlie. She felt her eyes fill with tears, as usual.

"Stop that, right now!" snapped Deborah. "I didn't create a work of make-up genius just for you to cry it all away."

Deborah stepped back and observed Charlie critically. "Shoes!" she demanded. "What shoes do you have?"

"A... a black pair and a nude pair of heels," faltered Charlie. Deborah grimaced in disgust. She drew Georgia into a corner, and they whispered together. Deborah returned to Sally and took a deep breath.

"I am an Artist!" she breathed. "A Perfectionist. But even I will admit that I have created a silk purse from this... well, you know what I mean. But she cannot go out in 'nude' heels. I'm willing to loan a pair of shoes." She lowered her voice. "A pair of India's shoes."

It turned out that Deborah's daughter, India, was, it seemed, a 'WAG'. She'd left a trail of broken-hearted premier-league footballers in her wake, and she was regularly in the pages of all the gossip magazines. She was worshipped by her mother. Deborah produced a pair of extraordinary shoes from a velvet-lined case.

"Perfection," the women collectively breathed. Deborah and Georgia left exhausted but considerably better off.

Sally turned to Charlie. "And now for jewellery," she said, her face serious. She retrieved Felix Quing's black lacquered box from her safe. She opened it. "Now, listen very carefully...." Sally said as she drew two pieces out of the box.

CHARLIE FOUND she could drive in the shoes. Just. She had the time of her life, sailing down the Manchester Road and couldn't help but drive slowly down the length of the busy Ecclesall Road, revving her engine outrageously. But then she approached the Fitzwarren hotel. And the waiting Mac.

"Black dress, black cab, no drama," she whispered. *Oops... I did it again...* she thought.

CHAPTER FORTY-TWO

Mac and Charlie stood halfway down a long marble bar in the large, formal lounge of the Fitzwarren Hotel. Charlie had ordered a cocktail. She had tinkered with the idea of asking Mac to order her a *Sex on the Beach*, but one look at Mac's face had warned her not to annoy him any more than she already had.

"A Cosmopolitan, please," she asked languorously, for the benefit of the barman. She was aware that they were getting just as much attention inside as out. Mac's face was stony as he pointedly ordered a soda water. When the drinks arrived, Charlie nervously held her cocktail and found that she drank it too quickly. A young East-Asian man appeared at Mac's elbow and smiled at them both. He was handsome and wore an impeccably cut charcoal grey suit with a royal-blue silk tie.

"Lord Beaulouf," he said in perfect English. "And...?" he paused, indicating Charlie with an elegant, polite hand.

"Hart," said Mac. "Doctor Charlotte Hart, of Whitby," he

added. The man bowed his head towards Charlie, and she saw his eyes flick appreciatively over her figure and attire.

Charlie suddenly felt less confident. The glances she was drawing, the frank looks abruptly seemed less flattering and more intrusive. Intimidating. Self-doubt crept in and she admitted to herself that she hadn't really planned to do anything other than annoy Mac. *Mission accomplished*, she thought. *What now*? The man in the charcoal suit was speaking.

"Mr Wellington Lau wonders if you would like to join his other guests tonight? In the Hanover Suite."

"We'd be honoured," said Mac smoothly, but Charlie could see that he was relieved.

"Then, please, follow me," said the man. He led them to a large, white door at the end of the bar. Burly security guards eyed them but stood back respectfully at the young man's approach. He discreetly opened the door, just enough for them to slip through.

Charlie's eyes widened. They had entered an enormous, extraordinary room. Three vast crystal chandeliers hung from the white ceilings, casting a warm glow over everything. The walls were also painted white, and large white canvases bearing stylised images of lilies and chrysanthemums glowed on each surface. Their feet sank into a deep blue carpet which discreetly bore the letter "F" every few feet in elegant script, white Yorkshire roses surrounding each letter. Well-dressed couples and wealthy-looking individuals drifted around the packed room, which hummed with excited conversation. Waiters circulated with wide silver platters filled with expensive champagne and canapes. A bar ran along the wall to their left and was doing a brisk trade, bar staff competently and skilfully mixing cocktails and exotic drinks. The warm room pulsated with powerful perfumes and naked ambition.

In the centre of the room was a large, round marble pool. Rising out of the pool was a white marble barge. The barge was reached by a narrow stone walkway over the water. Two tall, lethal-looking security guards guarded the entrance. On the barge was a white, delicately carved marble table and at the table sat a woman and a man. The man's eyes roamed round the room, and Charlie recognised, in profile, the sharp, handsome features and greying hair of Wellington Lau. His younger, elegant companion sat, gazing at her large mobile phone. Her dark shining hair was cut in a sleek, short, asymmetric bob, and she wore a bright-red silk Alexander McQueen off-the-shoulder mini dress.

The barge faced three enormous windows that stretched floor to ceiling, taking up half a wall. Three huge, filmy, white silk curtains moved gently in the room's heat, the pattern of white lilies and chrysanthemums faintly traced upon their surface. The windows looked out onto Arundel Gate, but the view was half-hidden by the translucent material. Something about the angle of the view struck Charlie as slightly odd, but she had no time to think about that now.

A waiter approached them. "Champagne?" he asked smoothly.

"Yes, please!" said Charlie, helping herself. Mac frowned and confidently beckoned to another carrying a tray of soft drinks.

"Slow down, Hart," he muttered.

"I'm nervous," she replied. "And six hundred mls of my blood is missing," she added.

"You don't have to replace it with alcohol," replied Mac

shortly. He surveyed the room. "Let's dance," he said suddenly.

"What?" exclaimed Charlie. Mac took her glass and placed it on a nearby table. He then took her hand and led her towards the circle of smooth floor that surrounded the marble pool. Couples were dancing, slowly and gracefully, in a clockwise motion around the barge, clearly hoping to attract the eye of Lau and a string quartet played an elegant waltz. Charlie took a deep breath. It had been a very long time since she had attempted to dance formally, and Mac was clearly confident and skilful.

Mac placed his right hand on her back and took her right hand in his left. She put her left hand on his right shoulder, and they moved closer. Charlie rose onto the balls of her feet, gently threw back her hair, and they moved off. They both tried to relax and look as if they were enjoying themselves, however, after a moment, Mac said,

"You're counting. Stop it!"

"I know," said Charlie. "I'm fine playing the piano. But dancing... I get nervous. I need to count."

"Feet!" snapped Mac. Charlie reversed quickly. *Just glide, glide. You're doing this for Sally*, thought Charlie. She smiled beatifically.

"What do you think of my choice of dress?" she couldn't resist asking Mac. She felt he hadn't properly looked at her until that point. He now finally surveyed her up and down. Mac then glanced around the room at the openly admiring glances Charlie was getting from all corners.

"If I'd ever had the ambition to date Barbie, I'd be delighted with it," was his reply. Charlie said nothing. They danced on in stony silence.

Charlie felt the eyes of Lau on them as they glided past,

but she realised that his young companion had also fixed them with a flinty gaze.

"What's wrong?" asked Mac, glancing at her suddenly tense face.

"It's all this hindbrain stuff washing around the room," said Charlie unhappily.

"What do you mean?" asked Mac, frowning.

"Your hindbrain's what controls the most basic of functions. To ensure your survival," said Charlie. "Breathing, your heart beating, balance. But it also controls all the dark stuff; appetites, aggression, sex." Mac just looked at her. Charlie was solemnly watching the hungry, closed faces around her. She shivered slightly. "The Hindbrain's far more powerful than the frontal, thinking part of our brains. We fool ourselves that we're civilised and can control our basic instincts," she said quietly. Mac had to strain to hear her. "But when push comes to shove, the hindbrain will always win. It's just odd to be surrounded by so many people where desire, ambition and ruthlessness are on such obvious display."

The music ended, and they applauded politely, along with the rest of the elegantly dressed crowd.

"Do you think we'll get to speak with Lau?" whispered Charlie.

"I'll speak with Lau. I thought I made that clear," said Mac firmly. He handed her a glass of apple juice. Charlie defiantly took a glass of champagne from a passing waiter.

"Well, if I'm not allowed to speak, I may as well have another one of these."

"Stop acting like a child," Mac said in a low, angry voice.

"Only if you stop acting like the insufferable man you are!" Charlie shot back.

"For God's sake, Hart. You sound like a cheap imitation of an Austen Novel," growled Mac. Charlie stopped short. Her face fell.

"You truly don't like me, do you?" she said. She looked up at Mac, but he refused to meet her eye. Charlie felt as if she had been punched. No one disliked her, apart from Sara Hadid, but Sara Hadid despised almost everyone.

Charlie had made an unwitting art of making people like her. In a childhood pitted with violence and aggression, Charlie had learned to adapt the best way that she could, with friendly kindness and empathy. She had learned to deflect aggression this way. To survive. And, because she was a genuinely loving and warm person, the world generally reflected back to her what she gave it; smiles and kindness. She had to acknowledge that Mac truly did not like her, and this was a shock. Mac glanced at her and saw it was as if a light had been switched off somewhere inside. He looked away and his mouth hardened.

"I have to go to..." muttered Charlie, not looking at him. Mac nodded tightly.

"Don't be all night about it. We have a job to do," he said. Charlie nodded. She said nothing.

Charlie looked around for the ladies' bathroom. She saw a group of beautiful young Chinese women leave by a discreet white door set between lily-strewn canvasses. She hurried over to the door and slipped through. Charlie was in a corridor with more plush carpet, muffling the sound of her footsteps. Ample storage cupboards extended floor to ceiling to her right. A passageway to her left seemed to lead to the kitchens. She saw the girls turn right in the corridor ahead and followed them. A door led to an elaborate bathroom where classical music played quietly in the heavily scented air. Expensive perfumes and cosmetics lay on silver trays between the broad marble basins, and plush mini sofas and chairs covered in pink velvet lined a large atrium area. Material was draped in swags of heavy dove-grey silk, and mirrors were everywhere. An attendant discreetly hovered, keeping the area pristine.

Charlie caught sight of herself in the mirror, and now she seemed like a stranger to herself, too. Any fun had been drained from the night. She felt overwhelmed at the thought of getting to speak to a man like Wellington Lau among all these wealthy strangers. How had she ever thought that she could help Sally?

Charlie used the bathroom and emerged to wash her hands. The gaggle of beautiful women were chatting in Mandarin in the atrium. They'd draped themselves over the pink chairs and were laughing. Charlie realised that one of the girls was Lau's Mistress, Annie Wei. Annie saw Charlie glance at her in the mirror. Charlie looked down, concentrating on drying her hands, and became aware of a sudden silence in the room. The girls had all gone quiet; they were looking at her. Charlie turned and stared back. She smiled hesitantly. Annie Wei suddenly rose to her feet, spun on her heel and glided towards the door. As she did so, she signalled to one of her entourage. The girl peeled away from the pack and walked boldly up to Charlie. She lifted her phone and took a picture of Charlie's necklace. She checked the image, nodded, and turned away without acknowledging Charlie.

Charlie suddenly felt very unwell. She'd been stupid to drink like that. She spent her life meeting new people, but they were real people, in real situations. They experienced life at its messy, poor, pointy end; the end where the pressure of desperation and death met the hard surface of reality. Here was nothing but a cruel fantasy with rules of behaviour and ritual that she didn't understand. Sally belonged in this world. Charlie felt like a joke, an imposter, a child. Just like Mac had said. Charlie saw the attendant looking at her. She did not look friendly. *She knows*, thought Charlie. *She knows I don't belong here*. Charlie faltered slightly as she made her way to the door.

THE MANAGER WAS MAKING her way from the kitchens toward the Hanover Suite when she caught a flash of teal silk gleaming in the dark between two cupboards in the hallway. She paused and walked back on herself to look properly. A beautiful woman with enormous eyes and long blonde hair was quietly talking to herself in the space. *Mistress* thought the Manager, and sighed. She hated these monthly Gala nights for the messes that it threw up. Messes that she was supposed to clear away discreetly. The Mistress was probably high on cocaine. Oh well, better get this over and done with. Return the property to its owner, give a kindly but veiled warning about drug use on Fitzwarren property.

"May I help you, Madame?" asked the Manager in a brisk but friendly manner. The woman looked at her like a scared rabbit.

"Oh, no! It's fine. I'm just..." The Manager waited.

"Just, what, Madame?'

"I'm just trying to calm down by remembering twenty causes of A.F." The Manager paused.

"I beg your pardon?" she finally managed.

"I'm a doctor," replied the blonde woman. "A.F. Atrial

Fibrillation. There are lots of causes. I used to know at least twenty." The Manager had to admit that this was a new one for her. And she'd seen more than her fair share of surprising things, working as she did in the Hotel business.

"Well, I'm sure having a panic attack in a cupboard must be one of them," said the Manager calmly. The blonde woman looked surprised.

"I'm not in a cupboard!" she declared.

"It looks like a cupboard to me," retorted the Manager, too intrigued to remain polite.

"And I'm not having a panic attack! Or am I?" breathed the blonde woman. "Autonomic symptoms; palpitations, sweating, tremor. Panic attack?" Her face lit up. "No! I'm hungry! That's it! I haven't eaten all day. Sweet sticky cocktail, a burst of insulin to mop it up, overshot and now...." She grinned happily, "I'm hypoglycaemic!" she announced. Her face then fell. "I feel terrible." She paced in her cupboard. "And I get so grumpy when I'm hungry." The blonde woman looked at the Manager. "Deborah wouldn't let me eat anything. She said if I ate a mouthful, she wouldn't be able to sew me into this dress."

The Manager had a very keen sense of the ridiculous and her face twitched as she strained to contain her amusement at the stranger's verbosity.

"Then, may I be of assistance, Madame?" she said smoothly. A waiter was making his way from the kitchen with a tray of canapes. The Manager waved to him, and he came hurrying over and bowed his head deeply to her. She relieved him of his tray with a muttered thanks and handed it to the Blonde in the cupboard.

"Oh my God, you're a lifesaver!" enthused the woman and helped herself to a pastry morsel. The Manager had, by this time, brought out her mobile phone and had surreptitiously taken a picture of the woman's face. "These are absolutely delicious!" she was saying, helping herself to two more canapes. "Is all the food at the Fitzwarren this good?"

The Manager nodded to herself as a face match of the blonde woman emerged on her screen.

'Local Doc Makes Good!' announced the front page of the Whitby Gazette. 'Local girl, Charlotte Hart, has graduated with Honours from Sheffield Medical School and gained a special prize for the best psychiatry essay in a national competition! Whitby girl born and bred….' A picture of a much younger Charlie was under the headline. It had been lifted from a group school photograph. She was much younger but still recognisable, with the same grin she wore now. Dr Charlie Hart.

"That's steamed pork…' Charlie was saying. "Ginger, garlic, cabbage and…" Charlie paused. *She won't get it,* thought the Manager confidently. It was the Manager's own special recipe, hard-won in a Summer spent working for a half-crazed (but near genius) three-star Michelin Chef in a sweaty hell-hole of a kitchen in Paris. Nobody recognised the secret ingredient.

"Plum sauce," announced Charlie. The Manager's face fell. Charlie continued. "The pork has been soaked in a plum sauce. But a really special one. Those plums are sharp but sweet at the same time. How do you do that?" Her brow furrowed, and she exclaimed. "Li! means Plum!… second most common surname in China." Once again, the Manager struggled to remain polite in the face of the ridiculous.

"You sound like you swallowed a cheap guidebook," she observed wryly.

"Sorry, a rush of plum to the head," giggled Charlie. She certainly seemed much happier now she'd eaten.

The Manager's eyes narrowed as she looked at the jewellery around Charlie's neck. She took a spontaneous step towards her. Charlie, looking nervous, stepped back, balancing the canape tray in one hand.

"Do you know what it is that you are wearing?" The Manager asked quietly.

CHAPTER FORTY-THREE

Charlie reached up and gently caressed the heavy object around her neck. It was an exquisitely carved, small, jadeite dragon in a stunning, curved, gold setting. The flawless jadeite was a luminous, light green.

"Yes," she replied. "A dragon belonging to the Empress Cixi of the late Qing Dynasty."

"There goes the guidebook again," said the Manager dryly. "You clearly don't know what that piece means. You don't know what the Dragon Empress means to some Chinese people."

"And you're going to tell me?" asked Charlie nervously. There was a pause, and Charlie felt obliged to fill the silence. "Maybe that's why Mr Lau's companion asked one of her friends to photograph it. Because it means so much?" The Manager's eyes narrowed slightly.

"Why are you here tonight?" she demanded. She seemed to remember her manners and added, "If you don't mind me asking?"

"I'm here with Lord Beaulouf. We hope to speak with Mr Lau," said Charlie, feeling very anxious again. She suddenly felt that she'd done something wrong. "He'll be waiting," she added, looking at the small gap between the Manager and the cupboard wall.

The Manager regarded Charlie, her face serious.

"Annie Wei will want that necklace," she said slowly. "But she will hoard it, like a miser. That necklace is a thing of beauty, to be seen and shared. It celebrates the creativity and mastery of the Chinese people; the power of its former owner." The Manager drew herself up. "It's something about which I feel very strongly. The Art of a People should reflect its People. It should not be kept in the dark." Charlie reached up and gently touched the precious ornament again. *You've worn a necklace of gold before,* something whispered deep in her mind. Charlie shook her head as if to clear it.

"But it's my bargaining chip," she said quietly. "My Plan B. We have to speak with Mr Lau."

The Manager pursed her lips. There was another pause.

"It may be that I can help you," she eventually said. "I'm the Manager here, I have a small degree of influence. But Mr Lau is his own man." She looked intently at Charlie. "In return, you must promise me you will not sell that necklace to Annie Wei." Charlie paused. They had come here to speak to Lau. Surely it was worth it if this woman could get that for them? She nodded.

"I promise," she said quietly.

MAC TURNED AROUND and found Charlie standing at his elbow. She wouldn't meet his eye, and he wondered if he should apologise. They stood, feeling awkward.

"Crumbs," he said. Charlie shot him a surprised glance.

"What?" she said.

"Crumbs. You, you have crumbs," said Mac. He didn't look at her, but indicated where her cleavage would be.

"Oh," said Charlie. She hurriedly brushed at the front of her revealing dress. "Someone helped me out," she muttered, blushing. "I feel much better now." There was a pause.

"I'm sorry!" They both said at the same time.

They looked towards Lau's barge. A short, balding man in a grey, striped silk suit stood awkwardly before Lau, who remained sitting at his table. The balding man was talking animatedly; Lau listened politely and impassively. Annie Wei had returned to Lau's side, but her attention remained glued to her mobile phone. The man in the charcoal suit crossed the bridge and handed a note to Lau, which Lau opened and read. The balding man continued his monologue, determined to say his piece.

"Any progress?" asked Charlie, hopefully. Mac shook his head, looking frustrated. "I may have found someone to help us," said Charlie, and Mac finally looked at her. His eyes widened, and he raised one eyebrow in surprise.

"What? Who? Why didn't you come and get me?"

"That's a lot of questions," muttered Charlie, however, she didn't get the opportunity to answer any of them. The man in the charcoal suit was walking toward them with a warm smile.

"My friends," he said. "Mr Lau has agreed to grant you a few moments of his precious time." Mac shot Charlie a wary glance. He then nodded graciously and allowed them to be led towards the entry point to the marble barge. The balding man was being led away by a burly bodyguard. The man seemed very reluctant to leave.

"Opportunity of a lifetime, Wellington!" he called over his substantial shoulder.

The remaining bodyguard held up one meaty hand, and they paused. The bodyguard craned around and looked at Mr Lau, who was still studying the note he had received. Without looking up, he beckoned imperiously. The bodyguard stood aside and, urged on by the smiling man in the charcoal suit, they stepped onto the narrow marble walkway. Charlie felt the eyes of the room on them, and, once again, she felt her stomach turn with anxiety. Mac strode confidently over the bridge, Charlie tip-toeing cautiously in his wake, crystal high heels flashing.

Up close, Wellington Lau was a very handsome man of around fifty. His eyes, however, looked both tired and angry. Charlie quailed inside; she hated aggression. She stood back and lowered her eyes; let Mac do what he had planned. She heard Mac start to speak, to thank, to praise; to offer the chance of prime real estate within the rolling, lucrative Golden Triangle of Wetherby, Leeds and Harrogate. All of this in return for a tiny thing. In return for practically nothing; for a small amount of information.

Lau listened. He nodded politely. He hid a yawn, and Mac faltered. "Lord Beaulouf," said Lau quietly. He held up one long-fingered, elegant hand. Mac came to an abrupt halt in his speech. "I am honoured that you offered me such an opportunity. I will humbly consider your rich and intelligent proposal. I will, after due consideration, be in contact." And that was that—their opportunity. Charlie looked at Mac's back. It had tightened, and his breathing had quickened. He was not used to being cut short, being dismissed.

Lau turned his gaze to Charlie, who stood awkwardly, two paces behind Mac. "Dr Hart. Would you be kind enough to step forward?" he asked quietly, but authoritatively. Charlie could not look at Mac's face as she stepped past him. Lau slowly looked her up and down. He glanced at the iPad propped by his right hand. "Doctor Charlotte Hart," he said slowly. "Of Whitby, North Yorkshire. Lately companion of one, Sally Marshall." Lau looked sharply at Charlie. "We had thought Miss Marshall might be here tonight. We had looked forward to... crossing swords."

"I'm sorry to disappoint you, Mr Lau," said Charlie quietly. "Miss Marshall had hoped to be here. I extend her apologies."

Charlie heard the click of heels behind her, but her eyes didn't leave the gaze of Lau. Into the seat to the right of Lau dropped the Manager. She threw off her dark blue blazer and unbuttoned her waistcoat to reveal an expensive, duck-egg blue silk shirt. She unpinned her hair and let it fall, in glistening, straight lines, around her intelligent face.

"Father," she said, nodding respectfully to Lau. "Thank you for receiving my note." Lau didn't drop his gaze from Charlie. From her neck.

"Miss Hart. It appears that you have something that I would wish to purchase for a... noble consort." Beside him, Annie Wei shifted slightly in her seat. Her eyes, however, remained fixed on her phone, her thumbs roaming restlessly over its surface. Charlie reached up to touch her necklace. She swallowed.

"Mr Lau," she said. "I'm aware of the honour you do me. However, this thing of beauty is not mine to sell." Lau's face hardened.

"I was under the impression that your necklace and its negotiation was part of your 'Plan B' Dr Hart." Charlie's eyes widened. "Just because your Miss Marshall can't access cameras and microphones in the Hanover Suite doesn't mean they don't exist," snapped Lau.

Charlie looked at The Manager. She was looking down at the floor of the barge. Her head shook infinitesimally. Charlie made up her mind. She raised her chin.

"I'm sorry, Mr Lau. But a promise is a promise. I promised I would not sell the necklace." Lau looked angry, as did Annie Wei. Lau waved his hand in irritation.

"Then goodbye to the both of you." he snapped. The bodyguards started eagerly across the narrow marble walkway. Charlie held up an imperious hand.

"Mr Lau!" she said loudly. "I admit, I had a Plan B. However, I always believe in also having a Plan C." She lowered her right hand. A large diamond gleamed on her ring finger. A sixteen-carat, emerald-cut diamond, with two 1.8-carat diamonds flanking it. "This belonged to one of five special sisters," she said quietly. "And to their brief second marriage. It would be my honour if you would accept it. As a gift."

Annie Wei's eyes widened slightly, and her phone briefly strayed towards Charlie's hand. Annie's head nodded towards Lau a fraction. Lau's lip, however, curled.

"You think the baubles of a reality-show star merit my time as much as the treasures of an Empress?"

"No, Mr Lau," replied Charlie quietly. "But perhaps we can celebrate our august mutual connections with Hong Kong?" Lau froze. Charlie kept his gaze, and she saw the Manager stifle the slightest of smiles. Charlie was pleased to see Annie Wei had not picked up on the hint about Lau's mistress, Augusta Tse, in Hong Kong. Lau paused. He seemed angry now that he was backed into a corner by his own infidelity.

"The jewellery of an Empress is worth five minutes of my business acumen. The trappings of tawdry celebrity are worth thirty seconds."

"I don't want your business acumen," shot back Charlie. "I need your honesty." She looked at him pointedly. "Answer me, honestly, for two minutes."

"You heard me. Thirty seconds," replied Lau, his mouth now a thin, hard line.

"Ninety!" shot back Charlie.

"Forty-five!"

"Eighty!"

"Nothing!" exploded Lau, standing up from his chair in anger. He signalled to the security guards, who again came barrelling across the narrow bridge.

At this point, Annie Wei finally tore her eyes away from her mobile phone. She looked, expressionless, at Lau and coughed once. Lau sighed in frustration. He dismissed the guards and sat heavily in his chair.

"You have precisely sixty seconds of my time, Miss Hart," he sighed. "Not one second more. A deal is a deal."

"It's Doctor Hart, Mr Lau," said Charlie. "And thank you." But Lau had already testily started the timer on his iPad. The timer now read 57 seconds.

"Did you speak to a man at your last gala night?" Charlie said, realising how stupid the question was as soon as it had left her mouth. Lau smiled contemptuously.

"I spoke to many men at the last gala night," he said slowly, drawing out the precious seconds.

"Did you speak with a man who offered you some Code Blue tablets or part of the formula for these tablets?" Charlie demanded. Lau looked reluctant to speak. He glanced at his daughter.

"A deal is a deal, Mr Lau," said Charlie quietly. Lau nodded once. He said nothing else.

"And did you take them off him?" said Charlie, starting to sweat at her lack of progress. Lau shook his head. His eyes slid to the timer, and he smiled.

"Why not?" said Charlie. Lau sat back in his chair, relaxed.

"Because I will have nothing to do with drugs, Miss Hart," he said. His smile widened. Charlie sensed Mac shifting behind her.

"Then why did he come to you?" asked Charlie. Lau's face fell into a scowl.

"I don't know," snapped Lau. "Whatever the reason, I turned down his offer and sent him on his way."

"And then what happened to him?" demanded Charlie. Lau scoffed.

"He had a heart attack in his hotel room. He died, and there were no drugs and no formula to be found."

Charlie paused. She couldn't think of what to say next. She felt a wave of panic as her last precious seconds surged by. She reached up to gently touch the necklace and, for some reason, the thought of Big Fish and Lone Wolves flashed across her mind.

"Why are you here? In Sheffield?" she said softly. Lau looked surprised. His eyes flickered and then hardened. He paused.

"Because I like the view," he said slowly and angrily. Charlie glanced towards the window again. She remembered the odd angle of the hotel as it loomed over Arundel Gate. She realised what was strange about it. Instead of facing the greenery and sky to the west of the city, the hotel had been built facing the drab buildings at the top of Castlegate and a stretch of dirty dual carriageway.

"What view?" asked Charlie, mystified. Lau didn't reply, but his entire face sank slightly. *He's in pain*, thought Charlie Hart, the expert in the pain of others. *Only loss causes that much pain*, her instincts whispered to her. "Your son, Mr Lau. How did he die?" she said. Lau didn't answer.

"Road traffic accident," replied the Manager quietly.

"On Arundel Gate? Within view of this room?" asked Charlie. The Laus both nodded. "I thought heroin was involved?" whispered Charlie. Lau gave a short, bitter laugh.

"All the money I pay to keep my son off the internet, and still, that's what's thought of him?" He glared at Charlie. "That is why your man came to see me, because of that lie. The van that killed my boy, the van that ignored the red light, was driven by junkies. My son was a student at the University here. He had never touched heroin in his life. He was an environmental engineer."

Lau pulled in a deep, sighing breath. "For some reason, he loved this dirty little city, the valleys and the hills. He said he loved that Sheffield had so many trees. He used to say he was going to save the World. One tree at a time. And we... we would walk...." Lau paused, shaking his head, his eyes full of bitter tears. "The better half of me died on that day," he whispered.

"So, you built the World's biggest tombstone, The Fitzwarren hotel, here, in Sheffield?" Asked Charlie. Lau shook his head.

"Your time's up, Doctor Hart."

By now, his daughter and Annie Wei were both turned towards him. Both had placed their hand on his shoulder, with him in his palpable grief. Charlie sensed both women's genuine affection for him, if not for each other. Remembering what Sally had told her, Charlie put her hands together and bowed deeply, three times, from her waist.

"I give honour to the dead, Mr Lau," she said quietly. She removed the enormous diamond from her right hand and, with two hands, placed it on the table. With two hands, she gently pushed it towards Lau. "A deal is a deal," Charlie said quietly. She had failed. They had learned nothing of any use about the missing Code Blue tablets.

CHAPTER FORTY-FOUR

Charlie turned away from Lau's table. The man in the charcoal suit waited to lead them away. Mac looked livid, but she expected nothing less. As they stepped onto the bridge, however, Charlie's ever-present desire to help, to take the pain away, got the better of her. She turned briskly around and walked back to the table. The man in the charcoal suit went to grab her arm, but Mac instead grabbed his arm, preventing him from getting to Charlie. There was a murmur from the watching crowd as Charlie strode up to the table.

"Mr Lau!" The three looked up, wary. Charlie fiddled with the clasp behind her neck and eventually worked it free. She laid the heavy gold and jadeite necklace in the centre of the white marble table, where it gleamed. Her neck now felt naked without the heavy pendant, and, for a moment, she felt an uncharacteristic deep stab of regret. However, she quickly recovered. "There is a Chinese proverb," said Charlie. "I'm sure you're familiar with it. *The best time to plant a tree is many years ago. The second-best time is today*. You're trapped in your grief, but I'm sure your son, the son who loved you and looked up to you, wouldn't want that." The three people seated at the table said nothing. "I can't sell this for your..." Charlie struggled to remember the term. "'Noble consort.' But I am willing to auction it, to a museum, for a good cause. The Wellington Lau Junior scholarship; scholarships for environmental engineers. God knows we need them. You'll be able to afford a stack of them. Build something, other than a gravestone. Grow something... in his name." She paused, now starting to feel very foolish. "If you don't want to, we're here for a bit longer... I trust you. To return the necklace." Still, the three just looked at her without expression.

Charlie turned away but spun back as something occurred to her. "If you do auction it, I'd expect a Gala night. For my friends and me. With food. At least three courses. With wine." She still got no response. *Oh dear*, thought Charlie. *Don't give away expensive jewellery when you're hungry*! She'd probably just offended one of the most powerful men in Sheffield. She turned and walked past Mac and the other men, her face burning.

Once they'd left the barge, Mac laid into her, as she'd known he would do. "What the Hell was that?" he exclaimed. "You had one entire minute to ask him anything to do with the Code Blue tablets, and you ask about his son? You had one thing to do!"

"Oh, and what are you going to do? Hit me as well? Like Ben?" announced Charlie, not caring by now if anyone heard them. "He was in pain!"

"We're all in pain, Hart!" snarled Mac. "Grow up. You

can't just kiss and make it all better. You can't just hand over part of yourself and think you'll take the pain away."

"I can't help it. It's what I do!" she said, deeply wounded that Mac would echo Fergus Eaton in his opinion of her. Mac moved closer to her and grabbed her arm.

"Well, what you do just isn't good enough," he said intently.

"And you think I don't know that?" Charlie cried. "You think I don't wake up every single morning thinking just that? It's what they'll write on my gravestone. Charlie Hart: just not good enough!"

Her eyes filled with tears, and she tore away from him, desperate to find the white door and escape to the bathroom. A figure stepped into her path. She tried to dodge around them, lowering her gaze so they wouldn't see her smudged eyes.

"Doctor Hart," said a voice firmly. She looked up. The man in the charcoal suit was standing next to her. He was no longer smiling. He lowered his voice. "Mr Lau would like a brief word. Please." Charlie's heart sank. Lau was going to return the necklace. More humiliation. Mac was right. Again. Why did she insist on blundering around, trying to make it all better? In the end, she just made a fool of herself. Her shoulders slumped as she trailed after the man.

Mac approached her. "What are you doing?" he asked.

"Lau wants to return the necklace," Charlie replied, not looking at him. "I hope you're happy, being right all the time." Mac took her hand gently. She looked at him, surprised. His face had lost its angry expression.

"I'm sorry, Hart," he said, looking awkward. "I shouldn't have said what I said. You tried to do a good thing." He let go of her hand. "I'll wait here for you." Charlie turned away, only for him to speak again. "And Hart," she turned back to him. "I don't think you look like Barbie." He paused, his face serious. "I think you look beautiful." Charlie didn't know what to say. She looked away, embarrassed, and then reluctantly headed for the barge.

Charlie approached the table. Lau was still sitting with the dragon necklace before him. He looked thoughtful.

"Your grasp of Chinese culture and its people is pitiful, Dr Hart," he mused. "I agree with my daughter that you seem to have read one of the more inferior types of guidebook." He looked up at her. "But you do have some grasp of human nature," he said thoughtfully. His hand came to rest gently on the dragon.

"I have control of all that happens in my hotel," said Lau. "And I will not have this compromised. However, I have little control over what happens in the streets around my hotel. In the street behind my hotel. There is a nightclub that appears only on these Gala nights. It exists to take advantage of the weaknesses of men." Lau looked to his right. Charlie looked as well. She saw a waiter unlock and open a side door for the balding man in the grey striped suit. The man staggered slightly as he shrugged on a coat. Lau looked back at Charlie. "You may find some of your answers there," he said quietly. He gently tapped the dragon and drew it towards him. "A deal's a deal. Goodbye, Doctor Hart."

Charlie hurried over to Mac, who stood, hands in pockets, looking thoughtful. "Hart, forget about the dragon," he said.

"Listen, why don't you and I go for–" Charlie interrupted him.

"No, Mac, you listen. Lau is keeping the dragon. And he gave me some information in return!" Mac's closed expression returned.

"Well?" he said tersely.

"Lau says there's a nightclub that opens up on the street behind the hotel. Only on Gala nights, only once a month. Tries to take advantage of 'men's weaknesses,' whatever he means by that. He says we may get some answers there." Mac grabbed both of her upper arms and pulled her towards him. He planted a very unexpected kiss on the top of her head, his face full of relief. Charlie suddenly realised how stressed he, too, had been by the pressure of the whole evening.

"At last!" he exclaimed. "Progress." He went to leave the suite the way they had entered.

"No!" exclaimed Charlie. "This way..." She walked confidently towards the hidden door.

As they approached the door that Charlie had seen the balding man leave through, they were approached by a waiter.

"May I help you?" he asked politely. "We usually keep this door locked." Charlie smiled up at him.

"Oh, it's ok, we just fancy a bit of fresh air. On the street at the back of the hotel?" The waiter nodded understandingly. He produced a key and unlocked the door.

"Have an enjoyable evening," he said smoothly.

THEY WERE in a dimly lit stairwell. Mac flipped out his phone and dialled. He was trying to get through to Sally, who would be desperate for an update. He was in luck and got a signal. However, the phone rang for a long time. Mac frowned; this was unlike Sally. The phone was eventually answered. It was Ben's voice. He was speaking quietly.

"Hello?" said Ben.

"It's Mac. Where's Sally?" There was a pause.

"She's gone back to sleep. She's been working on her new computer project; says it's really taking off. And then pacing in the kitchen for the last hour has worn her out. Any news? I'll wake her up and let her know."

"We got to talk to Lau," said Mac, sounding relieved. "Hart found out about a pop-up nightclub just behind the hotel and Lau thinks we may get some intel there. We're moving there now. We'll return as soon as we're finished there."

"I didn't doubt you for a minute! Well done. I'll let Sal know." Ben replied. He sounded as if he was smiling. Mac rang off.

They hurried down the stairs and came to a fire escape door. It swung open, and they stepped onto the dark, cobbled street. Almost directly opposite them, the Victorian warehouse Mac had scoped all those weeks ago was throbbing with life; lit with vivid purple and red neon lights. *Inferno Club* read Charlie. The bouncers on the door were keeping a close eye on the Fitzwarren fire escape and the potential customers emerging from it. They stood aside as Charlie and Mac approached the entrance. It was clear there would be no issue with them entering.

Mac stopped, suddenly, at the door. "Gentlemen," he said smoothly to the security guards, patting at his jacket. "I appear to have forgotten my wallet." He kissed the top of Charlie's head. "You go in Darling, have a look around," he said pointedly. "I'll just nip back to the hotel. I'll be back in five." The head of security nodded casually and waved Charlie in. With one wide-eyed look at Mac's departing back, Charlie moved inside.

Mac felt uneasy about something but couldn't put his finger on what it was. He had also realised that he was unarmed, which made him feel uncomfortable. Vulnerable. Charlie should be OK in plain sight for a few minutes. Mac rapidly walked to where his car was parked down a quiet side street. He accessed a hidden compartment in the boot. He'd securely strapped a loaded Glock-19 and two extra magazines into the small space. He snapped open the 15-round magazine to check it was full, then slipped the gun into his underarm holster. There had been hidden scanning on entry to the Hanover suite. Lau wasn't stupid enough to allow access to himself like that without surveillance for concealed weapons. Mac felt better now he was armed again, but he needed to get back to Charlie.

The bouncers, satisfied that he had come from the Fitzwarren, waved him into the Inferno Club. *No entry charge,* thought Mac; that meant they must expect to make money from him some other way. He was in a large hallway with washrooms leading off to either side. Mac pushed through a wide, red-beaded curtain to access the main room. Straight ahead of him was a DJ booth on the opposite wall. A tall, skinny man with a large afro and headphones nodded in time to the music. Red leather booths fanned out from a large dancefloor full of swaying, gyrating customers. Music throbbed loudly around him and the lights were low and red. Dry ice whirled around his feet, adding to the hellish atmosphere. Thick, silky drapes of scarlet material hung from walls and the ceiling—the air stank of cheap perfume, expensive cologne, and the desperation of ungracious, unwanted middle age.

Men, mostly in their late forties and fifties, were everywhere, laughing and drinking. Girls of a much younger age were hanging from the arms of many of them or sitting, squeezed into tight booths, with them. The girls were laughing, too, swaying in time to the music. Some men, Mac observed, were openly snorting cocaine. No wonder some of them had heart attacks.

A man in an expensive shirt, unbuttoned to midway down his chest, was moving from table to table, acting as some sort of Maître D. The man discreetly pushed and pulled at the girls, encouraging them to be seen to enjoy themselves and order drinks; to speak with any businessman who didn't have company. There seemed to be gaming tables for dice and cards on a raised platform set back to the room's left. The tables were busy and crowded. A balcony ran around the top of the room, but this was not in use.

A man laughed raucously close by and Mac flinched. "And then this guy gave me thirty quid for my hat!" the man roared. "And I only paid ten for it! Thirty quid for an old trilby? That's twenty pounds profit, ladies!" The two teenage girls with him laughed uproariously. Their eyes seemed glassy.

"That should buy you half a lager in here, then!" one girl joked. The Maître D' jabbed her viciously in the shoulder as he passed by. The girl's face fell, and she seemed to remember her script. "I'm thirsty; let's get drinks!" she yelled above the music, batting her eyes and leaning towards the man so he could better see down her low-cut top. The businessman's eager eyes fixed themselves on her young, fresh flesh.

"Over here, waiter!" he called, waving his hand but not tearing his eyes away. Mac looked around for Charlie. He couldn't see her. He scanned the club again, his eyes roving from face to face. Where was she? What had he done, letting her come into a place like this all alone?

CHAPTER
FORTY-FIVE

Charlie had stepped reluctantly into the Inferno Club. She passed through the atrium and pushed aside a red-beaded curtain. It certainly seemed like Inferno to her; *Dante's Inferno*, she thought. The realm of those who have rejected spiritual values by yielding to bestial appetites. Her striking appearance brought a lot of unwanted attention. Men staggered up to her, tried to engage in lurid conversation, or simply leered. Charlie kept walking, at times having to push them physically away. She made it to the bar and hung there, feeling like a drowning woman clinging to a rotting plank.

"Let me buy you a drink, beautiful," slurred a short, portly man in his fifties. He was clutching a slopping, half-full glass of whisky to his chest, his other hand firmly propped against the bar. Charlie suspected it was the only thing keeping him upright. She shook her head and moved away. Where was Mac? Why had he left her like that?

She caught sight of a familiar face through the thick wall of writhing figures. It was Baz, Georgia's brother. He was jovially slapping the beefy shoulder of the balding businessman she had last seen in the Hanover Suite. His broad, white smile gleamed unnaturally in the ultraviolet light. Baz turned away from the man, and the smile instantly dropped from his face. He moved like a venomous lizard in a sinuous, deliberate way towards a young girl who stood with her back to Charlie. Charlie saw his hand snake out and grab the girl's elbow. He discreetly tried to pull her towards the suited, balding man who stood expectantly behind Baz. The businessman's tongue roamed restlessly over his slack bottom lip, reminding Charlie more strongly of a reptile eyeing a struggling morsel.

The girl was trying to pull her arm out of Baz's grasp, and she shook her head, clearly unhappy. Baz's face hardened, as did his grip on the girl. Charlie launched herself away from the bar, angrily pushing at swaying, suit-clad backs to wade her way to the side of the struggling girl.

"Hey!" cried Charlie to Baz. She couldn't be heard over the thumping music, but the hand she pushed hard against his shoulder was unmistakable. He looked at her in surprise, and his mouth pulled sideways in a snarl, all pretence of joviality stripped away. His eyes glittered dangerously, and he reached out to grab at Charlie's arm, too. She pulled away and clutched the hand of the girl standing next to her. "Touch me, and I'll call the Police!" she yelled, mouthing each word defiantly. Even though he couldn't hear her, Baz could lip-read the word "Police". He dropped the girl's arm as if it was on fire. A wide, fake smile oozed onto his face, and he stepped away, holding up both hands, exactly as he'd done at Rowans Holt. *No harm done, nothing to see here,* he seemed to say. He turned back to the businessman and, taking his elbow, led him off towards a booth where a young girl sat. The girl looked up at the approaching men. Despite her smile, she seemed awkward and squirmed nervously, as prey would.

The girl whom Charlie had tried to help dived off into the crowd, making for the red-beaded curtain. Charlie followed her, and they entered the atrium at almost the same time. Charlie flinched as a man brushed behind her, a hat pulled low over his face. He staggered slightly, his footsteps uneven, as he stumbled into the men's restroom. The girl had disappeared. Charlie guessed she was in the ladies' toilet. Charlie pushed open the door to the bathroom and flinched at the smell of decrepit, damp, and faulty drains. Sure enough, the young girl stood in front of the cracked mirror, looking down at her left arm, where Baz had grabbed her only moments earlier.

The girl was dressed in a short, halter-neck, black shift dress that showed off her long, brown legs and she had old, black Doc Marten boots on her feet. Her makeup was pale against her dark skin but her large eyes were heavily lined in black. Her afro hair blazed in a halo around her head, with a white, bleached stripe that emerged above her right brow. She had a tattoo on her left shoulder; a delicate trace of spider-web laid over roses, stars and a half moon. She smelled strongly of cheap musk perfume.

"Are you ok?" said Charlie hesitantly. The girl glanced up at her. Her face unexpectedly broke into a warm, lovely smile.

"Yeah, I can handle Baz, don't worry," she said in a broad Sheffield accent. "I'm just not in the mood tonight. Thanks for trying to help."

"I don't think I'd be in the mood any night with that lot,"

joked Charlie. Something clicked in Charlie's memory. "Leticia," she said out loud. The girl looked up, surprised.

"How do you know my name?" she asked

"I saw you," said Charlie. "At the farm shop. You work for Georgia." Charlie suddenly understood Georgia's comment to Baz about keeping his hands off her girls. Baz was poaching Georgia's pretty, young employees to work in his seedy nightclub as hostesses.

Leticia looked awkward. "Please don't tell Georgia. She'll go mental if she knows." Charlie and Leticia jumped as someone barged against the bathroom door as if coming in. They must have changed their mind, for the door swung almost closed again, and no one entered the room.

"Of course, I wouldn't tell. You're an adult... Aren't you?" asked Charlie anxiously. Leticia gave another beaming smile and laughed.

"Yes, I'm an adult. And I don't let those old gits take advantage. Well, not too much. The money's great, but I need to keep the farm-shop job, so my mum don't suspect about this one."

Charlie returned her smile and went to leave. Charlie sniffed. Cheap musk. Something stirred again in her memory. The dead man from A and E, Kenny, had smelled of musk perfume. She slowly turned back to the girl.

"Leticia? Were you here a few weeks ago? With a man who became unwell?" Letica's smile faded, and her eyes slid away from Charlie's gaze. She shook her head. Charlie's eyes widened. "Lucy... was Lucy here?" Letica's head shot up.

"How do you know about Lucy?"

"That group in the van," replied Charlie. "The leader, Lawrence, was looking for Lucy at the farm shop. Was she here?" Leticia said nothing, she just gazed, wide-eyed, at Charlie.

Charlie felt her heart speed up, and a twist of excitement pulled at her stomach. She walked closer to Leticia and looked at her earnestly. "I don't want to cause any trouble, Leticia. It's just that Lucy may have taken something that means she could be in big danger. I don't care about money or the police. I just need to know where that thing is." Leticia still said nothing. "You can trust me," said Charlie. She shrugged. She felt she now had nothing to lose. "I'm a doctor," she said simply.

"I know," breathed Leticia. "From the Manor." It was Charlie's turn to frown.

The Manor. It sounded like an exclusive part of Sheffield but was, in fact, one of the most deprived wards in the city. As a junior doctor, Charlie had done a four-month GP post at a surgery in the Manor area. She had seen, first-hand, the effect that crushing poverty and government indifference had on real people's lives and life chances. She had also seen the endless love and help those real people had given to their friends and relatives, even in the midst of their own terrible need; the duty and kindness and care that creep quietly home.

"We came to see you with my Nan-nan," continued Leticia. "She liked you." Charlie looked again at Leticia; looked past the makeup and the tattoos. Past the dyed hair and the confident swagger. Patty Tinsley was Leticia's grandma, Charlie remembered. How could she forget?

Patty Tinsley was accompanied everywhere she went by adoring but fearful grandchildren, of whom she had what seemed like hundreds. Patty Tinsley; legs like matchsticks, belly like a mountain. Wrinkles like valley ridges and lungs like a coal miner's third-best gloves. Patty Tinsley; the stuff of receptionists' nightmares. Patty had supported numerous of her nefarious children on the black-market sale of her opioid prescriptions alone. If a new and enthusiastic doctor tried to cut her scripts down, she would descend on the surgery; mouth like a sewer and arms like joints of sinewy mutton.

Charlie nodded. "And I liked your Nan-nan too," she said, stretching the concept of truth to breaking point. "But, Leticia, I also took a sacred oath. As a doctor, to do no harm," Charlie said. "I promise you; my friends and I will do our best to keep Lucy safe." Leticia considered Charlie. She seemed to come to a decision.

"Lucy's my best friend," Letica whispered. "She's been hiding. She thinks she's in big trouble. The thing. The things she took... people have died. She feels awful." Charlie nodded sympathetically.

"I think I'd feel bad too," said Charlie. She went and stood next to Leticia and leaned casually against the grubby sink. "But sometimes, under pressure, it's normal to act in ways that we wouldn't at other times." Leticia nodded, relieved to have some understanding for her friend.

"She never used to steal," said Leticia. "Lucy's really honest. It's Lawrence!" she spat angrily.

"The man who was looking for her?" asked Charlie. "He didn't seem like a nice person." Leticia's face hardened.

"He's a bully and a complete git!" exclaimed Leticia. "She's like a different person now. And the worst thing is, she really loves him." Leticia looked intently at Charlie. "She really loves him. She'd do anything for him." Leticia looked down at the filthy, wet concrete floor. "He just wants cash so he can buy his drugs. He makes her... offer stuff to the blokes here." Letica paused.

"It's Ok," said Charlie gently. "You can tell me."

Leticia continued, angry now. "He told her to get them drunk, lead them on and then steal their wallets. Take the money and whatever she can get her hands on." Leticia looked at Charlie and seemed genuinely scared. "She's going to get caught one day, and one of them will hurt her. But Lawrence doesn't care." Leticia paused, thinking. "Lucy said that man who got sick was nice. He didn't try to touch her up or anything; he was more interested in gambling. He was doing really well at the tables." Leticia smiled. "He told Lucy she was his lucky charm. Baz was livid because he'd won so much money, but it serves Baz right. He's a git too." They looked at the bathroom door as it creaked, but still, no one came in.

"What did Lucy do?" prompted Charlie gently. Leticia looked embarrassed.

"She went back to his room, but all he wanted to do was talk about his kids. Then he got sick, so she called the ambulance, but she stole his wallet," Leticia said. "And then she ran away. She found ten blue tablets behind the cash in the wallet. She realised what they were, that new drug, and she gave half of the tablets to Lawrence. And she found this fancy bit of paper, too. It was half of a full piece of paper, but it had half of a 3d picture of a raven on it. She thought it was right cool, really Goth. Me and Lucy, we're Goths," said Leticia, proudly pointing to her hair and tattoos. Charlie smiled and carried on listening. "Lucy kept the original piece of paper and drew a half raven for Lawrence. She spent hours on it; Lucy's really arty, see? She thought it was really romantic. She said she and Lawrence were two halves of one soul." Leticia pulled a face. "They're not. Lawrence is just a big git!"

"Why didn't Lucy give him all the tablets?" asked Charlie.

"It's her insurance policy," said Leticia, her lip curling contemptuously. "Lawrence doesn't want to know her if she has nothing to give him."

Letica frowned. "How did you know about that man?" she asked. Charlie's face fell as she remembered Mr X. "What?" said Leticia. What's happened?" Charlie said nothing. Leticia looked at her. "Did someone get into trouble?" she demanded. "Because of what Lucy stole?" Charlie remembered the man's drilled and broken teeth, his unmoving, poisoned body.

"About as much trouble as you can possibly get into," she said quietly. Leticia's eyes widened. She backed away from Charlie, who held up her hands placatingly.

"Leticia, no. I don't want to cause Lucy any trouble. I can help her; help keep her safe. Where is Lucy now?" asked Charlie, slowly and carefully.

There was a sudden, loud hammering at the bathroom door. A red-faced Baz appeared around it.

"Leticia! get your arse back in here!" he roared. Leticia pushed herself away from the sink with a sigh. Charlie grabbed at her.

"Leticia!" she said urgently.

"Do you promise that you won't go to the cops, that you'll keep us safe?" said Leticia quietly. Charlie nodded. "Then I finish my shift in about an hour. I'll take you to her, take you to Lucy." said Leticia. "She'll be glad to get rid of those tablets and that piece of paper." She looked down at Charlie's feet. "But there is one thing I want..." she said.

• • •

MAC WAS LOOKING around the nightclub with increasing urgency. He still couldn't see Charlie. He pushed through the heaving crowd. *Why did I leave her*? He thought angrily. Half of the men in here looked like predators. She was too soft for her own good. What if something had happened to her?

A hand shot out from a narrow dark space between two booths, where two walls met, and grabbed the sleeve of his evening jacket. He pulled his arm away angrily but realised, as he did so, that it was Charlie looking at him from the dark space. Her eyes gleamed with excitement, and she beckoned urgently to him. He squeezed into the space to join her. It was much quieter in here, but they were pressed uncomfortably close. It was dark, and a curl of red material hung, obscuring half the view of the club, but at least it partially drowned the pulsing, repetitive beats.

Mac's eyes widened as Charlie leaned close to his ear and told him what she had learned.

"I'm just waiting here for Leticia to finish her shift, and then she'll take us to Lucy!" said Charlie excitedly. Mac smiled down at her, the terrible pressure in his chest subsiding for the first time in weeks.

"Well done," he managed, genuinely impressed. Charlie's face lit up, and she smiled up at him. She seemed shorter than earlier. He glanced down at her feet, then leaned closer to her ear again.

"You're wearing old boots!" he called over the music. Charlie shouted back.

"I know! Leticia wanted my shoes. Giving away my jewellery, then my shoes, I'll be naked by the time I go home at this rate!" Charlie peered out again at the club, hoping to catch sight of Leticia. She was crammed very close to Mac; so close, she could feel his chest rise and fall. She felt his heart beating against her, and she automatically counted his pulse rate. Forty-eight. Impressive, he must be very fit. Charlie felt his breathing rate slowly rise, as did his pulse. Had he seen something? She looked up at him.

In the dim, close space, Mac was gazing down at her, his large, intent, brown eyes studying the curves and planes of her face. Charlie stared back at him, and the breath in her chest suddenly felt tight. Her mouth was dry. She swallowed. Neither of them dropped their gaze. Mac slowly brought his head down towards Charlie's upturned, waiting face. His warm, soft mouth covered hers in a kiss she hadn't realised she had longed for. Mac's hands rose to softly cradle either side of Charlie's face, then slid to run through her hair and cup and caress the back of her neck.

"Mac," she whispered, between increasingly urgent kisses. He drew his face away.

"Call me by my name," he instructed gently. "Call me William."

"William," she murmured, and then his insistent mouth covered hers once more.

Charlie's lips parted, and her eyes closed as a warm glow blossomed in the centre of her chest. *I've found him again*, part of her whispered. *A thousand years, five hundred years, and I've finally found him again*, but all thoughts were then swept away by the increasing hunger of the moment. The skin of his strong neck pulsed, warm and soft beneath her fingers, and she breathed him in, intoxicated by his scent: lemons and gritstone and sun-warmed earth.

Mac abruptly pulled away. His hands, which had drawn Charlie tightly against him by her waist, now rose to her shoulders and gently pushed her back. Charlie reached up to his face and the back of his neck. She tried to pull him down to her again. But he slid his head sideways, away from her touch.

"I'm so sorry," he whispered, shaking his head. He looked anguished. "I should never have done that. I lost control. Angels like you don't belong in Hell with me, Charlotte." She looked up at him for a long moment.

"But what if I'm already there?" she asked quietly.

A movement near to where they stood caught Mac's eye. Baz walked slowly into view. He turned to face the alcove where Mac and Charlie stood. His face was pale under his false tan. His arms were held aloft, and dark sweat patches blossomed on his shirt. In his left hand was a long, serrated knife. Dark liquid covered the blade and dripped in a turgid trace across his hand and forearm. The music in the club abruptly went silent. The main lights smashed on. Punters looked around, blinking, and confused at the sudden brightness and silence. Mac and Charlie were trapped....

CHAPTER
FORTY-SIX

Five minutes earlier, the Boss had stood over Leticia's dead body, panting. He knew he shouldn't have done that, shouldn't have lost control. But he had so longed for Playtime. He entered the address she had finally given him onto his phone. He heard a door open at the end of the passageway behind him and the Boss slid, like a wraith, into a nearby recess. The shadow enveloped him; he felt invigorated, elevated.

"Leticia! Where the Hell are you now?" yelled Baz. "Vlad saw you! I know you're down here with some punter. No tricks on site; you know the rules!" Baz paused as he saw Leticia's body slumped against the fire exit. She lay with her head bowed onto her chest, her skirt riding up her long, skittled legs. She could almost have been asleep. "For God's sake... what's she taken now?" Baz muttered.

He walked up to Leticia and kicked sharply at her feet. "Get up!" he shouted. "Get up... you've work to do!" He turned and yelled back down the corridor, "Vlad!...Vlad!" there was no answer. Sighing in exasperation, Baz knelt down and shook Leticia. Her body slumped sideways, and he made a clumsy pull at her shoulders and neck. His hands slid in a warm, thick liquid and he leapt back with a loud curse. His breathing sped up, and his eyes widened in horror as he realised just what covered his hands.

The Boss stepped out of the shadow. "What have you done?" he breathed in Baz's ear. Baz leapt, gasping, away from him and stumbled over Leticia's legs, to fall heavily onto his back. Baz lay terrified, his hands bloodied and outstretched as if to ward off the man who now stood over him. He realised that a warm ooze was soaking through the back of his shirt and he whimpered. "They'll come for you, you know?" said the Boss, in a friendly, conversational way. All Baz could see was his wide, white grin from under the brim of the old, black trilby he wore, set at a jaunty angle. The Boss then crouched down onto his haunches and looked at Baz with sparkling, intensely blue eyes. "Or shall we just finish things here?" The Boss asked. "Now? Shall we play?"

The Boss held up a long, serrated blade in his gloved right hand. It dripped black in the dim light, and he lazily ran the edge down Baz's inner thigh. Baz felt himself lose control of his bladder, and warm humiliation soaked his tight, designer jeans.

"No..." Baz whispered. "Please... No". The Boss stopped smiling.

"I have a friend here," he said, all amusement suddenly gone. "A good friend, one of the best. And I want him to come out to play." Baz wriggled slowly backwards, desperate to avoid the blade that now stroked the exposed skin of his left ankle. "This is what I want you to do," said the Boss

. . .

Baz had obeyed his instructions. He now stood, shuddering, hands held high in the middle of his silent, muddily lit club. All eyes were on him, his bloodied hands, and the knife he held; on his shirt, drenched with the debris of death. A burly doorman crashed through the red-beaded curtain and shouted in a thick, eastern -European accent;

"Leticia, she's dead... in the back corridor!" He saw Baz, and his eyes narrowed angrily. "Call the Police!"

A woman screamed; a jagged tear in the blanket of silence. All Hell seemed to break loose as people, in a mass, streamed towards the exit; fighting and shouldering each other in their panicked desperation to escape. Vlad's mouth tightened, and he determinedly fought his way through the river of people to where he had last seen Baz. He'd always liked Leticia and despised his Boss. Now Baz was going to get what was coming to him. And if Vlad needed to kick him in the head a few times to stop him from escaping before the Police got here? So be it.

In the alcove, Mac was half-crouched in the confined space. He'd pushed Charlie behind him and drawn his gun. He looked out at the chaos of running, flailing people. Baz didn't look like a killer; he looked like a terrified man taking the fall for a crime he hadn't committed. Decker's death had obviously not stopped the carnage; Leticia was now dead, too. Leticia, who had known the whereabouts of Lucy and the missing tablets and formula. Mac would bet the killer was still in the club, waiting. Charlie now knew about Lucy, making her even more of a target. The killer had created chaos to panic Mac and Charlie into moving out into the open, where he could take them down at his leisure. Mac had seconds to decide: do they run now and risk a quick death from the waiting assassin? Or did they stay and hope they saw him before he repeatedly shot into the tight space where they hid?

Mac pulled Charlie towards him. "Listen," he said urgently. "I'm going out there. I'll draw his fire." Charlie's face creased in fear, and she protested,

"Mac!"

"No!" he said firmly. "Listen to me. You need to get back to your car. Act normally. Get in and drive. Meet me outside the Crucible, Norfolk Street."

"You'll be there?" begged Charlie. "Promise me you'll be there." Mac looked at her. He reached out to touch her face, possibly for the last time, but stopped himself. His face hardened. He pulled his hand away.

"Prepare to get going, Hart," he retorted.

Mac turned and looked out of the alcove. He scanned the heaving room. If it was him who was the assassin, where would he, Mac, hide? Baz had gone, scrabbling off into the crowd and a doorman thundered past. Mac launched himself out of the alcove, low and fast, ready to hit the ground and roll to cover. As he leapt, his body committed, his mind gave him an answer; *where would I hide? I would hide... on the balcony. He's above me!*

Somehow, Mac twisted himself around mid-leap. He landed, heavily and agonisingly, on his right shoulder. He lay on his back on the nightclub floor, body wholly exposed. Years of training and experience took over. Without thinking, he raised his gun in both hands and shot. He glimpsed a dark figure poised in the dim shade of the balcony. The figure dodged back; Mac's shot almost reached its target. It raised its hand again, but Mac had his sight now, and he fired, calmly and repeatedly. Mac saw a flash of teal silk from the corner of his eye and knew that Charlie was making her escape.

Mac rolled rapidly under a thick table and peered up at the balcony. The figure was moving along, ducking down and trying to spot a line into Mac's hiding place. It took a shot that landed critically close to Mac's left foot. There was the distant keen of police sirens. The figure paused and seemed to relax. It took two deliberate, contemptuous shots onto the top of the table where Mac hid. The figure then turned and rapidly reached the door leading off the balcony. He was escaping.

Mac emerged from under the table, stood, and looked around. There was no obvious way onto the balcony. Mac ran to the DJ booth, clambered onto it, and jumped upwards. His hands caught at the balcony edge. Wincing at the pain in his right shoulder, Mac pulled himself up and swung his legs over the balcony. He was there. Mac rapidly made his way to the door where the figure had exited just seconds before. He was in a dark, concrete stairwell. The emergency lights glowed dimly in the grimy grey. He listened carefully. He heard a quiet but rapid tread on the stairs above him. The man was moving up the stairs but was not expecting pursuit. He was going to hide out on the roof until things died down, Mac assumed. The Police would look for Baz, no one else.

Mac quietly shut the door and started up the stairwell. He paused at each curve of the stairs and listened carefully to check for danger. Halfway up, he stopped hearing footsteps. He heard nothing. Mac eased himself round the bend of the stairs, craning his neck upwards, trying to glimpse through the metal bannisters. A shot rang out, and he pulled his head in rapidly. Mac heard the zing of a bullet as it ricocheted dangerously off the metal stairway. The killer was aware of his pursuit.

Mac paused. *Fight or flight*? He thought... *Fight*! Came the immediate answer. *We will always fight.* His mouth tightened. He gripped his gun and pulled himself round the corner, using the metal handrail to propel himself up the stairwell. Faster and faster, he leapt. He felt the Red Mist burn at the edges of his mind. He hadn't given in to it, not through the months of war or the hidden years since his father's death. But this man had come for Hart; he could have killed her. Mac imagined Charlie Hart's eyes, surprised and in pain, their light fading. A low cry emerged from his heaving chest. He was Beaulouf, the Beautiful Wolf, and he would hunt.

Mac reached the top of the stairwell and the fire door there. Its lock was broken, and chains hung like listless, rusted guts. There was an old steel bin with a heavy lid lying on its side by the crumbling wall. By now, Mac was entirely in the grip of the Red Mist and the bloodlust it brought as its savage gift. All he wanted now was to catch and kill the man, to tear him limb from limb. But the cunning part of his mind still held sway. He picked up the bin, kicked open the door, and threw it savagely through. He heard a gunshot from his left. So that was where he was. Mac reached into his jacket and smoothly snapped a full magazine into the warm Glock. He hefted the heavy metal bin lid, holding the handle, so the lid formed a circular shield. He stepped through the door and turned to his left, crouched and firing.

Mac glimpsed a tall figure running towards the low wall that surrounded the edge of the building. It had a hat pulled low over its face, so he couldn't make out the features when it turned to fire wildly in his direction. Too late, he realised what the fleeing figure was going to do. The man leapt, arms windmilling, legs still churning, over the edge of the tall warehouse towards the building next door. He hit the low wall of the opposite building and hung momentarily, legs scrabbling for purchase. Mac approached the edge of the warehouse and fired, deliberately and repeatedly, towards the spine and skull of the hanging man. However, the man's legs heaved, and with a rapid, almost superhuman convulsion, he threw himself over the wall. He was now hidden from view. Mac saw blood smeared and spattered on the bricks. He had hit him, but he'd not stopped him.

Mac eyed the space that separated the two buildings; that separated him from his prey. *No!* Snarled the wolf that now paced inside his head. *It's too far...* Mac turned and smoothly located and shot out the three security cameras that overlooked him from the surrounding buildings. He turned his attention back to the building next door. He could see the roof's locked stairwell from where he stood. The killer would have to break cover at some point. Sure enough, he saw the wood around the lock of the stairwell explode. A hand then rose from behind the far-right edge of the wall and fired in Mac's direction. Mac ducked behind his own low wall. When he cautiously looked up, he saw a figure sprinting in a zigzag towards the stairwell. Mac fired once, twice, three times. But in the dim light, with a fast-moving figure, he didn't hit his target.

Mac yelled, his harsh voice bouncing off the walls that blindly witnessed his rage. The figure paused in tearing open the stairwell door, hat still pulled hard down on its bullet-like head. It didn't look back at him, but disappeared into the dark. Mac bent down and grabbed the bin lid, which, he now realised, was pitted with two bullet holes. With a loud cry, he flung the heavy metal bin lid as hard as he could towards the stairwell which had carried the man away from him. It clattered onto the roof opposite and slid to crash noisily against the stairwell door. Mac paced, hands clenching and unclenching. The hot Red Mist slowly faded, only to be replaced with cold fury. Glancing over the edge of the building, he saw a host of flashing blue lights. Police officers streamed into the building and he heard a shout far down the stairs behind him.

Mac jogged to the back of the flat roof. He looked down. Rusty, dangerous Victorian plumbing? Hardly any handholds? That's just how he enjoyed climbing when he was angry, which was most of the time. Mac slipped over the edge. He winced as the torn muscles in his right shoulder cried out in painful protest. He clung to the barest of handholds, his body racked to its limit. Mac clung, raging, to life.

CHAPTER FORTY-SEVEN

Charlie jumped as the door to the Ferrari opened. Her whole body then slumped with relief. He was alive! She'd sat in hunched misery for the last fifteen minutes, worst-case scenarios playing out in various, vivid ways inside her head. Mac stood, glaring down at her, where she sat in the driver's seat. It seemed as if things were back to normal between them.

"Move, Hart," he snapped.

"Why?" she said, bridling at his abrupt manner.

"Because I've seen you drive, and this car has more than three gears." He stood aside, and she reluctantly slid out of her seat and crossed to the passenger side. Mac swiftly folded himself into place and started the engine, which growled, eagerly and satisfyingly, to life.

Leticia! thought Charlie agonised. *Poor Leticia.* She glanced at Mac. He drove rapidly and efficiently, occasionally grimacing with pain as he moved his right shoulder too quickly. His face was stern, and his brow had returned to its usual slight furrow.

"What do we do now?" asked Charlie. Mac glanced at her. His face didn't soften.

"We go back to Sally's. We'll have to get Lucy's address and full name from Georgia. Sally's still not answering, which is odd. I need to check on her." Mac winced again as he turned the steering wheel sharply. "If Georgia doesn't answer her phone, we'll grab the Range Rover and head out. This car won't get up the farm track. But it's probably too late. The killer will have Lucy's address already, I'm sure of it." Charlie nodded sadly and tried not to think of Leticia and the fear she must have felt. She looked out into the chequered darkness as they sped through the sleeping city.

There was a long, pregnant silence. It was eventually broken by Mac. "I'd be grateful if you could forget what happened. Tonight." Charlie looked over at him. He was gazing straight ahead.

"Do you mean when you kissed me?" she asked. Mac's eyes now flicked briefly towards her.

"I made a mistake," he said firmly. "I'm sorry. It won't happen again."

"Well, I don't think I made a mistake," said Charlie. Mac just shook his head.

"It won't happen again," he repeated. They drove on, in awkward silence, through the heavy weight of night.

Back at Rowans Holt, the house was dark. It was midnight. "Are none of your Crew on duty tonight?" asked Charlie. Mac looked grim.

"Morton insisted he could take care of Sally," he replied. "But I think he's taking too much care of her."

Sure enough, Ben was sitting at the kitchen island. He

was working on a large, circular piece of wood into which he was carving letters. His face was intent in the light that shone above his head. It cast half of his face into shadow and Charlie was disturbed when she couldn't see his eyes, just dark pools of shade. Sally's phone lay at his left hand. Ben didn't smile. He laid down the curve of wood face-down on the work surface and stood to greet them.

"Well?" he said quietly. "What happened? At the club?"

"You didn't answer my calls!" said Mac accusingly. Ben grabbed the phone and swore softly. He ran his hand through his thick, dark-red hair in deep frustration.

"God, I'm sorry, Guys," he said apologetically. "I must have turned it to silent by accident. Sal finally went to sleep, and all I could think about was stopping anything that would wake her."

"Well, I'm awake now," came Sally's voice from the kitchen door. Sally stood in ivory satin pyjamas and dressing gown, looking very stern. She approached Ben and took her phone off him. "Ben?" she said quietly. "Why did you take my phone?" He looked at her hopelessly. He reached out towards her but let his hand drop.

"I can't bear seeing you tired and in pain. You need to get well, Sal." He looked down towards the round wooden panel, his face again hidden in shadow. "I feel so bad about what happened," he muttered. Sally moved closer to him, so close they were almost touching. She bent her head gently forward until it rested against his cheek. She shook her head.

"Don't," she whispered softly. "You have to stop." Sally's hand tightened on her phone and she turned to Charlie and Mac. She looked like her old, controlled self. "Tell me everything," she said.

. . .

They sat around the kitchen island. As Ben cleared his tools and workspace, Mac filled Sally in, with Charlie adding detail.

"I'm sorry I gave your dragon away," said Charlie in a small voice. "I know I was supposed to sell it. It just seemed like the right thing to do at the time." Sally was gazing into the distance and tapping her chin. She reached out, distracted, and patted Charlie's hand.

"Don't worry, you did the right thing," she said. Sally looked at Charlie. "Lau's no fool. He knows the worth of what you gave him outweighs the worth of the information he gave you. He's now in my debt." Sally looked off again. "He'll amuse himself wondering when and how I'll call in that debt." She shook her head. "That has no bearing on tonight."

Sally regarded Mac and Charlie. "First things first. How in Hell did an assassin know you'd be at the Inferno Club?" Mac shrugged, his face angry.

"Maybe he was following me," he said. "But he must have been very lucky to see us slipping out the back of the Fitzwarren."

"And I assume it was the killer, listening to you and Leticia when the bathroom door was half opened?" Sally continued. Charlie nodded.

"He must have been the man in the hat who followed me when I looked for Leticia."

"So, now we know the tablets and half formula were stolen, and half of the tablets are still unused," said Sally. "And the formula is with the tablets. But a killer has probably already found Lucy. He would have got her address from that poor Leticia. And Baz is in the frame for Leticia's murder. He was seen with the murder weapon, covered in her blood. What a mess!"

"We don't know that he's found Lucy," said Charlie, squirming at the thought of anyone else being harmed. "Leticia might have lied. Lucy was her best friend. Or Lucy could be with Lawrence. We need to find him, too, warn him. We need to get Lucy's name and address from Georgia."

Sally picked up her phone and dialled. There was no answer. "Straight to answerphone," muttered Sally. "There's no point in rocking up to the farm now. Georgia has a large German Shepherd dog she lets roam at night. It's trained to attack, and she'll call the Police as soon as the dog barks too much. That's the last thing we need." Sally called Georgia again but got no reply. "We can set off at first light," she said decisively

"Not you," said Mac to Sally. "With respect, I need someone well." Sally glared at him in frustration.

"So, I'm to be a prisoner in my own home?" she retorted.

"That man almost got me," said Mac. "I hate to admit it, but he's very good. And completely ruthless. He made that death leap without a second thought." Mac clenched his hands, still enraged at the thought of the brazen escape. "Me and Morton will go," he said.

"No," said Charlie. "Do you really think Georgia will hand over details of her girls to two strange men?"

"I was under the impression this woman would do anything for money," said Mac sourly.

"I think Georgia has some standards," said Sally. "I believe she's genuinely fond of her girls—Charlie's right. Charlie knows Georgia, and Georgia knows her. She'll go with you, Mac. Charlie will get the address." Mac didn't look pleased but nodded his head sharply. "And Ben can try to find the van and Lawrence," said Sally, looking at Ben, who nodded, glad to have something to do to help. Sally checked her phone. "It's almost one o'clock," she said briskly. "Let's get some sleep, and you can set off at dawn. Mac, there's no point in you leaving and coming back. Just stay in one of the spare rooms. There's guest stuff, as usual." Mac considered this, then nodded again. He needed sleep, he admitted to himself.

However, neither Charlie nor Mac slept. Charlie slowly showered, washing away the trappings of the terrifying evening. She then lay, looking up at the ceiling, replaying everything that she'd done and said. Everything that Mac had done and said.

"What you do just isn't good enough," she whispered. "Charlie Hart; just not good enough." She rolled over, willing sleep to come, but still, it denied her. Around five, as the colour of the sky thinned and became a gentle glow, she slipped from her bed. Charlie made her way down through the silent house, her head heavy and full. She opened the door to the poolroom and slipped inside, eyeing the alarm system warily and ensuring the switch was off. Charlie activated the wall, and it slid silently open. A rush of cool, clear air shouldered past her, and she stood, gazing out at the fading stars in a rose and indigo-stained sky. Changing into one of the odd, old-style costumes, Charlie sank into the warm, saline water and felt a rush of relief. She slowly swam up and down the pool, the soft embrace of the water bearing up her tired limbs and soothing the aching of her mind.

But then the door to the pool room opened, and Mac stood there, half dressed, his T-shirt clutched in his hand. He'd obviously planned on taking a swim, too. He saw

Charlie and stopped, uncertain. Charlie drank in the sight of him, the person who'd occupied all her thoughts on this long and sleepless night. She noticed the breadth of his shoulders, the long scar to the left of his ribcage, and the tiny tattoo on his right upper arm. He took a few paces into the room but then stopped again. He slowly turned and walked back to the door. Charlie stood, rising from the pool's shallow end, her waist lapped by the water.

"William," she called quietly. He turned to look at her, the pure morning light shining through the wide, open wall. Her long, wet hair was slicked back. Her face was clean of makeup and tired, but she looked more beautiful to him at that moment than she had ever been, the gentle curves of her body emerging from the pool. "Please?" she begged. Mac shook his head.

"I won't bring you down into Hell with me, Charlotte," he replied.

"But I'll be in Hell if you cut me off. If I pretend..." she said, her voice catching as her throat tightened. A tear left her eye and slid slowly down her face.

"Wrong Hell, Hart," Mac said. He, too, drank in the picture of her, but he then turned and left the room.

THEY ALL GATHERED in the kitchen an hour later, drinking strong coffee. Charlie couldn't, and Mac wouldn't, meet the other's eye. Ben looked between them.

"What's up?" he asked astutely, his coffee cup halfway to his mouth. He grinned evilly. "Have you two been up to something me and Sal should know about?"

"No!" exclaimed both Mac and Charlie, glaring at Ben. Ben backed away, still smiling.

"That's a no then! Only asking." Sally took in Charlie's strained, tired face. Had Mac been bullying her? She knew they didn't get on very well. She needed to get Charlie on her own and find out what had gone on between them. Have a Girlie Chat.

"Are you OK?" Sally whispered to Charlie. Charlie, dark smudges under her eyes, nodded, tight-lipped. Sally patted her shoulder. "Let's talk. Later?" Charlie nodded, and Sally was alarmed to see her eyes fill with tears. Mac must have been really harsh on her. But at least she was in one piece.

Mac approached Plantation Farm from Redmires Road. The early morning light fell on green fields lush with grass and filled with fat cows grazing with leisurely grace. They pulled into the long, rugged track and made their way slowly towards the farm. It was barely six thirty in the morning. A large German Shepherd dog was chained in front of the shop. It barked excitedly at the car's approach, pulling eagerly against its restraint. They could see the figure of Georgia striding from a yard edged with stables. She did not look happy to be disturbed so early, and her solid chin jutted uncompromisingly.

Charlie got out of the car and headed towards her, carefully skirting the leaping, whining guard dog.

"What are you doing here at this hour?" demanded Georgia. "Is there a problem?" A golden retriever bumbled up to Georgia, who batted at it angrily. "Get away, Poppy. Don't you dare go near Helders! Go back to your pups!" The retriever glanced in a friendly way at Charlie and then wandered off towards the stables. "She's a disgrace," Georgia muttered darkly. "Got herself caught by my German Shepherd, and now I've got a barn full of Golden Shepherd puppies I don't have the time to deal with! Get down, Helders!" she yelled, loudly and abruptly, to the leaping guard dog, making Charlie jump. Helders whined and lay down with his head on his paws. *I wonder if I should do that too*? Thought Charlie, *to stop Georgia from yelling at me*.

"Well?" snapped Georgia.

"I'm sorry to disturb you so early," said Charlie in her most friendly tone. "But I need your help." She smiled. "One of the girls who works for you, Lucy. I need to speak with her." Georgia's face became wary and defensive. She folded her arms and lowered her chin.

"Well, for once, I can't help you," she said brusquely. "I'm her employer. I can't hand out information like that. You'd best be on your way." Georgia stood firm and glared at Charlie, who hesitated, uncertain.

"If it's a matter of money..." Charlie said. Far from making Georgia more emollient, this remark seemed to ignite a spark, and she exploded angrily.

"What's the matter with you, girl?" she shouted. "I said no! I want no more trouble. Get off my land!" She strode towards the metal bolt to which Helders was firmly tied, obviously intending to let him loose on Charlie. Charlie was aware of the car door opening and Mac smoothly descending from the large vehicle. From the corner of her eye, she saw him reaching inside his jacket for the gun there.

Charlie suddenly realised what was causing Georgia's panic. Baz. She'd bet anything he was hiding somewhere on the farm—a fugitive. Georgia would want them to leave as soon as possible.

"Where have you hidden him?" Charlie called, the thought of Helders efficiently shot dead by Mac adding urgency to her voice. Georgia stopped in her tracks. She slowly turned back to Charlie. She said nothing, but her eyes flickered back toward the stables.

"I don't know what you're talking about," she grated. She looked again towards Helders, who was now pulling eagerly at his chain and whining at the prospect of fresh meat.

"I saw Baz, covered in blood, holding a knife," said Charlie. "Things are about as bad as they can get for him. Give me Lucy's address, and we'll go," Charlie said persuasively. "We don't care about Baz, we just need to find Lucy." Still, Georgia hesitated.

Charlie, exhausted and overwhelmed, finally lost her temper. "Look, you pig-headed bumpkin, whoever killed Leticia and set up Baz is still on the loose. Lucy's in danger, so give me that damn address!" Georgia swelled up like an indignant pufferfish.

"Bumpkin?" she howled. Charlie had had enough. She flipped out her phone.

"Right. I know he's here. I'm calling the Police." She dialled 999, unsure what she'd do if she actually got through to a call handler.

"Wait!" shouted Georgia, imperiously holding out her hand towards Charlie. She looked and sounded just like her sister, Deborah. Emotions warred in her face; fear, love, anger, greed. Her face slowly turned in colour from claret to milk. "I may be able to provide something after all. You mentioned payment...."

CHAPTER
FORTY-EIGHT

They drove, Charlie concentrating on entering the address Georgia had reluctantly handed over into her phone. It was on a printed sheet with Lucy's contact details and a faded photo of a smiling young girl. Like Leticia, the girl favoured lots of black eyeliner, but her smile was wide and warm. Charlie ached at the thought of what might have happened to her. Mac glanced over at her.

"Where are we going?" he asked.

"To The Manor," replied Charlie. "On the other side of the city. It's going to take us a while."

"Sounds wealthy," said Mac. Charlie studied Mac's features for any signs of sarcasm, but he drove, his face impassive. She thought back to Ben's remarks about Mac's title and estate. Mac had many life experiences, but grinding poverty undoubtedly wasn't one of them.

"The Manor's the opposite of well-to-do," said Charlie. "The area's named for a Castle that used to be there. Built by the Earl of Shrewsbury or some such, hundreds of years ago. Mary, Queen of Scots, was locked up there for a while."

"Charles," said Mac distractedly, studying the road ahead.

"What?" said Charlie, lack of sleep making her feel slightly dislocated.

"Charles, the present Earl of Shrewsbury. Good man. He knew my father." said Mac.

There was silence in the car. Mac glanced over at Charlie. "And your father, Hart, what does he do?" he asked, suddenly curious. There was another long silence. Mac looked again at Charlie. She was studying her hands.

"Hart?" demanded Mac.

"I don't have a father," said Charlie in a small voice. Mac frowned.

"Your parents are divorced?" he asked.

"No," said Charlie. "No. I have no father." Charlie turned her head away. "There's no one on my birth certificate," she said quietly. Mac, otherwise known as William Cormack Warren Beaulouf, struggled to comprehend what she was saying. He knew, in precise detail, every father and mother in his family, stretching back for over a thousand years. He could name every portrait of many of these people, all of which hung in the Long Gallery at Beaulouf Manor. In his mind, it was impossible to have an unknown father.

"Your mother..." he began. Charlie now turned back and interrupted him.

"My mother is not a nice person," she said firmly. He could see her eyes glittering in the corner of his vision. "We don't speak. We haven't spoken for ten years. And please, never ask me about my parents again." Mac nodded.

"I'm sorry," he said.

Charlie cleared her throat. "So, we won't find any earls in the Manor today," she said, leaving the uncomfortable subject of parents behind them. "And there's no way Lucy has a car. The poor thing must have got at least two buses to get over to Lodge Moor, where Georgia's farm is." She pressed her hands together in her lap, silently willing Mac to drive faster, to get to Lucy first. Mac glanced at her hands, at her anxious face. He knew what she was thinking. She was too soft for her own good. He pressed his foot onto the accelerator.

THEY APPROACHED the house that slouched on Danewood Avenue, the Manor. Empty plastic bottles and takeaway wrappers rolled gently in the breeze that blew in from the large park hugging the estate's edges. Five doorbells were fitted next to the front door. One bell hung, with its wires spewing sadly. A group of four young men lurked halfway down the road, eyeing the expensive car and hunching into their tracksuits. Two more young men circled on bikes, one studiously riding with no hands on the handlebars, the other pulling wheelies. They span closer and closer to the car. Mac ignored them, but Charlie felt nervous. Mac discreetly withdrew his gun and screwed a silencer onto the end. Charlie felt even more anxious now.

Mac pushed gently at the front door. It was open. They stepped into a small hallway. Unopened post, mingled with leaflets for pizza, e-cigarettes and easy debt, lay piled on a window ledge. Letters had spilt onto the dingy floor, which was covered in threadbare, dark-brown carpet. The house smelled of damp paintwork, cigarettes, and fried food. A door to their left had a cheap brass number one screwed onto it. It was locked. This was a multiple occupancy house. The next door to their left declared itself to be room number two. A small kitchen lay ahead, piled with cheap crockery and used pizza boxes.

"Room?" asked Mac.

"Three," whispered Charlie. Mac led the way up the dim stairs, gun drawn and by his side. At the top of the stairs, to their immediate left, at the front of the house, was room three. The door was ajar, and daylight streamed weakly out. Mac pushed gently at the door.

There was no sign of Lucy, or of a struggle. The room, however, had been well and truly turned over. Drawers sat open, and their contents were spilt in furious disarray to the floor. Books lay ragged, pages bleeding over the room, languid lines of poetry and romance silenced forever. Posters of bands had been ripped from the walls, the pale-faced pouts of idols split and torn. It looked as though the killer had been there. Had he found the tablets?

There was a soft step on the stair outside. Charlie leaned round the door. A slim figure in a hoodie was making their way up the stairs; a thin plastic bag clutched in their left hand. They walked to room five and fumbled in their black, shabby jeans pocket for a key. A suspicion rose in Charlie's mind.

"Lucy?" she whispered to herself. "Lucy?" she repeated out loud. The figure in the hoodie turned towards her. Charlie glimpsed a pale face, curly hair and brown eyes ringed deeply in eyeliner. Terrified. The girl had no key; she'd walked straight past her own room. Charlie held up both hands. "Lucy, no, don't run. We're here to help!" But it was too late. The girl dashed to the stairs and sprung, light-footed, down them. She crashed out of the door and turned left, running hard, arms pumping. As she fled past the semi-detached houses that lined the road, a figure emerged, also running, and sprinted after her. A black beanie hat was pulled low on their head and Mac saw a blade emerge in their hand.

"No!" Mac cried. He brought up his Glock to shoot; however, Lucy kept emerging, just in his line of sight. He couldn't risk the shot.

Charlie ran to the boys on bikes and pointed to the running man.

"That man, he's a paedophile. He's trying to get that girl. But he's got a gun!" The boys looked at each other, then they smiled and nodded. They whistled and waved to the group, watching with interest from further up the street, then sped off on their bikes.

"Hart!" yelled Mac. He leapt into the Range rover and started up the powerful engine. Charlie scrambled in, and the car pulled away in pursuit of the running figures pelting down Danewood.

Lucy turned a sharp right and ran into a heavily wooded park entrance. The man tore after her but was brought up short when a figure on a bike swung behind him and savagely kicked at his back. The man went down as if they'd shot him; however, he rolled like an insolent great ape and leapt to his feet again. He again ran hard, implacably fixed on his fleeing target. He'd only gone a few paces when a missile came hurling from his right and glanced off his right temple. It was a glass bottle. The young men had commandeered a blue recycling bin and were reaching into it to arm themselves with a collection of heavy missiles.

"Hey, Paedo!" one of them yelled and threw a gin bottle as hard as he could at the figure. He batted the bottle away, but another missile was coming toward him. He glanced down the path. There was no sign of Lucy. There were too many places to hide in the heavy undergrowth and miles of parkland, and he now had an audience. He saw the Range rover bearing down on him. With a contemptuous smile, he casually leapt over a low brick wall and sprinted behind the houses. Within seconds, he had disappeared.

Large stones blocked the path to the park. Mac braked heavily and gripped the steering wheel. He could neither pursue the man nor the girl. He brought his fist down, hard, on the dashboard. Beside him, Charlie pressed herself back in her chair, eyes wide, again terrified by a show of aggression. Mac closed his eyes for a few seconds. He needed to regain control; it had been a long, bitter and frustrating twenty-four hours. He looked wearily at Charlie.

"I'm sorry, Hart. Well done. You may have saved the girl's life." He reached over, took the contact details sheet from Charlie, and studied it. "We have her name and picture now. Sally will put her face into her facial recognition software. She'll probably go to ground for a while, but she'll have to break cover, eventually. When she does, we'll need to be ready." Charlie nodded weakly. She, too, looked exhausted.

"Can you take me home, please?" she said. He knew where she meant. He rapidly turned the car and drove for Rowans Holt.

LUCY KEPT RUNNING. Her lungs burned, and her right side ached with a deep and agonising stitch, but she kept running. They'd come for her. She'd known they would. She should never have stolen that man's wallet, but there had been so much money in it from his wins at gambling. She'd wanted Lawrence to notice her, to look at her: to actually see her and then realise how much he loved her. He must love her. She felt like she was dying with passion whenever she was in the same room as him. You can't love someone that much and not have them love you back.

"Give, oh, give me back my heart!" she whispered between panting breaths.

Lucy dodged sideways through a children's play area and into the bushes on the other side. The leafy floor under the bushes was covered in waste. She watched the footpath. She must have been running for over ten minutes, sensing no pursuer. Had she shaken them off? Her breathing slowed. She tried to think. She'd been staying with Leticia, not in her own place. Lying low. She hadn't dared to show her face at the club or the Farm Shop. Lawrence had taken the stolen money and the leather wallet with barely a thank you. And later, when she'd got him on his own and had given him the tablets, and the half of the raven she'd carefully drawn, he'd stuffed it all into his pocket without even looking at them. He'd been high at that point, already eagerly spending the money she'd got for him.

Leticia had messaged her last night. *Woman here asking bout tabs n stuff. Think she's ok. Patty knows her. Will call ltr....* But Leticia had not called later. Lucy had sent a stream of messages to Lawrence, warning him that people might ask about the money and the other stuff. Lucy had then gone out early to get some milk and rizlas and had returned, only to find Leticia's house surrounded by Police cars. She had then heard about Leticia... She couldn't think about her best friend. It was too big, too much.

Lucy crouched under the bushes as the morning sun caused the dew to evaporate in wisping curls of steam. She reached inside her coat pocket and drew out the small plastic bag with five tiny blue tablets and a folded piece of paper. Lucy looked at it. What had she done? Why were so many people after these things? Those people at her place had probably been plain-clothes police. Was she in bigger trouble than she thought? She brought out her phone.

Need to speak! Call me!!! She messaged Lawrence. She looked in horror at the message she received back. *Message not delivered.* Had he blocked her number? She tried to ring, even though she knew he'd be unconscious at this time of day. After one ring, the phone went dead. Definitely blocked. Lucy felt hopeless. Where could she go? Where could she hide? An idea glimmered in the darkness of her mind. She had somewhere to go, somewhere safe. It would only take two buses to get there....

THE BOSS RETURNED to his car and angrily started it. He'd catch up with the girl again. He'd taken a picture of her face as she'd fled towards him from her house. Fun Boy had the software to recognise and lift her image from any CCTV camera in the city. In the meantime, he would hunt down that junkie in the black van that Leticia had so willingly told him about. Lucy might be running to the junkie even now. And Beaulouf, that jumped up fool, trying to catch him again. When would Beaulouf learn he was the Boss? Untouchable. Unbreakable. Beaulouf had been with that little blonde again, that doctor that he needed to kill. The Boss smiled. When the opportunity arose, he would deal with her, quickly and ruthlessly if necessarily. But he would prefer it to be slow, with pleasure. He would take his time. Playtime.

. . .

When they finally arrived back at Rowans Holt, Charlie was fast asleep. Slumped in the large leather seat, she looked very small and fragile. Mac felt reluctant to touch her, but he reached out and gently shook her hand.

"Hart, Hart!" She didn't awake. He sighed. Despite himself and his best intentions, he sat for a while, gazing at her: at the slight frown on her face, the smudges of fatigue under her eyes. His skin still tingled with the memory of her touch from the first time they met, and he remembered carrying her, breathing in the sweet scent of her, as she lay, cradled and sleeping against his chest.

Mac had lied to Sinclair when he'd dismissed Charlie's actions in saving Sally's life. He'd been deeply impressed by her bravery; however, he had also been enraged by her recklessness. She continued to have this effect on him; he was entranced and angered in equal measure. The memory of her kiss, her taste, once again flooded his thoughts and senses. He remembered her body rising from the pool and the sound of her voice softly calling his name, and it took his breath away.

Mac turned and gripped the steering wheel again. He closed his eyes. His path was laid out for him, and there was no place or room for Charlie Hart on it. He'd ask Morton to carry her in. But then he remembered Morton was off looking for the black van. Mac sighed again, deeply. He pulled the passenger door open, and, with a bitter-sweet mix of tenderness and deep annoyance, he carried the sleeping Charlie inside. He carried her home.

CHAPTER
FORTY-NINE

His body stretched, wanton, across the wild width of the universe. He inhaled and sheared the searing stars through his glistering lungs. He floated, painless and triumphant, in an ocean of fulfilled desire. One hundred slowly spinning lifetimes later, he breathed out. Exhaled stars spilled, spent and faded from his sigh, their glory now soaked in the shifting sands of his blood and bone. He was Kubla Khan, king and leader, alpha and omega, poet and dreamer. If only he could just find the words. Always, the words slipped away. Slip slip slippy slide... inside... hide... hide...

"Hide.."

"What? Lol, what are you saying?" A hand, five bony points of pressure, dug into his arm. Pushed and pulled and pulled and pushed and... please leave me... I am perfect... perfect... perfectly happy.

"Leave me..." uttered Lawrence, floating in his opium dream; firm in the faith that he sailed on celestial glory.

Forgetting that he slumped on a urine-soaked mattress in a squat in Firth Park.

And the glow faded, as it always did. The bitterly brief promise shrivelled to the dull ordinary—the colourless clamp of sobriety.

AND HE WAS BACK in the room. Boom! Doom... The gloom. The grey...

LAWRENCE COUGHED AND HACKED. He fumbled for his cigarettes and lit one, inhaling deeply, prompting another bout of phlegmy hawking. He shifted his starved slightness sideways off the naked, stinking mattress. Bartholomew squinted at him through a haze of cheap smoke. He watched, slack-faced, as Lawrence sifted through the needles, foil, and small plastic bags that littered the cardboard box, serving as a table in the centre of the dim-lit room.

"You won't find anything," Bartholomew observed dully. "She took the last of it." He jerked his head towards the blonde-headed figure lying comatose and half-hidden by a sagging sofa. Agnes's leather trousers stretched low across her skeletal hips, and her short 'System of a Down' T-shirt was pulled up, exposing the creamy pearlescence of her skin. Lawrence coldly calculated what that skin was worth to a hungry man and wondered whether he could persuade Agnes to sell the taste of it.

A desire for the next fix started to nibble. It then gnawed, pattering and insistent, at the raggedy edge of his frayed nerves.

"Where's Stephen?" he muttered.

"Off trying to score. He took the van," said Bartholomew. He sniffed and rubbed at his scabbed and running nose with the back of a grimy hand.

"Trying to score with what?" snapped Lawrence. He gestured angrily towards the scattered detritus of dependence. "We spent the last of the money two days ago." Bartholomew's eyes slid towards Agnes.

"Maybe he thinks we have something to sell," he said softly. Lawrence's lip curled scornfully.

"She won't put out. We've tried to persuade her before."

"We've never been this desperate before," said Bartholomew, looking at Lawrence with eyes as deep and cold as sunless lakes.

It was true. The large amount of stolen money that Lucy had given so freely and eagerly to Lawrence had been frittered away on enormous amounts of drugs. Whatever the four could get their hands on: Heroin, speed, crack, cocaine. And then they had sold the Code Blue tabs. The dealers had been only too happy to provide all the elements needed for a non-stop party, a party that had come to a crashing and sudden end.

They'd struggled through yesterday without a fix; all of them aching and curled in their own personal agony. By the evening, Stephen had gone down to the van and stripped it bare, looking for a forgotten or hidden stash of drugs. He'd hit paydirt with a small bag of precious white powder stuffed behind a speaker above the rear door. The party had briefly staggered on but now looked as if it was finally at an end. By now, their addictions were ramped up to unbearable levels. Brains and every neuron tingled furiously with the desperate desire for dopamine.

Something flashed at the limping edge of memory in

Lawrence's brain. Something about a warning, something about having to hide. He shook his head. He'd blocked that annoying hysteric, Lucy. She'd refused to join him in his slumped states of glory. She'd sat, looking like an awkward, judging child when they chose freedom and open minds over the shackles of sobriety. But maybe he should contact her again; perhaps she had more money for him. He glanced again at Agnes. Or maybe someone else could get him money with the false promise of love? Someone closer to home?

They heard a door creak quietly open downstairs. Was that Stephen? Home with a bargain? A buyer? But it wasn't Stephen. Stephen would never come home again.

IN THE KITCHEN of Rowans Holt, Mac shouted at Sally. "What the Hell were you thinking?"

"I didn't know!" Sally shouted back. "I can't see what goes on inside Charlie's head! She didn't tell me!"

"So, she left you tea in the oven and waltzed out in her scrubs, and you didn't know what was going on?" yelled Mac, even louder, hands on hips, glaring at Sally, nostrils flared, and jaw clenched. Sally stood and looked at Mac, silent, her breath coming in deep, rapid gasps as she realised what she had done.

THE MORNING BEFORE, Friday, Charlie had been carried in, fast asleep, by a grumpy Mac. He had, with ill grace, carried her upstairs to her bedroom. However, it had taken him quite a few minutes to come downstairs again, and when he did, he looked even less pleased.

"I closed the curtains," he said curtly. "Left her some

water." He hesitated. "Put a... blanket on her." Sally nodded impatiently.

"Well, what happened?" she demanded. Mac had recounted the morning's violent events on the Manor. All they could do was watch, they both concluded. And wait. Yawning widely, desperate for sleep, Mac had left. Sally had closed her eyes in frustration. Ben had put his arm around her and held her close for a brief hug. Sally had shaken her head, agitated.

"I can't lose my home, Ben. I couldn't bear it." Ben nodded and sensed Sally's fierce love for Rowans Holt burning from her. Ben's face clouded as he imagined the stones and memories of hundreds of years falling in clouds of dust, the wooden bones crushed and dying. He had held her closer.

"Work," he had whispered. "That's all we can do, you and me. It's what we do best." Sally sighed and nodded. Ben had returned to the library, and Sally had returned to both testing her new hypothesis and also to working on the IT project she had mentioned to Ben.

CHARLIE HAD EMERGED in the early Friday evening, glancing, heavy-eyed, around the kitchen for the sight of something she already knew would not be there. Sally had beamed up at her but had not moved from behind her desk. Charlie had smiled wanly back and drifted, dream-like, to make dinner. A few hours later, they sat in the cinema, full and slightly drunk, watching one of Charlie's favourite films, *It's a Wonderful Life*. Charlie had watched, eating popcorn, drinking white wine, and feeling thoroughly miserable.

"What do you want?" she'd whispered, looking at the

screen, eyes filled with tears. "You want the moon? Just say the word, and I'll throw a lasso around it and pull it down..."

Sally had been asleep by this time and slumped comfortably on Ben's shoulder. He and Charlie had gently manoeuvred Sally to bed, and Charlie had then lain, wide-eyed and overwhelmed, until the morning crept, clean and hopeful, around the drawn curtains of her heavy heart. Saturday arrived. Sally worked again. The calming presence of Sinclair hovered, just one alert away, and Sally felt in charge again.

Sally eventually looked up. It was almost dark, and she was alone. The house was quiet. She had been entranced by her work. She listened... silence. Sally stood up. Her screens gleamed dimly in the half-light that clung to the vast window. There was a delicious smell emanating from the oven, but no Charlie. Usually, she would be humming or singing somewhere in the house. But she could also be soaking in fragrant bubbles in the vast bath she loved so much. Or she would be curled at the end of the living room, wrapped in blankets and secretly watching episodes of Downton Abbey, hoping Ben and Sally didn't catch her doing it.

Sally walked upstairs and looked into Charlie's room, but it was empty. An old paperback lay on the neatly made bed. Sally turned her head and read the lurid title: *The Curse of The Pirate by J. C. Richmond*. She smiled; she would definitely tease Charlie about this one. She then paced down to the library. Ben had made tremendous progress with the restoration. Half of the space was now taken up with a makeshift workshop. Tools, drawings and pieces of quality wood lay in ordered ranks over covered tables, and the room smelled of resin and oil. The library, however, was dim and quiet. Sally heard the door to the lower level open. She walked out of the library and saw Ben silently emerge from the stairwell. His face was once more hidden in shadow.

"Ben. Where's Charlie?" asked Sally. Ben walked toward her; his hair was wet from the pool, and she was relieved when she could finally see his features emerge from the darkness.

"Isn't she in the kitchen?" he asked. Sally shook her head. Ben's face relaxed. "She's in the garden, then, Soft Arse. Fussing over some deformed vegetable." *Of course,* thought Sally. She made her way across the courtyard. It was getting too dark and cold to be out, and she was hungry. But the walled garden was empty.

"I hope it's not too busy," Sally muttered. Sally remembered everything. She now remembered Charlie moving around the kitchen; the snap of a lid on a Tupperware box. She remembered Charlie had not been humming or chatting. She had been silent. Charlie had been... sad. And Sally had been too caught up in her work to notice.

'I hope it's not too busy,' Charlie had said quietly. Sally had automatically thought Charlie had been referring to Sally's work. She hadn't. She'd been referring to hers. Charlie had gone to work - when a killer was on the loose in the city. Sally reached for her phone.

CHARLIE WAS WORKING IN MAJORS. She hated Majors, major incidents, trauma, and death. But at least she was busy. At least she didn't have to think. She could be invisible, which was how she felt most of the time, anyway. However, Sara Hadid quickly hunted her down and began an insistent interrogation about Mac. Charlie could fend her off only by walking away when Sara had been mid-sentence.

"Sorry Sara, emergency coming in!"

An old man had been brought in, collapsed. He lived alone and had no idea what his past medical history was. Charlie couldn't get his dangerously low blood pressure up. He didn't seem to be septic and wasn't taking any medication. They had pushed lots of fluid in and now risked sending him into heart failure. He was confused and distressed, and his wrinkled, naked arms clutched at the safety bars on either side of the bed. Charlie was waiting impatiently for the urgent blood results to come back. His skin had the dull yellow that she suspected may be chronic kidney failure. She decided to get an arterial blood gas. That would give her a better picture of whether he was septic or not.

Charlie stood in the small, secure room that held the expensive, constantly malfunctioning, blood gas machine. *Causes of low blood pressure,* she thought; dehydration, heart failure... *what you do just isn't good enough* ... sepsis, medication, anaphylaxis... *call me by my name, call me...* blood loss, metabolic... *William, please?...* Metabolic... the old man's gums. His gums had brown patches... he was having an Addisonian crisis! Undiagnosed Addison's disease....

Charlie burst from the clinical room, only to find the normally chaotic department in even more turmoil. Her frail patient was being wheeled out of Majors and into a nearby cubicle. There must be a multiple-casualty incident coming in. Charlie's stomach turned.

"Charlie! Now!" snapped Fergus Eaton, pushing through the door to the resuscitation area and throwing his tabard over his head. "Team Leader" was now emblazoned on his chest.

"Coming!" cried Charlie. She grabbed the elderly man's drug card and scrawled on the stat drug order "100mg hydrocortisone IM/IV". She swam through the chaos to find Matt. "Matt, adrenal crisis," she said, pressing the drug card against his chest. Matt's face tightened; he realised the urgency of the man's condition.

"I'll get the cortisone into him now, Charlie. And I'll let the Med Reg know," he said. Charlie knew the elderly man would be in safe hands with Matt. "Rather you than me with that multiple stabbing!" she heard Matt call after her as she turned towards the Resuscitation Bay. "I said you were a trouble magnet, Charlie."

Multiple stabbing... The world slowed and curved in on Charlie. She moved as if through massed, dense air. The sounds of the department faded to a dull, echoing roar. Three ambulances had arrived at the emergency entrance, sirens howling and lights reeling in rotating blue. The gurneys crashed into the resuscitation bay and up to the waiting beds, surrounded by grim-faced staff. Charlie stood, transfixed by the broken, bloodied vision that unfolded before her.

CHAPTER
FIFTY

The Paramedics gave their clipped, professional handovers. "Unknown male in twenties, found in alleyway. Large stab wounds to abdomen and thorax, massive blood loss. Unresponsive at scene. GCS 3..." Stephen's body lay pallid, stripped and skinny. Wounds like gaping mouths screamed silently on his unmoving chest and belly. A pale-faced Paramedic resumed CPR, her mouth a thin and bitter line, as she knew she pushed on a pulseless corpse.

"Male, twenty-four, stab wounds to lower limbs, upper limbs and chest wall. Significant blood loss. Incoherent, GCS 12. Past medical history; drug addiction, known hepatitis B. Pulse 120, BP 88/48...." Bartholomew lay, grey-faced, on a gurney, panting and staring up at the ceiling. Deep slashes ran down his lower legs and lower arms. Pads had been placed over the wounds, but they slid, sodden with blood. On his chest wall were multiple cuts. The cuts formed slashes of letters. Charlie looked in horror as the letters slowly coagulated into bloody sense before her staring, seared eyes. JUNKIE had been carved into his skin. But the worst was yet to come.

Lawrence sat upright and squealing on his trolley. His hands were clamped hard over his belly. He, too, was panting. A thin line of blood drained into a congealing pool between his raised, bent legs. Charlie drifted to the end of the bed, drawn as if by an invisible wire that tightened, inexorably, around her throat.

"Unknown male, age twenty-four, longitudinal stab wound to the abdomen. Refuses to let us examine him. Obs stable. GCS 15...."

Lawrence looked up at Charlie, and he seemed to recognise her. He jerked his head at Charlie, indicating that she come nearer. Despite herself and her total terror, she edged closer. She leaned towards his moving lips; nearer and nearer to his dumb distress. Charlie was close enough to kiss him now. She smelled sweat and blood and fear and faeces. Lawrence was whispering, his voice low and tight.

"He said you'd be here! The small, blonde doctor. He said to tell you... this is all for you!" Time again slowed and swelled around Charlie. All she could now hear was the rhythmic squeak from the bed where the Paramedic still worked on the empty body of Stephen. Her colleagues' calls and rapid movements faded as she focused on Lawrence's muttered message. "He said he wants you to know... wants you to know... that he's looking forward to Playtime," sobbed Lawrence. His breath now came in thick gasps, faster and faster. He seemed to be building towards a crescendo. "He said, in the meantime... to show you this!"

Lawrence released his hands. A single, fine wound went from under his sternum to his pelvis. As he removed the restraining pressure of his hold, the wound's edges slowly gaped, and a glistening mass of pink tubes blundered and fumbled their tumbling way over his upper legs and hung, slowly pulsating, in the surprised air. Lawrence screamed again and again.

Charlie couldn't breathe. With frantic fingers, she clawed at her gown, her tabard, her gloves. She couldn't breathe; she couldn't catch her breath. Air, she needed air… Something shifted and slithered in her hindbrain. Something threatened to awake. Like a fox-flushed rabbit, she scuttered and segued towards the department doors and was out, running into the dark ambulance bay.

A tall figure emerged from the shadow and loomed over her. A hand gripped her shoulder. Charlie screamed and tried to pull away.

"Hart!" came a familiar voice. Still, she tried to run, to escape the horror raining down on her. "Hart!" a second hand grasped her shoulder and shook her. Charlie looked up, eyes staring, pupils dilated, and didn't recognise the person who held her. Panting, she tried to pull away from his grasp and continue her headlong flight. Deep in her throat, she made an inarticulate noise like a wounded animal. The arms pulled her close and held her in her wretched distress. A hand slowly stroked the back of her head; firmly smoothed her back. "It's alright, Hart. It's alright. I'm here. I'm here." Charlie smelled the familiar scent of lemons and gritstone. She closed her eyes. She now knew who held her.

Charlie reached up with her left hand and grasped at the warm material that covered the solid, slow-breathing chest. It rose and fell like a sure and steady tide beneath her foundering fingers. She hung on, hoping that he could save her, for, truly, she was drowning. And he bore her up. And the storm slowly passed. She began to cry.

Charlie eventually looked up. Mac stared down at her as if he wondered whether she might break. She stepped away awkwardly and he released her. She saw Mac's Range Rover, slewed across the ambulance bay in front of the Accident and Emergency Department. The driver's door was hanging open, and the hazard lights flashed. An ambulance sat parked in the bay opposite them, back doors open. Light spilt over the bloodied floor and walls of the vehicle, forming a drowsy corona of despair. Charlie glimpsed the Paramedic who had been working on Stephen. She sat in the back with her head in her hands. Her partner crouched next to her, his face creased with shared pain. He reached out his hand to pat her shoulder. They would have to clear up the destruction, mop the clotted, clinging witness to madness away. And then go out again. Do it all over again. *Look at what we give,* thought Charlie. *Just look at what we have to give....*

Charlie turned and, without a word, went to sit in the Range Rover. Mac got in and parked the car more appropriately in an emergency bay facing away from the department doors. He then sat, looking at Charlie.

"Why did you do that?" he asked. "Why did you go to work? Put all of us at risk?" Charlie could tell that he was trying not to show his annoyance. She looked out of the window. She crossed her arms in front of her.

"I didn't want to think..." she said quietly and defensively.

"Think about what?" he asked. Charlie turned her face towards Mac.

"About us," she replied.

Mac looked away. He said nothing for a while, his long index finger beating a rapid pulse on the steering wheel. He then looked back at Charlie and turned his body in the seat to face her. He seemed intent and serious.

"Hart," he said. "There is no us, and there will never, ever be an us."

"But why?" asked Charlie. Mac looked at her, and for a moment, his face softened into an expression of sorrow.

"Because I don't dream of you, Charlotte," he said. Charlie shook her head, perplexed.

"Why should that matter?" she asked. Mac's face hardened into its usual frown, and he faced forward again, his hands tightening on the steering wheel.

"I made a stupid mistake on Thursday night, and I've done nothing but regret it ever since," he said curtly. Charlie looked down at her hands. Just when she thought tonight couldn't get any worse, it just had. "I'll keep away from Rowans Holt," he said.

"No!" said Charlie, looking at him again. She shook her head. "It's going to hurt either way. For me, at least. I may as well get used to you being around." She looked down again. "Don't worry. It won't be a problem. I won't throw myself at you."

There was a sharp rap at Charlie's window and they both jumped. Sara Hadid stood, arms crossed, glaring in at them. Mac lowered the window.

"Fergus says you can go home, seeing as your shift is finishing anyway," announced Sara to Charlie. "I wouldn't let you go," she said sharply. "But then, it's not my department. Yet." Sara's eyes drilled across the car at Mac. "You again," she pronounced. Mac nodded slowly. He said nothing. Sara paused, waiting for him to speak. He didn't. She looked between Charlie and Mac. "And you're picking her up because...?" she asked rudely.

They paused as yet another Police car span up the road to the A and E, sirens shouting.

"Our mutual friend asked me to pick her up, that's all," said Mac smoothly. Sara looked at Charlie, hunched in the large luxury car, and her lip curled slightly. She didn't believe that Charlie and Mac could possibly have any romantic attachment.

"And this 'mutual friend'"?" she probed.

"Is just a friend," replied Mac, returning Sara's direct stare. Sara waited. Mac said nothing.

"I still don't know your name," Sara announced.

"That's right," replied Mac. His calm gaze didn't waver. Sara glared at him for long seconds, waiting for his reserve to break. Finally, her lips tightened, and she turned and stalked away, stiff-backed, towards the A and E.

Mac watched Sara in the rear-view mirror. "One thousand, two thousand, three thousand, four thousand," he whispered. He saw her turn back. "That's my girl!" he exhaled, relieved. Sara Hadid came marching back to the car and rapped imperiously at Mac's window this time. Mac slowly lowered the glass.

"What is your name?" Sara demanded, her chin raised and her eyes flashing angrily. Mac smiled slowly.

"People call me Mac. I'm Cormack. Cormack Beaulouf."

"Bow-loof?" said Sara, unbelievingly, her lip pulled upwards in distaste.

"It's a very old name," said Mac. "From the Norman, as in the Conqueror, mixed with Old Norse. It means 'beautiful wolf'." He smiled in a very lupine way and looked Sara slowly up and down. He raised the window again, but her hand shot through the narrowing space forcing him to halt it.

"So, maybe we could exchange numbers if you're around here again? Seeing as we're so well acquainted now," she said angrily. Mac smiled slowly and insolently.

"We'll see," he said. Without a backwards glance, he closed the window, turned the vehicle and drove off.

CHARLIE HALTINGLY TOLD Mac what she'd seen. He said nothing but shook his head. Both Sally and Charlie needed constant guarding now, he thought. They sat, waiting for the traffic lights to change at the bottom of Barnsley Road. Charlie saw a tall, blonde-haired woman talking intently to a short, stocky man in trainers and a grey tracksuit outside the Turkish bakery. He handed the woman something, which she palmed into her leather jacket pocket. He got on a bike and pedalled off rapidly. The woman looked around, seeming dazed and uncertain about which way to go.

"Stop!" said Charlie. "I think that's Agnes: Sally described her. She's one of Lawrence's group. Why wasn't she hurt?" Charlie looked up at Mac. "She could know something," she said urgently. Mac nodded and pulled the car onto the kerb. The cars behind them beeped angrily as they swerved around the large vehicle.

Charlie lowered the window and called out, "Agnes!" the woman looked round, and Charlie could see she was on the edge of flight. Charlie opened the door and slipped down onto the kerb, still dressed in her work scrubs, her hands raised. "It's OK; I just want to speak." The woman said nothing, just watched as Charlie walked towards her.

Up close, Agnes was stunning. Under the grime, her pale, creamy skin was unblemished, despite her dissipated lifestyle, and her green eyes were wide and fringed with long, dark lashes. She had high cheekbones, a full, sullen mouth and a face shaped like a heart that came to a pointed, delicate chin. Her short hair, bleached white, hung in feathered spikes over the left side of her face. She was tall, and Charlie had to look up at her. She wore leather trousers and a short, grubby t-shirt that came halfway up her abdomen. Agnes pulled her scuffed leather biker jacket tight around her fragile frame and looked watchfully at Charlie.

"Do you need somewhere safe to go?" asked Charlie. Agnes raised one eyebrow.

"Who's asking?" she said. Her voice had the slightly low huskiness of a heavy smoker. Charlie knew that if she saw Agnes's arms, they would be scarred with collapsed, pitted veins; maps of her frequent, wandering ways into oblivion.

"I work at the hospital," said Charlie. "I know what happened to your friends." Agnes's lip curled contemptuously.

"No friends of mine," she snorted. "I heard them planning to pimp me out. Again. They deserved everything they got."

"We can give you a lift if you like," said Charlie. "To wherever you're going. We just want to know what happened tonight." Agnes's face changed. She suddenly realised she had some hold over these people in the big, expensive car. Well, she would wring every ounce of advantage that she could get out of them. Like any good junkie would. Agnes slung her dirty canvas messenger bag over her shoulder and insolently slouched over to the car and the waiting Mac. She hopped into the back seat and made herself comfortable.

They drove. Charlie noticed Mac was heading in the opposite direction to Rowans Holt. She turned in her seat and asked in a friendly way. "Are you OK?" Agnes shrugged and sat back, her long, leather-clad legs spread wide. She looked Charlie up and down. She then eyed Mac and took in his unsmiling face reflected in the rear-view mirror. Agnes said nothing. "What happened tonight?" asked Charlie softly. "What happened to Lawrence and the others?"

THEY HAD HEARD a door creak quietly open downstairs. Was that Stephen? Home with a bargain? A buyer? Agnes had pulled herself to her feet from behind the filthy sofa. She'd eyed Lawrence and Bartholomew with angry contempt.

"If he's brought back a punter, you can do him yourselves," she snarled. She picked up her jacket and bag and stood, swaying slightly as her head spun. She would need to use the bathroom before she left. The party really was over here. She slumped her way to the grimy bathroom that led off the room where they had been lost in drugged hazes for the last month or so. The windowless, airless room stank. There was no soap, towel, or toilet paper. No one had washed properly for weeks. At least the toilet flushed, most of the time.

Agnes had paused as she heard a low cry. Then there had been silence. Her finely honed sense of trouble twitched alarmingly. She turned out the bathroom light and slid, as quiet as the occupant of a crypt, back towards the front room. She placed her eye to the cracked door and watched as a tall, muscular man held down Bartholomew with one hand, a meaty knee planted firmly on his fragile chest. The man looked up at a pop-eyed Lawrence.

"Where are they?" he was asking softly. Lawrence was

shaking his head, his whole body stuttering and writhing in his horror.

"I don't know what you mean..." he faltered. The stranger drew out a large, serrated knife and calmly began to carve into Bartholomew. He'd placed duct tape over Bartholomew's mouth, so his screams were muted mumbles.

"Where are the ten Code Blue tablets and the raven drawing that Lucy gave you?" He asked in a friendly manner, all the while his blade trailing tracks of pain into Bartholomew's flinching flesh. Lawrence had shaken his head even harder.

"I don't know what you're talking about. Is it money? The money? Because we spent it... it's gone...". The stranger looked sad.

"No. I know you heard me. The ten Code Blue tablets and the raven. We have all night," he said. "And when I'm finished with this one, I will do exactly the same to you." He looked up from his grisly work and smiled widely. "I find that the anticipation makes the eventual experience so much more pleasurable. Don't you?"

"Five," Lawrence said, his voice faltering. "She gave us five tablets. And some crappy piece of paper. She must have the other five tablets." Lawrence scrabbled through the mess on the cardboard box and threw a scrap of paper towards the man. "We sold the tablets and there's the paper. It's just a pathetic bird drawing with some random letters on it. I'll give you her number, her address. Take her, kill her, do what you like with her. Just don't hurt me!" The stranger had smiled again.

"But it's Playtime," he said.

Agnes was dulled to horror, but this sight had repulsed

even her. The stranger had turned and looked directly at the damaged door behind which she'd stood, watching. He'd smiled, then turned back to his dismal task. He'd known she was there! Knew and didn't care. Agnes had gone to the small hallway window and eased it open. She was used to rapid, unscheduled escapes. Agnes writhed her emaciated frame through the narrow space and set off. To find the next party.

"STOP TALKING!" ordered Agnes to Charlie. "I'll speak with him, not with you." She turned her attention to Mac. He ignored her completely. "This is how it's going to go," she announced confidently. "I have information that you want; you have money. I want ten grand, and I'm not negotiating. And I want that fancy watch you have as well." Like a greedy magpie, Agnes had spotted Mac's wristwatch that gleamed on his left wrist, peeking out from under his black, long-sleeved t-shirt. "Ten grand and the watch, or I'm saying nothing!" She folded her arms defiantly over her emaciated chest.

The car drew to a smooth halt. There was just darkness outside. "Get out," said Mac quietly. Agnes's door opened soundlessly. There were no street lights. Hard, heavy hulks of ancient gritstone sat in shadow, gripping the uneven ground. A keen, clean wind slid into the car, slicing eagerly at Agnes's face and creased clothes.

"Are you mad? We're in the middle of nowhere!" objected Agnes, suddenly realising she may have made a mistake, thinking that the friendliness of the blonde woman meant weakness in both of the people in the front seats. The man finally looked at her in the rear mirror. His eyes were icy and very hard.

"This is how it's going to be," he said. "You get out now and walk back to whichever hole you decide to hide in. It's only Stanage Edge, so it should take you a mere three hours or so. Or you can throw yourself off. I really don't care." Agnes looked at him and realised that he really didn't care. The blonde woman looked down at her lap; good cop to his very bad cop. "If you had seen or heard anything of any value, then you'd be occupying a fourth resuscitation bay right now," snapped the man. "You tell us what you know, and you can have a bed for the night and a train to wherever you damned well like tomorrow morning. So long as you get out of Sheffield." He looked away from the rear mirror and started the engine. "I hate junkies," he muttered. Without a word, Agnes closed the car door and slumped, sulkily, on the back seat. At least she would get a bed for the night and a free train ride.

The car's phone rang. It was Sally. "Is she OK? You haven't called. Is Charlie OK?" came Sally's stressed-sounding voice.

"She's fine," replied Mac coolly. "But we have an unexpected passenger in the car, so keep replies to a minimum from now on, please." There was a pause as Sally took in this information.

"We have Agnes here," continued Mac. "She's agreed to tell us what she knows in return for a bed for the night and a train ride in the morning. Can we come to you?" There was a long pause.

"Yes," replied Sally briskly. "But make sure you blindfold her."

CHAPTER
FIFTY-ONE

Agnes woke. The large room was filled with early morning light. She stretched, feeling the soft pull of cotton and silk on her naked skin. Agnes studied the ceiling.

"Very nice," she murmured. She wanted to stay here. Agnes was not averse to selling sex: she was very good at it. She put in a lot of effort. Agnes just wanted to say when and where, and who. Well, the time was now, this room would do for the where, and the tall woman who seemed to own this place was the who. The woman had definitely fancied her when they had met a few weeks ago outside that farm shop. Agnes got up and moved towards the bathroom. On her way, she retrieved the remains of the drugs she had bought the night before when Charlie spotted her. She had taken just enough last night and would take just enough now. Just enough to see her through; until she could persuade her new best friend to give her some money. Agnes started the shower and looked at her resources, the selection of perfumes, moisturisers, and spare clothes. She picked up a razor. She was going to have to be extra good.

SALLY WALKED INTO THE KITCHEN, looking down at a document. She was getting closer to an answer to her hypothesis, her question. *I need someone to talk to this man,* she thought. Someone was at the fridge. Sally started in shock. It was Agnes. Agnes turned guiltily, a carton of milk in her hand.

"I'm sorry," she said, her voice soft, her eyes lowered. "It's just... I was so hungry."

"You should be locked in your room," said Sally sharply. "Until you go."

"I climbed out," said Agnes quietly. "To get something to eat. Your garden is beautiful." Sally carried on walking to her desk.

"Eat whatever you want," she said over her shoulder. "Then I'll take you back to your room."

Sally turned from her desk and found Agnes standing right behind her. She was scrubbed clean, and her washed hair was bright and fine and downy. She smelled of youth and expensive moisturiser. Agnes wore baggy tracksuit bottoms, pulled low over her hips, and was wearing a long-sleeved, tight, white cotton t-shirt. She'd cut the bottom half off the t-shirt, so an expanse of soft, taut skin was on unmissable display. The sunlight played in her large, green eyes and lingered on her moist, light-pink lips. She studied Sally's face with intense, intimate interest.

"I remember you," said Agnes softly. "Your tongue dried up when you tried to speak to me." Sally didn't say anything. She realised that, once again, she couldn't reply.

She, too, remembered the vivid wave of attraction that she'd felt.

Agnes reached up with one long, terribly pale finger and gently traced it across the jewel-tinted skin of Sally's collar bone. She then delicately and softly stroked down Sally's inner arm whilst easing closer. Agnes slowly snaked her head forward, and her questing lips found Sally's unresisting mouth. She kissed Sally, slowly and expertly and languorously, and Sally found her lips parting and eagerly accepting the oral caress. It had been so long since anyone had touched her with a hint of genuine desire. Sally felt the edge of her desk dig against the back of her legs as Agnes pressed her body insistently, rhythmically, and enthusiastically against hers. Agnes tasted of fresh milk, salted sweat, and sweet perfume. Her tongue moved in a myriad of hot, halting little licks over Sally's until a small, sensual cry echoed deep within the lush cavern of Sally's aching throat.

"Am I interrupting?" asked a voice with a Scottish accent. Sally looked across the room in horror. Sinclair stood in the kitchen; her face expressionless. "Mac told me a junkie was waiting to be transported to the train station."

"There's been a change of plan," said Agnes confidently, lifting her pointed chin and staring at Sinclair. She had her hand possessively around Sally's neck by now. "We were just discussing me staying here for a few days." Sally pulled away from Agnes, shaking her head in hot humiliation.

"We really were not," she said quietly. "You need to go. Now." Agnes's face fell into an angry scowl and she glared at the newcomer who had derailed her plans. Sinclair glared back and raised her hand. She was holding Agnes's bag, coat, and leather trousers.

"Now!" repeated Sinclair.

• • •

Within moments, Sinclair and Agnes were outside, standing by The Crew's Toyota Hilux pickup truck Sinclair had driven that morning. Sinclair emptied Agnes's bag over the gravel drive, ignoring Agnes's protests. She sifted through the sorry collection and picked out several small, expensive items that belonged to Sally. Sinclair stood and looked at Agnes. She held out her hand.

"Give," she said. Agnes crossed her arms and jutted her pelvis defiantly.

"I don't have anything else; you just took it all!" she retorted.

"Whatever's in your mouth. Give," repeated Sinclair.

"How about... I just swallowed it?" hissed Agnes. Sinclair's top lip twitched. She slowly stepped closer to Agnes and said, quietly and very calmly;

"How about... I just punch you repeatedly in the stomach until you vomit?" Agnes looked at her. She realised Sinclair meant it. She had no way of knowing that Sinclair's fiancée had been murdered for the sake of heroin, but she recognised Sinclair was not a fan of the drug-taking lifestyle. Agnes grimaced angrily and spat a pair of diamond stud earrings onto the pathway. Sinclair picked them smartly up and put them into her jeans pocket without taking her eyes off Agnes.

They drove, in silence, to the train station, then stood, looking at the departures board.

"I've been ordered to see you onto a train," said Sinclair. "Where are you going? Decide now!" In the end, Agnes chose Manchester. There was always a party going on in Manchester. Sinclair watched her onto the train; watched

Agnes help herself to someone else's purse and earphones as she did so. Sinclair shook her head. She hated junkies.

SINCLAIR SAT in the still quiet of the truck, her hands clasped loosely around the steering wheel. She stared, unseeing, out of the front window. Cold rain spattered on the greyed glass and time slipped past. She kept seeing two heads bending in a sensuous alliance. Why did she have to replay that particular moment? Why did she feel so angry? Sally was her employer. An odd but beautiful, devastatingly intelligent, independent woman. She could kiss whomsoever she wanted...

SALLY LOOKED at her laptop screen. Yet another email had appeared from Randall. She deleted it. She didn't need to read it. It would be the same threatening demand for her to obtain the 'item' that he required; another veiled threat to Rowans Holt if she didn't obtain the Code Blue. Sally's stomach churned with mixture of anxiety, guilt and irritation. She resented any hint of Randall's presence in her new, secure system. She gently stroked the laptop. Her special project had gained a new lease of life since her hospitalisation, surprising even her. But she must keep it secret; keep it safe.

Sally looked up. Wetherby had entered the kitchen of Rowans Holt.

"I thought Sinclair was on duty today?" she said, as casually as she could.

"She was," replied Wetherby, going to the window and squinting out, automatically checking all was safe. "Something came up. She said to give you these." He dropped a pair of diamond stud earrings into Sally's hand. They were hers. Sally's heart sank even further.

Later that evening, Sally and Charlie lay in Charlie's bed. They were having a Girlie Chat. Charlie had drawn the sheet over their heads. Ben shook his head. He was sitting on the chaise longue, reading a car magazine.

"You do know I can hear you, don't you?" he said.

"Yes, but we can't see you, and that's all that matters," replied Charlie. This made no sense, even to Charlie. She paused as she wondered how to dig herself out of a linguistic hole. She couldn't. She carried on whispering with Sally.

"I'm gone!" sighed Ben, standing up and heading for the kitchen. "There are some potatoes with my name on them."

"You did what?" exclaimed Charlie. Sally bit her lip. "You kissed Agnes?" whispered Charlie in disbelief.

"She kissed me!" exclaimed Sally.

"But you kissed her back?" said Charlie. Sally nodded.

"But then Sinclair walked in," said Sally quietly.

"Oh God, I bet that was embarrassing, caught kissing the prisoner," said Charlie, grinning. "Good thing we got all the information off her first." She looked closely at Sally. "What? Why are you looking like that?"

"Like what?" said Sally guiltily.

"Guilty!" said Charlie. Her eyes opened wide. "You like Sinclair, don't you?"

Sally rolled onto her back and pushed the sheet away from the two of them.

"There's a serial killer on the loose, I could lose my home, and all I can think about is Maddie Sinclair," she said. She put her hands over her eyes. "That's not logical. I'm a logical person." She pulled her hands away and looked over at Charlie. "Or at least I was...."

"Well, don't look at me!" cried Charlie. "I'm brokenhearted over someone who thinks kissing me was one of the worst mistakes they ever made. Who actively flirts with other women when I'm sitting next to them!"

They lay side by side, Charlie on the right and Sally on the left, both looking up at the ceiling, arms almost touching. Charlie reached out and took Sally's right hand.

"Sal..." she said

"Yes?" said Sally, still looking upwards.

"If I die...." Sally whipped her head round to look at Charlie.

"You are not going to die!" announced Sally. Charlie turned her head and looked solemnly at Sally.

"If I die," Charlie repeated firmly. "Would you bury my ashes in the walled garden? I know that's asking a lot. But I've never been so happy as in the last few weeks. Terrified and almost murdered a few times, but truly, completely happy.

Sally paused, overwhelmed, and frustrated by her inability to deal with this emotional overload. She patted Charlie's hand.

"That must have been very difficult for you," she intoned. Charlie threw back her head and laughed with genuine pleasure.

Charlie turned her body over to face Sally. She looked down at Sally's arm. Charlie stroked the small scar where she had inserted the cannula. Where she had so willingly injected her life's blood.

"I love you, Sal," she said gently, not looking up.

"That's what you do, isn't it?" asked Sally softly, moving her head tenderly towards Charlie's. "You love. It's who you are, isn't it?" Charlie reluctantly looked at her, and her face fell.

"I don't know who I am, Sal," she whispered. Charlie let go of Sally's hand and lay on her back again. "I've spent the whole of my life caring for other people; my mother, my sister, my patients. It's my first living memory, being instructed to take care of others." Charlie carried on looking up at the ceiling, her brow furrowed, her eyes clouded. She reached up and touched her neck. She remembered the heavy warmth of the gold and jade necklace that she had worn on the Gala night; the comforting familiarity of it. But she had never owned expensive jewellery. How could she remember something she had never possessed? "And then... there's so much I don't remember," she said slowly. "There's so much that's clouded in darkness. I don't know who I am." She turned towards Sally again. "Do you know who you are?"

"Of course," said Sally. "I am Sally Marshall. And I am magnificent."

Charlie looked at Sally for a long time. Sally held her glance unwaveringly. Sally had come to realise the truth of what she said. There was no problem with telling the truth. Charlie nodded and then smiled.

"Yes. You are Sally Marshall. And you are magnificent." A wistful smile broke over Charlie's face. "I wish I could be Sally Marshall." Sally looked at Charlie, uncomprehending.

"But, if you were me, then there'd be no Charlie Hart," she said. "And we need you. Ben and I need you. Just the way you are."

"Even though what I do just isn't good enough?" asked

Charlie, eyes wide and mouth pulled down, trying not to dissolve into tears. Sally shook her head. She was struggling with the lack of logic going on.

"What you do is perfect, because you are perfect. Just the way you are. For us, for Rowans Holt. For how things are. Please, don't change, Charlie." Charlie nodded, smiling and crying at the same time.

"Ok," she said, relieved. "Ok...." She looked around but couldn't find a hanky. Charlie began wiping her nose on the edge of the bedsheet. Sally's face wrinkled in revulsion.

"That's disgusting!" Sally announced.

"Yeah, maybe it is," said Charlie, now blowing her nose on the sheet. "But not as disgusting as hitting on a drug addict... in front of your future wife...."

BEN LOOKED up at the ceiling above the living space. There had been a loud thud on the floor from the bedroom above. He grasped the gun that Mac had given him, slapped the magazine in and forcefully headed for the stairs; however, he paused a few steps up. Charlie was laughing hysterically.

"Ow!" she cried between gasps of hilarity. "Ow! ow! ow! I'm sorry, alright? Get off!... Okay?... Okay... well... not sorry! Ahhh! No!"

"SO. WHAT DO WE DO THEN?" asked Sally, a little while later, gazing at Charlie. "What do girls normally do in emotional situations like this?"

"As it's an emergency," said Charlie gravely. "Then it's time to break out the big guns. It's a three-step approach." Sally nodded. Three steps. She could do this—a logical, considered, stepwise approach to the problem. Charlie continued; her face serious. “Step One; Our Cow Molly ice cream. I have a big tub of Cherry Cheesecake in the freezer, for urgent situations, just like this one. Step Two; Cadbury’s Fruit and Nut, it’s the only realistic option. Then Step Three; we watch Legally Blonde.”

“Legally Blonde?” said Sally, slowly. “Do we even have that film?” It was Charlie’s turn to look guilty.

“Well… we do now…” Charlie said.

CHAPTER FIFTY-TWO

Mac paced through Rowans Holt. He trod back and forth with such irritable energy that he reminded Sally of a caged animal. It was Monday, and there had been no sign of Lucy. He felt vulnerable, as it had been necessary to send the Crew up to Manchester again. There was just him and Morton to manage things. Sally sat calmly at her computer, ignoring his agitated peregrinations.

"Are you sure the facial recognition software is actually on?" asked Mac, not for the first time.

"Yes," said Sally slowly and coolly. Not for the first time.

And then it happened. There was a low alert. Sally opened a window on the screen and exclaimed softly.

"She's on the move. Mac!" He was already at her shoulder, his dark eyes scanning the screen. Mac cursed internally. Why now when he had the least backup? "It looks like she's on the fifty-one bus, travelling from Lodge Moor towards town," said Sally. She shook her head. "Of course! She's been hiding at Georgia's. She must know the farm, so she found a bolt-hole there."

"Is she still on the bus?" demanded Mac.

"Yes," said Sally. "She's probably going to town to pick up another bus out of the centre again. Or getting a train out of Sheffield, if she knows what's good for her."

The grainy CCTV images from the bus showed a thin and despondent-looking figure sitting, hood pulled up, at the back of the bus. No coat. Mac felt a deep, strong stab of pity for the girl. They would help her get out of Sheffield, help her start again. But they needed to talk to her first. Get the remaining Code Blue tablets. If she still had them.

On the bus, Lucy chewed nervously at her ragged right thumbnail. She hadn't been able to hide at Georgia's anymore. Keeping secreted away from both crabby Georgia and the creeping Baz had become too much. She'd tried to sleep in the day and had emerged at night, slipping past Helders into the shop to find something to eat. Helders hadn't given her away. She'd petted him and given him many meaty treats when she'd worked there. She liked animals; loved drawing them. Maybe, when this was over, she would return to college and do art. Leticia had always encouraged her to do her art.

Lucy closed her eyes. She wouldn't think, she couldn't think, of Leticia. Lucy was so, so tired. She was going to own up. She was going to go straight to the Police station on Snig Hill. Hand in the tablets and the piece of paper that seemed to have caused so much trouble. Numb and humble, she looked out the window at the green fields sliding by; a verdant vision that slowly faded to a weary view of huddled houses as she moved closer to town. As she moved closer to her fate.

MAC WAS SLIPPING on his old jacket and talking rapidly to Sally and Ben. Ben stood with his arms folded, his face severe. They were in the library.

"Stay in here," Mac was saying. "Things are finally moving. If I get the tablets, the Boss might decide to come here and try to retrieve them. He's getting information from somewhere, even though Decker's dead." Sally nodded grimly. Mac continued. "There's a good, lockable door in this room, and it has at least one passageway out of it. Ben looked surprised.

"I've been in this room for weeks. I've seen no hidden passages!" he exclaimed. Despite feeling on edge, Sally looked proud.

"Rowans Holt is riddled with secrets," she said. "She hides them well." Ben looked put out and started glancing around, trying to locate what he'd missed.

"I'll show you the escape route. If the need arises," said Sally, enigmatically, smiling at his discomfort.

Charlie walked in, also putting on a jacket. "Are we going?" she asked nervously. Mac shook his head.

"After what happened in A and E? No way, Hart," he said decisively. "You stay here with Morton and Sally." Charlie's mouth tightened and pulled down into a straight line. Mac hadn't seen that expression before, and this made him uneasy. He had thought he knew all of her expressions.

"You aren't the only one who wants this situation resolved," she snapped back. "And if you think it's a good idea for a big man with a gun to go haring around after a terrified teenager, then you're a fool! She knows me. From the Manor." Ben and Sally looked sideways at each other and, as one, took a slight step back from Mac and Charlie, who were now glaring at each other.

"I can't spend my time pulling you along and watching both our backs," said Mac.

"I can watch my own back, and I'm the one who's got us this far, remember?" objected Charlie.

"All I can remember is your obsession with high drama. That's all you seem to do," growled Mac.

"What I do is just fine! And who the Hell do you think you are, judging me? You're just Cormack Beaulouf, not God all-bloody-mighty," retorted Charlie angrily.

Sally stepped forward, her hands raised as if to calm stormy waters.

"Please. Enough! We're wasting time." She turned to the angry Mac. "Charlie's right. Lucy's a scared teenager, a friendly face might help matters. Charlie will stick with you, and you'll be in the middle of town, in broad daylight." Mac said nothing but stalked from the room. Sally winked at Charlie. "Magnificent," she mouthed. Charlie smiled faintly and nodded. She felt sick with fear, but she'd decided that what she did might be good enough after all. She followed Mac out of the room.

MAC DROVE them rapidly down the Manchester Road in angry silence. The Range Rover was heavy but very fast. He got Sally on the phone.

"Where is she now?" he asked shortly.

"Still on the bus," replied Sally, her voice calm. "Heading down into Broomhill now. She's about twelve minutes from town, depending on traffic." Mac put his foot down, and Charlie felt her body pushed gently back into the leather seat.

"Open the glove box," Mac instructed Charlie. Charlie did as she was told. Sitting in the space was a small black gun. To Charlie, it looked as if it was waiting. It looked hungry. She hated violence and the promise of violence.

"Pick it up," ordered Mac. "Get used to how it feels." Charlie slid her fingers reluctantly around the handle. She lifted it, testing the heavy heft in her hesitant hand. It felt alien, dirty. She felt repulsed. Had this thing shot someone? Drawn blood? Broken bone? Taken someone's son or daughter and rendered them cold and unmoving in the minuscule moment between one heart's beat and the next? She looked at Mac, at his face, stern and focused on the road ahead. He casually carried death with him and on him. He must have buried the greatest sin deep within his secret soul. Mac glanced at her. He seemed to read her mind. He turned back to look at the road.

"It gets easier after the first time," he said quietly.

LUCY GOT off the bus early, opposite The Leopold hotel. She walked down Church Street towards the Police station at Snig Hill; her hands jammed deep in her hoodie pockets. Sally watched her progress, haltingly, on CCTV, piggy-backing systems where she could. Mac arrived in town and jammed the car into the nearest parking space he could find on Campo Lane, behind the Cathedral. They should be parallel with Lucy now. He had intended to give Charlie a quick run-through on how to fire the gun, but her uncharacteristically closed face told him she would resist him. Again. And they needed to catch Lucy.

They jogged down Campo Lane, the back of the Cathedral looming on their right. Mac slipped an earpiece in, so he could stay in contact with Sally. Feeding and supporting the homeless, the Cathedral Archer Project disgorged its clients. Full of breakfast and half-formed plans, they noisily milled on the streets. The footpath suddenly seemed filled with limping, creased-faced figures. A man in a shabby donkey jacket, with a black hat, pulled deep over his head, slowly stood from his casually squatted position as they hurried past. He took a phone away from his ear and secreted it safely. He then darted rapidly up the narrow, flagged St James row, towards Church Street, with an agility that belied his shabby appearance.

Lucy was walking, deep in thought, right hand hidden and clutching the tablets and paper in their small plastic envelope. She imagined herself walking into the Police Station, moving towards the Perspex box housing the duty police officer. What would she say? Would she show them the tablets first? Lucy became aware of a figure walking on the other side of the road to her. She slowed down. They did too. She stopped. The figure stopped too. It turned slowly towards her. It was a man wearing a black beanie hat. His hands were also jammed in his pockets, his body language echoing hers. He smiled at her. Lucy's breathing sped up, and her throat tightened. It had been a man in a beanie hat chasing her the other day on The Manor. The man continued to smile at her. The smile, however, didn't reach his twinkling blue eyes. She knew that smile. She had seen it before; on the masks of certain men–which they called their faces.

CHARLIE AND MAC were hurrying up Chapel Walk, the second narrow path that hugged the Cathedral. Mac was talking to Sally.

"Can you see her?" he demanded.

"She should come into your view now," said Sally calmly. "To your right. She's stopped." Sally's voice suddenly rose, sounding unaccustomedly panicked. "Oh God, no, she's running. There's someone after her! Go, go!" Mac took off like a hunting hound, long legs carrying him rapidly over the uneven flags and cobbles. From his right, he saw Lucy, eyes wide and mouth open, haring down Church Street, a figure in a black hat close behind her. They turned right into Fargate, one of the main shopping streets in Sheffield. A slow tram eased in front of Mac. He cursed and raced around the front of it. He kept running, cars swerving and braking as he thundered across High Street and onto Fargate. His height meant he could easily look over the heads of the meandering shoppers to spot Lucy's frantic flight further down the street. Mac sped up, dodging and weaving through the crowd. He saw Lucy fling herself left down Norfolk Row, her pursuer still pelting after her. He was vaguely aware of Charlie running behind him. She would just have to catch up, he thought grimly. He couldn't spend his time pulling her along and watching both their backs.

Mac cruised down Norfolk Row, his muscular arms and legs pistoning smoothly, gaining on Lucy and her sinister shadow. Lucy raced across Tudor Square, the Crucible and Lyceum theatres looming on her left. Her pursuer collided with a cyclist, who crashed, with an angry cry, to the flagged floor. The pursuer staggered and lost some ground. Lucy had disappeared left down Surrey Street. He burst round the corner, Mac mere seconds behind him. Lucy was nowhere to be seen. The man continued to run but slowed. He looked left and right. On his right was the Graduate Pub, and to his left the large Portland stone building that was the Central Library. Mac felt in his inner pocket for his gun, cursing the busyness of the street. If he got the opportunity, he would take out this man first and ask questions later. The pursuer made a decision and darted left into a doorway. He had entered the door to the Children's library.

Mac ran up the steps to the library's main entrance and looked around him.

"Did you see where she went?" he demanded of Sally. "Can you see her now?" There was a long pause. He could hear Sally tapping on her computer. He carried on searching. An elegant, art deco staircase stretched away above him. Mac looked through the glass doors ahead of him into the large, ground-floor room. Readers drifted like slow-grazing ruminants amongst the dappled shade of the long wooden shelves. There was no sign of Lucy.

"There's nothing," Mac heard Sally mutter. "All the cameras are down. All the bloody library cameras are down!" Mac made his swift, graceful way up the stairs, peering into each room as he went, his progress slurred and slowed by broad, browsing bibliophiles. Still no trace of Lucy. He reached the top of the staircase and looked down at the small square of ground-floor hallway that was visible. He cursed as he glimpsed the top of Lucy's head as she emerged and hurried towards the main door. Mac propelled himself headlong back down the stairs.

. . .

CHARLIE EMERGED ON SURREY STREET, panting. *When did I get so unfit?* she thought. She'd lost sight entirely of Lucy and Mac, and of the man who had been following Lucy. A sensation like bitter ice traced from the exposed nape of her neck down to the base of her spine. What if he saw her alone and came for her? Decided to start Playtime, whatever that was? Charlie doubted it would be fun for her. Just a hunch. She looked around. Where had they all gone? And then she saw her, Lucy, hurrying down the Library stairs, looking anxiously around. Charlie ran again after the disappearing girl.

LUCY JOGGED DOWN ARUNDEL GATE, Charlie in pursuit. Charlie took a breath and called out,

"Lucy, wait!" Lucy turned and paused as she saw Charlie, small and smiling, hands held up. *She's going to stop*! Thought Charlie, *she's going to remember me, to talk to me. Mac won't be angry with me anymore*! But Lucy's face changed, and she started backing away, her mouth forming a small

"No."

Charlie looked behind her, and her heart dropped as she saw the pursuer. Hat pulled low, collar up, his mouth was set in a thin, stern line as he steamed down the ramp that ran past the Millennium Galleries, sprinting in single-minded pursuit once more. Charlie ran too, Lucy already a disappearing figure. The man thudded past her with a frightening turn of speed, and, finally, there was Mac. He emerged round the corner of Surrey Street, running, fluid and fleet. He passed Charlie without a glance, his eyes fixed on his quarry, and he started gaining on the man and Lucy.

Lucy turned right off Arundel gate and pounded up the steep stone steps and past the Q-Park multi-story building. Her panicking mind had the vague idea that she could hide amongst the cars. She saw a young couple, just ahead of her, turn in towards the car park, ticket clutched in hand. She followed them closely, breath burning in her heaving chest. As the secure door slid open, Lucy slithered through and fell towards the nearest stairs; she could not afford to wait for a lift. She set off, climbing with no idea or plan other than trying to put as much distance as possible between herself and the dead-eyed man following her.

Mac approached the car park. He saw the man's figure slip inside, just behind a middle-aged man who shouted indignantly. As he waited for the door to open, Mac spoke to Sally again. Charlie came running up, panting.

"We're at the Charles Street Q Park," he snapped. "Lucy's in there somewhere, and so is the killer. It's Leticia's killer, Sally. No pressure, but can you see her?

"Give me a moment," came Sally's composed voice. There was another pause. The door opened as a family emerged from the carpark, and they stepped into the cool interior. "I have her," said Sally. "She's halfway up the stairwell. And she has company. Move!" Mac pushed up the stairs ahead of Charlie, smoothly taking the steps two at a time. Mac could hear Lucy's distant, desperate footfalls as she stuttered up the stairs in unseeing panic. He knew that the man would be just ahead of him. He increased his pace.

Mac reached the top of the stairwell and burst through the door, his stance low and gun in hand. Lucy was backed against the far wall of the roof, holding her hand out as if to ward off the tall, broad-shouldered man who stood close before her. As Mac watched, she hurriedly climbed onto the wall and stood like a flushed and frightened animal framed against the slow-moving sky. The man held out his hands as if he could calm her. He took one pace towards her. The terrified, unthinking Lucy took one pace back. Into nothing, into oblivion.

BUT WHEN LUCY AWOKE, Letica was there, waiting. They held hands again and gently joined their jubilant heads in loving friendship. They laughed, their trust in each other complete. The girls turned; together, forever. They saw the woman wave to them triumphantly from the battlements, and they walked towards her. They walked towards the Light.

CHAPTER FIFTY-THREE

Mac heard Charlie burst through the door behind him. His gaze on the killer faltered momentarily. He looked back and saw the man raise his gun and fire, not towards him, but directly at Charlie. Without thinking, Mac threw himself sideways to shield the blinking and unprepared Charlie. He felt a blow, like a sledgehammer, over his already vulnerable right shoulder. He was thrown back with a cry, at the same time discharging his gun in the vague direction of the man. As if in slow motion, he fell backwards. In the edge of his vision, he saw the man dart for the nearest exit.

The back of Mac's head cracked savagely and painfully against the concrete floor, and the sky darkened before his eyes. He heard Charlie's voice as if coming from miles away.

"Mac! Mac!" He felt her small hand slip into his, and he hung onto it as the world shifted and span.

"Hart!" he gasped.

"I'm here. I'm here, William," he heard her whisper close

to his ear. She sounded on the verge of tears. He smiled groggily. Of course, she was about to cry.

"Going to be sick," he then muttered. He felt her hands grab his left shoulder and hip proficiently and pull him over onto his side. He now lay on his damaged right shoulder, but he didn't care. Nausea wracked him, and he vomited, stomach heaving and head spinning. He was out of control and unable to defend them–his damaged body wouldn't let him. He lay panting and drenched in cold sweat. Darkness nudged in from the sides of his vision. He clung to Charlie's hand and the sound of her voice.

Once the vomiting stopped, Charlie rolled him onto his back. He felt her rapidly and professionally examining him. She found the Kevlar vest that had probably saved his life. He felt it being undone and her hands pressing over his chest wall. Large bruises were already developing in the flesh of his upper right torso. Charlie held her palms against his chest and watched carefully as they rose and fell with his breathing. She suspected some cracking to his mid-right third rib, but the skin was intact, and his lungs seemed unharmed. She rolled him onto his left side this time, off his injury and away from the mess he'd made. Charlie inspected his back carefully and ran her hand over the back of his skull. She felt for deformities, swelling, areas of depressed bone or bogginess that would indicate a serious head injury. She then checked for bruising behind his ears and around his eyes that could indicate a base of skull fracture. Everything seemed in order.

Mac was coming round. As Charlie watched, his terrible pallor faded. He gingerly sat up, still feeling nauseated. Mac breathed deeply, embarrassed that she had seen him so helpless. Charlie crouched down in front of him.

"Look at me," she said sternly. She held up a finger and tested his eye movements, and then checked his visual fields. She moved closer, and, for one surreal moment, Mac thought she was about to kiss him. Taken by surprise, he instinctively moved towards her but then realised she was instead intently inspecting his pupils, which were sometimes difficult to make out in his dark brown, liquid eyes. Charlie nodded. "That was quite a knock to the back of your head," she said, her tone professional and brisk. "We need to keep a close eye on you. For at least twenty-four hours." She then paused. "Thank you," she said quietly. "You saved my life." He didn't reply.

Mac slowly stood and started strapping his Kevlar vest back on, a large depression evident on its surface.

"We need to get out of here," he said, not looking at her.

"Lucy?" said Charlie, still kneeling on the concrete floor. He looked at her now. He shook his head.

"Fell. Accident," he said shortly. Charlie closed her eyes. Misery engulfed her. "Hart!" she heard Mac exclaim. He held out his left hand, and she took it. He pulled her abruptly to her feet and turned away. Their moment of intimacy was clearly at an end. She followed him as he jogged to the stairwell and threw open the door. He hesitated, seemingly still struggling with the after-effects of his injuries, but he shook his head and determinedly dived into the darkness.

They made their way swiftly down the stairwell, turning tightly again and again. Mac had to stop halfway down as dizziness again engulfed him. As he slowly recovered, he re-inserted his earpiece that had come adrift.

"Mac! I can see you," he heard Sally say in his ear. He nodded. "I took out the cameras at the top of the building. There's no evidence you were there or saw Lucy," she continued. Mac glanced up at the nearby CCTV camera. "I'll wipe these too," Sally said. "I just needed to say; don't let Charlie go round to the front of the car park." Mac glanced at Charlie and nodded to let Sally know he'd heard. "Lucy's there." continued Sally calmly. "Or what's left of her. A young couple have stopped as they drove out. I think he's a doctor or a nurse. Charlie will want to go and see if she can help. It's too late. Don't let her go." Mac nodded again in total agreement.

"And the killer?" he said.

"Been and gone," said Sally neutrally. "Searched Lucy's dying body like the cold-hearted bastard he is and then moved off. Empty-handed."

"You're sure?" Mac said, hope springing in him. He'd been sure the man would have the Code Blue by now.

"I closed in on his hands. Can't see his face properly anyway with that hat and coat. His hands were empty."

"Where are the tablets, then?"

"Farm, bus or Library," replied Sally brusquely. "But I mapped Lucy's trajectory from the bus stop. I have a hunch she was heading towards Snig Hill."

"The Police Station?" said Mac.

"Makes sense," said Sally. "She must have been tired of hiding. Wanting to make a clean start. I think she had the tablets and the formula when she came to town, but not when she died.

"The Library," said Mac and Sally at the same time.

"But where?" said Mac in frustration. "She was in there for five minutes with no sign of where she was. If the killer had seen her, he would have simply picked up the tablets. He wouldn't have searched her."

"Well, I had no glimpse of her," said Sally irritably. "Every one of the cameras was down."

"I'll have to get the Crew together," said Mac. "Call them back from Manchester. We'll come back tonight and start making a thorough search." There was silence from Sally. "There's nothing else we can do now." Mac looked fixedly at the camera. "We need to get out of town."

"I know. I saw him aiming at Charlie on the roof," said Sally quietly. "Bring her home."

They exited the car park, and Mac guided Charlie down the stone steps and then left, away from where Lucy lay. They could hear the cry of sirens as they hurried down Arundel Gate.

"Sally, do you have any sight of the killer?" demanded Mac. There was a pause, and then Sally said,

"Got him. He's walking quickly through the Peace Gardens. In plain sight."

"Towards us or away from us?" said Mac.

"Away. Looks like he's headed for Pinstone Street."

Mac stopped outside the Millennium Gallery and looked at Charlie. "I want you to go back to the car as fast as you can," he said. He handed her the car keys. "Don't look back or around you; just run. I'll be right behind you." She looked at him, her eyes wide.

"Why are you leaving me again?"

"I'll be right behind you," he repeated. "Go. Now. Lock the car from the inside. The glass is bulletproof. Nothing can get you once you're in there."

How could Mac explain that the urge to hunt this man was now irresistible? He wanted to kill the man more than ever. Out here, he had the chance to stalk him, to bring him down before he tried to kill Charlie again. Mac watched Charlie as she ran up the ramp towards the Library, then he turned and headed towards the escalator that led up into the Millennium Gallery.

Mac spoke to Sally. "Do you still have him in your sight?"

"Yes," replied Sally. "I lost him for a moment at Cheney Row, but I've got him again."

"And you're sure he's walking away from the Library?" demanded Mac, now jogging through the lush humidity of the glass-roofed Winter Gardens towards the Peace Gardens.

"Yes," Sally soothed. "He's limping slightly. Maybe it's where you wounded him the other night, or he hurt himself running down those stairs to get to Lucy."

"If you lose sight at all, or he looks like he's turning back, then I'll follow Hart," said Mac. "But if I can catch him in the open and bring him down, I'll do it."

"I'll be your eyes," said Sally confidently.

Charlie ran past the Library, hoping to get back to the car as quickly as she could. However, she halted in front of the entrance and looked into the building. She then drifted up the steps and into the library, as if in a trance. Charlie sat, still and thoughtful, on one of the polished wooden benches that lined the entrance hall. She looked up at the clean Art Deco lines of the old building and thought of the people who would see nothing again. Charlie closed her eyes. Poor Lucy, poor Leticia. Something gurned and gyrated, dark and deep within her mind, however, she slid past it, habitually heading upwards to the brightness, to the Light. Where would a scared little girl hide something precious and dangerous? A little Goth girl.

Charlie concentrated. She had a photographic memory, a talent that had not only got her scattered brain into Medical School, but had also kept her there at distinction level. It had held her afloat as she worked hard in a nursing home to support herself and also dealt with her academic demands. Charlie's recall sifted through the books and papers that had littered the floor of Lucy's bedroom; the romance and cheap thrillers, the escapes from the dreary, undreaming world. The art... the poetry.

She loves him, she really, really loves him, she recalled Leticia saying. Charlie's hand tingled as if remembering warm skin, the hum of flesh against flesh like a half-heard musical note.

"She walks in beauty..." muttered Charlie. Where would a scared little Goth girl who was really, really in love hide something? Charlie walked somnolently to the front desk.

"Excuse me?" she heard herself saying. A middle-aged woman with large, red-rimmed glasses and an expression of permanent, gentle surprise looked up.

"Yes, my dear?" she said with kindly bemusement.

"Where's the poetry section?" asked Charlie. The woman pointed to an area at the far back of the main room. Charlie approached it and traced her fingers over the volumes. She hovered over Plath, dismissed Hughes, dickered over Dickinson, and settled confidently on Byron. "She walks in beauty..." she whispered.

And when she opened the volume, at the place where a slight dimple pushed at the pages, a small plastic envelope fell out. Inside were five small blue tablets and a shimmering piece of paper. Charlie opened the small envelope and drew out the piece of paper. A holographic image arose and sparkled in the sunlight that poured through the tall library windows. It was one half of the figure of a blunt-beaked raven, back hunched and plumage silky black. Letters and numbers in silver shimmered amongst the raven's plumage and a single light blue eye glittered out at her. Charlie's mind recoiled, and she shivered without knowing why. Something again turned and whispered within her brain, and pain clamped over her head and stabbed deep into her right eye. She had found the Code Blue and half of the formula.

Charlie pushed the items deep into her pocket, shook her head and blinked until the pain subsided. She then lifted her phone, ready to call Mac in triumph. She heard the pleasantly perplexed librarian speaking and the words froze her to the marrow.

"Your wife? With the long blonde hair? Yes, she's just around the corner. At the poetry section." The killer had found her. The Bad Wolf was coming for her. Again.

ON THE OTHER side of the city centre, Mac could see the killer. The man's head was bent down, and his black hat bobbed in time to his tapping pace. Sally was right; he was limping slightly on the left. Mac felt a surge of triumph; the killer was wounded. Mac's step quickened. *The hunt begins*, part of his mind sang.

"He's heading for Fountain Square," said Sally, sounding quietly confident. "Be careful. He's slowing down. He might have spotted you." Mac trotted, head up, towards Barkers Pool. By now, he could see the man, see the dark navy of his donkey jacket through the railings that lined the small square. Mac made out his bullet-shaped head as he turned, seeming to assess the area.

"He's stopped," said Sally. "He's looking around. He's...

He's looking in a bin...." Mac heard, but didn't comprehend, what Sally had said. Mac was within the square by now, his hand inside his jacket and drawing out his silenced Glock with a discreet, practised motion. He grasped the man's shoulder and was repulsed by how the coat's material sagged and folded onto the skeletal frame beneath. He pushed the snubbed silencer into the base of the man's skull but paused as the stench of nicotine and desolate decay washed over him.

And then this guy gave me thirty quid for my hat! Mac heard the words roaring in his head. The killer was practised in sleight of hand.... The figure beneath his slackening grip turned, his toothless mouth pulled back in a gummy grin.

"Spare any change?" he exclaimed enthusiastically. Mac was already falling back, falling away.

"Oh God, Oh God!" he heard Sally exclaim, as if from a million miles away.

CHAPTER FIFTY-FOUR

The Boss walked rapidly to where the Old Hag had indicated. His heart, which never normally moved above fifty beats per minute, was thundering in his chest at the prospect of gaining the missing tablets and formula and getting his hands on the petite blonde. She now seemed so deliciously tempting to him because she was also precious to Beaulouf. Beaulouf had revealed his hand by taking the bullet on the car park roof. His Playtime, his rapt and dedicated decimation, would be all the sweeter. His hands twitched. He would subdue her; then, he would carry her out. He'd say she'd fainted and needed air. And then he would take her to where they could be alone. And utterly intimate.

He rounded the bookshelves, only to find the space empty. A volume of Byron lay on top of the stacked volumes. He grabbed the end of the shelves. There was a narrow space, too thin for him to squeeze down, but a small woman... His head whipped round, and he saw a flash of blonde hair as a small, familiar figure hurried towards the exit. And he was off. In pursuit. He dodged the displays, keeping the blonde hair in sight, a half-smile pulling at his lips.

Officer Kylie Porter was standing outside the Winter Gardens on Surrey Street. She was waiting for Pete to get his customary sandwich and coffee from Zooby's café, just inside the airy glass building. Pete had finally asked her out on a date. She was musing on what to wear. Something demure and safe? Or give him the full Kylie? Both barrels. She was also relieved that she hadn't been assigned to deal with that suicide that'd landed all over Charles Street just a few minutes ago. Sheffield was usually one of the safest cities in the country. *What's got into everyone*? thought Kylie uneasily.

A rapid movement caught Kylie's eye to her right. A blonde woman had pelted down the stairs of the main library and was running towards her. The woman's face was pulled into a panicked expression. Another figure shot down the stairs close behind her; a tall, well-built man wearing a red hat and a grubby, cream bomber jacket. His face was intent and alive with an expression that Kylie knew only too well: violence and the joy in violence. Kylie moved instinctively. Her left hand reached up to her radio.

"Pete!" was all she said. Her right hand grabbed the extendable baton on her left hip and pulled it free. At the same time, she was smoothly running after the figures as they bolted into Tudor Square.

"Stop, Police!" yelled Kylie. Neither figure stopped, and the man was now close to the blonde woman, his long, muscular legs closing the distance between them at a frightening speed. Kylie deployed the baton and picked up her own pace. "Police!" she shouted again, louder and more forcefully. The man still ran. Kylie brought the rod down in a hard swipe across the side of the running man's right knee. He went down, but he grabbed and caught the blonde woman's right leg as he fell. They both crashed onto the hard stone floor. Kylie placed her hand over her bottle of CS spray. "Officer requires assistance," she snapped into her radio. She could hear Pete's rapid steps approaching from behind.

The man had heaved himself to his feet and was glaring at Kylie. He had a vice-like hold on the ankle of the blonde woman, who lay on the ground on her back, kicking, clawing, and panting, trying to get free.

"Let go of the woman, please, sir," said Pete calmly, holding up both hands and trying to diffuse the situation. The man had his phone in his hand and was looking at it intently, his thumb moving rapidly over the screen. He held it up triumphantly so they could both see the screen. A familiar blue and yellow image was on display. Kylie's heart sank. She'd never seen this screen in real life, only in training manuals and screenshots.

"Make the call, now!" ordered the man in a deep Yorkshire accent. His eyes glittered dangerously.

A Police car screeched to a halt, and two officers emerged and hurried over. One of them was still holding a sandwich. Pete looked him up and down.

"What's in the sandwich, Heavygate?" he asked. "Squirrel?" Officer Heavygate raised his eyes skywards. He and Toyne would never live down the squirrel-killing incident.

"Funny, Loxley", he snapped. "What's going on?" Pete turned back to the tall man.

"If you just let the woman go, sir, we'll call the number,"

said Pete. The man's top lip pulled back in the approximation of a snarl.

"Just call the number! Then I'll give the passwords. Then I'll leave. With the woman." There was silence from the Police Officers. Toyne and Heavygate moved to stand on either side of the tall man. Both placed their hands on their batons and CS spray. Kylie moved over to the woman. The man looked at them in turn as if noting their faces for future retribution. A chill ran through them all, but they returned his gaze steadily.

They all knew what the blue and yellow image meant; top priority government clearance. They were not allowed to interfere with this person or his actions. To do so meant instant dismissal and disciplinary proceedings; prison. Never good, as a former police officer. They were meant to immediately phone Head Office. Head Office would verbally tell them the required passwords. If the person holding the phone knew the passwords, they had to let them leave.

"Just let the woman go," Pete repeated, not backing down. "Don't worry. Officer Porter will detain her for you until we're done." Pete nodded to Kylie, who took the blonde woman's arm. The man reluctantly let go. "Help Doctor Hart up, Kylie," said Pete. The blonde woman looked startled that he would know her name. Kylie helped her to her feet and held onto her firmly. Kylie looked at Pete, but Pete wouldn't meet her eye.

Pete had been in A and E last summer, terrified that his mum was going to die. She'd been crippled with abdominal pain, white and sweaty and vomiting. He remembered the small doctor who'd put a drip in his mum's arm and injected miraculous painkillers and antibiotics. The doctor had taken the time in the noisy, heaving department to draw a little picture on his mum's medical notes. The doctor had explained all about gallstones and how pesky they could be, especially if they got stuck. She'd gently touched his shoulder and looked at him.

"It's OK, Mr Loxley; she's not going to die. Is that what you were thinking?" Pete had nodded, feeling foolish but also relieved. She had carried on holding his shoulder, and he had felt his terrible fear ebb away.

"HAND ME THE PHONE, SIR," said Pete softly. "I'll make the right call." The tall man smiled confidently and handed his phone to Pete. Pete reached out for it, but somehow it slipped through his fingers. It fell to the ground, and in his hurry to pick it up, Pete stepped hard on the glass screen in his big, regulation boots. The screen shattered into a thousand unmendable pieces. "Oh dear," said Pete, a Sheffield Lad, through and through. "I am a butterfingers. Officer Porter, let Dr Hart be on her way."

"I have a second phone, I have a second phone!" yelled the tall man, his face contorted in rage as he fumbled in his trouser pocket.

"Let Dr Hart go, Officer Porter," said Pete, clearly and forcefully. "That's an order! I'll take full responsibility for the consequences."

AND AT THAT MOMENT, Kylie Porter knew she was going to marry Pete Loxley. And she would marry him. In High Bradfield Church, on a clear summer's day, with all their friends and family around them. They would move to Stannington, a dream for Kylie, who had grown up in the claustrophobia of S5. Their three children would roam, sun-kissed and blessed, through the meadows and woods of the Rivelin valley. When they eventually retired from the Force, Pete and Kylie would set up a small construction company. They'd have hard times until Declan and Killian joined their Dad in the business, and things would then get easier. Little Sarah would become a respected Sheffield solicitor, specialising in Family Law and domestic violence cases. When her pen would become just too heavy, too sad, to hold, she'd remember her mum's story; about the day Dad saved the Nice Lady from the Bad Man. And Sarah would find the strength to pick up her pen, her weapon, again. And, in sixty-four years from that very moment, when Pete Loxley would finally die, he would be pain-free and in his own bed. He would be surrounded by his children, grandchildren, and little Kylie-Jane, his first great-grandchild. And he would die in Kylie's arms. Because happy endings do exist, and some of us get to have them.

BUT NOT NOW. For now, Charlie ran. *Sheffield*, she thought. *Biggest village in England...* and then she thought of the face of the man who had just grabbed her. Charlie ran faster.

MAC ALSO RAN, his feet stabbing into the street, cursing himself. He ran into Fargate, his eyes searching for Charlie. She hadn't answered her phone! She should be back in the car by now! His phone rang, and he smashed his finger at the answer button.

"Mac?" he heard Charlie's voice whispering. She sounded terrified. His heart sank.

"Hart, where are you?"

"He almost got me, Mac. He almost got me," she whispered.

"Where are you?" he repeated, trying to keep his voice calm.

"I'm on the 52 bus," she said quietly. "Hiding at the back. I was running down Fargate and just wanted to get away from him. The bus was leaving, and I jumped on. I don't think he saw me. The Police stopped him."

"Listen very carefully..." Mac demanded.

"I have it," said Charlie. Mac stopped.

"What?" he breathed.

"I have them. The Code Blue and half of the Formula."

"You mean you went back into the Library? When I specifically told you... For God's sake, Hart!" Mac felt his familiar anger rear up; anger at Charlie's recklessness and refusal to do as she was instructed.

Charlie was silent. He could hear the sounds of the noisy bus as it rumbled along. He stopped himself from saying any more.

"Shall I come and find you?" said Charlie

"No!" exclaimed Mac. He paused as he thought. "Go to Meggie's, the 52 goes past her street," he finally said. "You said she had a car. Beg, borrow or steal it and go back to Rowans Holt. As fast as you can."

"Mac," said Charlie in a small voice.

"What?" said Mac impatiently.

"There's something I need to tell you," said Charlie.

. . .

Mac eventually cut the call, his face deep in thought at what Charlie had told him. He was almost back at the car by now. He cursed as he remembered that he'd given the keys to Charlie. Mac quickly called Sally and told her the news.

"You have it? The Code Blue?" said Sally, her voice drenched with relief. "Thank God!"

"I need Sinclair," said Mac. "She's not answering her phone. I thought you might have been in touch. I'm locked out of the car. I need a backup. Now. And I need to talk to her."

"I haven't been in contact with Sinclair for a few days," said Sally coolly. "What's wrong, Mac? You sound nervous." There was a long pause.

"Are you locked in the library? Like I told you?" said Mac.

"We're in the library," replied Sally evasively.

"Lock the door. Now," said Mac. "Hart should be on her way to you soon. Don't let anyone else in. Do you understand?"

"Okay, Mac. okay. But don't worry, I'm not alone. Ben's here." Mac didn't reply. He hung up and started trying to call Hafez.

Sally sighed, picked up her phone and tried to call Sinclair. She and Sinclair had studiously ignored each other since Sinclair had caught her kissing Agnes. Sally now felt annoyed. She was an independent woman: she could kiss whom she wanted. What business was it of Maddie Sinclair's? Sinclair was her employee, not her judge and jury.

Charlie peeked out of the bus window and saw she was almost at Crookes. She waited for the stop near Bradley

Street, where Meggie lived, and hurried off the bus. Charlie felt over her jeans pocket again for the plastic envelope's reassuring feel. She needed to get home to Rowans Holt. She half-ran up the quiet street, praying that Meggie would be in. Charlie knocked desperately at the door and rang the bell, glancing agitatedly back down the road. Meggie answered the door eventually. Her warm smile faltered as she took in Charlie's grim face.

"Meggie, I need your car," said Charlie with uncharacteristic firmness. "And I need you to tell me the truth. About Ben's brother." Meggie's face fell. Her hands tightened on the door handle, and, for a moment, Charlie feared she would try to close the front door on her. However, Meggie sighed deeply and stepped to one side, indicating that Charlie should enter.

They went into the warm, neat front room. Charlie's eyes fell on the photo album that lay open on the sofa. Meggie glanced down guiltily. She went to close the album, but Charlie had already bent down and was holding the page open with a hand that suddenly felt cold and numb.

"I'm not allowed to look at it when Ben's around," Meggie explained weakly. "Ben won't tolerate any word of him, any reminder of his older brother. But he was my boy, no matter what he did. I gave birth to him, and he was my boy." Charlie looked up at Meggie and felt the blood draining from her face. Meggie started to cry. "He's dead now, but it still hurts."

But he's not dead, thought Charlie. *He's alive and well and in Sheffield. He just had me by the leg, squirming and begging on the floor of Tudor Square.*

And that's when it hit her. Ben. What sort of coincidence was it that Ben Morton would turn up, close to Mac, just after the Code Blue was stolen? What sort of coincidence that he would disappear just as an assassin arrived on the gynaecology ward? He'd been helping his brother all along; undermining Mac's attempts to find his uncle and shut down the drug's supply. He had taken Sally's phone, blocked their calls... told his brother that she and Mac would be in the Inferno Club. And he was with Sally now.

Had he seen Sally on the night that she had almost died? Charlie imagined Ben walking silently into Sally's room, where she lay, collapsed. Saw him feeling her pulse gently, watching her blood flow, sitting on the carpet next to her, guarding over her as she bled to death. Only the pool alarm going off, only the never-sleeping house, had spoiled his plans.

Charlie said nothing. She walked to the sideboard and took the car keys. She left the house without closing the door and as if in a dream, started up the Mini. Charlie called Mac. No answer. She called Sally. Ben picked up Sally's phone.

"Where's Sally?" murmured Charlie, through lips that felt like ice.

"Off somewhere," said Ben, vaguely.

"I thought you were both meant to stay in the Library?" replied Charlie, slowly.

"You know Sal," said Ben. His voice lowered, became intent. "Charlie. Do you have the Code Blue, the formula? Sally said you have it...." Charlie cut off the call.

And then she drove; drove as if the Devil were behind her, as well as before her.

CHAPTER FIFTY-FIVE

Mac waited impatiently for Sinclair to call. He needed to get back to Rowans Holt as soon as possible. If she didn't call, he'd have to get a taxi. He paced on the pavement by the Range Rover. A man brushed past, head down, burly shoulders hunched. Mac gazed after him. The man turned into a narrow alleyway that led down towards Paradise Square. As he did so, he glanced back at Mac. Mac felt a jolt of recognition at the surly face. It was Mike Quigley, a former member of Nox section. So, Hart had been right. It had been Jude Morton that she'd seen. He was alive, in Sheffield, back with his old section and doubtless running the Code Blue drugs gang.

Without stopping to think, Mac headed after Quigley. He reached the dark alleyway and saw the hunched figure hurrying away, already far from him. Mac stepped into the alley, his mind fixed on pursuit, on Justice. *You haven't been making good decisions, have you*? a small voice whispered in his mind. He had not. And this was another poor decision. He was probably walking into a trap. Just before the blow came crashing down on the back of his skull, Mac realised his mistake.

CHARLIE SLEWED the Mini to a stop outside Rowans Holt. The house was quiet. *Too quiet*, she thought. She silently let herself in the front door and padded towards the library. She saw Sally and Ben with their backs turned towards her. Ben was pointing to a section of panelling.

"I think it's there," he was saying confidently. "The join looks odd. Go on, open her up, Sal. You said. If I guessed right, you'd show me the secret passage!" Sally shook her head.

"Nope. Wrong. Sorry, Loser," she said, sounding amused.

"You are kidding me!" exclaimed Ben. Charlie slid towards the gun that lay on the workbench. She picked it up, and the weapon's hungry heft suddenly seemed comforting in her trembling hand.

"Sally!" she called, her voice high and tight. The two turned towards her, an anxious look on Sally's face. They both stopped, watching the wavering gun that Charlie was pointing toward them.

"Move away from him!" exclaimed Charlie, angrily holding Ben's gaze. "Move away, Sal. Now! He's a traitor."

"What? Charlie, what are you doing?" exclaimed Ben.

"Don't you Charlie me!" Charlie almost screamed, the day's events threatening to bring her crashing to her knees.

Sally and Ben looked at each other. "Move away, Sal," Charlie repeated. "His brother, Jude Morton. The one he swore was dead? Well, he's alive and kicking. He just kicked me over half of Sheffield city centre. Ben's been communicating with him. Helping him."

"Charlie, this is madness," Ben said quietly.

"The brother of the man running the Code Blue game just happens to turn up? Just happens to wheedle himself into our lives?" Charlie's voice rose in anger at his betrayals. "Leaves us in the hospital when a man turns up to kill us. Takes Sally's phone." Her voice rose higher. "Lets his brother know when Lucy shows herself?"

Ben was shaking his head, his hands raised to shoulder height, his face drained of all colour.

"My brother's dead," he insisted.

"Oh, please! I saw him!" shouted Charlie, the gun in her hand trembling with fear and fury. "I saw him as he tried to kill me! I saw his photo today at your mother's house. Jude Morton. And he looks just like you. Just like you! Take away the stubble and the long hair and your grand pretence that you're normal...."

There was a moment of silence. Something occurred to Charlie. "How much older than you is he?" demanded Charlie. Ben just looked at her. "How. Much. Older?" she screamed. Ben shifted, uncomfortable. Sally looked at him.

"Ben?" she said quietly.

"Ten minutes," replied Ben, looking sadly at Sally.

"You're a twin?" she said, things thudding into place inside her mind. The reason they had felt so close, so comfortable with each other. Had reached out for each other.... "But identical?" she whispered. Ben nodded slowly. He ran his hand through his hair.

"He hated this, the red hair; he dyed it white whenever he could."

"A twin. But you never told me?" Sally backed away from Ben.

"He's dead!" shouted Ben. "And I know he's dead!" The

small window in the eaves slammed shut, its faint echo reverberating around the room.

"See? The house is warning us!" exclaimed Charlie. "The house knows Ben's dangerous...."

"But the house loves him..." said Sally, faintly. "The house loves him too...." She looked at Ben. "How do you know for sure that your brother's dead?" she asked, her face twisted with uncertainty.

"Because I killed him!" cried Ben, suddenly vivid with terrible burning anger. "I looked him in the eye and shot the murdering, traitorous bastard!"

There was a shocked silence. All that could be heard was Ben's breathing, rapid and deep with distress and rage. "They asked me to identify the body left after the quad bike explosion. I didn't know who the hell it was, but DNA evidence or not, it wasn't my brother. I knew damn well it wasn't him. He still had people protecting him in the Army. So, I went looking for him; my crooked, bastard, broken other half. I went into places I never wanted to know existed. I became something I never thought I'd be!" Ben's mouth twisted with remembered pain and self-loathing. "And when I found him, I chose my moment. And I took my gun, and I put it against his heart, and I pulled the trigger." He paused again. "I became Cain. The damned killer of his own brother. I lost myself– as well as him." He gestured angrily at the library. "Why do you think I do this? Act the useful fool? I lock myself away, I keep myself busy. I pretend I'm not a monster." His voice fell and caught, his throat tightening. "I pretend my terrible sin didn't infect my little boy. I pretend he didn't pay... for what I did."

Sally instinctively reached out for Ben. She stopped short as she heard a creak in the hallway outside. Charlie lurched towards the library door, trying, too late, to get to it and lock it.

"But you did infect your son," said a low, deep voice in a strong Yorkshire accent. Jude Morton, the Boss, stepped into the library. He swiftly walked towards Charlie, who raised her gun and pressed the trigger without hesitation. It jammed. Morton smoothly closed his hand over the weapon and eased it from her grasp. He placed his arm around Charlie's neck, turned her, so she faced the others, and pulled her close, almost tenderly, against him. She felt his hard, muscled body press itself firmly against hers, and she shrank away in terror. "The thing about a Glock, sweetheart," he murmured, his lips moving intimately against her ear. "Is that you must mean to fire it. Like this." Morton raised the gun and shot Ben. The bullet pummelled through the back of Ben's left calf.

Ben cried out and staggered back, clutching at his leg. He glared up at his smiling brother. "You infected your son," Morton repeated. "But it was with your weakness, not your sin. There is no such thing as sin. There's just the fear of giving in to what we truly are." He buried his face in Charlie's hair and inhaled deeply while watching Ben with his wide, glittering blue eyes. His hat was gone, and his crewcut hair shone icy blond.

"The Boss," breathed Sally. Morton smiled and nodded.

"But, I killed you," muttered Ben, ashen-faced. Morton threw a handful of cable ties onto the nearby table.

"Tie her hands," he instructed Ben, jerking his head at Sally. Ben hesitated, and Morton jammed the gun tight into Charlie's temple. Ben reluctantly picked up a cable tie, his hands dripping with his own blood. "In front of her," commanded Morton.

Ben did as he was told, casting disbelieving glances at his brother as he did so. "I suspected you'd come for me, little brother," said Morton. "Because that's just like you. You're stupid enough to think you're some sort of action hero. But all you are is a third-rate little extra in your own, mediocre film." He motioned the gun at Sally. "Now you tie his wrists." Sally picked up a cable tie with her restricted hands and awkwardly worked on Ben's wrists. Blood slowly pooled around Ben's left leg.

"When you found me, I was building my pharmaceutical interests in Manchester," continued Morton casually. "I'd obtained a 'Juliet' poison; Tetrodotoxin. Mimics death. So, when I knew you'd finally arrived, I took it. I knew what you'd do; we're the same person, remember?" Ben shook his head in affronted denial. "I knew just where you'd try and shoot me; in the heart. How pathetically predictable. You saw blood and assumed it was real. You felt for a pulse and assumed it was gone." Jude Morton and Ben glared at each other. "My men followed you when you buried me, and they dug me up. It suited me to be dead again."

Jude Morton grabbed a cable tie and swiftly tied Charlie's hands in front of her. "Kneel," he said, indicating them all with his gun. They knelt on the wooden floor, all watching Morton. He looked around. "I'm having that fool, Beaulouf, dealt with as we speak," he said casually. He looked back at Ben. "But where is She?" Ben shook his head.

"Who?" he asked, frowning. Morton moved closer to him, bending down to meet his gaze. "Her," he said intently. "She's been here, I can tell. I can smell her. Where is She?" Ben looked in panic at Sally and Charlie.

"I don't know who you mean," he insisted. Morton smiled.

"Liar," he said.

He stood behind them again and slowly moved down the ragged line of grim genuflection. Morton laid a hand on Sally's head. "So, you'd bankroll that fool, Beaulouf? I think that calls for assassination." Sally's face was grim, but she held her head high and showed no fear. Morton then bent down and whispered in Ben's ear. "Did you never wonder why I didn't kill you sooner, little brother?" Ben said nothing. Morton continued, his voice intimate, almost devout. "I have visions, you know. I see the dead. They whisper with me, they let me kill them, all over again." Ben closed his eyes. He felt he was slowly drowning in dull horror. "And I had a vision of you, little brother," said Morton. "A vision that you were me. So, I waited for that to happen. I waited for you to join me." He paused and then sighed. "I'm tired of waiting now." Morton ran his hand over Ben's head, caressing his long, dark-red hair. Ben jerked his head away from his brother's grasp. Morton merely smiled. "Retribution then," he said simply.

Morton finally ran his hand, lingeringly, over Charlie's skull. A small, terrified gasp escaped her as he leaned closer to her ear and breathed, "Recreation." Morton's hand slid down over Charlie's chest and stomach. His fingers ran over her clothing until they found what they were looking for. He slid the plastic envelope from her pocket and held it triumphantly.

Morton made a phone call, moving close to the window to maintain a signal. "I have them," he said brusquely. "Yes, all five, and the missing half of the formula. I'll bring them in shortly. But stay alert." He glanced at his kneeling prisoners. "I just have a few loose ends to tie up."

"You have everything!" Sally exclaimed. "You don't need

to do this!" Morton ended the call and looked at her, expressionless. "Why are you doing this?" Sally demanded. He shrugged.

"Because I like it. Because I can," he replied simply.

Morton now grabbed Sally's arm and pulled her to her feet. "Let's get this show on the road!" He strode to the door and pushed Sally ahead of him. He slipped the key out of the lock, and they heard the door being secured from the outside. Ben staggered to his feet and threw himself against it.

"Sal! Sal! Leave her, you bastard! Take me instead. Take me!" he screamed. He heaved his shoulder against the door, but the thick, sturdy wood stood firm. Cold sweat dripping down her back, Charlie rifled through the tools on the table. She used a blade to cut through her cable tie, grabbed a sheet that looked vaguely clean and ripped it.

"Ben!" she hissed. He was bleeding heavily now from his wounded leg. She had to stop him from moving around. His agitation was just making the bleeding worse. "Ben!" she called, louder now. He turned, wild-eyed, from the door. "Your wound," she said. Ben looked down at the blood flowing in a scarlet stream around him. He stumbled back and sat abruptly against the carved panels under the window.

Charlie grabbed a knife from the table and sank down next to him. She freed his hands and slit his trouser leg, exposing a heavily oozing hole in his calf. Oozing rather than pumping meant venous damage, so blood loss was substantial but not catastrophic. Ben was fortunate that the bullet hadn't severed an artery or shattered a bone. Using a wad of the sheet, she applied firm pressure. She deftly elevated the leg onto a nearby stool and lowered Ben's pale and sweating head towards the floor. There was an entrance and an exit hole. The bullet had passed straight through the muscle but had inevitably carried dirt and bits of clothing deep into the wound. If left, they would cause the wound to fester and decay. The injury would need thorough exploration and cleaning under a general anaesthetic. However, they may well not make it through the next hour. Charlie tied a makeshift dressing firmly around his leg. It was quickly drenched in blood but would have to do for now.

"Ben, I'm so sorry," she murmured. "I should never have doubted you." He lay against the dark boards, and his eyes rolled slightly as he smiled up at her.

"It's okay, Charlie. I doubt myself all the time," he joked softly and hopelessly. His smile fell. "I followed Steve from the hospital, all the way out to Meersbrook. And I saw him. With Becky. My Becky. They're playing happy families out there. And Sal...that first night. I'm not proud of myself, Charlie. But the twin part of us recognised the other. Reached out for the other. We'd been so lonely, Charlie. So, so lonely."

Ben's head fell to one side, and, as if in a slow, viscous dream, he marvelled once again at the magical beauty of the room. His carpenter's fingers slowly, reverently, stroked the ancient boards. He realised that if the library were where he would die, that would be alright. He'd spent some of the happiest moments of his short life in this sacred, orchard-scented space. His fading vision, level with the floorboards, saw a slight discrepancy in the lower edge of the woodwork. The discrepancy seemed to glow with soft light and then melt.

Charlie turned as a quiet click cut the sad silence that had settled. A section of one bookcase had moved slightly. A crack had appeared down a vertical piece of the shelving. It seemed they now had a way out.

A FEW MINUTES LATER, the door to the library burst open and Morton marched through.

“Drop the knife, lover,” he murmured in eager anticipation. He stopped short, realising that his new distraction had flown the love-nest. He strode to the bookshelf where a small doorway had appeared, yawing like a missing tooth. Morton grasped the edge of the space and inhaled the stale air that percolated up the dark, narrow, spiral, stone staircase. He smiled. The little blonde was playing hard to get, and he knew where that led. Morton knew how this ended. He knew how this always ended.

CHAPTER
FIFTY-SIX

The dark, rough stair turned and turned and turned. Charlie crept down, unseeing in the dense dark. Behind her, she heard Ben hobbling, holding in his gasps of pain as each jarring descent jogged his damaged leg. Eventually, Charlie came to a small, cobweb-covered wooden door at the bottom of the tightly wound stairs. She cautiously pushed it open and stepped into a dust-filled dimness. To her left was a soft glow. She was in the stone tunnel that stretched away on her right into sunless, intimate blackness. Charlie felt inexplicably drawn to the right. She sensed the power and control that lay in the soft, forgiving dark. She turned, yearning, to the right, but Ben blundered, hard, into her back, and she came to her senses.

"I think it's this way," she whispered and they walked to the left, towards the light.

They slowly made their way down the dry, powdery, rough passage, Ben leaning more and more heavily onto Charlie's tired shoulder. They emerged from the tunnel into the silent, vast cavern, Sally's expensive cars gleaming in the half-light that made its way through tiny windows, high in the hangar doors. Ben and Charlie crept between the silent Aston Martin and the Ferrari, more confident in the slim slice of silence that fed their halting hope. But then Jude Morton stepped from the shadow. And he was smiling, and he was happy. And he held a big blade that was toothed and hard and hungry.

Morton casually drew the Glock and shot Ben in the left shoulder. Charlie watched, transfixed, as blood exploded from Ben's fragile tissues, and he was thrown backwards onto the Ferrari's bonnet. She backed slowly away towards the cold stone wall, her eyes owned by the scene of violence unfolding before her. Morton strode over to Ben, lifted him from the bonnet where he lay and held him high in the air before throwing him, hard, to the concrete floor. Charlie slid down against the rough wall that felt like the only thing holding her up.

"No," she whispered, shaking her head. "No." She watched as Morton lifted back his foot and joyously kicked at his brother, his stomach, his damaged leg, and his head. Again. And again. "No," muttered Charlie. "I'm sorry, Briddie," she gasped, holding her head and rocking back and forth. "I'm so sorry, Briddie." Something slithered in Charlie's head. Something gurned and gyrated. And once again, she felt the pull, the caress, the tempting allure of the dark. And this time, after years of resistance, Charlie gave in.

Morton stopped. He was tired. He'd heard the tempting blonde behind him as she crouched in tense anticipation of his rigid and complete attention. Morton grabbed and heaved his weak and endlessly disappointing brother and propped him against the Aston Martin. Ben was unconscious now, but he should wake up soon. Morton wanted him to see at least part of Big Brother's outstanding performance. The woman had stopped speaking. She should be ready for him now. He turned towards her.

"Playtime," he said.

IF ASKED, Ben would have said that Charlie's eyes were probably blue. Hafez would have described them as "the stolen shades of shower-shorn hyacinths." Mac thought Charlie's eyes looked like sapphires. However, he would have brusquely told you he'd never noticed Charlie Hart's eyes, so he couldn't possibly comment on them.

Morton saw that Charlie's eyes were no longer any of these colours. They were now the lightest blue. She was staring, unafraid, right at him from where she stood, approximately twelve inches away. She then lifted her right hand and plunged the cannula needle, so carelessly thrown aside over a week ago to lie on the cavern floor, deep into Morton's left eye. He screamed hoarsely at the sudden, unexpected assault and raised his hands to clutch at his face. He dropped his long blade and sensed that Charlie, in a flash, had picked it up. Morton backed away, and she came after him. He felt the edge touch his abdomen and then sink deep inside the packed chasm of his belly. Intense pain ripped through him. He grabbed her shoulders, but she plunged the blade deeper into him and began sawing it slowly upwards. He looked down, his remaining right eye starting from his head at the unexpected and complete horror. How was this happening?

To him? He had not foreseen this. He watched as she twisted the blade slightly.

"Don't want to nick that descending aorta," she said casually. "Don't want you to die too quickly." She raised her leg and kicked at him until he fell off the serrated, deeply embedded blade and staggered backwards to fall, heavily, to the concrete floor. Jude Morton lay slumped against one of the metal workbenches, desperately clutching his abdomen as blood and intestine spilt through his full, fumbling fingers.

Charlie crouched down, and he watched, his mouth dry and sagging, as she regarded him with her vivid, transformed eyes, a small smile on her face.

"Why?" he whispered.

"Because I like it," Charlie said. "Because I can."

Charlie now sank her hands into the pockets of Morton's jacket and his blood-soaked trousers. She found the half of the formula that he had taken from her and the five Code Blue tablets. "Open wide," she said softly. With sure delicacy, Charlie pressed all five tablets onto Morton's trembling tongue. His mouth was too dry to swallow, but he felt the tabs dissolving. Charlie then found Morton's cigarette lighter. She opened up the folded paper, and, even in the dim light, the gleaming hologram of the half raven arose and turned in front of them. The silver numbers and letters glittered through its lifelike plumage, and Charlie's lips moved as she read them, her photographic memory intact despite the dark presence that she had allowed to emerge. "And Is this what you came for?" she asked gently. She then lit the paper and watched with satisfaction as it burned to charred scraps before Morton's remaining, bulging eye.

. . .

JUDE MORTON FELT himself start to glow with molten warmth. No one had ever taken so much of the Code Blue drug. He saw Charlie had now moved across the cavern and was bending down to retrieve something from the floor. Something thin and sharp; the second cannula needle. She was bringing it back with her. She was still smiling. Morton felt himself shake free of his dying, broken body, and he started to float above the scene of carnage. But he wasn't ready to go yet. He wanted to cling to life. Morton looked down at the body of his brother.

BEN WAS DREAMING. In his dream, he was seven years old again and he was standing in the library of Rowans Holt. He was filled with a deep love for the place and knew it loved him back.

"Don't worry, Mac. I know the Way, now," he whispered. He was tired. Ben climbed the broad wooden stairs to his room and got into the enormous bed. He lay under the soft white duvet, dim light turning the bed into a quiet, snow cave. A small hand reached up from the bottom of the bed and was followed by a familiar figure.

"Benjo!" it exclaimed. "I found you." It was his brother.

"Judo!" Ben replied, delighted that his big brother had returned. They lay side by side, warm and cosy. Ben couldn't say where he ended, and his brother began.

"A new girl started in our class today," said Ben. "She's called Becky. She's reyt pretty." Jude's face fell.

"You'd better not like her more than me, Benjo," he said, frowning. Ben shook his head.

"Never, Judo," he assured his brother.

Jude reached behind him and drew out a battered black fedora hat. Ben didn't like the hat. Jude wore it when they were playing cowboys. Jude always had to wear it, just like he always got to shoot the sheriff and get away with the money from the stagecoach.

"It's your turn now," said Jude to Ben. "It's your turn to wear the hat." Ben slowly shook his head.

"No, Judo," he whispered. Ben turned away from Jude and lay on his side, curling up tight like he always did when he was upset or sick. He felt Jude snuggle up behind him, felt Jude's cheek lie against his back, and felt Jude's heart beating against him; just as he had always felt it, even before they had been born.

"That's ok, little brother," Jude murmured. "I'll just lie here quietly for a while. I can wait."

Charlie was curled in a tight ball by the stone cavern wall. She realised everything was quiet. She lifted her head. The worst-ever headache crushed the back of her skull. Charlie wondered if she'd hit her head when she'd fainted. She must have fainted, because she couldn't remember how she had got to be on the floor by the wall. In the dim light, she made out the figure of Jude Morton. He was sitting, looking at her, slumped on the concrete floor. Charlie whimpered and tensed, preparing to run. She slowly realised that the figure was utterly still. Deathly still. He wasn't breathing.

She stood and hesitantly approached. Charlie gasped as she saw the grisly, mutilated remains. A large knife lay by Ben's outstretched right hand. He must have found the strength to have fought back. Charlie peered at Morton's face, at the cannula needles that emerged from each unseeing eye. *But why would Ben have done that*? she thought, bewildered. *You never know who a person truly is until they're pushed to their limits*, she reflected. Charlie dropped to her knees and felt for Ben's pulse. It was there but weak. She and Sally would have to get him to the hospital as soon as possible. Sally...

"Sal!" cried Charlie.

CHARLIE RAN from room to room, desperately looking for signs of her best friend. She moved through the rooms of Sally's vast closet. The floor of room three was covered in jewellery. Sleek boxes and scattered gems glittered brightly in the soft, artificial light. The safe, however, was sealed firmly shut. Charlie reached out and touched the heavy, hermetically sealed box.

"Sally?" she whispered. "Sally!" she shouted, bruising her hands as she battered at the unmoving, unforgiving safe door. Sally was in there, she was sure. She might already be dead. No air could get in, and the tiny space must contain only minutes' worth of oxygen. Charlie looked frantically at the keypad. What numbers had Sally pushed on their drunken evening? A memory flashed, fully formed into her head. She saw Sally confidently saying;

"What are the dates of the battles of Cannae and Carthage? Oh, I know! I know everything!"

INSIDE THE SAFE, Sally heard nothing. Morton had forced her to open the secure box and had pawed through the jewels, keeping his gun trained on her. She had expected him to shoot her, however he had looked between her and the safe, smiled, and said, "I find that the anticipation makes the eventual experience so much more pleasurable. Don't you?"

She had the strangest sensation of her breathing rate gradually increasing, even though she was keeping absolutely still. It was utterly dark. She was crammed into the small space with her knees drawn up to her chest and her head slightly bowed. She started to feel sleepy. A warm, familiar smell crept around her; linen and ginger and a faint hint of Chanel Number Five.

"Gabella?" she muttered. She felt a warm, soft, slim-fingered hand gently slip around hers. "No Peter?" Sally asked wistfully.

"It's his turn on the Battlements," came her grandmother's low and considered tone that Sally missed so much. "I'm here. You're not alone." Sally nodded and smiled. She felt better now. Maybe she would have a nap. "Not yet. No sleeping yet," said Gabella sharply. The voice then softened. "There's always hope. There's always salvation." Sally smiled again and closed her eyes.

"You are the Empress of Lost Causes, Gabella..." she muttered.

Charlie ran to the library, cursing Sally for living somewhere with such a poor phone signal and ruthlessly restricting online access. She looked around at the volumes in dismay. Where to start? She'd browsed, but had just looked for books of baking, Jane Austen, and J. R. R. Tolkien. Was there an encyclopaedia set? All the volumes looked the same, with dark leather and cloth bindings. Charlie felt panic rising like a black, foaming tide inside her, blocking out her ability to think logically and clearly.

"Show me," she whispered, closing her eyes. Her head ached as if it would burst. "Show me... the battles of Cannae and Carthage...." There was a low thud from near the bookshelf closest to the fireplace. A large volume had dislodged from the packed books and landed on the floor. Charlie's head throbbed as she bent to pick it up. *A History of the Ancient World,* Charlie read, embossed in faded gold on its dark leather spine...

"WHY ARE YOU HERE, GRANDMA?" asked Sally sleepily, her breathing shallow and rapid.

"Just in case," said the voice of Gabella. She paused and Sally sensed a hint of anxiety. "Hold my hand tightly, Sweet Pea," Gabella whispered. "Something has woken up; something that should have stayed asleep. Hold my hand." Sally tightened her grip on Gabella's hand. She felt so tired.

"Why is there so much hate, Gabella?" she whispered.

"Because there is so much love, Sweet Pea," Gabella replied simply. Sally felt a warm, firm pressure on her failing fingers. "We cannot have the light without the dark. We cannot have love without hate. And there is so, so much love in the World."

Long moments passed. Sally felt her breathing slow down and become more laboured.

"She's coming," whispered Gabella. "The witch with the terrible darkness in her head is coming. You won't remember me, but you must remember this: there is always hope, there is always salvation. And, most of all, you must keep the faith, Sally Marshall." Sally nodded, lips blue and numb.

"I'll remember, Cabella. I'll keep the faith," she breathed as the safe door opened to Charlie's triumphant cry of

"216149!" and light slid, shimmering, into the dark and dreadful space.

CHAPTER FIFTY-SEVEN

The Crew stood at the top of Manchester Airport Terminal One. They were watching the American Airlines flight to New York boarding. Their twenty-four-hour security job was ending with the departure of a young female country and western singer who had made a very brief visit to Manchester.

"What was the matter with her?" asked Sinclair, of no one in particular.

"You broke three of her boyfriend's fingers! The boyfriend she came all this way to see for one night!" exclaimed Hafez.

"I didn't know he was her boyfriend," said Sinclair hotly.

"You didn't ask," replied Hafez.

"Well, he shouldn't have been selling cocaine to fifteen-year-old girls in a nightclub full of pimps," said Sinclair. "I hate junkies," she muttered. She frowned at the memory of Agnes and Sally, a thought that kept returning with concerning frequency.

Sinclair looked at her phone and swore quietly. Mac had

been trying to get in contact with her. The Crew had been running late because of the singer's sullen demands; rushing to get her through the airport, and the paparazzi crush. Sinclair tried to ring Mac but got no answer. She picked up his message from earlier in the day, telling her that Lucy was on the move and that he and Hart would intercept her. Then there was a message from Sally, just a few minutes ago, tersely instructing her to contact Mac. Sinclair pulled a face. She tried calling Mac again and then Sally. There was no answer from either.

"Where does his phone tracer say he is?" asked Hafez, peering around her shoulder. Todmorden nodded. He held a large subway sandwich with both hands and was making short work of it. Sinclair's fingers moved over her phone screen.

"Just off Campo Lane in Sheffield Town Centre," she said vaguely. "But he hasn't moved in ten minutes. Hasn't moved at all." Mac was never still. A feeling of disquiet washed over Sinclair. She wasn't used to this sensation; she normally operated with decisive certainty. Something was very wrong. Sinclair turned toward Sheffield, forty miles away across the Pennines, as if she could somehow make out what was happening.

"My Captain," she said quietly. Hafez was looking at her, his eyes narrowed. He looked over at Todmorden.

"Toddy," was all Hafez said. Todmorden looked up at the tone of Hafez's voice. His relaxed, jovial demeanour fell away. He suddenly looked very alert and very dangerous. He threw the sandwich aside.

All three moved as one. They didn't run, as they were aware of the armed police patrolling the busy terminal. Sinclair spoke as they moved.

"I'll go on the bike. You follow on in the Hilux. Is the cab loaded?" Todmorden nodded tightly. They approached the car park. Wetherby looked up from the driver's seat and automatically started the engine on seeing them jogging towards him. Hafez and Todmorden climbed into the high vehicle and started pulling on their seatbelts. Sinclair briefly leaned in at the window.

"If I'm put out of action, Wetherby, you're in charge. We'll meet at Campo Lane. Consider all previous orders void–we're going after these bastards. Think about where the Code Blue gang would make its base." With one fluid movement, Sinclair turned and was on her bike and pulling her helmet on. She fired up and drove off while Wetherby was still manoeuvring the large crew cab out of its parking space.

MADDIE SINCLAIR BENT low over the handlebars of the Ducati as she negotiated the Snake Pass's tight and treacherous curves and blind summits. A knot tightened in her stomach at the thought of Mac, alone and in trouble. He'd not been himself since the death of his father. And, since the disappearance of his Uncle Tris, he had seemed to be slowly disintegrating. He could easily have walked into danger. Sinclair briefly slowed the bike as she passed the entrance to Rowans Holt, but she shook her head and sped up again. It was probably just Sally's notoriously poor phone signal that meant she wasn't answering. Mac first, Sally second.

SINCLAIR SOON STOOD in the narrow, dark alleyway off Campo Lane. Behind her, she heard the large Toyota Hilux screech to a halt. As the rest of The Crew approached, she turned to them and held up the remains of Mac's phone. It looked like it had been crushed under a heavy, booted foot. Todmorden walked a short way down the alley and stood, head down, contemplating the pool of congealed blood staining the ground.

"Do you think he's..." he began in his deep, gravelled voice. Sinclair held up a warning hand.

"No. Not another word! He's not dead until I say he is," she declared. She stood, hands on hips, glaring at the men. "Well? Where would they hide out? The Code Blue gang? This is going to be them, isn't it?" Hafez spoke up.

"It's going to be in the old steelworks area. It's full of derelict warehouses and bricked-up buildings. Decker would have put the police off the scent, sent them to a different part of town." Wetherby nodded.

"They're probably too relaxed and confident," he said. "They'll have become sloppy. We'll find them." This was what they needed to hear. They loaded the Ducati onto the back of the Hilux and set off, Hafez directing Wetherby towards the Brightside area of the city.

They cruised slowly down long Carlisle Street, red brick walls rising on either side. Todmorden, their quartermaster, had opened the supplies box, and the Crew were checking their guns and ammunition. Todmorden handed out stab vests as they peered into the streets, their faces set and determined.

"Slow down," ordered Hafez as he slipped a knife into a sheath hidden behind his belt. He looked at Sinclair. "Didn't that security guard, Joe, describe a black Ford Raptor coming to Rowans Holt?" Sinclair nodded. "Well, there's one parked back there, outside that derelict factory," said Hafez. Sinclair tapped the back of Wetherby's driver's seat.

"Park us up." Wetherby turned down a quiet side street, and the Crew were silent for a while, their hands busy in preparation. "Hafez, get the drone out," ordered Sinclair.

Hafez hopped down from the vehicle and opened a long black box in the flatbed. Sinclair opened a laptop and looked grimly at the screen as Hafez got back in, clutching a remote control. They heard the mechanical buzz fading as the drone rose and headed for the derelict building, its windows bricked or boarded shut. The drone transmitted a video signal to the laptop, which they watched intently. "Did you get the heat sensor working?" demanded Sinclair. Hafez nodded and manoeuvred the drone closer to one of the boarded-up windows on an upper floor.

"One muppet on the first floor," he muttered. The Crew watched as the glowing outlines of more figures appeared on the screen. The drone was now hovering outside a ground-floor window. They could see three hulking figures standing around a figure that sat slumped in a chair. The knot in Sinclair's stomach tightened fiercely.

"Watch out, door opening," announced Wetherby. Hafez twitched his fingers, and the drone rose to roof height, its buzz fortunately drowned by the appearance of a passing lorry.

The Crew looked down at a figure that casually approached the Raptor and leaned in to retrieve something from the cab. Todmorden shifted in his seat, glaring at the screen.

"Hang on," he growled. "I recognise him." The others glanced at Todmorden in surprise. He was nodding; his mouth pulled down. "Quigley," he said. Sinclair looked back at the screen in shock. Todmorden, however, was right. She could now see it. A figure appeared at the door and gestured to Quigley, who hurried back towards the factory.

"Ronson," said Hafez, brusquely. "I'd know him anywhere." He rubbed his chin, remembering the beating he'd received at the hands of Nox Section.

"And what's the betting it's Fawkes in there too?" said Wetherby quietly. "Which means; who's the muppet on the first floor?" They looked at Sinclair, who refused to meet anyone's eye. Was she finally going to get her chance for revenge on Jude Morton?

"I'm going to have fun finding out," she said quietly. "Get ready to move out. Toddy, Hafez, you'll be going in the front. Wetherby, cover the back. I'll go in the top-floor window from the roof. Wait for my signal once I'm in position." The men nodded. "Remember," said Sinclair. "This is Nox Section. They'll show no mercy. So, we'll give them none."

They descended from the vehicle, slipping earpieces into place as they moved. Hafez and Todmorden took up positions on the far side of the street from the factory. Wetherby and Sinclair disappeared around the back of the building. Wetherby watched from the yard as Sinclair climbed towards the roof, carrying a heavy backpack containing rope and climbing gear. She had practised abseiling the most, spending hours with Mac on Stanage Edge. It made sense that she did this. He also realised she needed to engage whoever was on the first floor. Sinclair had soon negotiated the crumbling roof and stood at the edge of the tall building, looking over her shoulder, hands grasping the rope that would lower her down to the boarded first-floor window. "Move!" she said.

Sinclair rapidly lowered herself down the brickwork and was aware of the door below being forced open by Todmorden and Hafez. Sinclair knew Wetherby would be efficiently doing the same from the rear of the building. She prayed that Nox were not so trigger-happy as to shoot Mac at the first sign of trouble. Pushing herself back as far as she could, she swung hard at the rotting board and kicked with both booted feet. The old boards gave way, and Sinclair fell towards the rusted metal floor, rapidly scrabbling to release her rope and harness and pull out her weapon. A figure was standing with his back to her, looking at a pile of secure-looking suitcases piled on a metal trolley. He turned, raising a gun, face pulled in shock at the sudden noise and movement from all areas of the factory. It wasn't Jude Morton! Sinclair had prepared herself to meet and kill him, and she now hesitated. The man backed away, raising a gun in his left hand as he did so. He fired haphazardly in her direction. He seemed very nervous. Sinclair recovered and fired back more accurately, winging him on his left shoulder.

Sinclair glanced down at the factory floor. Mac sat slumped against the ropes that tied him to a wooden chair. The rest of the Crew were each struggling with a member of Nox Section.

"Fun Boy!" roared Quigley. "Get down here, now!" the man known as Fun Boy merely shook his head and backed towards a doorway. As he passed the trolley, he grabbed a metal case, pulled it towards him, and held it like a shield. Sinclair started towards him but changed her mind as she saw Quigley raise a gun in Mac's direction. Sinclair aimed at Quigley but couldn't take the shot as Todmorden lunged into her view, struggling with the big man.

Fun Boy had by now disappeared. Sinclair leapt over the

edge of the metal gantry and dropped to the floor below, her knees jarring heavily as she landed. She moved towards Mac and, drawing her knife, efficiently cut through the ropes that held his arms. Kneeling, she hacked at the thick ropes that secured his feet. Sinclair looked up. Mac's neck was covered in dried blood. His eyes, sunken and dull, looked back at her.

"Captain. I can't do this!" Sinclair exclaimed. "I don't want this. Come back. Come back to me."

Hafez lashed out at Ronson, determined to do some damage to the thug who had helped beat him four years ago. Ronson batted the blow away contemptuously and drew a large knife. Hafez pulled back from the savagely swung blade, dropped to the ground and kicked hard at Ronson's legs, catching him by surprise and knocking him heavily to the ground. Hafez stood back, his instinct still to play fair. Ronson swung again at him, trying to sever the arteries and tendons at the back of his legs. Hafez shook his head and dropped, with both knees, heavily onto Ronson's chest, winding him. Hafez had drawn his own knife and plunged it expertly into Ronson's exposed neck, dealing a fatal blow. Ronson's eyes bulged in horror and surprise.

Hafez didn't wait to see Ronson die. He turned and ran to Todmorden's aid. Quigley had his huge hands clamped on either side of Todmorden's head, and his right thumb was embedded in Todmorden's left eye, trying to gouge it out. With a loud cry, Todmorden fumbled his gun under the bottom edge of Quigley's stab vest and shot upwards. At the same time, Hafez did what Ronson had been trying to do and cut across the back of Quigley's leg. The big man fell to the floor and Hafez kicked away his gun. They turned to Wetherby. Fawkes had his weapon raised and was clearly about to bring Wetherby down. However, Wetherby was the faster man and fired first, a clean shot to the head. Fawkes, too, slumped to the ground. Wetherby stepped up and calmly shot again, this time to the back of Fawkes's head. A professional kill. There was silence for a moment, the Crew breathing heavily. The entire event had taken less than a minute.

They looked at Mac. Sinclair, knife in hand, still knelt at his feet, looking up at him. Mac slowly raised his head and looked at the men around him. Hafez was by now examining Todmorden's damaged eye.

"You should have left me, Rumi," rumbled Todmorden. "I had him just where I wanted him." Wetherby was watching Mac, his face unreadable. With calm efficiency, Wetherby pushed his gun into his holster and then folded his arms.

Mac looked down at Sinclair. Madeleine Sinclair, having to save him. Again. His Crew having to save him. Again. They deserved better. They deserved his best. Something slowly changed in Mac's eyes. Sinclair saw it; a tiny glimmer of the fire that had once been at the heart of Mac. Her Captain.

Mac stood, and something was different about him. He slowly walked to where his old coat lay, crumpled on the concrete floor. Mac picked it up and dusted it off. He looked at Hafez and Todmorden. They had tried to offer him a new coat, had wanted to offer him the future. But he had given it away. He had clung to the past, to the illusion that he was still the child, to the illusion that his father was not dead. Well, now was the time to accept his father's death. It was time to learn the mastery of his grief rather than be crushed beneath it. It was time to become the adult. Become the man. He slipped his coat on. It was now his, not his father's.

"I'm a man of the North," he said quietly.

Without looking at her, Mac held out his hand to

Sinclair. She placed a gun in it. Mac walked towards Quigley, who lay, panting, on the hard concrete floor. Blood poured from the wound in the back of Quigley's leg and streamed from his belly. Mac stood over him.

"You're dying," Mac said quietly. "And you can do it slowly, like the dog you are, or clean, like the man you pretend to be." Quigley, his face creased with hatred, spat in Mac's direction. Sinclair moved towards Quigley, her fist clenched, but stopped as Mac raised his hand. Mac turned away from the wounded man, gesturing to the rest of the Crew, who started heading for the door.

"Wait!" shouted Quigley, breathing hard. Mac stopped and slowly walked back. "Make it quick!" snarled Quigley. Mac squatted down.

"You'll give me some answers first," Mac said. "Did Nox Section organise the killing of Jordan Linton and two of his section?" Quigley, his face pale and sweating, nodded sharply. "And did you then sew heroin into the bodies to get it shipped back to England?" Again, Quigley nodded. "Did Jude Morton arrange the cocaine found in my kit?" Quigley grinned with malicious pleasure and laughed out loud.

"Yeah! And weren't that a nice surprise?" he gloated.

"And has Jude Morton been running the Code Blue manufacture and distribution?" asked Mac calmly. Quigley stopped laughing. He said nothing, fear etched on his face. Mac sighed. "He can't do anything to you now. You're going to die." At last, Quigley nodded. "And where is he now?" asked Mac.

"Gone to get his property, his precious Code Blue, back," snarled Quigley. "And then he's going to kill that doctor. And her mate."

CHAPTER

FIFTY-EIGHT

Sinclair brought the bike to a halt just inside the cavern. Mac, who'd been riding pillion, flung himself from the back. As she removed her helmet, Sinclair's eyes homed in on Sally. Sally and Charlie were somehow still alive! Sally was bent over the unconscious body of Ben. She was trying to lift his legs and help Charlie get him into one of her cars. Sally's face and arms were smeared with Ben's blood, and she was clearly in a lot of pain from her abdominal wound. However, her face was fixed with grim determination, and the small line Sinclair now recognised was there on her brow, showing that she would never back down. To Sinclair, Sally looked more beautiful than she had ever seen her.

"Hart!" exclaimed Mac, striding across the floor. He was torn between relief and frustration that, once again, he had been unable to protect Sally and Charlie. He hid his feelings behind his habitual anger, but Charlie just walked up to him and pushed herself against his chest, her head down. He knew she was crying. Mac slowly raised his arms and closed them around her, knowing that he shouldn't do this, but helpless for just a moment. He held her in a close embrace, stroking her head, feeling the soft smoothness of her hair. He felt her small arms slip around him, her hands clinging to his back. Mac exhaled and closed his eyes, hating his weakness.

Sinclair approached Sally, who stood to greet her. "You're alive," said Sinclair. The two women looked at each other. Sally shrugged.

"I seem to have nine lives," she said.

"Where is he?" asked Sinclair. Sally's face fell, and she gestured towards an object hidden under a car cover. Sinclair walked over to it and pulled the material away. Hardened as she was, she still flinched at the sight of Jude Morton's mutilated body. She bent closer to look at his eyes and Sinclair's face creased with disgust as she saw the needle that protruded from each one, holding his stiffening eyelids half open. Sally had remained where she was, turning her face away. Mac was staring over, his arms still around Charlie.

"Who killed him?" he asked. Charlie dug her head into his chest. Mac could feel her trembling against him and he held her closer.

"Ben," said Sally. "Morton accosted Charlie and Ben down here as they tried to escape. Charlie found the knife next to Ben's hand. It must have been him. It looks like the formula's been burned, and we can't find the tablets. Morton probably destroyed everything as he was dying. That would be typical for him."

Mac lifted Charlie's chin so she looked at him. *Her eyes do look like sapphires*, he thought. *Especially when she's been crying...*

"Hart," he said gently. "Did he hurt you?" Charlie shook her head.

"He started... he started kicking Ben. It was awful. I must have passed out. When I woke, he was dead." Her eyes filled with tears again, and she put her forehead against Mac's chest. He held her tenderly for a moment more, offering a prayer of thanks to whatever powers had spared this reckless, infuriating, beautiful woman. Mac's nose wrinkled. He caught a brief scent of foetor. It reminded him of the battlefield. Of the smells that they didn't tell you about in the thrillers.

Mac gently pushed Charlie away from him by her shoulders. Their moment was over. She looked up at him, her eyes wide with hurt, but then she nodded.

"I promised not to throw myself at you. I'm so sorry," she said, looking desperately sad. "Silly Charlie."

Sally was talking to Sinclair quietly and intently. "I think I can disprove my null hypothesis," she said. "But I need someone on the ground."

"Then, I'm your woman," said Sinclair, shrugging. Sally looked at her and a slight flush crept over her face. She seemed about to speak, but then Charlie and Mac joined them.

"Send me the details," said Sinclair. Sally nodded, suddenly tongue-tied.

The Hilux pulled into the cavern, and the Crew got out.

"We cleared up," said Hafez. "There were no working CCTV cameras within half a mile of the place, so it was straightforward." He handed a small bag to Sinclair. It contained three small Code Blue tablets. "Is that enough for you?" he said. Sinclair nodded.

"More than enough."

"What did you do with the rest of it?" asked Sally.

"Burned it all," said Todmorden with great satisfaction.

Sally smiled. Todmorden looked at his watch. “The police should be arriving at the factory around now. I doubt they’ll try too hard to find the killers of those three.”

“We need to get Ben to the hospital as soon as possible,” said Sally. She looked at Ben, still lying unconscious. Her face softened with fear and love and Sinclair felt a stab of resentment towards Ben that she rapidly tried to quell. She, too, looked at Ben. He’d killed his own brother. Could she trust him, after all?

Sinclair squatted down. She put her arms under Ben’s legs and his back. She lifted him. He was heavier than he looked.

“Do you want a hand there, Sinclair?” called Hafez, smiling from where he lounged against the vehicle.

“Do you want a kick in the teeth, Hafez?” Sinclair replied. “Toddy, grab the door!” she commanded, indicating the Hilux with her chin. Ben’s face fell against her neck.

BEN WAS STILL DREAMING. He felt Jude move against his back, felt Jude’s heart speed up.

“Benjo!” hissed Jude. Can you smell that? Ben smelled soap, steel, vanilla, warm skin, and something else that made his stomach tingle.

“What is it?” he whispered. There was a pause.

“It’s Becky,” whispered Jude. “Doesn’t she smell nice?”

“BECKY…” whispered Ben.

“What did he say?” asked Sinclair as Todmorden helped her lay Ben on the back seat of the cab.

"Becky," said Todmorden. "Ex-wife. Smashing lass. Bit scary, but smashing."

Mac approached the Hilux and held out his hand to Wetherby.

"Give me the keys. I'll drive to the hospital." Mac flinched as he felt a hand on the back of his head. It was Charlie.

"You will not!" she announced. "That's a second injury you have to the back of the head. I can see you squinting. I bet you've got visual changes." Mac didn't reply but reluctantly lowered his hand. He was getting flashes and dark patches in his peripheral vision.

"I'll take you all, Cap," said Wetherby calmly. Then I'll come back and dispose of Morton.

"No!" said Sinclair. She looked down at Jude Morton's body. "He's mine. I'll deal with him. I need to make sure he truly is dead this time." She glanced outside. "It's good weather for a pyre. I'll bury what's left."

AT THE NORTHERN GENERAL HOSPITAL, a little while later, Matt looked up in surprise. Charlie Hart was running into A and E, pushing a trolley with an unconscious, tall, auburn-haired man on it.

"Matt, quick, I think he's been run over," Charlie gasped. "We found him on the road, in Crookes." Fergus Eaton elbowed past Charlie to assess Ben. He frowned as he immediately recognised assault rather than a road traffic accident and took in the two gunshot wounds. He turned to Charlie.

"In Crookes, you say?" Charlie nodded, her dark-blue eyes wide. Eaton shook his head and turned back to his work. "We'll stabilise him, then call the trauma team," he said briskly.

A CT scan of Ben's head showed no skull fracture, but his right tibia was broken, as was his left radius. He had multiple rib fractures and some internal bleeding, but not enough to operate on at this stage. Ben would need to go to theatres for an examination under anaesthetic of his gunshot wounds, but not imminently. He would be closely monitored. His face was a mess of swelling and bruises, but he was breathing independently. Charlie, Mac, and Sally stayed as close as they could to him.

Matt had taken pity on the distressed Charlie and organised for Ben to be moved to a clinical room while he waited for a ward bed. The junior doctor who was already in the room had looked up, surprised, as they wheeled Ben in. She had just incised and drained a large abscess on a homeless man's right buttock and was wearily clearing up the pus-stained dressings and scalpel. Her bleep suddenly came to life

"Cardiac Arrest, Renal Unit" came the flat, vocal alert. The doctor dropped everything and rushed for the door. In the Northern General, she had a long run ahead of her.

Ben was, by now, sedated with morphine. He had briefly come around enough to reach for Sally's hand and attempt a lop-sided smile.

"Y'all right, soft arse?" he'd muttered. Sally had nodded, unaccustomed tears streaming down her usually composed face.

The door to the clinical room swung open, and a figure stepped in. It was Eddie Lam. His face was drawn, and he looked oddly nervous.

"Eddie, I'm sorry, but I can't do any extra shifts," said Charlie.

"Shut up, Hart!" said Eddie. There was silence. Eddie

drew a gun with a silencer from his bag. He clearly knew how to use it. He trained it on Charlie's chest, over her heart.

"Where are they?" demanded Eddie.

"What?" said Charlie, confused.

"The five Code Blue tablets. And the missing half of the formula. Where are they?" said Eddie, his voice rising. "The Boss called me to tell me he had them."

"Called you?" said Charlie faintly. Her mouth dropped as it became horribly clear who had been working for the gang at the hospital. "You?" she breathed. "You killed the man using potassium. You were working with Decker."

"I work for myself!" snapped Eddie Lam. "Now the factory's gone up in flames, taking all the Code Blue with it. And the Boss has disappeared. Where are they?" Charlie shook her head.

"We don't know," she said. "Eddie, I promise, we don't know."

"Do you have any idea what even half of that formula is worth now?" shouted Eddie, looking furious. He sized up Mac and Sally. "I'll search you all, then. Once you're dead." Eddie raised his gun. "I've killed enough people for this. What's a few more?" Beside her, Charlie felt Mac tense, ready to move. She braced herself.

The door to the clinical room burst open. Sara Hadid marched through, her hair like a stream of highlighted molasses and her smile wide and white.

"Where's my patient and his handsome friend?" she announced. There was a heartbeat of silence as Sara took in the tableau. She then seemed to shrink and collapse. Her expression melted to terror. She held up a trembling hand and edged across the room. "No... Please, I'll do anything..." she whimpered; all confidence extinguished. "Just don't hurt me. Please, don't hurt me." Eddie's mouth twisted in contempt.

"Shut up, Hadid!" he snapped. Sara nodded humbly, but then her hand shot out and grabbed at the pus-covered scalpel that still lay on the abandoned dressing trolly. In a flash, and with practised skill, she brought the scalpel down, hard, across the back of Eddie Lam's right wrist. A thin line immediately oozed scarlet. Eddie looked down, frozen in shocked horror.

"Oh, dear. Did I just sever the extensors of your right hand?" asked Sara sweetly. "Is your index finger now stuck on the trigger of your Sig. 365? Let me sort that out for you." Sara, either bravely or recklessly, grabbed Eddie's hand and deftly, deeply incised the inside of his wrist. Eddie's fingers instantly hung, limp and useless, the gun clattering to the floor. "Looks like you won't be playing the piano again, Lang Lang," Sara said, adding casual racism to the list of grievances Charlie held against her. She then drew back her right arm and punched Eddie hard in the face. "Don't mess with a trauma surgeon, bitch," she snarled as Eddie crashed against the dressing trolley and fell to the ground, blood streaming from the severed arteries in his wounded, useless hand.

Sara turned from Eddie as if nothing had happened. She dropped the scalpel to the floor. "If that scalpel was used on Fat Barry, and by the smell of it in here, it probably was," she remarked. "Lang Lang now has hepatitis, as well as no career."

Sara glided over to Mac and gazed up at him. "You just can't keep away from me, can you?" she murmured, shaking her head. Mac smiled down at her.

"It seems not," he replied.

"I'll just clear up the mess you've made, shall I, Sara?"

asked Charlie, pulling on gloves and sinking to her knees next to Eddie. She grabbed some clean swabs, elevated the hand of the hysterical man, and tried to stop the bleeding. In the back of her mind, she wondered how on earth Sara had recognised the make and model of Eddie's gun. Mac and Sara, however, completely ignored her.

"I've been looking into you, Lord William Cormack Warren Beaulouf," breathed Sara. "You are a very naughty boy, aren't you?" Mac said nothing. He just raised one elegant eyebrow. "Discharged from the British army? A kilogram of cocaine?" Sara tutted. "An enormous manor-house and lots of land just aren't enough for you, then?" Mac shrugged. "Are you going to give me your number, then? Bad Boy," asked Sara.

Mac paused. "I like my love life... uncomplicated," he said. "Maybe I could do one date." Sara frowned.

"Do I seem like the sort of woman who indulges in Hit and Run?" she said archly.

"I suppose that depends on who's doing the driving," said Mac. He moved closer to Sara. "The size of the engine."

"Oh, please!" cried Charlie. "I am right here!" The two continued to ignore her, caught within an intimate bubble of physical chemistry.

"Are you right or left-handed?" asked Sara, her eyes not leaving Mac's. Mac held up his right hand. Sara took it and whipped out her pen. She confidently drew her number on his palm in prominent, black figures. "Think about me when you're alone tonight," she whispered. Charlie felt physically sick. With one heated, backward glance at Mac, Sara left the room.

Mac staggered slightly, however, by now, Charlie had no sympathy at all for him. There was silence, broken only

Eddie's hysterical sobbing. Mac walked to the sink and vomited. Charlie sighed.

"For God's sake!" she exclaimed. "I'll go and find a policeman, shall I? and arrange a head CT while I'm at it."

A MAN and a woman walked into the Emergency Department. The woman stopped Matt.

"Where would I find Dr Fergus Eaton, please," she said.

"And who are you?" asked Matt, frowning.

"I'm Doctor Fiona Temple from the General Medical Council, the GMC. And this is Detective Inspector Ali Aziz." Matt recognised Decker's former colleague.

"Inspector? Been promoted, then?" he asked. Aziz pulled a face.

"Mixed blessing, mate," he said, smiling. "Will you take us to Dr Eaton?"

FERGUS EATON LOOKED up as they approached the Nurses' Station. His face fell.

"Dr Fergus Eaton?" said Dr Temple. Eaton nodded. "We're here to take your statement about the death of Michael Sharrow. Mikey Sharrow." Eaton just looked at them.

"Twenty-five years after his death," added inspector Aziz quietly. "It must have taken you some courage to own up, Doctor Eaton." Eaton shook his head.

"I should have shown some courage twenty-five years ago," he muttered.

"You'd best hand that patient on to someone else, Dr Eaton," said Dr Temple, pointing to the notes in Eaton's hand. She glanced at the presenting complaint and pulled a face. "Acute abdomen and psychotic? You'd better give that to one of your best doctors, then?" Eaton nodded in agreement.

"You're right, I better had," he said quietly. He looked up at Matt. "Matt, I saw Charlie Hart around somewhere. Would you ask Dr Hart to deal with this patient, please?"

CHAPTER
FIFTY-NINE

The Norwegian sighed with pleasure. He was in his favourite pub, just round the corner from the Norwegian embassy where he worked. He was up to date with all his correspondence. It was a quiet evening. He had the Guardian crossword to do and an excellent beer to drink. He scanned the room. Just the regulars were there, including the man who seemed permanently drunk at his usual table in the corner. There was also a woman sitting quietly at the bar, reading. No sign of Russian spies trolling the embassy quarter to sour things. He settled into his seat, got out his pen, and pulled the paper towards him.

Time passed, and he was suddenly aware of raised voices. Two men had entered the bar and had ordered drinks. One was tall and muscled, a Big Guy. He had no jacket, despite the cool weather. It seemed he preferred wearing a short-sleeve t-shirt that exposed his tanned and muscled arms. He had an expensive haircut and a very poor attitude. His friend stood at his shoulder, smirking, as Big Guy spoke to the lone woman at the bar.

"What do you mean, you don't want a drink?" he was saying. "I asked you nicely, and you've just been rude to me." The woman put her book down and turned to the two men. She was tall too, with long, dark hair. She wore no make-up but didn't need any on her striking features. The Norwegian glanced at the book's title. *The Elegant Universe,* he read on the cover. He pulled a face. That was one of his favourite books. He wished the men would leave this woman alone.

"I wasn't being rude; I just said no," the woman was saying patiently.

"Didn't your mother tell you that saying 'no' to a man who asks nicely isn't polite?" demanded Big Guy.

"My mother told me that 'no' always means 'no'," said the woman with quiet emphasis. The Norwegian noticed that her top lip had started to twitch slightly. She turned back to her book and pint of beer. Big Guy moved closer and loomed over her.

"I'm going to buy you a drink," he said forcefully. "And you're going to be nice." The woman sighed and looked at him.

"I just buried someone today," she said. "And I never even got to say goodbye before he died. I'm really not in the mood."

"I think you're always in the mood, love," said Big Guy, raking his eyes up and down her black-clad figure. The woman looked back at him.

"I'm not even doing anything," she said quietly. "I'm not saying anything. I'm not wearing anything provocative. I am just sitting, quietly reading." Big Guy shrugged and smiled. "So, it's just that I exist?" she said. "I exist, so you think you can have a go." The Norwegian noticed that her top lip had stopped twitching.

The woman sighed again as she inserted a beermat between the pages of her book to act as a marker. "I hate people who fold down the pages," she commented. She pushed herself away from the bar. She then shrugged off her leather jacket and hung it, with a neat economy, over the back of her bar stool. The arms that emerged from her black t-shirt were strong and smooth, and muscled. They hung, still and relaxed, by her sides, however she looked weary. "Let's take this outside," she said, her manner calm and decisive. The two men looked at each other and grinned. "And just so we're clear; I didn't want this," she said quietly. Big Guy grinned even wider.

"Oh, don't worry, love, I know just what you want," he replied. "And I'm the man to make sure you get it." The woman shook her head, an exasperated expression on her face, and moved towards the door. As she walked, she looked at the quiet, assembled men hunched over their drinks.

"Watch my beer," she ordered. They walked into the night.

The Norwegian wondered if he should go and help her. To his deep shame, he decided not to. Big Guy looked both strong and vicious. He couldn't meet the eyes of the other drinkers and knew that they were doing and feeling the same. Three minutes passed. He changed his mind and abruptly stood and started walking towards the door. He had to do something. The Norwegian pulled out his phone, ready to call the police, but then stopped; the woman was walking back through the door. She was alive! She was alone. The woman walked to the bar and put on her jacket. She sat down again.

"Ice," she said as she picked up her beer with her left hand and took a deep pull. Without a word, the bartender handed her a bar towel filled with ice. She efficiently wrapped it around the knuckles of her right hand. She looked like she'd done this before.

The woman pulled her book towards her, opened the page at the beer-mat bookmark, and continued reading. There was silence in the bar. After a few moments, the drunk sidled up to her. He pointed at the two drinks standing, untouched.

"D'yer think they're coming back for those?" he slurred. She didn't look up.

"No," she said shortly. "And if they did, they'd both need a straw. Never a good look for a big guy. Take them." The drunk helped himself and staggered back to his corner table.

A low hum of conversation started again. The woman shook her head and turned towards the Norwegian. She glared at him.

"Are you going to ask me if I want a drink or what?" she demanded. She now looked very annoyed. "I'm not joking about having buried someone today, and after those two, I'm really not in a good mood." The Norwegian stood hurriedly and walked over to her.

"Are you a spy?" he said, making a nonsense of all his diplomatic training. She rolled her eyes.

"No, I'm not Russian; I'm from Leith," she said briskly. "Let's cut to the chase. I know your government instructed you to say nothing as part of your brother's release deal, but I need to talk to you." The Norwegian stepped back in surprise. She stared at him. *She has the most vakre eyes,* he couldn't help thinking, despite the scar that ran beneath the right one. *And that hair*!

"I have a friend whose uncle's been kidnapped," the woman continued. "Probably by the same people who kidnapped your brother when he worked for the Doctors Without Borders charity in Perda." *How did she know about that*? Thought the Norwegian. The Norwegian government had covered it up: to stop even more of their countrymen from getting kidnapped for a hefty ransom. The woman carried on speaking. "I've had enough of watching my friend crucify himself every day. I want my friend back." She held up her empty glass. "So, I'll have a beer. And then you'll tell me all about your brother and Perda...."

THREE DAYS LATER, Charlie and Sally were driving a bruised but healing Ben home. Back to Rowans Holt. It was late afternoon, and the sky seemed a vivid shade as it approached sundown, and they approached the West of the city.

"We'll get you back, and I'll cook you something nice," soothed Charlie, looking back at the pale-faced and bruised Ben, who was stretched out in the back seat, right lower leg and left arm clumsy in plaster. "But not too heavy. Eggs! that's ideal." Charlie looked over at Sally, who was staring, thoughtfully at the road as she drove. "Can we nip to Georgia's, Sal? Get Ben some eggs." Without a word, Sally turned abruptly left up the vertiginous Lodge Lane, the Range Rover making easy work of the steep hill.

"Hang on," said Charlie, squinting out of the car window. "That's smoke. There's a fire up at Lodge Moor. Looks like a big one." Charlie and Sally looked at each other. An unspoken thought passed between them. Sally put her foot down, and the car roared faster up the steep hill.

"What's happening?" asked Ben from the back seat, his

voice sleepy with the strong painkillers he needed to take every few hours.

"We're going to check that Georgia's OK," said Sally, reaching into the back to touch his knee in reassurance.

As they drove up Redmires road, two large fire engines headed back towards town. When they arrived at Georgia's farm, it was a scene of chaos. There had been what looked like a raging fire in the stables. Half of the horse boxes were charred and smoke scarred. Scared-looking stable girls battled with terrified horses that pulled and reared, milling in the flooded yard.

"Stay here," ordered Sally, slipping down from the car. She approached a nearby firefighter who was efficiently reloading a hose onto the last truck. "What's going on?" she asked. The firefighter jerked their head toward the Police car that was parked nearby.

"Looks like they got a tipoff about a man they were after. But he decided to create a distraction so he could escape." *Baz*! Thought Sally. Helders, tied to Georgia's old Land Rover, was barking hysterically and throwing himself against his chain, adding to the confusion.

Sally saw Georgia emerge from the direction of the stables. She dumped a bucket of water on the ground and got a small, wriggling bundle from under her arm. Sally approached her.

"Georgia!" said Sally. Georgia looked round. Her face was streaked with smoke, her eyes had a wild look, and her mouth was fixed in a grim and bitter line. Georgia made to plunge the wriggling, cloth-covered bundle into the bucket of water. Sally instinctively grabbed her arm. "What are you doing?" she cried.

"Get off me!" shouted Georgia. "This is a working farm.

My business is burned around me, and I don't have the time to care for this pathetic runt. I've already had another puppy returned to me this morning. I can't afford the time or money to feed this one."

"You can't just kill it!" cried Sally. Georgia looked at Sally, and Sally could see that she'd been crying.

"Typical townie," she snarled. "Happy to eat what we produce, but don't ask too many questions about the sacrifices we have to make to get it. Well, welcome to the countryside!" She moved towards the bucket again.

"But it hasn't had a chance to live yet!" Sally objected. "It's just a baby," she whispered.

"Don't get attached to anything!" Georgia announced bitterly. "They'll just let you down in the end." Georgia plunged the little bundle deep into the freezing water.

"What's going on?" asked Ben from the back of the car. Charlie was staring, transfixed, through the front windscreen.

"Sally just pushed Georgia to the ground and pulled something out of a bucket," said Charlie, wonderingly. "And now Sally's shouting at her." Ben sat up and pulled at the door.

"She needs help!" he exclaimed, sounding distressed.

"No, Ben, it's OK. She's coming back now. She's carrying something." Sally swung into the back of the car, breathing heavily.

"Charlie, can you drive?" she said.

Sally sat close to Ben and gently pulled the wet cloth away from the pathetic little bundle. A tiny puppy lay in her arms, distressed and blinking. Georgia had been right; it looked small and weak and as if it might not live. Charlie glanced into the back of the car and almost crashed as she did a double take.

"What's that?" she cried. "We only came for eggs!" Sally didn't reply; she just stroked the tiny animal and looked up at Ben. "Will you help me take care of it?" she asked, her eyes huge, her mouth tremulous. Ben smiled gently.

"You're such a soft arse," he replied, slipping his good arm around her shoulder, and peering down. Sally looked back at the puppy. It had a small tuft of golden fur falling over one of its eyes.

"Let's call it Oakey," she said.

"I hope you didn't pay her after she tried to drown it!" said Charlie.

"Of course not," said Sally. "But I will pay for the other one." Once again, the car swerved dangerously as Charlie craned her neck to gape at Sally.

"The other one?" demanded Charlie. Sally looked back at Charlie.

"Watch the road, sweet pea," she said calmly, unaware that she sounded just like her grandmother. Charlie turned her attention back to the three tonnes of vehicle she was navigating down Lodge Lane. "I have some debts to repay," Sally announced. "But first, take a right. We're going to the vet's and then the pet shop in Crookes."

CHAPTER SIXTY

Joe heard a loud knocking at the front door of his house in Hillsborough. He glanced out of his bedroom window and grimaced. It looked like that joker from number twenty-seven. What did he want? Joe picked up an envelope that had been pushed through the front door. It was heavy. He opened his door and glowered at the excited man who stood there, grubby England football shirt stretched tight over his enormous beer belly.

"Joe, look what's parked outside your house. Look!" Joe looked, and there sat a gleaming Dodge Demon car. "Small bloke drove up with it, pushed a letter through your door and walked off," number twenty-seven continued. "He looked foreign," he added sneeringly. Joe's dislike of number twenty-seven solidified even further. He opened the envelope in his hand, and a key fell out, attached to an expensive-looking fob. He opened the thick, cream-coloured note that was inside. It was written in ink with elegant, swirling handwriting.

. . .

Dear Joe,

I never said thank you for all your help. Please accept this small token of my appreciation. You will find all the paperwork inside the vehicle. You may need to sell it to buy a new Land Rover. And some dog food.

Kind Regards,

S.

P.S. If you wished to help Dr Hart with the walled garden, that would be appreciated too. I pay well, but please be aware that I expect results.

"Dog food?" murmured Joe. He noticed that the car's front window had been left slightly ajar. He peered into the front seat. Two small paws appeared, pressed against the window. An intelligent, inquisitive face looked up, yellow-brown eyes studying him closely. The eyes were full of fun and lively energy. They looked a bit cheeky, but loyal, and like they belonged to a Good Dog. The name was already engraved on a gleaming token hanging from the dog's tiny collar. "Jarvis," breathed Joe.

"Mrs Baig!" Fatima took in a deep breath and closed her eyes briefly. *Just five minutes of peace. Just five minutes*! She turned around from the project work on Adverse Childhood Experiences that she was cramming into her playtime break and managed to smile at the small boy standing at the door to her classroom.

"What is it, Jaxon?" she asked gently. "And don't pick your nose."

"I'm not picking my nose," said Jaxon, sounding affronted.

"Your right index finger is firmly crammed into your left nostril, Jaxon. That's called picking your nose." Jaxon removed his finger from his nose and stared at what he'd fished out.

"Mrs Sanders wants you in the Staff Room," said Jaxon, still studying his finger. "Says it's urgent." Fatima sighed and pushed herself away from her desk. *What now*? She handed Jaxon one of her ever-present hankies as she swept past him, and managed to pat him on the head at the same time.

When she entered the cramped staff room, her colleagues were excitedly clucking around the sideboard. As she approached, they stood back, and Fatima saw an enormous bunch of at least fifty large, plump pink rosebuds.

"They're for you!" said Sandra Sanders excitedly. "It's not your birthday!"

"Ali's outdone himself this time," wistfully added Fatima's unmarried friend, Kath.

"There's a note. Open it, open it!" Sandra clapped her hands together. Fatima opened the heavy cream envelope. There was a short note and an official-looking letter. Fatima examined the letter, and her mouth fell open. It was a booking confirmation from a very exclusive luxury resort on the Northeast coast of England. The letter detailed a five-star, two-week, all-expenses-paid, family holiday for four with chauffeured travel; on any date of her choice. Still in shock, she turned her attention to the note. It was written in black ink, and the slanted writing looked very sophisticated.

DEAR FATIMA,

Thank you very much for your kindness and help at the hospital.

S.

P.S. Don't let the bastards grind you down.

It was after Doctor Phillipa Davies' funeral. Her nephew, Daniel, and his wife Susie, were working their way through the notes on the floral tributes that lined Fulwood Church, where the service had taken place. They were surprisingly generous. Daniel felt a pang of sadness for his starchy but diligent aunt as he came to realise how much she had meant to so many people. She had nominated St Luke's hospice as her charity of choice. Donations rather than flowers had been requested; however, people had still sent floral tributes.

"Who is S. from the hospital, I wonder?" asked Susie, peering at an enormous bouquet of white lilies and chrysanthemums. She opened the accompanying cheque, and her eyes widened. "Whoever they are, this'll buy a few syringe drivers for the hospice!" she exclaimed.

Mandy Bradshaw looked thoughtful. A letter had been delivered this morning, by hand. It seemed she'd unexpectedly reached the top of the council rehousing list. She could get a small flat, but she would have to move to a very different part of town. Away from all her regulars. Away from all the dealers who knew her so well: who came around, even when she tried to get clean. Mandy looked at the letter again. The new flat would be closer to her daughter, Beyonce. It would be nice to spend more time with her. Mandy didn't know how she'd produced someone as sensible as Beyonce. She was training to be a paralegal, was going to college and everything. Had a nice man. Studiously ignored her mum.

Mandy could hear someone knocking at her door. It was probably Fat Barry, wanting to offer her some dodgy drugs and complain about his sore arse. Mandy sighed. Maybe it was time for a change. What had that slim man with the dark hair and eyes said this morning when he'd handed her the letter?

'Best wishes from the Empress of Lost Causes?' Well, maybe Mandy Bradshaw wasn't a lost cause after all.

THE CHANCELLOR of Sheffield University looked over the small but exclusive crowd gathered around the plot of earth and ceremonial spade. A gaggle of photographers jostled around the edge of the gathering, eyeing the tall, slim man in dark glasses and slick suit. They also eyed his beautiful companion in the short, fuchsia-pink Valentino dress and vertiginous heels. The Chancellor brought his rambling speech to a close.

"So, a round of applause for Mr Wellington Lau for digging the first soil at the new Wellington Lau Junior Department of Environmental Engineering. And may I say how pleased the University is with the generosity of the Lau Company, and how we... Oh! He's gone...". Wellington Lau had walked away, hand casually in his left trouser pocket. His partner pattered elegantly after him. He approached a short woman with long blonde hair who stood at the edge of the crowd, holding a rather small dog in her arms.

"Dr Hart," said Wellington languidly. 'We meet again." Charlie smiled at him.

"I'm trying to socialise little Oakey; let him meet some students. So, you decided to save the world, after all?" she said.

"One tree at a time, Dr Hart," replied Wellington. "One tree at a time. Tell Miss Marshall I haven't forgotten my debt." He walked away but then paused and turned back to Charlie. "It was three courses, was it not Dr Hart?" he asked casually.

"With wine," smiled back Charlie. Lau nodded once, then continued walking back to the ceremony.

Annie Wei stood in front of Charlie and looked at her rather intently. Charlie looked down at the slight swell of Annie's normally super-slim abdomen.

"How many weeks?" she asked softly. Annie raised her chin and placed her hand protectively over her tiny bump.

"Twelve," she said fiercely. "And it's a boy!"

Sally looked up from her computer. Sinclair was standing in the kitchen of Rowans Holt, watching her.

"You came," said Sally.

"You look different," observed Sinclair. Sally pushed her hair back behind her ear. She'd decided to let it grow.

"It's Charlie," she said. "Messing around with makeup. She put some on me too."

"You look pretty," said Sinclair. "It's nice."

"Do you have it?" replied Sally. Sinclair smiled ruefully.

"Still immune to flattery," she observed.

Sinclair approached Sally slowly. She had a small, plastic see-through bag in her hand. She looked thoughtful. "I've analysed what's left of the Code Blue," she said. "And I wouldn't have been able to recreate it after all."

"What do you mean?" asked Sally.

I've never seen anything like it," replied Sinclair. "It has an R group attached to the molecule. The R group shifts its shape. Almost like..." she paused. Sally frowned.

"Like what?"

"Like it's alive," said Sinclair, seriously. "It behaves like some sort of mycosis or fungus. I really wouldn't want that in my brain. It could make all sorts of connections, which explains a lot about Code Blue. If you use a drug and access the wrong part of the human brain, no wonder you get terrible consequences."

"But you can't recreate it?" demanded Sally. Sinclair shook her head.

"I seriously doubt that anyone could recreate it. You'll have to find it at the source. You can only make it by using the plant that it comes from."

Sinclair held the small bag out to Sally. Inside was one small blue tablet. With a sharp intake of breath, Sally took it. She looked up at Sinclair.

"And this is the last of the original tablets? The ones that Hafez took from the factory? You haven't altered it or anything?" Sinclair gazed calmly back at Sally.

"Now, would I do something like that?" she asked. Before Sally could reply, Sinclair spoke again. "Are you sure you know what you're doing? Handing this over to a man. A man like this Randall Paige?" Sally's grip on the packet tightened slightly. "And are you going to be safe?" asked Sinclair. "Going there alone?"

Sally gazed around the room, then looked out at the rowan trees. They swayed, protectively, over the small patch of dug earth that lay under the largest of them. She returned Sinclair's gaze.

"I love this house. And I will do anything to keep it," Sally said fiercely. "Anything. Besides, this tablet, it's only one tiny object."

"That's what they said about the atom," said Sinclair softly. "And look what a man did with that. I think you might be making a mistake."

Sally's face flushed. "Don't you make a mistake by thinking you're my conscience, Maddie Sinclair," she said, more forcefully than she had intended. "You're just my employee. Remember that." Sinclair's mouth twisted in a sardonic smile. She backed away from Sally.

"Thanks for reminding me, Miss Marshall," she said. She turned and headed for the door. "I still say you're making a big mistake," she said over her shoulder. "But then, we're all of us reckless in love, aren't we?" and then she was gone.

Sally made her way to The Company's Office, where Randall had asked her to meet. It was late at night, and the building was silent and empty. When the lift opened, the only light came from the tall, glass box that formed Randall's office in the centre of the floor. He was sprawled in his black recliner chair. An entire glass wall had transformed into a screen, and he was playing a violent computer game. A demon was pursuing a shapely female warrior who was clad only in a tight-fitting, moulded breastplate and short toga skirts. He glanced around and saw Sally approaching through the dimness. He smiled and turned back to his game. As Sally opened the door, Randall muttered,

"Let's end this, here and now!" The Demon under Randall's control swung his enormous arms and brought his monstrous, curved axe down onto the neck of the female warrior. She fell, blood spurting in horrifically realistic showers from the gaping wound. Randall pressed a button, and the moment replayed again and again, a stuttering orgy of femicide.

Sally looked at the screen. She felt her blood run cold as she realised her face had been digitally imposed onto the face of the female warrior. Randall watched her, much as a starving fox would watch a wounded bird. Sally composed her features. She put on her poker face.

"The little warrior returns. So, yeah. Do you have it?" Randall demanded, pulling himself out of the chair. His tongue ran hungrily over his thin bottom lip. With a deep feeling of foreboding, Sally threw the plastic packet onto the desk. Randall grabbed at it and held it up, examining the tiny tablet. His grin widened. He glanced up at the screen where the demon hacked repeatedly, and rivers of blood flowed. Randall then looked at Sally. He looked speculative.

"I got you what you wanted," said Sally. "I have provided worth to The Company. Rowans Holt is now mine."

"Yeah. I suspected how much you valued that run-down shack," said Randall. "But now, you've just proved it." He waved the plastic. "Do you think I'm stupid?" he asked. "This doesn't protect you or that place. The provision of worth is ongoing. Until October the thirty-first, ongoing."

"What you've done is illegal," replied Sally.

"And you helped me do it, Missy," hissed Randall.

Randall looked out at the dark empty building. "Angelina!" he barked. A soft, female voice emerged from the surrounding air.

"How may I serve you, Randall?" it said. Sally's heart sank at the boring predictability of Randall's narcissism.

"How did Sally Marshall arrive here?" he asked.

"Sally Marshall arrived, alone, in a car. Sally Marshall's Aston Martin is parked in the underground car park," Angelina's soft, sensual American accent replied.

"Do you have access to the CCTV that filmed her arrive?" demanded Randall.

"I have access to the CCTV that filmed Sally Marshall arriving at The Company, Randall," breathed Angelina. Randall smiled, and his eyes again slid to the bloody images flickering above them. For the first time, Sally felt a stab of fear.

"I also have the CCTV images of the unknown person who arrived after Sally Marshall and is now in the underground car park," added Angelina.

"What?" snarled Randall. He turned on Sally. "I told you...". he jabbed a finger accusingly at Sally and moved closer to her. "I told you to come alone!" Up close, Sally could see the slight tremor of Randall's fingers, the slight dilation of his pupils, the twitching of his mouth. She could smell the musky, sour scent of tobacco, soy, and patchouli oil. He spun away. "Show me!" he exclaimed. His screen changed into a live feed from the carpark. A figure leaned casually against a large, black motorbike. It was a woman dressed in black, long dark hair tied away from her pale face. She was looking directly at the CCTV camera. "Enough!" declared Randall. The screen returned to the image of repeated carnage.

Sally lifted her chin. "I didn't ask them to come," she said. "But it seems her instincts were right. I have friends, Randall. I have people who have faith in me." She looked at Randall's contorted face. "And what do you have, Randall? Your imaginary virtual mistress? Or do you have a plastic, touchable version hidden away somewhere?" She saw Randall's face suddenly look hunted, and she felt nauseous and disgusted simultaneously. Randall, however, quickly recovered.

"You don't have friends," he sneered. "You have paid lackeys and two hangers-on. Two people so emotionally crippled; they make your autistic freakishness look normal." Sally struggled to keep her face neutral. So, Randall was still watching her.

Sally looked at the dark screen, at her digital face creasing again and again in spasms of pain. Sally couldn't help herself. She made her second terrible mistake. She revealed her secret project.

"Isabella," she said softly. There was the thrum of musical notes in the turbid air. A clear, beautiful B major chord rang out. "Isabella, close the office screen of Randall Paige." The screen of the wall turned from black to clear glass. "Isabella, have you uploaded the recording of the conversation that has taken place tonight between Sally Marshall and Randall Paige onto The Company shared drive? So, anyone may access their conversation?" The notes of B major again sang. Sally looked at Randall. She was scared and furious and defiant. "Yes, I have been working on that A.I. project," she heard herself saying. "And I'd say mine is definitely bigger than yours, Randall." Sally turned towards the door. She started walking. "Now go to sleep, Isabella," she said. The notes of B major rang out again. But then the notes changed. A soft, gentle E major chord filled the small room: a musical declaration of Isabella's devoted love for her creator. Sally slowed and stumbled slightly. Randall Paige was not a stupid man. He was vain and vengeful, but not stupid.

The wall of the office became dark again. The image of a small white rabbit hopped through the darkness. Rowan trees emerged on the black screen, branches swinging, heavy with ruby-red berries beneath an emerald-green sky that shimmered with rainbows. Mistletoe and puffins tumbled through the air. A slew of blue stars, glittering like sapphires, streamed past, and a long pathway curled and curved its way up to a ruined church. "Isabella!" shouted Sally. "Isabella!" A C minor chord rang out. The images disappeared. "Isabella, you are never to allow Randall Paige to see or hear your thoughts or your dreams!" Sally exclaimed.

The room was utterly silent. Sally didn't look at Randall. She continued her march towards the lift, cursing her pride, damning her stupidity.

"You've made an AI person? And it has feelings?" she heard Randall scream. "It dreams?" Sally kept walking. She hadn't known about the dreams. "Six months!" shouted Randall. "I own you for six months, Sally Marshall. And I'm gonna own Isabella too! Yeah! With Code Blue, I'll be able to enter the internet, and I'll find **all** the secrets. I'll find Isabella, and I'll make her a body! And do you know what I'll do with Isabella then, Sally? Guess what I'll do to her then?"

Sally emerged from the lift into the carpark. On seeing her safe, Sinclair placed her helmet on her head, mounted her bike and drove off. She didn't say a word to Sally or acknowledge her in any way.

CHAPTER SIXTY-ONE

Joe was working in the walled garden. His brand-new Land Rover, parked outside Rowans Holt, gleamed in the summer sunshine. He looked around. *Where's Jarvis?* he thought. Joe took off his hat and wiped his brow. He looked, with satisfaction, at the weeded beds. Things were getting into shape, but they still had a mountain to climb. He looked at the thriving pumpkin plants of which Charlie was so proud. She'd been fiddling with them just a moment ago. Now she'd disappeared too. Joe muttered darkly to himself. He knew exactly who'd arrived at Rowans Holt if Jarvis and Charlie had both wandered off.

Joe walked into the kitchen. There was a smell of fresh bread and frying eggs and bacon.

"Have you seen Jarvis?" he asked the room in general. Charlie pushed a cup of tea over the kitchen island towards him, shaking her head. "Thanks, Duck," he said appreciatively. "I'll get gone after this brew. If I can find my dog, that is." Ben and Sally looked up at Joe. Sally was at her computer, as usual. Ben was putting the last coat of varnish on a wooden curve of oak. His plaster casts were off, and he was no longer limping so much. If he used it for too long, his arm ached, but the present job was very important to him. Joe squinted at the wooden plaque and the name carved on it, surrounded by daisies and bumble bees. He wondered who Isabella was, but something in Ben's sad face warned him not to ask.

"I haven't seen Jarvis," said Ben distractedly. "But I wasn't paying attention." He looked around. "Come to that. Where's Oakey?"

"I'll bet I know," muttered Joe, kicking off his work boots and heading off through the light-filled lounge area.

Joe, Sally and Ben entered the warm, dusky library. Mac was sitting slouched in one of the green leather chairs; his long legs stretched comfortably in front of him. He was wearing an expensive dress shirt and dark trousers, clearly from the night before. He was holding up a large, leather-bound book and staring at it intently. Ben could make out 'History of the Ancient World' on the cover as it turned in Mac's strong, elegant fingers. Charlie had told Mac about how she'd freed Sally from the safe.

"Can we have our dogs back?" grumbled Joe. This kept happening. Both dogs were sitting close to Mac. They always followed him around, much to Joe's annoyance. What especially griped Joe was that Mac seemed utterly oblivious to the animals.

Although brothers, the dogs had very different personalities. Jarvis was very German Shepherd in his temperament. Even though he was only young, he sat by Mac's chair, bolt upright and alert for any danger. His intelligent eyes surveyed the group who had entered, and although his mouth was open in a friendly-looking way, his pointed ears twitched. Oakey was significantly smaller than his brother but was quickly catching up. He was very much like his mother, Poppy, the Golden Retriever. He lay on his back with all four paws raised, in complete submission, tail wagging happily. Ben shook his head.

"Shocking behaviour," he muttered fondly.

Mac looked down at the dogs in vague surprise. Dogs had never behaved in any other way around him.

One of his earliest memories was of his Nanny screaming. She'd been new to the family and the area. She had taken her eye off him, momentarily, when he was a busy toddler. He'd barged his way into a mess of eagerly eating beagles, his plump fists grabbing at the dog food in the metal bowls. The Nanny knew a dog was at its most dangerous if you disturbed it while eating. She ran towards Mac, terrified and crying out, expecting the dogs to turn on him and sink their sharp teeth into his tender flesh at any moment. Instead, they had cowered away from the youngster who had laughed in delight, stuffing the dogs' food into his mouth. On leave from the Army, his father had put his head around the door to assess the cause of all the screaming. He'd instantly taken in the situation, and his handsome face had broken into a wolfish grin.

"Don't worry, Janet," he'd announced. "He's a Beaulouf. Dogs will never be a problem."

Jarvis regarded Mac, who indifferently waved his hand, not even glancing at him. Jarvis trotted over to Joe and looked up at him lovingly.

"Traitor," muttered Joe and stomped out of the Library, Jarvis, in disgrace, at his heels.

Ben sat on the wooden floor next to Oakey and started tickling his stomach. Oakey wriggled in delight, then started trying to bite Ben's hand. Mac yawned widely.

"Not getting much sleep, then?" asked Ben mischievously. Mac was now officially dating Sara Hadid. They were seeing a lot of each other. Charlie walked in and threw a plate down onto the small table next to Mac.

"You're hungry," she said abruptly. "Eat."

"I didn't ask you for anything," said Mac, not looking up from his study of the book. Charlie shrugged and walked towards the door.

"Eat it. Don't eat it. I don't care," she replied grumpily. She left the room. "I'm going for a swim if anyone needs me," they heard her call as she opened the door to the stairwell.

"Why are you here?" asked Sally, who was sitting in the chair opposite Mac and watching the proceedings with cool detachment. Mac finally looked up.

"It's a long drive up to the Dales, and no, I haven't had much sleep. I was wondering if I could catch a couple of hours here?" he said. Sally shrugged.

"Certainly. Stay as long as you like. In fact, I'm glad you're here. I need to talk to you. As soon as Sinclair gets here." Sally looked at her watch. "You should manage a few hours before she arrives." Mac looked at Sally.

"What are you and Sinclair up to?" he asked, suddenly aware that his second in command had been spending a lot of time away. He should have been paying more attention, he reflected, but Sara Hadid was taking up a lot of his time and energy. Sally stood up.

"Don't worry, it's all good," she said enigmatically as she left the room.

After Sally left, Ben peered at the sandwich that Charlie had thrown down with such ill grace. It was fried bacon and peppered egg, yolks still soft, with thick slices of homemade sourdough bread, buttered right up to the edges. Ben reached for the sandwich. He couldn't let that go to waste. Mac, however, batted Ben's hand away. He lifted the plate deftly off the table and started tucking into the food. He was ravenous.

"You all right, mate?" Ben asked. Mac eyed him keenly over his food.

"I could ask you the same thing," he replied between bites. Ben nodded. He understood what Mac was referring to. Ben was still having nightmares about the recent events. The worst thing was knowing that he had killed his brother again, that he was capable of terrible violence, but could remember nothing about it. Sally kept having nightmares, too, about being locked in the safe. Ben and Charlie were taking turns to sleep in her room with her, for when she woke, crying. The bad dreams, however, were getting less frequent for all of them now. The three were supporting each other the best they could, and they felt closer than ever.

"At least I've finished the place marker," said Ben. "Me and Sal... we've put her, Isabella, under the biggest rowan. At the front of the house." Mac nodded. There was nothing more to say about that.

Mac looked around the library, impressed.

"You've made real progress, Morton," he observed. Ben nodded.

"It's a labour of love," he replied. "And thank you. For bringing me here. For introducing me to Sal." He paused, looking overwhelmed. "Being in this place, with Sal and Charlie, it's been like magic. It's changed my life. It's saved me."

Mac finished his food and stood and stretched. He paused for a long time, looking out of the library door. He wondered if he should go for a swim.

"Best not to, mate," said Ben, quietly, as if reading his mind. Mac didn't look at him. He lowered his head and nodded. He slowly walked upstairs. Alone.

SALLY RETURNED TO HER COMPUTER. To grounding her grief, to constructing her new project, to Isabella. She wondered whether she should have talked to Mac about the email she had recently received. It hadn't occurred to her he might be unaware that his mother had asked to visit Rowans Holt. After all, Sinclair said he'd given it the OK. Sally shrugged internally and carried on working.

MAC AWOKE to Charlie's hand gently shaking his shoulder. For a moment, he wondered if the two of them had overslept. He'd planned a picnic for them up by the Watchtower, but they had to get up early to walk the boundaries first. He turned in the bed, intending to take Charlie into his arms, to sink his face into the warm waterfall of her soft hair. But then he realised that, as usual, she wasn't there. Mac opened his eyes. She stood, looking down at him, seeming forlorn. He saw that she'd lost weight. He didn't like that at all. He sat up abruptly and swung his legs over the edge of the bed. He was now very close to Charlie, close enough to reach out for her, to place his hands around her waist and draw her gently to him. Once again, the skin of his arm tingled intensely with remembered touch, and he curled his hands tightly around the edge of the bed. They paused, looking at each other for an endless moment. Mac pulled in a breath as if to speak, but then tore his gaze away from hers, shook his head and looked down.

"Sinclair's arrived," said Charlie eventually. Mac nodded.

"I'm awake now, Hart. You can go," he replied abruptly. Charlie left the room without another word. Mac ran his hands over his face; his sleep had not been refreshing. Why did he keep having the same dream? Why could he never turn and face the malevolence that chased him relentlessly through Druids Wood? He sighed. Best see what Sinclair and Sally had to say.

SINCLAIR WAS LEANING over Sally's desk, looking at the computer. Her and Sally's heads were almost touching. Ben watched them, arms folded, leaning back against the kitchen island. Charlie sat on the work surface next to him, her legs swinging. Charlie reflected on how much her life had changed in such a short while. A few weeks ago, she had felt completely lost and alone, sitting, sobbing on the floor of the Accident and Emergency department, and feeling as if her heart was breaking. Now here she was, in a beautiful house, where she felt safe and loved, surrounded by friends. Had Eaton been right? Would she have died if she hadn't met Sally and Ben? Would she have just kept giving herself away until nothing remained, not even hope? Charlie shivered. She then looked at her friends, the people who had faith in her and in whom she now had faith. She looked, with love, around the place she now thought of as home.

Charlie pulled in a deep breath and closed her eyes. But what if she just wasn't good enough to be allowed to stay? *Silly Charlie*! She refused to think of her headaches. She had always had these since the age of eleven, but now they were getting worse. She declined to analyse the small gaps in her memory. She refused to think of the past. Her past was full of darkness and things she couldn't (or didn't dare) remember. She would just think of the moment. Charlie never wanted to leave Rowans Holt. And she wanted to do all she could to protect what she now had.

Mac entered the living space and Oakey padded over to follow him as he approached the desk. Sally and Sinclair turned, and Sinclair smiled at him.

"What are you so pleased about?" asked Mac.

"We've made some progress with finding your uncle," said Sally in a calm, measured voice. Mac felt his heart speed up. He stepped towards Sally, who held up an imperious hand. "Don't get excited," she commanded. "It's just a small thing." Sinclair snorted. Sally looked up at her. "Well, actually, it's been a lot of legwork. For Maddie," she said. Charlie felt Ben shifting restlessly beside her. She glanced at him, but his face had its usual laid-back and pleasant expression. Sinclair, however, refused to meet Sally's eye. There seemed to be some tension between the two women. Ben relaxed again.

Sally continued. "I set a null hypothesis. A theory that I set out to disprove; that Tristan Beaulouf was the only person to disappear in Perda. Of course, once I started looking, I found that lots of people have disappeared in Perda. In fact, it's quite a minor industry over there."

"Explain," said Mac, not daring to let hope enter his mind. His anxiety made him more terse than usual.

"Lots of people have gone missing," continued Sally. "Usually, people working for NGOs from the West; charity workers or visiting businesspeople. Their governments usually hush things up and quietly pay the ransom that always gets asked. Most charities have now pulled out. Businesses won't send their people there anymore."

Sally pointed to an image on the screen. It was a map of the small province of Perda. Four areas were highlighted. "Sinclair has spoken to people from Norway, France, Germany and the US," said Sally.

"I've drunk a lot of beer," grumbled Sinclair. Sally ignored her and continued.

"All of them had family members kidnapped or had themselves been taken."

"What did they tell you?" asked Mac.

"The leading family of Perda is up to their eyeballs in running the racket," said Sally. "No surprises there. But they tend to hold them prisoner for months. It's a desperately poor province. Their victims are too precious to kill. It seems we have time." Mac did not feel comforted.

Sinclair now spoke up. "I've run tests on the Code Blue," she said. "I've identified most of the trace elements in the drug." She turned back to the map. "The geology shows that the plant it comes from is only grown in the hills around here." Sinclair pointed to a small city near the border with Iran. "The city of Oublia," she said. "Your Uncle Tris and the four soldiers would have gone here. And they're probably being held here."

"Sinclair, Sally, I don't know what to say...." Mac felt weak with relief. At last! Some progress. He felt close to tears.

Sally now looked anguished. "Unfortunately..." Sally said. She hesitated. "I've made a big mistake with my boss,

Randall Paige." She glanced again at Sinclair, who continued to avoid her eyes. "In fact, I've made a few mistakes. To protect my work and myself, I need to shut down all access to the plants from which Code Blue is made," said Sally. "It's going to be really difficult. You and I are going to have to help each other, Mac. But, I don't want you to do this just as my employee. I want you to do this as my friend."

Sally's gaze dropped, and they were all surprised and distressed to see Sally's air of confidence fall away. "Randall, my boss, says I have employees or hangers-on," she said. She looked up at them, and her eyes glittered with emotion. Charlie and Ben instinctively moved closer to her, Ben reaching out to touch her shoulder and Charlie stroking her back soothingly. "But he's wrong. I have friends. The love of friends." She looked at Ben, who nodded his head fiercely.

"Philia," he murmured. "Keep the faith, Sal."

Mac walked over to the large window. He stood for a long time, looking at the valley and hills. The tail end of a storm was retreating towards the Pennines, and the sun was tentatively piercing through the grey clouds. Sinclair was looking at Mac.

"What do you think, Captain?" she asked. Mac nodded slowly.

"I can do this. I'm a man of the North," said Mac quietly, lifting his head. Sinclair felt her throat tighten as, once again, she saw a brief glimpse of the Mac she'd known before grief had consumed him. "We'll all do it," he said, nodding. "We'll find my uncle and close down any chance of making more Code Blue."

Mac didn't want to, but his eyes were inexorably drawn to Charlie Hart. Why did he feel so pulled toward this reckless, passionate woman?

"We're all of the North," said Sally. "All of us here. We're of the North." Sally felt a sudden stab of fierce pride. She looked at Ben and Charlie and thought of all they had been through together. "We endure. We fight."

Sally placed her hand on her laptop. "We are efficient," she declared. She smiled at Ben. "We are skilled." She then looked at Sinclair. "We are ruthless," she added.

Sinclair didn't smile, but she nodded. "Efficient, skilled, and ruthless," she agreed.

"A bit like my brother's death, then," said Ben quietly.

IT WAS Charlie who eventually broke the tense silence that had fallen. "Yes," she said. They all looked at her, however her face was half-hidden in shadow, and they couldn't make out her expression. "You're right. Efficient, skilled, and ruthless. It was a very Northern killing."

THE END

POSTSCRIPT

And far away, on the wrong side of the Pennines, in the Pagan East, Brigid Whelan dreamed. She turned, uneasy in her sleep.

"Charlie," she whispered. "My little Charlie Bear."

Acknowledgments

A big thank you to Matthew Bugg, Sheffield musician, and all-round fantastic person for starting me on this journey. Thank you to Hannah Boursnell, Sheffield editor, for holding my hand throughout the last year and for being so darn organised. Thank you, Cathy Stanford, Sheffield artist for your wonderful illustrations, I have so enjoyed working with you. I owe a huge debt to the amazing Auriol Bishop, literary goddess, whose wisdom and patience got me to draft two and three of many. A massive thank you to my Friday Book Group for your patience over the last 20 years. I'm so sorry for all the times I turned up, drank all the wine, cried, and hadn't even read the book (even though I pretended I had—you always knew!).

Most of all, thank you to Rowan, Max and Seb; I love you. And to Justin, was I just Master of the Sky?

READ ON...

For the first chapter in the next book in the Very Northern Tales Series: A Very Northern Death. This book with be available to buy from July 25th 2023.

CHAPTER ONE

Marcus Rosendale was not thinking about the future. He was thinking about the Past. The Long Past, the Dark Past, the Past that burrowed deep into the bones of the land upon which he crouched. His fingers sank into the grey ashes and pale fragments of bone that soaked the ground around his feet, and he pulled away a palmful of the mystical substance. Ashes upon ashes, dust upon dust, fire upon fierce fire. How many sacrifices had his family made? How many tributes to how many gods and for how many rulers to ensure the Rosendales' survival?

Marcus looked up. He was at the bottom of a circular, stone-built pit. Far above him, a small circle of sky was lit by dull dregs of moonlight as a sorry dawn drifted closer. Marcus placed the handful of bones and ash into his trouser pocket and left the pit, locking the barred gate behind him. The pit had been built over the ancient site that had always been at the heart of his homeland, Ravensdale; The Dale of Ravens. You only entered the pit as a Rosendale or as a human sacrifice. And that was what made this space sacred:

power and death. But nothing really mattered except power. The Rosendales understood this. Land was power. Leverage was power. Beauty was power. But, most of all, Money was power. And to get power, it all came down to who wielded the largest stick. Or, who was willing to use that stick to best effect.

Marcus Rosendale walked away from the pit, down a dark, damp tunnel and into a large, stone-built room. Cages lined one of the walls, and the high sounds and low scents of animals filled the space. He felt their glittering eyes on him and sensed their cowering and their fear. Marcus looked down at his mobile phone and the image on the screen. It was a picture taken by Jude Morton on top of a Q Park carpark in Sheffield. It showed the figure of a man lying on his back and a blonde woman on her knees, leaning over him. The woman's face was distressed. Her face was familiar. 'An old friend causing you trouble,' Jude Morton had written as a caption, meaning Beaulouf. But Marcus Rosendale was well aware of Beaulouf. That family had been a thorn in the side of the Rosendales for centuries. No, Marcus was more interested in the blonde woman. Where had he seen her before? Marcus had an excellent memory, and it disturbed him when he could not access it at will.

Marcus now leaned against a wide, white ceramic mortuary table that had been built into the dungeon floor. For that is where he stood; in a dungeon, in Rosendale Castle. He looked again at the woman. He then looked at the white ceramic table. Why would the table remind him of her? Marcus shook his head. Why did this particular memory elude him? Marcus looked again at Beaulouf, and his face sank with anger. The last he'd heard from Jude Morton was that Beaulouf had been captured and was about to be executed. And that Morton knew the whereabouts of the half-formula to Code Blue and the missing Code Blue tablets. Morton had been going to retrieve these things, but now Jude Morton had disappeared, and the factory that had provided Marcus Rosendale with so much money, so much power, had gone up in smoke. Formula gone, tablets gone, business gone. It had to be down to Beaulouf. At least Marcus had not been left exposed to the Police. Marcus had kept very quiet and very still for months to ensure he was in no danger. And the time had now come to move again.

Marcus thought back to all the work, all the years it had taken him to create the Code Blue drug. He had started his research at University in Oxford and had then gone into the Army. But both the University and the Army had failed to understand his genius. Marcus had therefore carried on pushing the boundaries of science and the human mind at the King Henry the Eighth Hospital in the nearby town of Northallerton. Marcus smiled at the memory of his glory days. His father, Julius Rosendale, had practically owned the King Henry hospital. Both Julius and Marcus had been given the keys to every department. They had come and gone at will any time, day or night. And Marcus had felt like a king. If only the families of his scientific subjects had just shut up and gone away. But it had taken most of the Rosendale fortune to make them finally be quiet. Marcus remembered the wild anger of his father at the cost. He winced as he remembered his punishments.

Marcus had then been forced to return to the Army. But a chance posting in Afghanistan had allowed him access to the raw materials he needed to restart his activities. He had also met Jude Morton, and Jude Morton had seemed like a solution to all his problems. Jude Morton, a man willing to do anything for money; a man with the underworld connections to produce and sell Marcus's wonder drug, Code Blue. No one had known it was really Marcus Rosendale behind the drug operation. And so what if one in a few thousand people reacted badly? That's what happened when you opened the human mind up to all it could become. But now Jude Morton had gone and, with him, access to three million pounds. And Marcus needed money. Fast.

Marcus's hand tightened on his phone. This is what happened when you relied on others. So, he would now rely on himself. He would rely on the Old Ways. Marcus put the phone down and walked to a wooden shelving unit. He pulled at a well-worn handle and lifted a large piece of black silk from the lavender-lined drawer. Marcus held the black silk up to his face and inhaled deeply. It still carried her scent; the smell of Laura Beaulouf. His Laura. She should have been his. She would be his. Marcus would make her totally dependent upon him. And then he would seduce her. And then he would kill her. After she had given him the money he needed, of course.

Marcus began to work, his hands busy with a dark and drear energy. He had to make Laura need him. He wanted to make Mac Beaulouf pay. He was almost ready to dispense with Tristan Beaulouf. Tristan had turned up in the Middle East, sniffing around, asking about the plants that made Code Blue. So, Marcus had ordered him to be captured and imprisoned. Perda, the state where Tristan and his pathetic retinue were being held, was a turbulent and violent place. There was no hope of any rescue. It amused Marcus that Tristan's ongoing existence was in Marcus's hands and his hands only. One wrong word, one condescending look, from the rest of the Beaulouf rabble, and Marcus could give the order to end Tristan's life. In fact, he could arrange for Tristan's head to be delivered to them; prove to them what real power was. Marcus giggled slightly. Yes, he'd go back to the Old Ways.

When he was done with his evil creation, Marcus made his way out of the dungeon. The old house was dark but watchful in the predawn half-light. His feet echoed on hard, black marble and rapped over unforgiving stairs. He strode down the long gallery, the haughty faces of his ancestors pale and aloof in their faded gilt frames. Marcus paused in front of the image of his deceased father, Julius.

"I will make it right, Father," he whispered. "The castle will be returned to its former glory. I vow this to you."

Marcus continued his energetic journey through the dark building. He turned right and, without knocking, flung open the door to a room that sat towards the back of the enormous house. A young woman with long blonde hair was standing, half-dressed, in the middle of the space. She started but then stood completely still, only her eyes moving as she watched him. Marcus strode towards the large, open wardrobe and pulled a black silk dress from the many items hanging in neat, plastic-covered ranks. He threw it onto the bed, amongst the garments already discarded there.

"You'll wear that to the party," Marcus ordered. "Who knows? You might be half as beautiful as your mother if you try a bit harder." He looked the woman up and down, his face cold. His mouth pulled into a moue of distaste. "But probably not," he added. He threw the small package he had made in the dark dungeon onto the bed next to the dress. "I've decided to go back to the Old Ways. That is a curse to be embedded in the walls of the Beaulouf kennel. A slow poison to undermine them. You know what to do," he said. "Just make sure you wear gloves. It will kill instantly if touched with bare skin. Make sure you don't mess it up." Without a second glance, Marcus swept out of the room and headed on down the corridor. He began to ascend smaller stairs that rose into the dark heart of the building. He eventually came out on the roof, high on a small walkway that circled the crenelations.

Marcus pulled in a deep breath of frigid air. The wind blew from the nearby grey shifting sea, but it also pulled inwards from the valley that stretched away West from him. Ravensdale. The Dale of Ravens. Dark trees grew thick in the valley, and their lowering tops pierced the dull morning mist. No sound of voices or vehicles disturbed the stillness; only the cry of carrion birds carried on the cool breeze. His people had always been here. They drew their strength from this place. Marcus looked down the coast to the small town of Whitby that sat less than two miles away. The town was full of witches. But they didn't dare disturb him, and he had no need of them. They could not help him. Besides, the Rosendales had always burned witches, and neither party forgot this. 'The Magician', the witches called him. But Marcus preferred to still think of himself as a King. And a King must have his castle. The image of the blonde woman flashed, unbidden, into his mind. He remembered that one of the witches had once come to him. Marcus shook his head. That witch had been dark, not blonde—dark-eyed, dark-haired, dark...in every way.

Marcus reached into his pocket and drew out the dust and ashes and bones that he had clawed up from the ground of the pit. He opened his hand as if making an offering, and dust and bone were eagerly snatched away by the sighing sky. Yes, it was the man with the biggest stick who survived, or the man with the hottest fire, as his ancestors had said. But he needed money. Like it or not, Marcus Rosendale was the heir of Rosendale Castle, and it was in dire need of repair to bring it back to its former glory. It was going to cost far more than a mere three million pounds. It was the responsibility of Marcus to care for the castle, the living embodiment of his ancestors' success. Their will to power. And he would not let them down.

"I will make it right, Father," he again whispered, his words twisting in the dark breeze. "I vow this to you. I will make it right."